RISE

RISE

Sara Jo Cluff

Rise

Paperback ISBN 9781686366529
Hardcover ISBN 978-1-7321832-6-1

Printed in the United States of America
First Printing, August 2019

Awkward Pepper, LLC
awkwardpepperllc@gmail.com

Cover images from pixabay.com
Cover design by Sara Jo Cluff

For Dad

The man who taught me the meaning of hard work

CHAPTER 1

Emmie

He sat before me, sweat and blood sliding down his cheek. I took the rag from my belt loop and wiped off some blood that dripped onto his eyelid.

"How bad does it look, Em?" Dante asked, his leg bouncing up and down. He always did that to keep his blood flowing when he was stopped even though I'd hold him countless times to conserve his energy.

Smiling, I slapped his bare shoulder, sweat flying. "Nothing you can't handle." I turned to Eric standing down below. "I need a butterfly bandage to hold his gash together."

Eric rifled through the medical bag until he found them. He took one out and reached up to me. "Here you go."

I wiped Dante's forehead before placing the bandage on his cut. "This should hold it for now. We'll take you to the infirmary once you win."

Dante looked past me at his opponent, his confidence slipping. "He's faster than me, Em."

"But you're stronger." Placing both of my hands on his shoulders, I rested my forehead against his. "You've got this. He's slowing down. We both know Santiago gets lazy and sloppy when his energy's drained. Get him to throw a few more punches into the air and then strike."

Dante nodded and pounded his gloves together. "Stomach, stomach, face, stomach, face."

"You can do this, Dante." I lifted his chin, so his brown eyes were level with mine. "You're going to win."

"I'm going to win!" he yelled.

I slapped the sides of his arms. "Go get him, tiger."

Dante stood, jumping up and down. He reached his glove out to me and I took it, kissing it for good luck. Glancing over at Santiago, I grabbed Dante's other glove and kissed it, never taking my eyes off Santiago. I pointed at him. "That one's for you."

Santiago scowled at me, but it turned into a smirk. Even though he was a fellow revolutionary, I still wanted Dante to put that boy in his place.

Our other revolutionary, Maya, was supporting Santiago that night, but she did it so he wouldn't feel bad. She'd told me before the match that she secretly wanted Dante to win.

I jumped down out of the ring and went to Eric's side. "We're going to win. I can feel it in my bones."

"We better." Eric ran his fingers through his thick blond hair. "I've got a lot riding on this match."

Our friend, Luke, laughed behind us. "He can't pull it off. He's too slow. Eric, you're going to be doing every single chore in our place for a month."

I tilted my head at Eric. "You went a month this time?"

"I'm like you," Eric said, smiling at me. He had some new teeth put in after losing a few of them while being held captive by Whit, a.k.a. President Randall, in River Springs. His perfect smile was back. "I can feel it in my bones. Dante's going to win."

"You better hope so," Luke said.

I looked back at my old Recruitment partner and Luke's girlfriend, Tina. She let out a deep breath as she rolled her green eyes.

Ever since Luke and Eric moved into the same apartment, they'd been betting on stuff nonstop. Everything was a competition for them. Even though it drove me crazy, I was happy to see them become such good friends. Last year they hated each other.

Bruce stepped into the middle of the ring, puffing out his chest. You could tell by his deep, brown eyes that he was Maya's little brother. He stood still until everyone in the arena was quiet. It had been a year since I'd first met Bruce and although he'd physically grown, his maturity level had remained the same. But it was what made him so much fun to be around.

Bruce cleared his throat. "Fighters ready?" Both Santiago and Dante nodded. Bruce held back a smile. He always tried to act tough when he stood in the ring, but the giddiness behind his eyes was apparent, reminding me he was only fifteen. "Round three starts …" Bruce's gaze swept between Dante and Santiago as he paused for dramatic effect. "Now!"

Bruce hopped out of the ring and the battle began. Just

like I'd thought, Santiago went immediately at Dante, swinging full force. Dante was able to dodge all of Santiago's punches, swiftly maneuvering out of the way each time. The fire behind Santiago's eyes began to fade. I took Eric's hand, squeezing it out of anticipation.

"You've got this, Dante!" I yelled.

The crowd went wild in the arena. Half of them were shouting out Santiago's nickname, The Bone Crusher. The other half were shouting Dante's nickname, The Inferno.

According to the statistics before the match started, the odds were in Santiago's favor. He'd been the top fighter in Scorpion City and that hadn't changed since he moved to New Haven. Dante hadn't beaten him once.

Even from down below, I could see the wheels turning in Dante's head. He was planning out his attack, wanting to make each swing count. Santiago went for Dante's abdomen, but Dante jumped backward, avoiding contact.

Santiago stepped back and then went at Dante again, landing two blows to his face. Dante stumbled backward, leaning into the side of the ring. He hesitated for a second and then shook his head like he was trying to shake off the hits.

That was when I saw it. That look Santiago got in his eyes when he thought he'd won. He smiled arrogantly at the crowd, pumping his arms up and down, trying to get everyone to yell louder.

Letting go of Eric's hand, I ran over to Dante's side of the ring. "Now Dante!"

Dante nodded and sprang forward, striking Santiago twice in the stomach. Santiago instinctively put his arms in front of his abdomen, freeing up his face. Dante's glove landed hard against Santiago's jaw, making Santiago throw up his hands. Dante went for Santiago's abdomen again, thrusting his arm with all his might.

When Santiago uncovered his face, Dante pulled his arm back and then threw it forward until it connected with Santiago's nose. Santiago staggered backward, trying to regain his bearings. Dante took the opportunity to land one more blow to Santiago's face and he fell, covering his nose with one of his gloves.

Bruce hopped back in the ring and bent down next to Santiago. He slammed his hand on the floor of the ring, counting out each number.

Eric came up behind me, putting his arms around my waist and pulling my back into him. I placed one hand on his and my other hand on my butterfly necklace as I looked on, eagerly awaiting to hear the final count. "This is killing me!"

"Six! Seven!" Bruce yelled out.

Santiago pushed his palms against the mat, trying to lift himself.

"Come on, come on," Eric said. "Stay down!"

"Nine!" Bruce shouted, his tone not holding back any excitement. I'd never heard the arena that loud before.

Santiago fell back down right as Bruce shouted out, "Ten!"

Bruce stood up, grabbed Dante's wrist, and threw his arm into the air. "The Inferno is the champion!"

I turned around and threw my arms around Eric's neck. Lifting me off the ground, he spun me around a few times.

When he finally set me down, I gave him a big kiss on the lips.

Dante stood in the center of the ring, pumping his fists into the air. The buzz in the arena vibrated through me as everyone stood and chanted, "Inferno." It seeped into my veins, making my blood pump faster.

Ten minutes later, we walked into the locker room. It had taken forever to get through the crowd since everyone wanted to congratulate Dante for being the first person to defeat Santiago.

Dante jumped onto the bench, holding his arms high in the air. Sweat slid down his forehead and bare chest.

I stood down below, my hands cupped over my mouth, cheering until my voice cracked.

Eric cupped his hands over his mouth. "Speech!"

Dante put his hands down and cleared his throat. "First and foremost, I need to thank all my fans for never giving up hope."

"Who says we never gave up hope?" Terrance, one of our military leaders, asked. He had a smile that stretched from ear to ear. "It sure took you long enough."

Dante laughed, rubbing his hand over his hair. After letting it grow out to a fro the previous year, he'd finally cut it back to a decent length. "I know, I know. But I'm here now and we won. I also need to thank my sister, Vivica, for actually being with me and not over with her boyfriend."

"Hey, I love Santiago," Vivica said, "but I still have a competitive nature. Someone needed to knock him off his pedestal. I don't think his head can afford to get any bigger."

Dante looked down at me and reached his hand out. I

took hold and he pulled me up on the bench next to him. I laughed as I strained my neck to see him. "How tall are you now? I swear you get taller every day."

"Six-four," Dante said, laughing. "My dad never thought I'd get this tall but look at me now." He put his arm around my shoulder and pulled me close. "Lastly, I need to thank my trainer and best friend, Emmie, for always being there for me. She's worked hard to get me in the shape I needed to be in. She's also worked hard on watching Santiago carefully, studying his techniques and searching for weaknesses."

"It took a lot of effort, but it worked out in the end." I squeezed Dante's waist, ignoring all the sweat. It was something I had to accept as his trainer. "I'm just glad you finally beat him. Now we can put you in the hall of fame."

"*We* won," Dante said. "This was a team effort. I think Emmie needs to be rewarded for all of her hard work." He smiled at Eric. "If you'd do the honor."

"Of course," Eric said, taking me by my waist and lowering me down. He dipped me, his warm lips pressing against mine, his hand cradling the back of my neck.

"Oh, get a room!" Tina said.

Dante tsked. "No way. Not until they're married."

Eric pulled me back up and glanced over at Dante. "Who says you get a say in this?"

Dante pointed his finger at his chest. "I do. I have no problem beating the crap out of you, Eric."

"Neither do I," Joshua said, cracking his knuckles. He was one of my half-brothers and a new pain in my side when it came to men trying to control my life choices. He was wearing his typical white button-down shirt untucked with the top button undone, his tie hanging loosely around his neck.

"Me either," Will said, straightening his glasses. He was a friend who I'd met back in Recruitment in our previous city of River Springs.

"Or me," Derek said. The other half-brother. He had Dante's giant face on his shirt, fire lighting up all around it with the caption, "*The Inferno.*"

I rolled my eyes. "Anyone else want a say in my and Eric's love life?'

"I think they covered it," Tina said, running her fingers through her long red hair.

Luke nodded in agreement.

A voice came through my communication device, so I pulled it out of my pocket.

"Emmie?" It was my best friend Dee.

"Hey, Dee," I said.

"Get to the infirmary now!" Dee exclaimed. I could hear the excitement in her voice.

"Is it time?" I asked, heading toward the exit. Everyone followed me out, staying close so they could hear Dee.

"Yes," Dee said. "Hurry!"

We ran outside of the arena and jumped into a few jeeps, driving as fast as we could. The street was covered in fresh snow at least two inches thick, but the jeeps had no problem plowing through it. Snow continued to fall all around us, covering every building and tree with its beauty.

One of my new favorite things to do was sit in my home next to the fire, curled up in Eric's lap with a blanket snugly around us, sipping hot cocoa and watching the snow fall outside.

Dee was waiting for us at the entrance to the infirmary. She had her brown curly hair pulled back in a low ponytail. "She's doing well so far. Dr. Stacey and Gideon are in the room with her right now." Taking hold of my arm, Dee steered me toward Marie's room. "I can't believe it's finally happening."

"I know," I said.

We stopped outside of her room. I peeked my head in and saw Marie lying on the bed, her face wet from sweating. Marie was our resident nurse in New Haven. She had left River Springs to join our revolution. Her husband, Gideon, was also from River Springs and was now an officer in our military.

Gideon smiled when he saw me. "Marie said that you, Dee and, Tina are all welcome in here if you want."

"No one else," Marie said through breaths.

"I wouldn't miss this for the world," I said, stepping into the room. Tina and Dee were right at my heels.

Dee sat down in a chair next to the bed, taking Marie's hand. I went on the other side of the bed and took her other hand. I couldn't believe New Haven was finally going to have its first birth. Gideon and Marie got married a month after the battle with Juniper City, which was Maya's old city. Dee and I were excited at the time to have the first marriage in our city. And now here we were a year later having the first baby.

"Just take slow, deep breaths, sweetie," Gideon said. He stood at the edge of the bed with Dr. Stacey. Marie nodded, inhaling as slow as she could under the circumstances.

Tina looked at Marie. "Do you mind if I watch?"

"I don't mind," Marie said. "Dee and Emmie can watch, too."

I shook my head. "I'm good."

"I have a weak stomach," Dee said. "I'll do better up here holding your hand and not seeing anything."

Marie tried to laugh, but it came out strained. "That's fine with me. It's nice having two hands to grip onto."

"I need you to give me a big push," Dr. Stacey said. Marie's grip on my hand tightened as she pushed. "Another push, Marie. You're almost there."

"I can see the head!" Gideon said. "Come on, sweetie. Our baby's almost here."

"One more big push," Dr. Stacey said.

Tina gagged. "I think I'm going to be sick. I shouldn't have watched." She ran out of the room with her hand over her mouth as Marie did her last push.

"It's a boy!" Gideon shouted. "It's our baby boy." Tears formed in his eyes as he looked up at Marie. "You did it, sweetie. He's here and he's beautiful."

The baby's cries filled the room as Gideon cut the umbilical cord and wrapped their baby up. Gideon glanced at Marie. "Do you want to hold him before I go clean him off?"

Marie nodded. "Yes."

I stood and stepped away to give Gideon room. Tears spilled down Marie's cheeks as she held their baby in her arms. She looked up at Gideon and smiled. "I love you."

"I love you, too, Marie." Gideon kissed her softly on the lips.

Dee ran out of the room. "It's a boy!" Cheers rang out

through the hall.

I put my hand on Gideon's arm and looked at Marie. "Congratulations to both of you. He's beautiful."

Gideon wiped some tears off Marie's cheek. She smiled over at me. "Thanks." She stared down at her baby boy, her eyes full of love. She kissed him on the head and looked back at me. "Is it still okay?"

I smiled at her. "Of course, it is, Marie. I want you to use the name."

"But you two were so close," Gideon said. "We don't want to cause any hard feelings."

"I'll be offended if you don't," I said. "Eric and I have already decided that if we ever have a boy, we're naming him after my father." I looked down at their baby. He had stopped crying and was just lying peacefully in Marie's arms. "I want to make sure someone uses his name and I wouldn't want it to be by anyone else than the two of you. Besides, Marie, you knew him longer than I did."

Gideon nodded and took his son from Marie's arms. "Welcome to the world, Mack Clark Saxton."

CHAPTER 2
Austin

Papers rained down on the ground next to me. My palms stung from slamming them against the top of the desk. Everything had gone wrong. I had every single detail planned out perfectly and she ruined everything in the blink of an eye. I should've known she'd do this. I shouldn't have expected anything less.

"Anger's not going to get you anywhere, Austin." Dean Johnson stood near the window of my office, looking out over the River Precinct in River Springs.

I wasn't sure if he was going to join our cause and support us after I killed President Randall, who was Dean's closest friend. Luckily, his daughter Amber had him wrapped around her finger. And I had tricked her into trusting me.

I glared at Dean until I thought my eyes might burst. I couldn't stand him or his annoying daughter, but I had to pretend if I intended to win the war. Then I could dispose of them both. "She betrayed us, Dean. She started a rebellion in *my* city!"

Amber came up next to me, batting her eyelashes and pouting like she always did. I wished she would grow her hair out, but she insisted on keeping it short. It didn't suit her facial structure at all.

"Babe, just calm down." I cringed at her voice. How had I once liked her?

"You forced her hand." Dean folded his massive arms and stared at me. "You didn't give her an option."

"Like hell, I didn't!" I fumed. How could he defend her? "She had a choice! She should've stayed and supported us!"

Amber ran her fingers through my hair. I wanted to back away, but I forced myself to stay still. "You killed her lover, babe. What did you expect?"

I'd expected her to be mad, maybe a little sad, but I didn't think she'd start a war in River Springs. I had other things more important to think about. Like capturing Emmie and destroying New Haven. "I didn't think she cared about him this much."

Dean laughed. "They'd been together for twenty years, Austin. You really thought she wouldn't have hurt feelings over you killing Whit?"

I needed to change the subject before I did something rash. I walked over to the window and looked out. My security detail was placed around the precinct, keeping every resident in line. They were ordered to immediately kill anyone who crossed that line. "Where do we go from here? We need to stop this war Janice started so we can move on. It needs to be quick."

Amber propped herself up on my desk and crossed her ankles together, swinging her legs. “They have a lot of weapons and ammo. It will be hard to get in.”

“We need to attack from all sides,” Dean said.

I nodded. “I like that idea. If we could somehow get our security to surround the perimeter, that would be beneficial.” When I leaned against the table, Amber linked her arm through mine. “We need to attack in the middle of the night. We need to use as little ammo as we can, so we have enough to fight the other cities.”

Dean shook his head and looked at me. He eyed Amber’s arm linked with mine for just a moment, then turned his eyes back to me. He didn’t like the two of us together, but I couldn't care less what he thought of our relationship. “We’ll need a lot of ammo if we plan on winning. There are too many of them.”

“If we could just get to Janice and kill her and her top supporters,” I said. “Then we might be able to get everyone else to surrender. When your life is suddenly on the line, you’ll do anything to stay alive.”

“I’m not sure about that,” Dean said. “I think a lot of them won’t go down without a fight.” He was probably thinking of Whit’s wife, Amy, who Dean had been sleeping with for years. It was another reason I didn’t trust him staying here. I needed to keep a close eye on him.

Amber gave a bored sigh. “Can’t we just throw a lot of bombs over there or something?”

I looked at her. “I need those bombs for my other plans.”

“Fine. What about grenades or the rocket launchers?” Amber asked, rubbing my arm.

I clenched my jaw as I thought about our ex-military leader, Mack, and how he'd somehow managed to get his hands on two of our rocket launchers. We only had five to begin with. "We only have three left and the rockets themselves are in limited supply. The area Janice is in is too big for the grenades to do any real damage. We need to find out where she's hiding."

"How do you expect to do that?" Dean asked.

"Let's send in a spy." I stood up straight and approached the window, just so I could get away from Amber. "Fine someone willing to go over there and find out her location. Give them a communication device and have them report back to us everything they find out."

Dean rubbed his hand over his bald head. "We've already tried that, and it didn't work. They check everyone who comes in for any communication device."

I closed my eyes, trying to keep my temper in check. "Send someone in, have them find out, and then have them escape and come back over here."

"We've tried that, too." Dean didn't hide his annoyance. "They killed the person before they could get back over here. Janice isn't too trusting. She knows what you'll try to do."

Opening my eyes, I slammed my fist against the window. "Then find another way! How hard can it be to find one person?"

Amber came up and wrapped her arms around me, rubbing her hands on my chest. Dean cleared his throat, so I took her hands and pushed them off me. Amber huffed, but I didn't care. We were talking about war. It wasn't the right time for her to grope me.

“It’s more complicated than you think, Austin,” Dean said. “Remember how close she was to Whit. He let her follow him around like a puppy. She sat in every meeting and heard every single word that came out of his mouth. She knows what to do. She’s smart and capable of stopping anyone from invading her part of the city.”

“Just send someone in and report back to me,” I said.

Dean nodded and left the room.

“You don’t have to worry about me touching you when my dad’s around,” Amber said from behind me. “I’m old enough to make my own decisions.”

I turned around to look at her. “It’s not about that, Amber. It wasn’t the appropriate moment for it.”

“I was just trying to console you.” She placed her hands on my chest. “You’ve been so wound up.”

She was right about that. Everything had been stressing me out. She annoyed me most of the time, but she was good for letting out some of that stress. I picked her up by her waist and set her on my desk. She bit her lip and wrapped her legs around me, pulling me close. I closed my eyes and tried not to think about the fact that it was her I kissed. She wasn’t half bad at it.

Right before I’d killed Whit, I had everything lined up perfectly. He was the last piece I needed to destroy and then it was on to victory.

But stupid Janice Woodard had blindsided me. I hadn’t seen her attack coming. If I would have known, I would have killed her too. I was just so mad at myself for making such a foolish mistake. I needed to repair the problem.

Before Janice's daughter, Emmie, started the revolution in River Springs, we had a stable seventeen thousand residents. Then she left and over time she managed to convince about three hundred to join her. It wasn't much, so I didn't worry about it. We still outnumbered them.

But Janice flipped out when she heard Whit was dead. She managed to talk someone in security into letting her do a broadcast that could be heard everywhere. Her voice rang out over the city, letting everyone know I killed Whit. She said that anyone that supported me should move to the River or Ocean Precinct. Anyone who stood against me and wanted to support her and the revolution Emmie started, she told them to join her over in the Lake and Mountain Precincts. She divided River Springs into two sections. She broke into our weapon supply and headed out, stopping anyone that tried to get in her way.

I didn't think anyone would support her or Emmie, seeing as Emmie had convinced less than three hundred to join her. To my surprise and dismay, several thousand did support them, leaving me with only nine thousand residents. Every day that number got smaller as people tried to escape and flee to the other side of the city. Some made it over there safely and some lost their lives along the way. It was such a waste, losing all those people, but they brought it upon themselves.

We tried to send spies over to get information, but they kept tight security around the perimeter of their territory. They put up barricades all the way around so no one could just walk in. They searched and questioned everyone that came through. We kept a close eye on the entrance to see who went in and out of their territory.

In the beginning, Janice was heavily involved. We saw her constantly near the entrance, talking to everyone that tried to enter. But as time went on, and the number of residents grew, she stopped showing up at the entrance. She was playing it safe. She probably saw it as being careful and wise, but I saw it as being a coward.

There were a few key players that we consistently saw at the entrance. They must have been her closest advisors and the people she trusted the most. I needed to find a way to get my hands on one of them. If we tortured them enough, they would crack. Everyone had a breaking point.

I needed to wipe out Janice's side of the city soon so we could move on to bigger and better things. We were losing valuable time and it had to come to an end.

CHAPTER 3
Emmie

President Mendes sat at the head of the table with her hands clasped together, her makeup making her hazel eyes pop. Her green blouse was too big for her. She'd lost weight over the past year. We had been working so hard to build up New Haven, so everyone worked long hours. She was also still adjusting to the loss of her husband Oscar, New Haven's previous Vice President, and the loss of her son Javier.

We were sitting in the conference room at the wood table and chairs, planning out our strategy for the upcoming weeks.

"Dante, what's the latest news?" President Mendes asked. Her orange blossom perfume wafted across the table.

Dante leaned back in his chair, his eyes filled with anger and sorrow. "They've captured them. We need to get there as soon as possible."

Ever since Dante left Kingsland, he'd been keeping in touch with an ally over there named Marcus. Things were fine up until about a month ago. Marcus and his supporters had been able to keep their involvement with the revolution a secret. But somehow the president of Kingsland found out their identities and started killing anyone who supported the revolution unless they all turned themselves in. They had barricaded themselves in a corner of the city since there were so many of them. But it wasn't long until they ran out of supplies and President Coleman was able to infiltrate their area.

"Where are they hiding them?" Vice President Jennings asked. He sat opposite the president, his petite frame not taking much room in his chair.

"That's the main problem." Dante rested his long arm on the back of the chair. "I have no idea. Marcus was only able to contact me for a few seconds to let me know they'd been found and then the communication went dead."

I twisted the ring Eric gave me around my finger. He'd asked me to marry him after he returned from being held captive in River Springs. He said he'd do it right one day but just wanted the assurance at the time. I more than happily said yes. Made of dark brown twine, the ring had started to fray from me turning it so much and the fact that I never took it off. "Do you know of any possible locations of where they would be?"

Terrance shook his head and sat forward, the muscles twitching under his tight military tee. "There were so many of them. Probably close to four thousand that supported Marcus. I'm sure President Coleman spread them all around the city so in the chance that we came to rescue them they'd be hard to find."

"How many still support the president?" Santiago asked. He leaned back in his chair, clasping his hands behind his head. His shaggy hair had grown so long, he'd started to tie it back with a hairband. He always kept an extra band on his wrist.

Anytime Vivica looked at Santiago, he would wink at her and move his eyebrows up and down. I had no idea how she put up with him.

Dante looked up at the ceiling, calculating it all out. He and I had become close friends since first coming to New Haven, so we could both read each other well. "My guess would be around ten thousand."

Santiago whistled. "Is it even possible to go rescue them?"

Dante gave Santiago a sharp look. "We have to. President Coleman will torture them for information and then kill them."

"How do you know he hasn't killed them already?" Gideon asked. His eyes looked tired, yet full of joy. He probably didn't get any sleep last night since he and Marie had just welcomed their first child into the world.

Dante swore under his breath. We all knew it was highly likely that had already happened.

Gently squeezing Dante's arm, I sat forward. "It doesn't matter. Those people are part of our revolution. If there is any chance to save at least one of them, we need to take it."

"Let's not forget about the fact that the same disease Lou and Dee had last year has been spreading around Kingsland," Vice President Jennings said. As always, his white polo shirt was perfectly pressed. "We have the cure and those people need to be saved."

He'd almost lost his daughter Dee from the disease. It was

probably hard for him to stomach other parents having to go through the same thing.

I nodded. "It makes this mission that much more important."

"We'll be going in blind," Hiro said. Hiro was a previous Juniper City resident and now a military officer for New Haven. He was short yet stocky. "We have no idea what we'll walk into."

Tina looked at Dante, tightening the band holding back her red hair. "Do you even know who the four thousand are? If we walked into your city, anyone could pretend to be a part of the revolution and then kill us when our backs are turned."

"She's right," President Mendes said. "There's no way of knowing who we can and can't trust."

"That leaves only one solution," Maya said. We all turned to her. She twirled her charm bracelets around her wrist. "We need to find and capture President Coleman."

Santiago smiled. "Hold him hostage. I like it." He held up his hand to Maya for a high five, but she ignored him. When Santiago glared at her and swore, Dante reached over and high fived him for her.

"We can set up an exchange," Terrance said. "They can have President Coleman back alive if they release the prisoners."

Vivica looked over at Terrance. She had her shoulder-length black hair slicked back. "Do you think they would trade the president for four thousand people? I don't think he's worth that much."

"What if we just asked for woman and children first and

then think of another plan?" Tina asked.

Gideon shook his head. "It has to be all or nothing."

"Let's take over Headquarters." For the first time that day, Dante had a spark of hope in his eyes. He grabbed a pen and paper from the middle of the table. He talked as he drew. "Let's make it a small ops mission. Just everyone in this room besides the president and vice president." He looked at me and Tina. "Eric and Luke can come too."

When we first came to New Haven, we agreed to not have the four revolutionaries go on missions together in case something bad happened. We were all so new to everything. Now we were more stable and knew our strengths and weaknesses. We'd had a lot more training and after the battle with Juniper, we realized the four of us worked best together, not separate.

"Bruce won't let you leave without taking him," Maya said. Her short black hair was in her typical fashion, spiked around her head.

I smiled at Dante. "Neither will Joshua nor Will."

Dante shook his head as he continued to draw. "Fine. What's that? Fourteen people?"

"Might as well make it fifteen," Terrance said. "We can have five groups of three surrounding the building."

"Who would number fifteen be?" Vivica asked.

The corner of my mouth turned up into a slight smile. I knew the perfect person. "Thunder Thighs." I immediately clasped my hand over my mouth. I had never spoken out loud the nickname I gave her back in Recruitment to anyone but Eric, Luke, Tina, and Dee.

Tina sat across from me laughing and clapping her hands together.

Vivica raised her skinny eyebrows and looked at me. "Who's Thunder Thighs?"

Tina laughed so hard, tears formed in her green eyes. I picked up a pen and threw it at her, smacking her in the cheek. "It's not that funny."

She nodded and let out a snort. "Yes, it is!"

Everyone in the room looked back and forth between me and Tina. I rolled my eyes and then tucked my hair behind my ear. "Her real name is Rachel."

"That girl from your old city who always looks ticked off?" Dante asked.

I nodded. "Yes, that would be her."

"You call her Thunder Thighs?" Maya asked with a sly smile.

My face reddened a little as I noticed all eyes on me, most of them questioning. I slowly nodded. "I gave her that nickname back in Recruitment when I didn't know her real name. She's very thick and muscular. It seemed appropriate at the time."

Santiago had a huge grin on his face. "I'm calling her that from now on."

"No!" I turned and pointed my finger at him. "You can't tell her my nickname for her. She'll crush me!"

Dante slapped me on the back. "I think you could take her."

Tina finally regained her composure. She looked across the table at Santiago. "Can we put that down as the next fight in the ring? Emmie and Thunder Thighs? I've been *dying* to know who would win."

"Do you have a death wish for me?" I asked Tina. "You know she'll kill me. There's no way I could beat her."

"Not with that attitude," Vivica said, folding her arms and pursing her lips.

Hiro cleared his throat. "Maybe we should go back to planning the infiltration of headquarters in Kingsland."

I really liked Hiro. He was such a hard worker and an amazing fighter, but sometimes he took life a little too seriously. He needed to lighten up just a bit.

"He's right," Vice President Jennings said. He gave me somewhat of a fatherly scolding look.

Ever since my father had passed away in the battle last year, he had taken it upon himself to become like a father to me. But so did Eric's dad Alexander, plus my two brothers, Derek and Joshua. It was becoming annoying. I went from having one father to four.

I sighed and looked at Dante's drawing. "So, where's headquarters located in your old city?"

Dante pointed to it on the paper. "Northside. I think it would be best to walk around the city from the outside and break-in on the north, right above headquarters."

Terrance and Vivica nodded in agreement. They were previous residents of Kingsland like Dante.

"What's security like?" Santiago asked, snapping the hairband against his wrist.

"Tight," Dante said. "They've beefed things up since the list leaked. It could be even more now that they've captured them. They have at least ten men outside on each side of Headquarters. Plus, another twenty-five on the roof."

"It'll be worse once we get inside," Terrance said.

Vivica nodded. "President Coleman has cameras installed at each corner of the building. Once we're spotted, they'll put the president in lockdown."

"If that happens, we're screwed." Dante rubbed his head as he eyed his drawing.

Santiago looked at Terrance. "Is there a way to shut down the cameras?"

Terrance scratched the back of his neck and thought about it for a minute. He had been their head of security before they left to join us in New Haven. "Possibly." Rubbing his square jaw, he sat forward. "But the second we take down the feed, they'll know something's wrong. They'll still put the president in lockdown."

"What exactly does that entail?" Maya asked.

Dante swore. "It means we're in deep …" I slapped him on the arm. He eyed me for a second and then finished his sentence. I rolled my eyes.

Vivica looked at Dante and shook her head. "It means they'll put him in a solid steel room below Headquarters. It's impossible to break in. Plus, they'll have it surrounded by at least fifty security guards."

"Not to mention the guards that will be in the room with him if by some miracle we break in." Terrance leaned back in his chair, the wood squeaking under his muscle.

"Is there a way to put the security feed on a loop?" Hiro asked. We all turned to him. "A continuous feed of the same minute or so. Get about a minute of tape showing everything clear and then play that same minute over and over until we're done."

I played with my butterfly pendant, moving it back and forth on the twine. "I'll ask Derek and Naomi."

"If we can do that," Dante said, "we might be able to pull this off."

"We'll have to be fast," Vivica said. "Once we're in Headquarters, we won't have much time until we're caught."

"How do we get inside Headquarters?" I asked.

"Roof," Terrance said.

Dante nodded in agreement. "We need to start by taking down the security on the ground at the back of the building."

"What weapons are we using?" Gideon asked. "Guns will be too loud."

I nodded. "We need to stick with bows and arrows and knives."

During the past year, we had come up with a design for a smaller version of a sword, but still longer and wider than a regular knife.

Terrance stood and went to a whiteboard on the wall. He picked up a marker to draw out the plan. "Okay, we'll have to wait until the sun goes down before we strike."

"Why don't we wait until the middle of the night?" Tina asked. "Wouldn't it be quieter?"

"It would," Vivica said, "but President Coleman won't be in the building anymore. He leaves somewhere between nine and ten."

Dante sat back in his chair and stretched out his long legs.

"They have a meeting every night from seven-thirty to at least nine. That would be the best place to capture him. He'll have his most important advisors, plus his top security with him. If we could get our hands on all of them at the same time, it would be very beneficial."

Terrance went back to drawing on the board, the smell of markers filling the air. "We'll go in five groups of three. We'll have to get over the brick wall as quietly as we can. We need to kill those ten guards behind Headquarters as quickly as possible. They can't have time to yell out or radio in our arrival."

Dante stood and went to stand near Terrance, taking his paper with him. "Once those guards are down, we need to climb up the back of Headquarters. Getting to all the security on the roof is going to be the trickiest part. There will be at least twenty-five of them and only fifteen of us."

"We won't have room or time for error," Terrance said. "Once we're in, we need to go to the main security room and take control of the room. If there is a way to run the continuous feed, we can set it up and then go from there."

"And if there isn't a way?" I asked.

Dante looked at Terrance and then over at me. "We'll just have to pray for the best and make a dash for the conference room."

The room went silent for a minute.

President Mendes cleared her throat and then stood. "Sounds like a plan. Emmie, why don't you and Dante go talk to Derek and Naomi. Everyone else, start preparing all the supplies you'll need for the trip. You'll leave first thing in the morning."

We found Derek and Naomi in the security room. When we walked in, they were sitting close together, and Naomi laughed at something Derek had said. She ran her fingers through his hair and then leaned in to kiss him.

Dante cleared his throat. "Shouldn't you two be working?"

They snapped away from each other and turned to us. Both were wearing shirts Derek had designed—a camera lens in the shape of a shield. He thought it was perfect because it symbolized them protecting the city through security.

Derek was beet red. "We were working."

"Uh, huh," I said, walking over to them. I took a seat in an empty chair. "Let's just ignore the awkward situation and cut to the chase." I looked at Derek. "Is there any way to make a continuous feed of a security tape?"

Derek nodded, his eyes full of excitement. "Yes. I learned how to do it, but never had a use for it."

"Well, now you do," Dante said. He had sat down in a chair next to me. "We're breaking into Headquarters in Kingsland and we need to be able to walk the halls without alerting the president that we're there."

Naomi raised her black eyebrows. "You know that's pretty much impossible." She was originally from Kingsland, too.

Dante took a deep breath. "We don't have any other option. They've captured Marcus and all of his supporters."

"Oh." Naomi's face fell as she tugged on her long black braid resting over her shoulder.

"You'll just need to get in the main security room," Derek

said. "You can contact me when you enter, but it's pretty simple. You'll need to record a certain amount of time and then put that feed on repeat."

"Seems easy enough." I stood, glancing over at Derek. "Thanks, Captain Awesome." I motioned between Derek and Naomi. "Keep it professional in here. You're working."

"Yes, ma'am," Derek said as he saluted me.

I sighed and left the room.

CHAPTER 4

"It's not funny!" I was in my room packing some things for the trip. Eric lay on my bed, holding his stomach from laughing so hard. "I don't know why everyone is finding it so funny. I could be killed."

"She's not going to kill you." Eric rolled onto his side and propped himself up with his elbow. He took some deep breaths to calm his laughter. "I won't let her."

I threw a couple of shirts in my bag with more force than necessary. "I'm making her a part of our team. I don't want to leave her alone with anyone else."

Eric groaned. "Seriously, Emmie? I don't want Thunder Thighs to be our third wheel."

I glared at him. "Rachel."

Her name didn't feel right on my tongue. I loved calling her Thunder Thighs more than anyone else, but I had to be more careful. I wanted to live.

"Thunder Thighs," Eric said, correcting me. "Can't we have Joshua or Will be with us?"

Putting my hand on my hip, I shook my head. "The teams are decided."

Eric stood and came up behind me, wrapping his arms around my waist. He kissed my neck. "Please?"

"No."

Turning me around, he pinned me up against the wall and gave me a playful smile. "Pretty please?"

For a second, I almost got lost in his blue eyes but then I pulled myself together. "No."

Eric pouted. He left a trail of kisses on my neck and cheek before he started nibbling on my ear. I tried to push him away. I wasn't going to cave. I couldn't cave. Holding onto me tight, he leaned his forehead against mine. He ran his finger down my cheek and then gently across my lips. "Please, Emmie?"

I touched his scar on his left cheek. He received a deep gash from a knife when he was being held by Whit. Everything on his body that had been broken or wounded had healed nicely, except his cheek. The scar had faded a little, but I had a feeling it would always be there.

Looking deep into my eyes, he kissed me. I tried to pull back, but I caved easily, melting into him. He always did that when he wanted something to go his way. Most of the time it worked.

After a few minutes, he pulled away, making me sigh. He kissed me on the forehead and then headed for the door. When he got to the doorway, he turned back around. "I'm going to go pack. I'll let Joshua know he'll be our third member."

"Nice try, Eric." I folded my arms, lifting my chin. "Rachel is our third member and that's final."

Eric frowned. "I'm losing my touch."

"Unbelievable." Dee paced in front of us, her hands balled in fists. I always thought she was so cute when she was mad, but she hated when I said that.

We were at the apartment she lived in with Tina. We had finished construction on some apartment buildings a few months ago. We had started building homes for each family but soon realized that wasn't practical in every situation, especially considering how broken every family had become after the battle. Dee had her family in New Haven, but she felt like she needed to get out on her own.

Will took a step toward her. "Sweetheart …"

Dee stopped and pointed her finger at him. "Don't you sweetheart me!"

Sighing, Will turned to me for help.

I held my arms open, facing Dee. "Sweetheart …"

As Dee let out a frustrated groan, Eric, Luke, and Tina laughed. Tina had her back up against Luke and he had his arms around her, holding her close. It had been about a year since they'd reunited, but it still made me happy every time I looked at them.

"I'm old enough to make my own decisions." Dee shook her head, her brown curls bouncing around. "I don't know why the five of you think you can boss me around."

"We're just trying to protect you." Will adjusted the black square-rimmed glasses resting on the bridge of his nose. They still had white tape wrapped around the middle from when they broke last year in the battle with Juniper. New glasses weren't easy to come by in New Haven. Not yet.

Dee stomped her foot. "I don't need protection! I'm the same age as all of you."

"Only Eric, Emmie, and I have turned nineteen," Luke said. "The rest of you are still eighteen."

Tina rolled her eyes. "You didn't have to get so technical."

Eric glanced over at Luke and then at Dee. "Everyone else in here has more experience than you."

Dee glared at him. "It's not my fault I came down with a disease. But I've fully recovered from it. I've been training with everyone else for over six months!"

She was right, but I didn't like the thought of her coming with us.

I walked up to her and put my hands on her arms. "The kids need you here. You're our best teacher."

"There are other teachers, Emmie," Dee said. "I want to come with you."

Luke looked over Tina's shoulder at Dee. "We've already set up the teams. You'll make things uneven."

Dee put her hands on her hips. "Really, Luke? That's the defense you're going with? Do you know how easy it is to change three groups of five to four groups of four? If anything, I'm evening it out! Sixteen is an even number."

Sighing, I tugged on one of Dee's curls. "You really want to go?"

"Yes." Dee looked me straight in the eye. "I want to go, Emmie. I want to be a part of the group. You can't just keep leaving me out. I know I'm tiny, but I can fight."

Tina let out a laugh. "She fought pretty well against Amber

and her bratty friends back in Recruitment."

I pursed my lips together. She had done well for herself. She was definitely fiery and determined. Her mad face softened in front of me, moving on to the sympathetic pout. I moaned. I'd had enough of that look for one day. "Fine. I think Dee should go with us."

Dee's eyes lit up and she clasped her hands together. "Really?"

Once I nodded, she looked over at Will. He looked from Dee to me to Eric and then back to Dee. Eric had just shrugged.

Will let out a long sigh. "If that's what you want."

"Oh, I'm so excited!" Dee threw her arms around my neck and gave me a big kiss on my cheek. I hugged her tight for a second, but then she wiggled free of my grasp and ran at Will. She threw her whole body around him and he held her tight while she kissed him all over his cheeks and forehead. Her curls covered most of his face, but I could see the blush. I loved the two of them together.

Eric rubbed his hands together. "Actually, this is perfect. Will and Dee can go with us and that way we can keep a close eye on her." He smiled at me, his eyes hopeful.

I shook my head. "That's not going to work. Rachel is going with us. But now you can have your other wish."

"What's that?" Eric asked.

I smiled as I put my arms around his neck. "Joshua can go with us."

Eric threw back his head and grunted. "I wanted him to replace Thunder Thighs, not come in addition to her."

"Why do you want Thunder Thighs on your team so badly?" Dee asked. She had finally lowered herself from Will, but he was still blushing brightly, straightening his glasses for no apparent reason.

"I accidentally let my nickname for her slip in front of everyone," I said. "Now everyone wants to call her that."

Eric kissed me on the cheek. "You can't keep her away from everyone for the rest of her life."

"Well, I'm going to try." Releasing myself from Eric, I straightened out my shirt. I headed toward the door of the apartment. "Now, if you'll all excuse me, I want to go see Mack one more time before we leave."

Marie sat in the infirmary bed and watched on as Gideon held Mack in his arms. Gideon was sitting in a chair right next to the bed. Both Marie and Gideon smiled when Dee, Tina, and I walked into the room.

"How's little Mack doing today?" I asked.

Gideon stood and brought Mack over to me. I carefully took him from his father's arms and held him close. He slept peacefully all snuggled up in a blanket.

"He's doing great," Marie said. "All his vitals are normal and he's eating just fine."

Dee and Tina stood next to me watching the baby sleep. Tina looked over at Marie. "How much did he weigh?"

Marie moaned. "Nine pounds three ounces. I hope my next one isn't that big."

I brushed my finger along little Mack's cheek and smiled. "He's already on his way to becoming big like Mack."

"I don't think Mack Clark would have wanted you stroking his cheek like that." Dee kissed little Mack on the forehead. "Or that."

Mack Clark had saved my life back in River Springs and then saved my life again during the battle with Juniper. He was killed right before my eyes just mere seconds later. I thought about him every day.

I laughed, thinking of Mack's tough demeanor. "No, he wouldn't have." Little Mack took a deep breath and let out a little sigh. "That seems about right." I looked up at Marie. "He's so adorable."

Marie smiled at Gideon. "He gets his good looks from his father." She held out her hand and he took it, kissing it lightly. He reached over and brushed some hair off her forehead.

"Are you sure you want to come?" I asked Gideon. "You can stay here. We'll find someone else."

Gideon shook his head. "Marie and I talked it over and decided it would be best if I went."

"Trust me, I don't want him to leave," Marie said, "but you need his expertise. This is a big mission you're doing, and you need our best fighters."

Dee flexed her arms. "That's why I'm going." Reaching over, she took Mack from my arms. "My turn."

Feeling Marie's gaze on me, I turned to her. She looked me in the eye. "Emmie, bring him home safely."

"I will," I said.

Marie was about to say something, but the nurse walked in, holding a tray of food. She smiled when she saw me, the warmth showing in her light brown eyes. I forced myself to smile, not because I didn't like her, but because every time I saw her, I thought of her father and brother who'd both been killed.

She was Vice President Oliver's daughter, Samantha. She had shoulder-length golden-brown hair that had a natural wave to it. There was something in her walk and the way she held herself that reminded me of her father. She also had that same loveable face and the eyes that held a bit of a mystery behind them.

Samantha set the tray on Marie's lap. "How are you feeling?"

"As good as I can be," Marie said as she picked up the fork on the tray. "Thank you, Samantha."

"You're welcome," Samantha said. "Do you need anything else?"

Marie shook her head as she took a bite of the potatoes. "Nope."

"Well, let me know if you do," Samantha said. As she passed me on the way to the door, she put her hand on my arm. "Be careful."

"I will," I said. Word must have already spread about our mission.

Marie lowered her spoon, her face serious. "Emmie, promise me."

I looked at little Mack in Dee's arms. He couldn't lose his father. We already had so many fatherless children in New Haven. We had to keep Gideon alive.

I turned back to Marie. "I promise."

We said our goodbyes to Marie and the baby. I kissed little

Mack's cheek before I left. When we passed the conference room on the way out, I ran in so I could grab my coat. It had been a cold winter just like the year before.

When we walked out of Headquarters, the sun had already set. I pulled my coat tightly around me and looked up at the stars. It was a clear night, so you could see countless stars lighting up the sky.

"Emmie." I turned to see Eric walking toward me. "Do you have a minute?"

"For you? Of course," I said.

Saying goodbye to Tina and Dee, I put my hand in Eric's. He took me to the ladder that led to an alcove. I had been up there many times since I'd first arrived in New Haven. I climbed the ladder first, with Eric right behind me. When I got to the top, I gasped.

The whole area was covered with strings of white lights, reflecting beautifully against the snow on the trees. On the ground were hundreds of butterflies and flowers of all different colors.

Reaching down, I picked up a purple butterfly. I ran my finger across it, noticing that it was paper that had been painted. Eric came up behind me and put his arms around my waist, looking over my shoulder at the butterfly.

I reached my arm around me and touched the back of his head. "How did you do all of this?"

I could hear the smile in his voice. "I had a lot of help."

Taking me by the hand, he walked me to the middle of the alcove. I put the butterfly in my pocket and then he took both of my hands in his, turning me so I faced him.

"Emmie …" He stopped and cleared his throat. His hands were slightly shaking, but I wasn't so sure that it was from the cold. "I still remember the first moment I saw you. You were standing in the Recruitment office, staring at your contract. I almost didn't stop, but something inside me told me I should. When you looked up at me, my heart stopped. You were the most beautiful girl I'd ever seen. Of course, I had to play it cool to keep up with my bad boy image."

His smile twisted as I rolled my eyes. "But I knew from that moment on that I had to get to know you. And trust me when I say it didn't take long until I realized I needed to keep you in my life. I was a little worried you'd get sick of me and would eventually brush me off."

I smiled. "I could never get sick of you. I was just glad to have a hot guy pay attention to me. I can't tell you how many flips my heart did when you were standing near me."

A smile pulled at his lips for a moment and then his face fell. "Emmie, those two challenges we did in Recruitment pained me. The one where I thought you were trapped and then killed, and then the underwater one. When Mack pulled your body out of the water …" He fought back tears. He looked up at the sky and blinked them away before turning his gaze back to me. "Watching you lifeless on the ground as Mack tried to bring you back to life, I knew at that moment that I was in love with you." He tucked my hair behind my ear. "Call me crazy, but I knew it. I know it was so fast. We'd only known each other a couple of weeks, but I couldn't help myself."

Eric reached up and wiped away some tears that were running down my cheeks. "Emmie Woodard, you are the most amazing woman I've ever met. You're strong, determined, fun to be around, and so kind to everyone around you. You've always put others before yourself. You're completely selfless."

I shook my head. "I don't know …"

Eric put his hand on my cheek. "You are. You have risked your life for everyone in this city without batting an eye. I don't know what this city would do without you. I don't know what I'd do without you. I want to spend the rest of my life with you."

He pulled something out of his pocket and then got down on one knee. Holding up a ring, he looked me in the eye. He smiled and sniffed as he wiped away a few tears from his eyes. "I was supposed to be manly." I put my hands over my mouth and laughed through my tears. Eric cleared his throat. "Emmie Woodard, will you marry me?"

I uncovered my mouth but continued to laugh. "Yes!" Standing up, he put his forehead against mine. My smile stretched from ear to ear. "Yes! Yes! Yes!"

Wrapping his arms around me, he pulled me into him and kissed me, his warm lips heating me on the cold night.

After a minute, I pulled back. "The ring! I want to see it."

"Oh, yeah." He took my right hand and started to put the ring on.

I twirled my ring made of twine that was already resting on my ring finger. "I don't want to take my other one off. It means too much to me."

The side of his mouth turned up. "That's why I made this other ring a little bigger so you could slide it over." He slipped it all the way on, and it fit perfectly. He let out a sigh. "Thank goodness."

Smiling, I pulled my hand up so I could get a better look at the ring. Unlike my first ring, it was made of silver. Butterflies were engraved around it.

“Oh, Eric, it’s perfect.” I put my hands on his cheeks. “I love you.”

“I love you, too.” Eric held me close and pressed his lips to mine.

CHAPTER 5

We were up before dawn. As the guys and Thunder Thighs were packing up the jeeps, Tina, Dee, Maya, Vivica, and Naomi circled me, wanting to hear every second of the proposal. They all took turns looking at my ring. I think Dee squealed at least ten times.

Terrance walked up to us, his stance wide thanks to all his muscle. "Listen ladies, I know you're excited, but once we set off, no more talk of the proposal, marriage, rings, or anything wedding related. We need all of you focused on the task at hand."

Placing her hand on her hip, Vivica rolled her eyes. "Can't we have two minutes of fun here? We've been preparing for this proposal for months. Excuse us if we're happy it finally happened."

"You've had your two minutes." Terrance folded his arms and looked at Dee. "And no more squealing."

Dee glared at him as he walked away. When he was a few feet away, a squeal sounded behind me. Terrance turned around so Dee threw up her hands. "It wasn't me. I swear."

A small figure bounded toward me, her long brown hair messy like she just got out of bed. When she got to me, she threw her arms around my waist. "Congratulations! I'm so happy for you."

She pulled back and I squeezed her cheeks together. "Thank you, Miss Rosie."

"Rosie, what are you doing up at this hour?" Santiago asked as he walked over to our group.

She stuck her tongue out at him. "I came to congratulate Emmie, dummy." She rolled her brown eyes at me. "Brothers."

"Tell me about it." I hugged her tightly. "Are you still going to be my flower girl? You haven't grown too old on me, have you?"

She shook her head. "I'm ten now, but I'm not too old. I still want to do it. Can I see your ring?" I held my hand out to her and she yanked it close. "Oh, Emmie, it's beautiful. I can't wait to find my Eric one day."

"Which will be at least twenty years from now." Santiago folded his arms. "And if I approve of him."

Rosie tapped her finger on her mouth, calculating it out. After a couple of seconds, her jaw dropped. "You can't make me wait until I'm thirty!"

Santiago smirked. "Oh, yes I can."

Rosie glared at him, rolling her hand into a fist. I put my hand on her chin and turned her face toward me. "You don't have to wait that long. Us girls have your back."

"Thank you, Emmie." Rosie hugged me and shook me side to side.

"You only have to wait fifteen years," I said, running my hand over her hair.

Rosie looked up at me, her voice coming out in a whine. "But, Emmie! I don't want to wait that long!"

"I'm just teasing you," I said. "When you find the right guy, you'll know it."

Santiago whistled. "That's if he's still alive when I'm through with him."

Vivica put her hand on Santiago's chest. "That's enough. You're going to give the girl a heart attack."

"We need to head out." Terrance's voice was loud enough so everyone could hear.

We said goodbye to Rosie and Naomi and went to join everyone near the jeeps.

Dante gave me a big hug. He kissed me on top of my head. "I know I already congratulated you last night, but I'll do it again. Congratulations, Em. He's one lucky guy."

"I know," I said, hugging him back. He laughed as we went to join Terrance up front. Santiago and Maya were already up there, standing next to him.

"Listen up." Terrance had his arms folded and his back straight as he stared out at all of us. Sometimes his demeanor reminded me of Mack. "This will only be about a five-hour drive, but I wanted us to get there in plenty of time so we could scout around while it's still light."

The four revolutionaries were leading the mission, but we asked Terrance to step in and help since he used to be the head of security in Kingsland.

Dante stood next to Terrance. "Emmie, Maya, Santiago,

and I will be the leaders for our groups."

"Vivica, Tina, and Luke are on my team," Santiago said. He rubbed behind his ear where the tattoo of a cross rested.

"I have Hiro, Will, and Dee," Dante said. I made him swear to me the night before that he'd protect Dee. I didn't trust anyone else but him to look after her like I would.

"Terrance, Bruce, and Gideon are coming with me." Maya fingered the sword pendant on her charm bracelet. She claimed it was good luck.

I cleared my throat and tugged on the end of my braid that hung over my shoulder. "That leaves Eric, Joshua, and Rachel with me."

There were a few snickers from the group, but I kept my face as straight as I could. It was going to be a long trip.

"The leaders will drive," Dante said. "Let's head out."

As I headed for our jeep, someone shouted my name. I turned around to see Derek running toward me. Well, it was more of a slow jog. He wasn't in shape. He was out of breath by the time he got to me.

He bent down, resting his hands on his knees and panting. After a few seconds of deep breathing, he looked up at me. "Were you really going to leave without telling me?"

I shrugged. "You weren't home by the time I went to bed last night."

"You could have woken me up this morning before you left the house." Derek stood straight, stretching out his back. He had started lifting weights to gain some muscle on his long, skinny arms, but so far, it wasn't working.

"I tried. I went into your room, shouted your name, shook

you pretty hard, and even threw a few things at your head."

He scratched his head. "Really? Well, that would explain the random items in my bed when I woke up." He eyed me. "Including a shoe. You threw a shoe at my head?"

"Yes." I twisted my ring on my finger. "And it didn't work."

"Well, now that I'm here and semi-awake, don't you have something to tell me?"

"You already know."

"I haven't heard it from your mouth."

I rolled my eyes. "Does it make a difference?"

Derek nodded. "Uh, yes, it does." He looked over at Joshua who was sitting in the back of my jeep. "I bet you told *him* already." They were both my half-brothers but from different sides of the family.

I rubbed my temples and groaned. It was too early for Derek and all his Derekness. "He was already awake since he's coming with me on the trip!" I sighed. "It doesn't matter. Derek, Eric officially proposed to me last night."

"What did you say?" Derek had his eyebrows raised, waiting in anticipation.

"No."

His face fell. "Why would you do that to him? I actually like the guy. He was going to take you off my hands!"

"Derek, of course, I said yes. I'm wearing the ring!"

He folded his arms and huffed. "Well, you haven't shown it to me yet."

I held out my hand and he took it in his, eyeing the ring way too closely. He scratched his chin. "I love the detail. This is some amazing work." He twisted the ring, examining every inch of it.

I snapped my hand out of his. "That's enough."

Derek's eyes lit up. "Did you see the flowers and butterflies I made you?"

"Yes, they were scattered all over the ground with everyone else's."

He furrowed his eyebrows. "Mine were different than everyone else's."

"How so?"

"Guess you'll have to wait until you get back and see for yourself. You kept them all, right? I mean, we poured a lot of time, sweat, love, and blood into those babies."

I raised my eyebrows. "Blood?"

Derek waved his hand. "It's a saying. But you kept them, right?"

"I did. Eric thought I was crazy, but I made him clean them all up with me so I could save them. They're in a box back at home."

He clapped his hands together in excitement. "Good! I can't wait until you see mine." He looked over at Eric who watched us from the passenger seat of the jeep. "She's already got you cleaning up after her, huh?"

Eric smiled at me. "She's worth it."

Derek pointed a finger at him. "I would have to disagree with you there."

Thunder Thighs grunted. "Me, too." She was sitting in the back next to Joshua. She looked him up and down, her eyes lingering way too long. Joshua glanced over at me and then slid farther away from her.

"Well, congratulations, little sis." Derek pulled me into a hug. "I'm so happy to finally get rid of you. It will be the greatest day of my life." He looked at Eric. "You have my permission to get married on your trip. That way you can just have her move in with you the second you get back."

"I wouldn't do that to her," Eric said. "I love her too much. She's getting the big wedding she deserves." His smile turned mischievous. "But I'm more than happy to have her move in with me when we get back."

Derek glared at Eric. "Not happening. No hanky panky until you tie the knot."

"I second that," Joshua said.

"Me, too." That came from multiple sources. I heard Dante, Will, Luke, Santiago, Bruce, and Gideon yell out.

"Can you just do it to piss all of them off, please?" Vivica asked. Santiago turned to her and shook his finger. Vivica rolled her eyes. "Oh, so you and I can …"

"Excuse me?" Dante asked. Using the top of the jeep as a handhold, he pulled himself up until he was standing and glared at Santiago.

Santiago gave an exaggerated laugh. "She's just kidding! We've never done anything like that. We're good, wholesome, clean people."

"That couldn't be farther from the truth," Tina said. Almost everyone nodded in agreement. Except for Dante. He was fuming.

"Enough!" Terrance glanced around at everyone. "We need to leave. Emmie, say goodbye to your brother."

I hugged Derek. "Bye, brother."

"Goodbye, sister from another mister." He laughed. "That never gets old."

"Yes, it does." I pulled away and looked up at him. "Love you."

"You, too," Derek said. "Drive safe."

As I was getting into the driver's seat, Derek called after me. "Oh, and feel free to name all of your children after me. Derek, Derekette, Derekina, Captain Awesome … anything along those lines."

"Not happening," Eric yelled out.

I looked through my rear-view mirror and saw Derek throw up his hands. "Just giving you some amazing options."

I took hold of Eric's hand. "Are you positive you want to marry into my family?"

Running his eyes over me, he winked at me. "You're hot enough." He leaned over and kissed me on the lips.

"Get a room," Thunder Thighs said.

"No!" I couldn't tell how many people had said that. I groaned and settled into my seat. I needed to move my wedding date to the closest day possible.

CHAPTER 6
Janice

The cold air pricked at my skin. Austin thought he could wear us down by making us uncomfortable, but it wasn't working, and it never would. He underestimated my will power. He underestimated a lot of things.

Shuddering, I stood and paced the room, trying to get the blood pumping through my body. We had turned the medical trade school building into our Headquarters. I didn't have much time to prepare my retreat after I heard Austin had murdered Whit. When I glanced over a map of River Springs, I knew I wanted to take over the Lake and Mountain Precincts.

The medical trade school building was in the Lake Precinct. It would come in handy if a battle began.

I'd gathered some supplies, made my announcement, and then immediately set off for Lake. I wasn't sure who'd support me. A part of me wondered if I would show up in Lake only to find everyone retreating to Austin's side. Or worse, staying there as if my announcement was meaningless. If that had happened, it wouldn't have been long until I was in Austin's custody.

Luckily, a little over eight thousand did support my movement. I still wasn't sure who supported me, Emmie, or just was against Austin leading Infinity Corp—which would, in turn, make in him charge of all River Springs— but right now, I didn't care. They were here, willing to fight off any and every one of Austin's advances.

My head hadn't stopped buzzing since I'd first arrived here last year. I was surprised we'd survived this long and that the revolution was still underway. My nights were restless. I was growing tired. Every time I felt like throwing in the towel, Whit came to mind. He was the one thing keeping me alive. I needed to get vengeance for his death.

Countless times I had told Whit that we couldn't trust Austin. We could never trust an Oliver, especially after what Frank did to our city. He turned his back on us and supported my daughter and her childish imagination. He'd gotten himself killed in the process, started a war in his own city, and turned our residents against each other. And now Whit was dead. None of it was necessary. It could have all been avoided. But arrogance and pride could ruin everything in the blink of an eye.

I pulled my cardigan tighter around me and sighed. I loved wearing skirts and dresses, but there were certainly days where I wanted to wear pants and bundle up. Especially when I was this cold. My button-down blouse and plaid skirt weren't providing much cover.

It all needed to come to an end, but I wasn't sure how I would accomplish that. We couldn't continue living on like we were. No one could function when you were always on alert. We had to keep security around the clock to make sure Austin wasn't trying to attack. He kept sending in spies, which was incredibly stupid of him. I was offended he found me so daft and naïve. I was smarter than him. I could win this. But I would need help.

The door to the room I paced in opened. I cringed when I saw Tami, Whit's daughter. Both she and her mom came to my side of the city. I was sure they didn't want to be around me or make it look like they supported me, but they couldn't stay over on the other side with Austin. He'd killed Tami's father and Amy's husband. The man I loved.

Tami looked nothing like her father, which helped ease the pain. I was glad Joshua had left. If it were him standing in the doorway, I couldn't have handled it. He looked exactly like his father. I closed my eyes for a second to try to compose myself.

"Austin sent another spy." Tami's voice came out sharp and closed off. She hated me. I didn't blame her. I'd broken up her family. Her hazel eyes showed no sympathy for me. Her face was tight and uninviting just like her mother's. She had her dark brown hair pulled back into a ponytail, making her face even more rigid. Tami couldn't pull off the dress she wore. She looked sloppy and the dress was too big, especially in the chest area.

"Do you have them in your custody?" I asked. I forced myself to keep my voice calm and even when I was around her or her mother. I didn't want them to see me suffer. They'd enjoy it too much.

Tami looked behind her and mumbled something to someone I couldn't see. After a few seconds, Tami let herself into the room. Amy followed, holding on to a short, blonde-haired girl. At least Amy looked decent in her sweater and skirt. More put together.

The girl she held was petite, making her easy to detain. She wore a Recruitment leader's uniform, even though last I'd heard, Recruitment had been temporarily removed from Infinity Corp until things were straightened out.

The room I was in had a table at one end where I could work during the day. On the other end sat one chair where we could question traitors. Amy shoved the girl down on the chair and then tied a rope around her body.

Amy stared at me for a moment, her gaze piercing. Her short black hair was a little disheveled. The spy must have put up quite the fight.

"Do you want me to stay?" Amy had to force the words out.

I glanced at the spy whose jaw was clenched like she was holding back the urge to scream out in anger. A smile came to my face, but I pushed it away. Tami stood near the door, looking straight ahead.

The three of us had come to an agreement. We all knew they loathed me, and I loathed them, but we had one thing in common: we wanted Austin to suffer for his crime. So, we decided to work together to accomplish our goal. It meant that we had to see each other more often than we wanted, but we tried to minimize the amount as much as we could.

"You can leave." I looked at Tami. "Both of you."

Tami opened her mouth to say something, but then snapped it shut. She and her mother left the room without another word.

I leaned back against my desk, taking in the spy. A little bit of blood dripped from her nose and her lip had been split open. I reached down for my cup of water sitting on my desk and took a sip, wetting my throat. "We've met, haven't we?"

She glared at me with all the hatred in the world. "Yes."

"When?" I swished the water around in my cup, keeping my gaze on her.

I wasn't sure she was going to answer, but after a moment, she spoke. "Over a year ago."

Setting my cup down, I stood and walked toward her. "Remind me."

"I was your daughter's dorm leader during Recruitment."

I eyed her Recruitment uniform. She must have just felt comfortable in it to still be wearing it. "That's right." Whit had questioned her, wanting to know about Emmie's every movement. I had been in the room during some of the conversations. Her name escaped me now. "You had to break up her fights."

Something crossed over her face, but I couldn't pin it down. Anger? Annoyance? Admiration? "Yes."

"She has a stubborn side, that's for sure. I would like to say she got that from her father, but I know she got it from me." I didn't realize how much those words would hurt as they left my mouth. Her whole life she had thought Philip was her father. He was the one who'd raised her. But Whit was her biological father. Some days I had wanted to take Emmie and Whit and just run. Live by ourselves without the rest of the world interfering. We could have been the perfect family. And now it was too late for that to ever happen.

"If you're trying to butter me up, it isn't going to work," she said.

The smile came and I couldn't push it away. I was really starting to like her. "You're going to have to remind me of your name. It's been a while since I last saw you."

She analyzed me, probably wondering if she should reveal it. She bit her lip before she spoke. "Jen."

I nodded. "Yes, that's right. Well, Jen, we seem to be in a predicament."

"No, we're not." Her voice was flat.

"You're tied up in a chair." I walked around her, keeping my pace steady and light. "You were sent as a spy."

Jen swore. "No, I wasn't. Tami hates me. She's doing this on purpose."

I stopped in front of her, tilting my head. "You know Tami personally?"

"Unfortunately, yes. We're the same age." She moved her nose from side to side as if there were an itch. Since her hands were bound, there was nothing she could do about it.

"You swear on your life that you aren't a spy?" I bent down so I could look her straight in the eye. Working for Whit, I'd become good at reading people.

Jen kept a firm gaze on me. "I'm not a spy. I wanted to get away from Austin and his strict military style of life. I prefer

President Randall's style over his." She didn't take her eyes away from mine. "And I always hated him."

I stood and started walking again. "You're quite honest."

"I don't like liars." She kept her head high, staring straight ahead as I walked in circles around her. She never once followed my trail.

"So, you came over here to get away from Austin …"

"I already said that."

Tucking my hair behind my ear, I walked back to the table. I leaned up against it, pressing my palms down on the top. "But you didn't support President Randall."

"I answered that, too." She licked the split on her lip and then spat the blood out on the floor.

"What about my daughter? Do you support her?"

My question surprised her, but I wasn't sure why. She stared at me for a long time. I didn't try to break the silence. I just stared back. She cleared her throat. "If you're making me choose between you, Austin, President Randall, Tami, or Emmie, I guess I'd have to choose Emmie."

My eyebrows rose. "You guess?"

"Honestly, I think you're all a little crazy. It must be something in the Oliver and Randall blood. But Emmie seems the most … sane."

"I'm not a Randall." Though I wished I was.

Jen smiled and then sucked on her bottom lip. "You constantly did one for years and years, so it's safe to say it rubbed off onto you." She laughed at her own pun. Her comment made me wonder how much about my affair had spread around the city.

"Jen, you've been quite frank about everything, so I'm going to trust that you're telling the truth about not being a spy."

Her eyes went wide. "Is this a trick?"

"No."

"What are you going to do with me?"

I pushed away from the table and went to her, untying the ropes. "If you work for me, I won't harm you."

She got up from the chair and turned toward me, her face skeptical. She rubbed her wrists. "Why should I trust you?"

"Because you need to." Placing the rope in the corner of the room, I went to my desk, sitting down in the chair. I gestured to a chair on the other side of the table.

Jen reluctantly walked over and sat down, sitting on the very edge of the seat. I turned my chair around and pulled a bottle of water out of a box behind the table. I set it on the table in front of Jen.

She sat completely still, looking back and forth between me and the bottle. If I said anything, she wouldn't take it. I waited patiently until she reached for it, opened it, and took a sip.

Sitting forward, I rested my arms on the table and clasped my hands together. "I can't say I completely support my daughter or her choices. I think she made a rash decision about a stupid prophecy that never even existed." It still bothered me that Whit never mentioned the prophecy in the twenty years we'd been together. Sometimes I wondered if he ever fully trusted me. I would never know that answer.

"I don't know anything about a prophecy." She held the

bottle of water in her hands, her grasp tight as if I might reach over and try to snatch it back.

I shook my head. "It doesn't matter. She started a revolution and the result was Vice President Oliver's death, President Randall's death, and a split in River Springs. I could dwell on all of this, but instead, I plan to fix it and move on."

"How do you plan to do that?"

"We need to end Austin's rein. We need to put Infinity Corp and River Springs back how they were."

Jen nodded in agreement. "The city was just fine before your daughter went on a hormonal spree and screwed us all over."

"How would you like to be a part of the solution?"

"What do you mean?"

I eyed Jen for a second. I hardly knew her, but I needed to trust my gut. It had gotten me this far in life. "I want you on my team. I want you to help in the capture of Austin."

Jen narrowed her eyes at me. "Why are you asking for *my* help? Two minutes ago, I was strapped to a chair."

"I like you."

Her eyebrows rose. "Why?"

"You're honest and you know what you want." I glanced at her bloody nose and lip. "And you obviously don't back down without a fight. Amy and Tami don't see eye to eye with me. I don't trust either of them."

She laughed. "Neither do I."

"Good." I sat back in my chair and crossed my legs. "But you and I agree on one thing, and that's restoring the city to its proper order. What do you say? Are you in?"

Jen bit her lip again and looked down at her bottle of water. "I don't trust you." Her eyes finally found mine. "I don't trust anyone. For how honest this city is supposed to be, it's full of a bunch of phony liars."

"I've been honest with you. Just like you've been with me." When she didn't respond, I continued. "Ask me anything you want."

She coughed and took another drink of water. "Anything?"

"Yes, anything."

"How long had you been sleeping with President Randall?"

I took a deep breath, relaxing my body. I needed to be calm if I intended to tell her everything. "It wasn't long after I started my job as his assistant. We had an instant connection."

Jen leaned forward. "Infinity Corp frowned on things like adultery. In the past, people have been seriously punished for it."

"President Randall never thought the rules applied to him." I smiled. "And I was too attracted to him to care."

She seemed to approve of my answer. "Did you love him?"

"Yes. With all of my heart." I truly did.

"And your husband?"

"I loved him as a father to my children. He raised them well. They would have turned out much worse if I had been more hands-on."

"Did you agree with the way President Randall ran Infinity Corp?"

That was an easy answer. "Yes. He did what was necessary for the good of the city."

Jen scoffed. "Rumor has it he tried to kill your daughter."

I shifted uncomfortably in my chair. That was one topic I hoped she wouldn't bring up. I had always agreed with everything Whit did. He always had good intentions. But Emmie was my daughter. *Our* daughter. He tried to kill her without telling me what was going on. He also kept the prophecy a secret. "President Randall always did what he thought was necessary to protect the city."

"He tried to kill your daughter and you consider that necessary to protect the city?" Her grip tightened around the water bottle. "From what? She was seventeen."

I almost lashed out, but I took a deep breath. "Well, Jen, if you look around, you can see what her choices did."

"Because he tried to *kill her*. Have you ever thought about the fact that if he hadn't tried to do that, Emmie would have stayed here, continued with Recruitment and started her job at Infinity Corp?"

"The prophecy stated …" The stupid prophecy. I didn't even believe it and here I was trying to use it as a defense. If I wanted Jen to help me, I needed to be honest. "I don't know what would've happened. Emmie was one for bending the rules."

She nodded. "That's true."

"But I didn't want my daughter killed if that's what you're asking. I would've handled it differently."

"How?"

She was really enjoying the questioning and using it to her

advantage. It made my need to have her on my side so much stronger. "I would've done what I should've done from the time Emmie was born. I would've been involved in her life. Kept her close so I could keep an eye on her. Anytime she tried to step out of line, I would rein her in."

Jen took another drink of water. "And if you couldn't rein her in?"

"I could. Everyone can be reined in at a price."

She shook her head. "I don't think Emmie could. She's too strong. Too determined."

I thought of that cute, blue-eyed, blond-haired boy she had a crush on. Eric. It would've been easy to rein her in if I promised she could have him. Or if I threatened to harm him. "She could. I know her weaknesses."

"What's my weakness?"

I looked her over, taking her all in. "You're too honest."

Jen cracked a small smile. She finished off her water and set the bottle on my desk. I took it and threw it in the garbage bin.

"Are you in?" I asked, watching her closely.

Her eyes validated her answer. "Yes."

CHAPTER 7
Emmie

I didn't know what I was expecting when we got to Kingsland. I'd never stepped foot into one of the other cities. It looked neatly structured like River Springs, but everything had more of an outdoor feel to it. Most of the homes and buildings were made of logs. There was something comforting about it that made me want to curl up and have a cup of hot cocoa.

We had driven around the east side of the city, a few miles out so we wouldn't be seen. We came to a stop on the north side, two miles away from the brick wall that stood between their city and the forest. There were a lot of trees around to give us the cover we needed.

We had all taken turns, going in our groups of four to scout out the area from a closer distance. From the fact that there were a lot of security guards on the roof of Headquarters, it was safe to say security was still tight.

When my group got back, Dante was standing near a tree by himself with his eyes closed. I went to him and put my hand on his arm. "How are you doing?"

Dante's whole body sighed. "I don't know. I didn't think it would be this hard to come back. I miss it." He took a deep breath and opened his eyes. "I miss the smell of the trees. I miss the sounds of the forest and the birds." He looked down at me. "I miss Whitney."

Whitney was his girlfriend back in his city. They weren't supposed to date, but they somehow managed it. She became sick with a disease and ended up passing away.

I rubbed his arm. "I'm sorry you have to go through all of this. Relive it all."

Sadness engulfed his eyes. He pulled me into a hug and rested his chin on my head. "I saw her brother, Brandon."

"Where?" I wanted to pull back so I could look at him, but I stayed in place.

"On the roof of Headquarters," Dante said.

"He's a security guard?" I asked.

He nodded against my head. "Yes. And one of us is going to kill him." He sighed. "I just hope it's not me that has to do it."

None of us would know what he looked like since we didn't grow up there. But Dante's sister would. "Ask Vivica to do it."

"Vivica was close with their family," Dante said. "She dated Brandon."

I thought back to when Vivica had told me their mom had died because she was distracted by a boy. I wondered if that was the boy she talked about. "Terrance, then."

"I can't believe this is finally happening, Em. It was easier with Juniper because I had no attachment to them. But these are the people I grew up with. People I once considered friends."

I lowered my arms and looked up at Dante. "I know. But it must be done. They're holding thousands of people prisoners. They'll all die if we don't do anything."

Dante nodded and stared up at the sky. "It doesn't make it any easier." A single tear slid down his cheek. "This mission is too important to mess up. Which is why I have to be the one to kill Brandon."

Once the sun had settled in for the night, we crept our way to the wall. We went in four lines, the revolutionaries leading each group. We had decided to wear all black when we first came up with the plan, so we would blend in with the darkness. But the more we thought about it, the less it made sense. Kingsland was surrounded by the forest, densely packed with trees. So, we went with our new camouflage uniforms that were a mix of black, green and brown.

We each had on a long sleeve shirt, pants, a thick jacket, and a beanie. Everyone had a bag slung around their shoulders with the supplies we would need. We also each had a bow and set of arrows, which was the weapon Kingsland security would be using. Dante had shown us how to conceal ourselves by putting leaves and sticks on our clothing, plus using face paint so our skin didn't stand out too much. We had earpieces in so we could communicate in case we were separated.

The one thing that gave me the most ease was the vests we were wearing under our shirts. Scorpion provided us with bulletproof vests. If anything, it protected our chest and abdomen, which were the weakest spots on our bodies. I happily took the small advantage.

We stopped about fifty yards out. Dante swore, so I went to him, keeping my voice low. "What's wrong?"

His voice was tight. "They installed lights."

I followed his gaze. Lights were on the other side of the wall, lighting up the area between the brick wall and the back of Headquarters. As soon as our heads were over the wall, we'd be seen.

Santiago and Maya joined us. Santiago folded his arms. "What should we do now?"

"We'll have to go farther down the wall." I glanced over at the brick wall, looking down both sides. The lights were only behind Headquarters. "If we went fifty yards down each side of the wall, we could jump there and then walk on the inside."

Dante swore again. "But before we would only have to deal with the security guards at the back and on the roof. If we approach from both sides, that means killing ten more on each side."

Maya ran her hand over her spiky hair. I expected to hear the clinking of her bracelets, but then remembered she took them off for the mission. They would cause too much of a distraction. "Why do we have to kill them all? Why not just the ones closest to the back?"

"It's a domino effect," I said. "Once you kill one security guard, the one closest to him will see. So, then we'll have to kill him, and so on."

Santiago shrugged. "So what? That's twenty more security guards dead. Twenty less we'll have to deal with if we get caught on the inside."

"We're still talking thirty on the ground and twenty-five on the roof," Dante said. "And there's still only sixteen of us."

I twisted my ring. "With the lights on, we're just sitting ducks on the ground. The guards on the roof will be able to hit us easily."

Santiago patted his chest. "At least they can't hit us here. Being hit in the arm or leg won't kill you."

"But being hit in the head will," Maya said, tapping her finger against his head.

"We need to take out the lights," I said. "We have to cover our entrance."

Dante shook his head. "They'll know we're here as soon as they see the lights get shot out."

"Then don't shoot them," I said. "We need to unplug them or something. Make it look like a technical malfunction."

Santiago nodded. "As they're scrambling around to see what happened, we start killing them one by one. If we're fast enough, it will be too late for them by the time they figure out what's going on."

"It's a long shot," Maya said. "It's risky."

"But we have to do it," Dante said. "We have no other choice. I'm not turning around and leaving."

"Let's do it," I said. They each nodded.

Dante looked at me. "Take your team and Santiago's team and head east. My team and Maya's team will head west. Once we're over the wall, we'll go from there."

We started to turn and walk away, but Santiago stopped us. "Uh, aren't you three forgetting something?"

I looked at him, confused. Santiago's smile twisted and he sat there tapping his fingers against his folded arms, waiting for us to figure it out.

After a moment, I remembered. We had started a tradition to say a prayer before we headed into battle. I rubbed my hands together. "Let's bring it in."

The four of us came close, taking one another by the hand. Santiago took a deep breath, calming his nerves. "Lord, give us the strength to carry out our mission. Help us to keep our eyes clear and focused, our hearts full and open, so we can win this battle for New Haven. Amen."

"Amen," Dante, Maya, and I said. We put our arms around each other and rested our foreheads together.

We kept our voices quiet as the four of us spoke at the same time. "For New Haven."

A murmur surrounded us, everyone else with us saying, "For New Haven."

I looked at my fellow revolutionaries. "Let's head out."

We split up and crept close the brick wall. My group followed right behind me, with Santiago's group behind us. Once we were well out of the range of the lights, we stopped in front of the brick wall.

Santiago pulled out a grappling hook with a rope attached, swung it around a few times, and then threw it up, the hook finding purchase on the top of the wall. He tugged on it a few times to make sure it wouldn't come loose. Once he was satisfied, he turned to me and nodded. "Ladies first."

I looked at Eric, Joshua, and Thunder Thighs. "Keep close together. Once we're on top, try to keep your bodies low while Santiago's group comes up. We'll have to wait until they're up so we can swing the rope over the other side and climb down."

They all nodded at me, letting me know they understood. I took hold of the rope, tugging on it twice.

Santiago snickered. "Don't trust me?"

I glanced over my shoulder at him and smiled. "Of course not."

I climbed, making it easily to the top. All the training helped me gain muscle and coordination.

A guard stood on the other side of wall, right below me. Motioning for the others to wait, I quietly drew an arrow and nocked it. I aimed it at the guard and took a slow, deep breath. Releasing the arrow, it soared downward, connecting with the guard's back. He fell to the ground and I waited, making sure there was no movement. When I was satisfied, I motioned for my group to climb.

Eric, Thunder Thighs, and then Joshua joined me on top. We stayed crouched down, close together.

As Santiago's team climbed, I spoke. "Once we're down, I want arrows nocked and ready to release. Shoot anyone you see."

It was dark, but I could see Eric's white teeth when he smiled. "Have I told you how sexy you are when you're in charge?"

Thunder Thighs grunted. "Gross."

"Seriously," Joshua said. "Keep those comments to yourself. That's my sister."

I smiled and winked at Eric. "Thanks."

Once Santiago's group was up, he tossed the rope over the other side and I climbed down as fast as I could. I jumped the last few feet and drew an arrow, scanning the area around me. As far as I could tell, the area was clear.

Once everyone had joined me, I contacted Dante. "We're down."

"We are, too," Dante said. "Head west until you get close to the lights. We'll talk again then."

"Yes sir," I said.

Dante laughed quietly through the earpiece as we started forward. There were a lot of trees in the area, so we went tree by tree, keeping as quiet as we could.

After about twenty yards, Santiago motioned for us to stop. He already had an arrow drawn, so he aimed it and released. A guard a few yards up fell over and we waited a minute before we moved on.

The lights were up ahead. Guards stood around the building, holding onto their bows, an arrow nocked, but pointed at the ground. At the snap of a twig, those bows would be up, and the arrows would be flying. I released one hand from my bow and held up my fist, motioning for both groups to stop.

My voice was barely a whisper. "Dante, we're right outside the lit-up area."

There was a minute of silence. Each second was agonizing. A sigh of relief almost escaped my mouth when I heard Dante's voice. "We're here."

"Everyone hold still," Santiago said. "I'm going to take a closer look." Santiago inched closer, keeping himself hidden by the foliage. He paused behind a tree and swore. "I see the breaker box. It's on the east side of the building between two guards."

"No sneaking up on it," Maya said. "What now?"

"We have the advantage of the trees," I said. "Revolutionaries, have two people from your team climb up. Once everyone is settled, we're just going to have to start shooting."

"Won't the guards on the roof notice?" Maya asked. "They'll alert security for sure."

There was a moment of silence.

"Then we'll have to be fast." Dante's voice was rigid.

I turned to my team. "Joshua and I will each climb a tree a little south from here so we can get the guards on the side of the building. Eric and Th … Rachel." I squirmed. I had hoped she hadn't noticed my misstep, but the look on her face told me she did. I just shrugged it off and continued. "You two will aim for the guards on the back of the building. Understood." They all nodded.

Santiago and his team came up next to us. "Let's have Luke and Tina head north with Emmie and Joshua to help with the side guards. Vivica and I will stay down here with Eric and … Rachel."

Thunder Thighs pulled her face tight, but I couldn't tell if she was confused or mad. Either way, she had to be thinking we kept forgetting her name, which was better than her knowing we just wanted to call her Thunder Thighs.

"Spread out." I took the lead, with Joshua, Tina, and Luke right behind me. When we had gone south a few yards, I looked at them. "Let's each take a different tree. Joshua, head south a few trees and aim for the first two to three guards. I'll take the second tree and Tina can take the third, both of us aiming for the middle guards. Luke, take a tree on the north side and take care of those guards. When you're settled in your tree, keep your eye on me. Once I give the nod, fire."

They each nodded and we separated. I found a tree I thought would be easy to climb and started up, careful of each step I took. We had practiced climbing trees as part of our training. Our primary goal was to go over different skills that would be beneficial to the different cities. We knew Kingsland was filled with trees, inside and out, so we made sure everyone in our military knew how to climb.

Once I was settled, I readied my bow and arrow and waited for everyone else to get into position. It was a good five minutes before we got the clear from each revolutionary.

I took two deep breaths to calm my nerves. "Revolutionaries, let's count it out." Their three voices whispered with mine. "Five, four, three, two …" I nodded and let my first arrow fly.

CHAPTER 8

The commotion after the first round of arrows was more than I expected. Dozens of lights turned on and guards shouted, frantically moving around. They all had arrows nocked, some firing them off. I instinctively wanted to nock another arrow, but something told me to refrain. I heard guards coming from behind us.

With all the shouting, I could speak without giving away my position, but I kept my voice low as I used my earpiece to communicate. "Joshua, Tina, Luke. Do not shoot. Stay hidden. Turn off your earpieces."

After I switched mine off, I slung my bow around my back and pushed my body into the tree. From where I was, I could see Tina do the same. Hopefully, Luke and Joshua followed suit.

Down below, a few guardsmen had captured some of our group. Our plan had gone completely wrong. At first, I was afraid they would just kill everyone they caught, but a guard came out from Headquarters saying that President Coleman wanted them taken alive.

I glanced down to see who they had. Everyone else with us had stayed on the ground. I wasn't sure what Dante's and Maya's groups had done.

Eric, Thunder Thighs, Santiago, and Vivica were being held on the ground. The guards had laid them all on their stomachs and taken their weapons. I felt bad for the guards holding onto them. Out of everyone in our group, they were four of our fieriest members.

A minute later, more guards came around the corner, dragging more of our members. I almost laughed when I saw Dee. She had gone completely limp. The guard carried her like a ragdoll. It was always her technique, which I usually made fun of, but it seemed to work every time.

I counted everyone else out. Dante, Gideon, Hiro, and Terrance were among the captives they threw on the ground next to the others. I didn't see Maya, Will, or Bruce.

The guards continued to search the area and I held my breath for most of it. I was afraid to move a hair on my body. We were lucky we were in camouflage; otherwise, they could have spotted us right away. The whole time I kept praying they wouldn't find us or the others. I wondered if they were up in trees like we were.

After ten excruciating minutes, they called off the search. One of the guards went to Dante and yanked him to his feet. They had taken everyone's weapons and earpieces, but they were still close enough that I could hear.

"Are there any others with you?" the guard asked.

Dante shook his head. "No. It's just the nine of us."

"Liar!" Another guard shouted out. He wore a short-sleeve shirt, which surprised me because it was so cold. But it made his massive muscles stand out. By the way Dante looked at him, and the way Vivica had flinched at his voice, I assumed it was Whitney's brother, Brandon.

Dante refrained from lashing out. "I'm not lying."

Brandon approached Dante. "Who sends only nine men on a mission like this?"

Dee gasped, leaving her ragdoll trance for a moment. "How dare you!"

"Dee, shut up." Dante's voice was quiet, but I could still hear.

"He called me a man! Unless you're blind, big macho tough guy, there are women here, also." When the guard near Dee went to strike her, she went back in rag doll mode.

The guard stopped mid-swing and stared at her. She didn't move an inch. He hesitated and then pulled back, leaving her alone. I still hadn't decided if bringing her was a good or bad idea. In our current condition, I was thinking bad. She was going to get herself killed if she continued to act like that.

Brandon stepped away from Dante and moved toward the back of Headquarters. "I know there are others out there. Show yourself."

I prayed everyone would stay hidden.

Brandon waited a couple of minutes and then turned back and sauntered over to Dante. He pulled something out of his pocket and twisted it in his hand. One of the lights reflected off the blade. It was one of our knives. Brandon went behind Dante, his movement slow and calculated. He took the knife and put it against Dante's throat, keeping his voice loud. "I'm going to be nice and give you ten seconds to reveal yourself. If not, we can all watch Dante die."

Every cell in my body screamed to jump down and run out there. I gripped a branch near me as tightly as I could, forcing myself to stay. We still had a mission to carry out. "Stay hidden," I said in a quiet prayer.

"You're wasting your time," Dante said, his voice confident. "There's no one out there."

"Ten," Brandon started. "Nine, eight, seven, six, five, four, three, two …"

"Wait!"

I closed my eyes and swore under my breath. Will. I heard the shuffling of feet and opened my eyes to see two guards holding onto Will, dragging him toward the others. They took his weapons and threw him on the ground.

Brandon stepped to the front of Dante and slammed his hand holding the knife into Dante's jaw, the tip of the knife slicing into Dante's cheek as he pulled his hand away. Dante stumbled a few steps but gained his balance back and stood tall. Brandon kneed Dante in the stomach and pushed him down on the ground.

As we all watched on, Brandon went and stood before the hostages. "No more lying. Next time, I won't be so nice." He looked out at the guards. "Take them inside and throw them in the cells for now."

I waited as they forced everyone inside. After five minutes, some of the lights turned off around Headquarters, but not all of them. There were still guards lined up on the side. I counted them out and was glad to see there were only four.

Another twenty minutes past without movement. I didn't want to risk using the earpieces again. Since Kingsland now had ten sets of them, they would hear anything we said if they were listening.

I held out my hand and signaled that I was climbing down, hoping Joshua and Tina would see what I was doing, and that Tina would pass the motion on to Luke.

Each step I took was precise so I wouldn't make any loud noises. Once I was on the ground, I moved a few yards east, away from Headquarters. I stopped and glanced around, hoping to see some familiar faces. Joshua stood a few yards south, so I signaled for him to join me. When he got to me, I put my finger up to my mouth, telling him to keep quiet. We started south until we came across Tina and Luke. I gave them the same signal and took the lead, heading back toward the brick wall.

There were two trees close together near the brick wall. I stood in between them and turned toward the others. They squeezed in until we were all close together. If anyone had personal space issues, they were going to have a serious problem with our situation.

I checked their ears and saw that they all had taken out their earpieces. I mouthed, "Are they off?" They all nodded. "Before we do anything, we need to find Maya and Bruce."

"How are we going to do that?" Tina asked. She had her hair pulled back in a braid like I did, so we could keep it out of our faces.

Unzipping the top of my coat, I reached inside to a hidden

pocket and pulled out a communication device. Each of the revolutionaries had one that we could use only to communicate with each other. I went off the hope that Kingsland security hadn't found that pocket in Dante's and Santiago's jackets yet. Pulling it up to my mouth, I pressed the button to activate it. "Cool Breeze, are you there?"

Santiago thought it would be cool if we all had code names when we used the devices. Mostly for fun, but also safety reasons. If an enemy got their hands on one, they wouldn't know we only went by our code name on that device. Santiago had given Maya the code name of Cool Breeze since he thought her personality was that of a cool breeze passing by on a nice summer day. Mine was Butterfly and Santiago's was Bone Crusher, which was his boxing name. Dante's was Bull's Eye for his amazing accuracy.

"I'm here, Butterfly," Maya said.

"We need to meet back up and go over our game plan," I said.

"Other side of the wall?" Maya asked.

I looked up at the wall. "It's our safest bet right now."

"See you on the other side," Maya said.

I was about to put the device away when I remembered Santiago had our grappling hook. "Uh, Cool Breeze, we're stuck on this side. Bone Crusher has our way out."

"I have ours," Maya said. "We'll climb over and then head east and then climb back over."

Bruce grunted loud enough to hear through the device, making me laugh.

"Contact me when you're back over here," I said.

We only waited five minutes, huddled together in silence between the trees, before we heard Maya's voice again. "Butterfly, we're over." She gave me her coordinates and I used my compass to locate them.

"I want a cool code name." It was the first thing out of Bruce's mouth when we found them. "Like Mighty Warrior or something."

"We have more important things to talk about," Luke said.

Bruce groaned in frustration as we came close together, using some trees as cover.

Tina sighed. "So how are the six of us going to do anything?"

"None of us are even from Kingsland," Joshua said. He had his arms folded and he pressed up close to me which I was grateful for. It was getting colder by the minute and I could use any warmth I could get.

I looked at my watch. "Well, it's a little after nine. We need to do something tonight. Once the sun is up, our window of opportunity is over."

"Can't we wait until tomorrow night?" Bruce asked. "That way we can get some good rest and think it over. We can contact President Mendes and Vice President Jennings and work something up."

I shook my head. "We don't have that kind of time. The others will be dead by morning."

Tina's eyes went wide. "You think so?"

"They have no reason to keep them alive," Joshua said.

"What do you suggest we do?" Maya asked me.

I thought over all our options. Rescuing everyone that came with us was out of the question. We needed to focus on Marcus and his supporters. We obviously couldn't rescue them, either. There were too many of them and we had no idea what Marcus or anyone else looked like. We couldn't trust anyone we met here.

So that left rallying everyone and getting them to agree with us, not President Coleman. But how could we get thousands of people to support or even listen to six outsiders? Six people they'd never seen before and had probably been fed lies about.

"We need to get supporters of New Haven out of hiding," I said. "We need to convince everyone that we're the good guys and are here to help."

Bruce swore, so Maya smacked him on the head. Rubbing the spot where she'd hit him, Bruce looked at her and frowned. "How come everyone else can swear but me?"

"First of all," Maya said, "I don't swear. In fact, a lot of our residents don't. You've just spent too much time around Dante and Santiago, and now Emmie."

"Hey!" I scrunched my eyebrows together. "I'm not as bad as they are."

Tina smiled. "Yeah, but they've definitely rubbed off on you."

I hated to admit she was right. I guess we would have to work on that, especially if young kids like Bruce were going to look up to us. "Fine, no swearing."

"We're losing focus," Luke said. "How are we going to convince them we're here to help?"

I thought back to when Dante first found out that a lot of Kingsland residents were coming down with the disease that Whitney, Eric's mom, and Lou had died from. The same one Dee had recovered from. Because we had found the solution.

I looked at the five of them staring at me, waiting for my response, and I grinned. "Because we have the cure."

CHAPTER 9

Somehow, we needed to find a way to address the whole city without interruptions. It was going to be tricky but had to be done.

I rubbed my hands together for warmth as we stood out in the cold. "Going into Headquarters is out of the question."

"We need somewhere else to go," Maya said.

Nodding, I pulled out a piece of paper from my pocket. As I opened it, a small object floated down to the ground.

Joshua bent down and picked it up, handing it over to me. "You dropped this."

When I took it from him, I smiled. It was the purple butterfly I had picked up when Eric proposed to me. I had transferred it to the pants I was currently in so I could take it with me.

I ran my thumb over it and then put it back in my pocket, and then opened the other paper. "This is a rough map Dante drew for me. We need to go somewhere else with less security than Headquarters but would still have some of the equipment we might need."

"What are you thinking we need?" Luke asked. He had his arms around Tina, holding her close.

"We need to be able to do a live feed to the entire city," I said. "We need to let them know what's going on."

Maya shook her head as she bounced up and down where she stood. "We need proof. They'll never believe us if we don't have proof."

"How do we prove we have the cure?" Tina asked.

"I don't know," I said. "I brought a sample of it with me, but even if we injected it into one of the sick patients, it takes days before you see results."

Joshua looked at me. "We also have a very limited supply of the cure. Even if we convinced them, we couldn't cure a lot of people."

"They have medical supplies here, right?" Luke asked. "We have the formula, you just need the supplies. We can't get back into River Springs, but there's a good chance we can find what we need here."

I sighed and stared up at the sky. "I don't think they'll have everything we need."

"Why not?" Bruce asked.

"Dante said they were more into herbal medicine here," I said. "They don't have a lot of the drugs we had at Infinity Corp." I rubbed my temples. "We need to focus on talking to everyone here. Once that's done, we'll figure out a way to convince them that we're the good guys, and then hopefully convince them in joining us and raiding Infinity Corp to get the supplies."

"So that takes us back to where do we go right now," Tina said.

On the map, I pointed my finger at our destination. "The President's home." They all looked at me, most with their eyebrows raised in surprise. "If President Coleman is anything like President Randall, he'll have a lot of equipment in his home. Whit wanted to make sure he could still run things and keep an eye on what happened in the city from his own home in the event something happened to Infinity Corp's Headquarters or he got stuck at home."

Joshua nodded. "That's right. He had his own version of Headquarters in a room connected to his bedroom."

"We're just going off of the hope that President Coleman will have the same in his home?" Tina asked.

"It's all we have right now." I looked down at the map. "According to this, President Coleman's home is only a half-mile east of here. Let's head that way. Everyone stay close together. Maya and I will lead, Bruce and Tina stay in the middle, and Joshua and Luke can take the back. Keep your eyes peeled for any movement. If you see a guard, kill him. We can't have anyone know we're here."

When they all nodded at me, I put the map back in my pocket, took my bow from around my shoulder, and nocked an arrow so I would be ready.

We proceeded slowly, all on high alert. If someone caught us, we were all dead. I kept my bow up with my arrow nocked, ready to be released at any moment. It was eerily quiet as we approached the president's home. Dante told me once that they had to be home every night by ten in their city. I glanced at my watch and it was only twenty past nine. Maybe they had changed their curfew to an earlier time with everything that had been happening in their city. Either that or they knew we were here and were waiting to ambush us. I really hoped it wasn't the latter.

I didn't realize I was holding my breath until it was almost gone. I slowly let it out as we crept closer. The home sat before us, but no one was outside. Motioning for everyone to stop, Maya and I split up, checking the perimeters to see if we could spot anyone. When we met back up, she shook her head and I did the same.

I huddled everyone together. "We're going in through the front door. Put your bows away and pull out your knives. Once we're inside, we'll be in close range of others, so knives will work better. If you come across a guard, kill them. Anyone else, we take them prisoner. Retrieve any belongings from the guards or prisoners and put them in your bag. Keep as quiet as you can."

Bruce bounced a little, his eyes eager. "I need to … relieve myself."

Maya rolled her eyes. "Be quick."

"You want me to go out here?" Bruce asked. He looked over at me and Tina, blushing.

"We're surrounded by a forest," Luke said. "Just go a couple of trees away and do your thing."

Bruce shook his head. "I'm not going alone."

"I'll go with you," Joshua said. He put his hand on Bruce's shoulder and steered him away from us. We waited in silence until they were back a minute later.

Bruce was all smiles. "I feel so much better."

"Good." As I spoke, I removed some of the foliage I had stuck in my clothes and hair. The face paint would unfortunately have to stay on for now. "Keep in a circle as we approach, with our backs facing each other. That way we can keep an eye all around us. Let's move."

We formed a circle and made our way to the door. I glanced around the area for any security device, but I couldn't see anything. When I got to the door, I turned the knob slowly. I was surprised when it just opened. Either these were very trusting people, or we were walking into a trap.

I inched the door open and stepped inside. Darkness engulfed the room, so I pulled out my flashlight and held it with my left hand, as my right hand gripped my knife. Above us was a chandelier made from antlers. Something caught my eye and I turned my flashlight to my left and nearly screamed out in fear. Hanging on the wall was an elk's head. Closing my eyes briefly, I took some deep breaths as I moved farther into the house. The door closed behind me.

When I looked to my right, I spotted a bear's head on that wall. The president must have been a big fan of hunting. The ground felt soft, so I looked down, only to confirm his love of hunting. A bearskin rug.

Bruce let out a yelp. He must have noticed one of the two guests on the wall.

Maya stood to my left. "Should we split up?"

"Not yet," I said. "Let's keep together as long as we can."

"What should we be looking for?" Tina asked from the right of me.

"A security room," I said. "Let's start on the first floor, right side. Everyone follow me."

The right side of the house proved to be empty. So did the left. Everyone followed me up the stairs. When we got to the top, I noticed a light on down the right hall. I motioned for everyone to keep silent and follow me.

Light came from one of the rooms. I crept up to it and peered inside since the door was open just a crack. I saw two teenagers sitting on a bed, very deep in conversation. The boy looked to be around seventeen or eighteen, the girl around fifteen or sixteen. From the girl's puffy eyes, she'd been crying.

They had a lot of the same features. Both had large, round brown eyes that fit their face perfectly. His black hair was cut close to his head, and her same shade of black hair hung to her shoulders, both gorgeous.

A picture of the two of them with their mom and dad sat in a wood frame on the nightstand. That must have been President Coleman and his wife, and the two teenagers sitting on the bed were his children.

The girl blew her nose into a tissue. "What do you think they'll do to them?"

"I don't know," the boy said. His voice was soft and soothing. "We'll just have to hope for the best."

A new set of tears fell from the girl's eyes. "Michael, I don't think I'm strong enough."

Michael took her hand in his. "You have to be. There's nothing we can do."

"Why can't we stop them?" Her voice was sad and angry at the same time. "They're going to hurt him. I just know it.

Dad's going to kill him."

"We don't know that," Michael said. He didn't look convinced of that. His gaze settled on the floor. "He may keep him alive."

The girl pulled her hand away and stood. "No, he won't. He hates Dante." My body tensed at Dante's name. "I've heard him say over and over again that he wanted Dante caught and killed."

Michael ran his hand over his head. "I don't know what to tell you, Zoe. Dad's going to do whatever he wants and you or I can't change his mind."

"We need to go stop him!" Her voice went up an octave or two.

"We can't!" Michael stood and went to Zoe. "There's nothing you can do to save Dante."

Zoe frowned. "But you just said …"

"I was trying to be nice," Michael said.

"So, you do think he'll kill him," Zoe said, her voice a whisper.

Michael looked at Zoe for a moment before he spoke. "Dante's not stepping out of Kingsland alive."

She broke down in tears again and fell to the floor. Michael sulked back to the bed and sat down. "Why do you care so much, Zoe? Dante left us. He and his family abandoned the city. They're traitors."

Zoe looked up at Michael, her face appalled. "They're not traitors! I know Dante and his family, and you should know them well enough, too! We grew up with them. They're good people. And now he and Vivica are going to die for no reason."

"People need to be punished for their crimes," Michael said. It sounded like he was trying to convince himself of the fact.

"Not by death," Zoe said. "They don't deserve that. They deserve people to stand up for them and support them. How do you know that Dad hasn't been feeding us lies?"

Michael sighed. "There's no point in arguing. We're two people. Dad has hundreds of security guards." He moved toward the door, but she stopped him.

"Michael, I love him," Zoe said.

Michael turned back to her. "Of course, you do. I love them, too. They're like family to us."

Zoe shook her head. "No, Michael, not like that. I *love* him."

"Zoe, you're only sixteen. You don't know what love is. You just think you love him."

"I know what I feel," Zoe said. "I've known it for years. I've just never told anyone."

They continued to talk, but I couldn't concentrate. My head was trying to piece everything together. I turned and looked at everyone with me. Tina had been standing right next to me, so she heard everything I had.

She must have been able to read my expression because she shook her head. "No."

"Yes." I stared at her, keeping my gaze firm. "I'm taking the chance."

Tina swore and Bruce turned to her. She smiled apologetically and then looked back at me. "It's too risky, Emmie."

In the room, Michael and Zoe were both sitting on the bed talking. They seemed to be on Dante's side, not their dad's. I could use that to my advantage. I removed my bow and quiver, handing them to Joshua. He took them reluctantly, his gaze going back and forth between me and Tina. She was still shaking her head.

"Can you please tell us what you're thinking?" Luke asked. "We can't read your mind as Tina can. Nor did we hear everything you did."

"It's the president's daughter and son," I said. "I'm going in there."

Maya put her hand on my arm. "Are you crazy?"

"You're just going to have to trust me." I tucked my knife behind my back. "Keep watch out here. If this goes bad, make a run for it and hide somewhere." Giving them a hopeful smile, I stepped into the room.

CHAPTER 10
Austin

When I was six years old, Joshua and I played hide and seek in his father's home. Over the years we found new rooms we'd never known existed and secret passageways that took us all over the home and Headquarters.

By ten, we knew the area inside and out. We used to listen in on meetings and would spy on the security detail. We even found out about Whit and Janice's affair. At the time, I felt so bad for Joshua. I could tell it genuinely upset him. I tried to cheer him up, but nothing worked. He finally came to accept it and moved on.

Listening in on all the meetings helped me gain a lot of knowledge. I hated how Whit ran the place and I could tell Joshua did, too. Whit was arrogant and self-centered. The only person Whit ever truly cared about was Janice, which crushed Joshua.

I also learned how much I disagreed with my dad. He was

too loving and trusting. His nature and Whit's nature should've balance each other out, but it didn't. I wanted to find that balance. That was how you ran a city. Rules and guidelines were needed, but the people needed to be heard as well.

Over time, I noticed Joshua turn to my father more for advice. My dad treated him as if he were his son, too. At first, I didn't care. Joshua needed a father figure in his life and his dad certainly wasn't fulfilling that role. But after a while, I got jealous. Sometimes my dad would spend more time with Joshua and forget about me. He kept telling me that Joshua needed just as much attention as I did, but I was his son! I was the one he needed to focus on. Me. Not him.

I had never meant for it to go this far. But everything unraveled so quickly right before my eyes. I had to put a stop to it before it was out of my control. I took drastic measures, but they were necessary. Amber sometimes told me I was turning out to be like President Randall, but that was far from the truth. I didn't want to be like him, and I never would.

Looking down at the city, I sighed. I'd never meant to hurt anyone. But I had these moments of rage I couldn't manage. My dad tried to help me over the years. It hurt me to see him upset that I wasn't improving, so I pretended my rage was under control, learning to hide it well. It lingered under my skin, waiting to boil over. One day it would eventually explode. I just couldn't afford for that day to be soon. I needed more time.

With River Springs split and my plans to end New Haven put on the back burner, I turned to Kingsland. I didn't want to seek help, but if I intended to win, I had to. It was easy enough to find someone there who would want to help. Dean did a little research into their city and found someone with a grudge against Dante and a sway on President Coleman.

Honestly, I felt bad for the guy. Brandon had lost his sister, Whitney, to a disease that seemed very similar to one that had been found in River Springs. Dante's father, Wallace Brown, had found a cure but had been keeping it from Kingsland. When Brandon found out, it was already too late. His sister had passed on.

He had been so close to the Brown family. He was dating Vivica, and Dante and Whitney had been secretly dating. He considered them family. But they lied to him and turned their backs on him and Kingsland. From the way Brandon described Dante, he reminded me of Emmie.

A knock at the door interrupted my thoughts. "Come in."

Dean walked into the room, unbuttoned his suitcoat, and took a seat in a chair near my desk. His suit was a tad too tight. He'd gained some weight since Whit died. "We sent someone in to spy on Janice."

Turning away from the window, I sat down in my chair so I could look at Dean. "Did they get in?"

"Yes. She's there and still alive." Dean smirked. "Janice already trusts her. She has Jen doing work for her. I think this time around our plan worked. We've just been sending in the wrong people."

"I'm glad to hear this." I sat back in my chair and clasped my hands in my lap. Things were starting to look up. "Any word from Brandon?"

Dean gave me a half-smile. "You're going to like this.

They've captured Dante and some of the residents from New Haven."

He was wrong. I didn't like it. It should have been *me* who captured them. Now I would have to twist it in my favor. "How many others do they have?"

"They have ten in all," Dean said. "Some of their key players, too. Vivica, Terrance, Santiago, Eric, and Gideon are among them."

"Not Emmie?" I asked.

Dean shook his head. "No, only two of the revolutionaries."

"That makes sense. Joshua told me they don't like all the revolutionaries going on missions together."

I let the wheels turn in my head. Attacking New Haven had proved to be a bigger problem than I'd originally thought thanks to all the setbacks. But the threat in New Haven had lessened. If we only had Emmie and Maya to get past, it wouldn't be hard. With Janice's side still a threat, we couldn't send all the military to New Haven. We needed to bring them to us.

I looked at Dean. "Let's send a small team to New Haven. They have something I want."

"What's that?" Dean asked.

I tried not to smile, but it came anyway. "Emmie. She won't have Dante, Santiago, or Eric guarding her. Or any of the others who would protect her."

"What about Joshua?" Dean sat forward. "Won't he try to stop us?"

My smile widened. "He's not working for them. He's

working for me. I'm sure he'll make it look like he tried, but he'll let her go."

"Tina. Luke. Others will try to stop us."

My smile disappeared. "Whose side are you on, Dean?"

He glared at me for a moment before he spoke. "I'm making sure you know what you're getting yourself into."

"I know what I'm doing," I said. "This isn't complicated. We send in a team, they capture Emmie, they bring her back here. It's a simple mission."

Dean sighed. "Fine. Do you want me to go?"

Standing, I went back to the window. "Yes." I pulled out my communicator. "Amber, I need you in my office." I watched over the city in silence until Amber joined us.

"Hey, babe, what's up?" Amber walked over to my desk and sat in my chair, twirling in it like a little girl.

I turned to face her, putting my hands that were balled into fists behind me. She could really grate on my nerves. "I'm sending you and your father on a mission."

Amber clapped her hands together. "Seriously? Where?"

"New Haven," I said. "I want you to go get Emmie and bring her back to me."

Amber stood and squealed in delight. "Really?" She stole a glance at her father. "I get to go get her?"

"Yes," I said.

She threw her arms around my neck, squeezing tight. "Oh, thank you, thank you, thank you!" Pulling back, she kissed me on the lips. When Dean cleared his throat, she finally released me.

I looked down at Amber. "I want her alive. She's bait."

Amber frowned. "But I can hurt her, right?"

"Of course." When Amber's eyes lit up, I held up a finger. "But not too much. We need her coherent."

"Fine," Amber said, rolling her eyes. "I'll hurt her just a little. But if she tries to escape, I'm not holding anything back."

I took Amber's chin in my hand. "Alive, Amber. I need her alive. I'll let you have fun with her after I've gotten my use out of her."

Amber squealed again. "I'm so excited! I finally get my own mission and it's to capture that brat."

"Our mission," Dean said, standing up. "I'm leading it. You're my second in command."

"Whatever." Amber jumped up and down where she stood. "I'm going to go pack." She turned to Dean. "When are we leaving?"

"Tomorrow morning," I said.

Amber pouted. "Why can't we leave tonight?"

"The trip's easier in the daytime." Dean opened the door. "Six, Amber. We're leaving at six in the morning." Before Amber could respond, he left the room.

Amber put her arms around my waist and pulled me close. "Am I staying with you tonight?" She batted her eyelashes and I had to hold down the bile.

"Not tonight." Putting my hands on her shoulders, I pushed her back. "You need to stay focused on the mission."

"I'll stay focused, I promise." She stuck out her lower lip and whimpered. She didn't realize how pathetic it made her look. I had no idea how it ever worked on Steven.

I turned away and went back to my desk, sitting down in

my chair. "I have work to do, Amber. You need to go get packed and get to bed early. We both know you're not a morning person."

Putting her arms around my neck, she kissed my ear and cheek. I took her arms and threw them off me. "I'm serious, Amber. Leave." If she stayed a minute longer, I would snap.

"You're lucky I love you," Amber said as she stormed toward the door. "Otherwise you wouldn't get away with this." She slammed the door on the way out.

Every time I saw her, it made the need to end the whole revolution more necessary. I couldn't stomach her much longer. Their mission had to be a success.

Once Emmie was in my custody, it would bring the New Haven residents to me. I could talk Brandon and others in Kingsland to come to my aide. With their help, it would be over within a month and River Springs would be exactly where it needed to be.

Completely under my control.

CHAPTER 11
Dante

Brandon's fist crashed down against my jaw again. He couldn't wrap his head around the fact that no matter how hard he hit me, I'd never talk.

I spat the blood from my mouth onto the floor in front of him. He had tied me to a chair and sat me in the middle of the room. All the other hostages were on the floor in a circle around me, their hands and feet bound.

Most of them had a hard time watching, for obvious reasons. Dee had closed her eyes and started humming. One of the guards kept trying to pry her eyes open, but every time he did, she tried to bite him. They finally ended up putting tape over her mouth and let her keep her eyes closed.

"Why are you here?" Brandon asked. He leaned down in front of me, resting his hands on his knees.

I eyed him. We used to be best friends. But everything had changed dramatically. I didn't understand why he had turned on me. "I missed those dazzling hazel eyes of yours." The punch that followed didn't surprise me. I spat the blood out of my mouth and turned my focus back to him.

A few of the guards suggested switching punching bags, but Brandon didn't care about seeing anyone else hurt. He wanted to see *me* in pain. Even though he'd punched me twenty times, I wasn't about to let him see me weak.

President Coleman stepped into the room. Brandon reluctantly backed away from me and stood near the other guards.

"Dante," President Coleman said as he approached me. "I was hoping to never see you again. Let's cut to the chase. Why are you here? Are you planning an attack?"

I looked up at him but kept my mouth closed. I'd answered the question multiple times and my response wasn't about to change.

President Coleman nodded at Brandon, so he punched me in the stomach. I kept my gaze forward and did my best not to flinch at the pain.

"It would be easier on everyone if you'd just talk," President Coleman said.

It was hard for me to look at him. He had the same eyes as his kids, and I cared deeply about them both. They were family to me. I wasn't sure their view on everything, but I'd held onto the hope that they were still good.

Staring straight forward, I sat up tall. "No, it won't. You'll kill us all anyway, so there's no point in me talking."

President Coleman smiled. "You think I'm just going to kill all of you?"

I forced myself to look into his eyes. "Yes, I do. Why would you keep us alive?"

"You have something we want," Brandon said. His voice was tight.

What could I possibly have that they would want? I stared at Brandon. "And what's that?"

Brandon opened his mouth, but President Coleman cut him off. "That doesn't matter right now. I need to know if my city is in danger."

"Of course, it is," I said.

"Others are on their way?" President Coleman asked.

I shook my head. "I meant your city is in danger because last I heard, there's a disease spreading." I saw Brandon flinch out of the corner of my eye.

President Coleman bent down to look me in the eye. "I meant are we in danger of being attacked?"

"By a virus?" I shrugged. "I'm not sure the specifics of the disease and how many it's affected here. If it keeps growing, I guess you could consider it an attack."

He backhanded me across the face. "You know what I meant!"

Smiling, I looked at him. "Hit me all you want, kill me if you want, but you're getting nothing out of me."

He hit me in the face again and turned to Brandon. "Switch him out for Vivica."

Brandon hesitated. He looked over at Vivica, who was sitting on the floor to the left of me. She stared straight ahead, showing no emotion. I almost spoke, but she glared at me.

"No," Santiago said. "Let me be your next target."

Vivica looked over at Santiago with a mix of frustration and surprise. I couldn't read Brandon's expression, but he glanced back and forth between the two of them like he was trying to decipher their relationship.

"I said Vivica," President Coleman said.

Brandon untied me and threw me on the floor next to Terrance. When Brandon walked away, Terrance turned to me and mouthed, "Are you okay?" I nodded in response.

Before Brandon could get to Vivica, Santiago hopped up and jumped in front of her, blocking Brandon from getting to her. It would have worked better if Santiago wasn't tied up; he ended up falling on top of her.

Brandon tried to pull Santiago up, but he squirmed and fought as hard as he could. Two other guards had to yank Santiago away and hold him back while Brandon grabbed Vivica.

"No!" Santiago shouted. "Leave her alone!"

I was surprised to see the sudden outburst from him. I hated him dating my sister, but I hadn't realized how much he cared for her. He had told me before that he was in love with her, but I didn't believe him.

Now I did.

Another guard came up to Santiago and punched him in the face three times, but that didn't stop him from fighting. They had to keep hitting him until he blacked out. When he fell to the floor, tears stained cheeks and I knew it wasn't from the pain.

Vivica had teared up, the annoyed look on her face telling me she was mad about crying. She hated to show her emotions in front of people. Brandon tied her to the chair, being surprisingly gentle. Vivica wouldn't look at him.

"Let's try again, shall we?" President Coleman said. "Vivica, why are you here?"

She stared ahead, fighting back the tears. When President Coleman nodded at Brandon, he just stood there.

"Hit her!" President Coleman yelled.

Brandon didn't move. The president backhanded Vivica across the face. I turned away, unable to see my sister in pain. It was hard enough having her up there.

"Tell me!" President Coleman practically spat the words out. He hit her again. "Tell me!" Again. "Tell me!" Again.

With each whimper from her mouth, I squirmed. Brandon had turned away and stared at the door. I could tell he was seconds away from running out.

"Tell me!" Again, and again.

"Stop!" I had expected those words to come from my mouth, maybe even Will's, but not Brandon's. He turned back around and walked up to Vivica, turning her face toward him. "Just tell him, Vivica. Please tell him."

"Screw. You." Vivica clenched her jaw tight, blood running down it.

"Why are you being so stubborn?" Brandon asked. His eyes pleaded. "It's not that difficult of a question."

No, it wasn't, but being quiet bought us time. All the hostages knew that. We had six others out there trying to rescue us and we needed to give them time.

"Why do you care?" Vivica asked. When Brandon didn't answer, she scoffed. "You're pathetic, you know that?"

Brandon looked surprised. "Me? Pathetic? You're the traitor!"

"Traitor?" Vivica shook in anger. "I'm the traitor? We left this city for a good reason and you stayed here supporting that monster!"

"Enough!" President Coleman yelled. Fear swam in his eyes, but I wasn't sure why. He turned to Brandon. "Maybe you should leave."

Brandon shook his head. "No. I want answers."

"I'm not telling you why we're here!" Vivica screamed, bubbles of blood sliding down her chin.

"I don't care about that!" Brandon's hands were balled into fists, his breaths coming out fast and ragged.

President Coleman stepped between Brandon and Vivica. "Leave, now."

Brandon pushed the president out of the way. "Just tell me why you did it."

"Did what?" Vivica licked her bloody lip. "Leave? To get away from all the politics." She nodded her head at President Coleman. "To get away from him. He's a liar and a fiend."

"No," Brandon said. "Why did you hide the cure?"

President Coleman pushed Brandon toward the door. Everyone else in the room turned to look at him.

"What are you talking about?" I asked Brandon.

He didn't take his eyes off Vivica. "Your family had the cure and you hid it. You could've saved Whitney." Tears streamed down his face.

"GET OUT!" President Coleman shoved Brandon, but he pushed back, knocking the president to the floor.

I shook my head in confusion. "We didn't have the cure. No one did."

Brandon pointed his finger at me. "Liar! I know you had it!" Coming over to me, he picked me up by my shirt and threw me against the wall. "I thought you loved her!"

"I did!" I choked back a sob. "I do! I still do! I'll always love her!"

"Then why didn't you save her?" Brandon's grip softened. "Why?"

"I couldn't," I said, tears falling. "I don't know what President Coleman told you, but we didn't have the cure."

"Guards!" President Coleman shouted. "Get Brandon out of here!"

Two guards rushed over and yanked Brandon away from me. I fell to the floor as they dragged him out.

Vivica looked over at me, trying to search for an answer, but I just shook my head. I had no idea what Brandon was talking about.

President Coleman was flustered. He looked over at a guard standing near the door. "Untie her. Maybe we should take a small break so everyone can regroup." He turned to me before he left. "You need to rethink your answer. The next time I come in here, I won't be so gentle."

I barely heard him. My mind replayed everything Brandon had said. Was it true? Had President Coleman told him our family had the cure and was hiding it? Was that why Brandon had turned his back on us so abruptly? If it was true, why did the president make that up? What was the point?

Vivica's scratchy voice caught my attention. "Do you

know what that was about?"

The guards had left us alone in the room. They were probably still listening to us, so we had to be careful of what we said.

"I have no idea," I said.

Eric looked at me. "It would make sense. That would be a good way to get people to turn on you and think your family was evil."

"But why that?" Terrance asked. "Out of everything he could have come up with, why did he choose to say you had the cure and were hiding it? What would even be the point of hiding it?"

I shook my head. "I don't know. None of this makes sense."

"Maybe he has it," Eric said. "Maybe President Coleman has the cure. Maybe *he's* the one hiding it."

"That doesn't make any sense, either," Vivica said. She scooted her body, so it was next to Santiago's. He still hadn't come to. They must have knocked him out hard.

Eric shrugged. "It was just a thought." He glanced over my face. "How are you holding up?"

"I'm fine." I looked at Vivica. "You?"

"I can take a few hits." She put her head against Santiago's.

I sighed. "He really loves you, doesn't he?"

Vivica smiled. "Yes, he does."

Santiago stirred. He opened his eyes and looked at Vivica lying next to him. Normally, Vivica would have been mad at a guy for trying to interfere. She hated being treated as weak and not being able to handle herself.

“Are you okay?” Santiago asked Vivica. The concern in his eyes radiated across the room.

Vivica leaned in and kissed him on the lips. “Thank you. I love you.”

“I love you, too,” Santiago said. As they gazed into each other’s eyes, I cleared my throat. They didn’t look at me, but everyone else did.

“I know this is hard,” I said, “but no one can tell them anything. No matter what we tell them, they’ll still end up killing us. They don’t want us alive and they know we can’t be turned back to their side, so death is the only option.” I glanced at Vivica and Santiago. “I know it’s hard to watch each other get beat up, but we have to stay strong. If at any moment you find yourself giving in, remind yourself of why we started this revolution. Remind yourself of New Haven and the people we’re fighting for. Remind yourself that we are warriors and we will not back down.”

We would never back down.

CHAPTER 12
Emmie

The moment I walked into the room, Michael and Zoe were both on their feet. Their eyes went wide when they took me all in. With my face still painted, I was probably quite the sight. I raised my hands to show I had no weapons and meant no harm.

Michael stepped in front of his sister, blocking her from my view. "Who are you? And how did you get in here?"

"It doesn't matter how I got in." I put my arms down and stuffed my hands in my pockets. "My name is Emmie. I'm friends with Dante."

Zoe peeked her head around her brother, looking at me with curious eyes. "How do you know Dante?"

I wasn't sure how much I should tell her. I was taking a big gamble being in the room in the first place. "That doesn't matter, either. What does matter is that he's being held captive by your father, along with nine others. I need your help."

"Why should we help you?" Michael asked.

Zoe stepped out from behind him and took a step closer to me. When she tried to move another step, he put his hand on her arm and pulled her back.

"I just wanted to introduce myself." She held out her hand to me. "I'm Zoe."

I eyed her hand before I shook it. "It's nice to meet you." I put my hand back in my pocket.

She nodded toward Michael. "This is my brother Michael, who has horrible manners."

Michael scoffed. "She broke into our house, steps into your room, claims she's friends with Dante and you immediately welcome her with open arms. I'll go get the maid and we can get a room set up for her and a nice warm meal."

"A warm meal?" The muffled voice came from outside of the room. I closed my eyes and sighed. Bruce.

Alarm crossed over Michael's eyes. "There are others with you?"

Bruce popped his head into the room to see what was going on and then stepped in. He had taken off his weapons, too. "Just me. I'm Bruce. A friend of Emmie and Dante." He walked up to Zoe and put his hand out.

She looked over at Michael, who shook his head. But Zoe just shrugged and shook Bruce's hand anyway. "Zoe."

Bruce reached his hand over to Michael, but Michael ignored his hand and bore his eyes into mine. Michael stepped forward until he was right in front of me. "You have two seconds to explain yourself and then I'm calling security."

"Two seconds?" Bruce stepped between Michael and me,

which was incredible since there wasn't much space to fit a person there. "Seriously? The two seconds are already up. She needs more time than that." He patted Michael on the arm. "Listen, let's just cut to the chase. Your father took our friends and we want them back. It's simple, really."

"And how do you suppose you're going to get them out?" Michael kept his feet planted where they were, our three bodies squished against each other.

I stepped back, pulling Bruce with me so we weren't so close to Michael. But he just took another step toward us.

"How many times do we have to repeat ourselves?" Bruce asked. "We'll get them out with …" He pushed his finger into Michael's chest, which again surprised me. No space. "Your help."

Zoe sighed and pulled Michael away from us. "What do you need us to do?"

"I just need a way to communicate with the citizens of Kingsland," I said. "Does your dad keep that kind of equipment in your home?"

"Yes …" Zoe started.

Michael cut her off. "Why would we give you access to that kind of equipment? This could be a trap."

Bruce laughed. "How could we trap you by talking to your citizens?"

"I don't know," Michael said. "It could be a decoy or something."

"There's no decoy," I said. "We don't have time for small talk." I looked at Zoe. "Can you take me to this equipment or not?"

“Yes,” she said as walked out the door.

“Uh, I should warn you …” I started.

Zoe let out a scream.

“That there are others with me,” I said in a mumble. Smiling at Michael, I took Bruce by the arm and left the room.

When I walked out into the hall, Zoe was frozen in place. Maya, Tina, Luke, and Joshua were all standing there holding their weapons, plus mine and Bruce’s. It was probably a terrifying sight to Zoe. Bruce shoved past me and went to collect his weapons from Maya.

Michael walked out and opened his mouth. I could tell by the look in his eyes that he was about to yell. I hurried and put my hand over his mouth. He stared down at me in surprise.

“I know this is awkward,” I said, “but you’re going to have to trust me. We aren’t going to hurt you, I promise.”

“Well, unless you try to hurt us,” Bruce said. Someone slapped him and I assumed it was Maya.

“Zoe can take us to the equipment, and you can stand guard.” I kept my hand firmly over his mouth and Michael didn’t try to stop me. “If at any moment we say something you don’t like, you can cut us off. Deal?”

Michael looked past me at the others. His gaze lingered a while, which I figured had to be on Zoe. He finally set his eyes back on me and nodded.

“And you won’t yell out when I release my hand?” I asked.

He nodded. I took my hand away and he smiled at me. “I can see why Dante would want to be your friend.”

“It’s creepy, isn’t it?” Joshua said. “They’re so much alike, sometimes it scares me.”

Tina laughed. "They're like twins who were separated at birth."

I rolled my eyes. "We aren't that much alike."

"Yes, you are," Luke, Maya, and Bruce said at the same time.

"Again, no time for small talk," I said. "Zoe, if you would please?"

Nodding, Zoe walked between Tina and Luke and headed toward the stairs. She passed them and continued down the hall until she came to a room on the right. She walked in, leaving the door open behind her. We all followed her into the room.

The room was full of computers. There were six large screens on the wall, each showing a different area of Kingsland. There were only two chairs in the room. Zoe sat down in one and Bruce sat in the other. The rest of us stood behind them.

"You can change the views," Zoe said, pressing down on a keyboard in front of her. The screens flickered, each time coming up with a new location.

"Stop." I stared at the screen in the upper left corner. It was Dante, Eric, and the others. They were all sitting on the floor, some lying down. I took a step toward the monitor. Dante had been beaten badly. "Can you zoom in?"

"I think so." Zoe fiddled with the computer until it zoomed in.

"Scan to the right," I said. The screen moved and I could get a better look at Vivica and Santiago. They were lying down next to each other. Vivica had been beaten, too. But nothing as bad as Dante. I was relieved to see that everyone else looked okay.

Zoe sniffed. I put my hand on her shoulder. "This is why we need your help. We need to make sure Dante stays alive."

Michael coughed behind me. "If we were to let you communicate with our citizens, what would you even say that could help free Dante?"

Turning around, I looked at him, keeping my hand on Zoe's shoulder. "Do you support your dad and the way he runs this city?"

"Yes," Michael said. The moment the word was out of his mouth, I knew he would be a problem. There was no way he'd let me talk to anyone once he heard what I was going to say.

"I don't," Zoe said. She put her hand on mine. Her eyes were filled with tears. "I think he's been lying to us and the rest of Kingsland." Michael opened his mouth to say something, but Zoe's eyes pleaded with him. "You can't possibly believe all the things he says about Dante. We've known him and his family forever. They're good people. I know they are."

"Our dad is a good person!" Michael said. "Why would he lie to us?"

Zoe shook her head. "I don't know, but he is."

"Enough," Michael said. "This is over. I'm getting security."

Sighing, I removed my hand from Zoe's shoulder. I nodded at Joshua and Luke. Before Michael could step out of the room, the two of them were on him. Joshua got in two solid blows to the head, knocking Michael unconscious. Zoe yelped out in surprise.

"He'll be fine," I said to her. "Luke, tie him up so when he comes to, he won't cause any problems." As Luke dragged

Michael's unconscious body to the corner of the room, I looked at Zoe. "So how do I talk to the residents?"

Zoe wiped the tears from her eyes as she watched Luke tie up her brother. She looked over at me, her face suddenly painted with regret. "Maybe this was a bad idea."

I knelt next to her, putting my hand on her arm. "Zoe, you said yourself you trust Dante. He's being held by your father and your own brother has said Dante will not leave this city alive. We need to make sure that doesn't happen. You're right; Dante and his family are good people. They only wanted the best for everyone when they left. Your dad has taken everyone who supports Dante and is holding them prisoners, too."

Zoe's eyes widened in alarm. "What? I didn't know that." She glanced at Michael on the floor. "You're not lying to me, are you?"

I shook my head. "No, I'm not. I'm sure if you continued scanning through all the security feed in the city, you'd eventually find them. Thousands of people are being held against their will. All they wanted was freedom." I rubbed her arm. "Dante said that a lot of your citizens are getting sick."

"They are," Zoe said. "How do you know that?"

"Dante has kept in touch with someone named Marcus. Do you know him?"

Zoe nodded. "Yes. He's a nice guy." A small smile formed on her lips. "He used to give me piggyback rides when I was little."

"So, you trust him?" I asked.

"Yes," Zoe said. "As much as I do Dante."

"Good," I said. "Now, we need to work together to free

Dante, Marcus, and everyone else. We need to rally everyone together. If we can do that, then they can all help us break into Headquarters, putting a stop to all of this."

"Why would they do that?" Zoe asked.

I looked up at her, her soft eyes filled with hope. "Because we have a cure for the disease."

CHAPTER 13

Zoe stared at me, trying to process what I had told her. Her voice was quiet when she spoke. "How is that possible? No one has been able to find a cure."

"We have," I said, standing. "Our doctors researched and studied it until they did." I pointed to Dee on the screen. "That's my best friend, Dee. Last year she came down with the disease. But our doctors cured her." I pointed to Gideon. "It was his wife, Marie, that put together the final formula. She administered it to Dee and now Dee's completely back to her old self, with no symptoms at all."

"And you think this cure will work on our citizens?" Zoe asked.

"Yes," Maya said, stepping forward. "From everything Marcus has told us, plus watching all the symptoms Dee had, we know it's the same disease. We can put a stop to it."

Luke sighed. "We don't have all day."

Tina gave him a sharp look. "They don't need your input right now."

"Fine," Luke said, folding his arms. "Continue talking about it all night. It's not like there's a time limit on Dante and everyone else's life."

Tina opened her mouth, but Zoe spoke first. "He's right. My dad won't keep them alive much longer. If you're going to do something, it has to be now."

"I know," Luke said. "Let's cut the chit chat and get going."

Joshua looked at Zoe. "Can we do a live feed from here?"

Zoe nodded, turning back to the computer. "Yes. There's an override system my dad had installed. It will automatically turn on all the televisions in everyone's homes and every building, plus it will have the audio come out of every speaker throughout the city. Just give me a minute."

As she typed away on the computer, Michael stirred. Luke had made sure to gag him in addition to tying him up.

"Want me to knock him back out?" Luke asked.

I shook my head. "He's fine. He can't move or talk. Just don't let him escape."

Saluting me, Bruce stepped in front of Michael. "Yes, ma'am. I'll keep watch."

When Bruce had his face turned toward Michael, I pointed at Joshua and Luke, telling them they needed to be watching, too. They both smiled and nodded. I appreciated Bruce and all the hard work he put in, but the boy was tiny. Michael could easily take him, even being bound.

"Okay," Zoe said. She handed me a small microphone and then pointed at a camera. "Just talk into the microphone and look here. When I press enter, this will go live. You'll be broadcasted all over Kingsland, including the room my dad will be in." She hesitated before she went on. "As soon as this is live, security will know you're here. They'll be storming in within minutes. You better be prepared for that."

"I understand," I said. "Where's your mom, Zoe?"

"She's sleeping," she said. "I'll go to her as soon as this starts and let her know what's going on. Hopefully, I can keep her calm and from coming in here."

I looked at Maya, Tina, Luke, Joshua, and Bruce. "This is it. The five of you have to keep me covered until I'm done."

"Before you start, let's barricade the front door." Joshua looked at Zoe. "Is there another way into this house?"

Zoe nodded as she stood. "There's a passageway from Headquarters to my parent's room."

"Where's your parent's room?" Tina asked.

"Right next door," Zoe said.

"Okay," Maya said. "Joshua and I will head downstairs and move any furniture we can find to block the front door. We'll lock all the windows and move furniture in front of them, too. Tina and Luke can do the same for upstairs and the passageway." She looked at Bruce. "Don't let Michael leave this room."

Michael started to sit up, so Joshua knocked him in the head again. "Just in case."

Maya looked at me. "Be thinking about what you want to say. This needs to be convincing."

"I know," I said. "Zoe, go to your mom's room and wake her up."

"Right now?" Zoe asked.

I nodded. "It's either you tell her now, or she wakes up in two minutes when Luke and Tina are in her room moving furniture around."

"True." Zoe glanced over my face, looking at me apologetically. "Please don't take this the wrong way, but maybe you should wash your face first since you're covered in that paint. The residents might not respond well with you looking like that."

Instinctively, I put my hand up to my face. I'd forgotten about the paint. I must have looked so strange to her. "Where's the bathroom?"

"I'll show you." Zoe turned and left the room.

I turned to the others. "Get started." They all nodded, following me out.

When my face was fully scrubbed and free of any war paint, I went back into the security room. Bruce stood tall, back straight, his face all business. Michael lay unconscious on the floor.

"What are you going to say?" Bruce asked me when I entered the room.

"The truth, I guess." Taking off my jacket, I folded it in half and placed it on one of the chairs. "I'm just not sure how I'm going to convince thousands of people to trust me over their president. I mean, I know I'm telling the truth, but they don't. I'm just some random girl who's going to show up on their screens."

"If only you had some proof," Bruce said. "Can you air the feed of Dante being held? I mean, he's pretty beat up. If they saw him, maybe they'd trust you."

I twisted my ring as I walked to the door. Furniture scraped across the wood flooring as they were pushed into place. "Maybe. But they'd have to like Dante to feel sorry for him. Over half of the city still supports President Coleman. They'll probably just be happy to see Dante in the shape he's in."

"True," he said, nodding. He scratched the back of his head and sighed. "I wish I was brilliant. Too bad I was only given brawn and good looks."

I smiled at him. Looking down at the still unconscious Michael, I let the wheels in my head turn, continuing to twist my ring. We needed proof that President Coleman was bad, but where would we get that? We couldn't get into Headquarters. I turned to Bruce who tapped his finger against his lip, deep in thought. "Hey Bruce, I have a task for you."

"My task is to keep watch over Michael." He folded his arms, trying to look tough and manly.

"I can keep my eye on him until everyone gets back," I said. "I need you to put your detective skills to work."

Bruce rolled his eyes. "I just told you I'm only good for my striking looks and massive muscles."

I rolled my eyes in return. "Oh, come on, we both know you secretly want to be a detective. You're always snooping around New Haven with that little note pad of yours."

His eyes widened in surprise. He absentmindedly patted his shirt pocket where he kept the pad. "I thought no one noticed that."

"You're talking to me," I said. "You know I notice everything that happens in New Haven."

"Blast!" He shook his fist. "I should've known you'd catch on to me. You always do."

"Well, I have a mission for you." Folding my arms, I looked him up and down. "If you're brave enough to accept it."

Bruce scoffed. "Of course, I am." He came up next to me, keeping his voice low. "What's the mission, boss?"

"I need you to snoop around this house and see if you can find anything that can incriminate the president." I kept my voice low, also, just to appease him.

"Like what?"

"Anything. Documents, photos, objects, anything that seems suspicious or off." I put my hand on his shoulder. "You need to be quick."

Squaring his shoulders, Bruce saluted me. "You can count on me, dearest Emmie."

"Good." I saluted him in return. His eyes lit up for a moment before he turned back to business. He marched out of the room, his arms swinging wildly.

As I waited for everyone to return, I paced the room, glancing over at Michael now and then to make sure he hadn't awakened.

I wasn't sure if Bruce would find anything, but I crossed my fingers he would. Otherwise, I had to hope my words would convince enough Kingsland citizens to trust me and turn on their president.

I could say I had the cure, but would they even believe me? Would I believe some person I'd never met before when they said they found the cure? I was a random stranger showing up on their screens, who could be lying.

Maybe I could talk Zoe into talking, too. If the citizens saw she agreed with me and trusted me, they might as well. Unless they thought I forced her to say all those things. Rubbing my temples, I wished away the stress headache pounding its way in.

"You about ready?" Tina asked from the doorway.

I sighed and sat down in a chair. "I hope so. This has to work."

"It will," Tina said, walking over to me. She squatted down in front of me. "I'm sending you positive vibes."

"Thanks," I said, resisting the urge to roll my eyes. I reached out and pulled her into a hug. "I just want Eric, Dante, Dee, and the others back."

"I know," Tina said as she rubbed my back. "We all do. Just be honest and open. They'll see the sincerity in your eyes."

"I hope so," I said.

Someone clapped their hands near the door. "Cute love fest, but let's get this party started." Joshua stood there with excited eyes. "I'm tired, I'm hungry, and I want to sleep in my own bed in the near future. So, end the hug and my wonderful sister can get talking so my wishes may come true."

Pulling away from Tina, I turned to Joshua. "I'm glad to know that out of everything that can come from my announcement, the one thing you're hoping for is the comfort of your bed."

Joshua shrugged. "Fine. I also hope for you to have the comfort of your bed." He smiled at Tina. "And your bed, too."

"What are you saying about my girlfriend's bed?" Luke

asked as he came up next to Joshua.

Joshua's face turned red. "Nothing. I just want her to be comfortable and to get some sleep." Luke raised his eyebrows, so Joshua continued. "I won't be anywhere near her bed, I promise. You can be there if you'd like, but I will be far away in my own bed, by myself. No Tina anywhere near me."

"Please stop talking," I said. Luke and Tina nodded in agreement. Joshua put his head down, muttering something under his breath. "Is everything set?"

Maya came into the room, pushing past the boys. "Yes, we're good. Luke, Joshua, and I will stand at the top of the stairs, weapons ready for when they breach the front door. Tina will stand guard at this door, being your last line of defense." She looked over at Michael. "Where's Bruce?"

"I sent him on a mini-mission to get me information," I said. "Maybe he'll find some evidence we can use against the president."

"Sounds good," Tina said. "Everyone ready?"

"Where's Zoe?" I asked.

"With her mom," Luke said. "It looks like everything's under control in there for now. We just need to get started."

Spotting some dirt on my pants, I brushed them off with my hands. "How do I look?"

Tina came over and smoothed out some of my braid, pulling out a leaf I'd overlooked. "With the war paint gone, you look like a regular person, which is what you want."

"Regular people don't wear bulletproof vests," Luke commented.

Smiling, Tina helped me take it off. "True." She set it

down on the chair and looked me over. "A lot less intimidating."

I turned and stared at the screen where Eric, Dante, and the others were. "Once I press enter, this goes live." I glanced around the room. "Our position will be revealed. Once they break through the doors—and they will—it's only a matter of time before we're all captured."

Maya nodded. "We know, but we have to take this risk. There's no other option now. We're too far in this."

"She's right," Luke said.

"Alright." Shaking my hands out, I took some deep breaths, preparing myself for my speech. "Everyone, get into position."

Luke, Maya, and Joshua left the room. I stared over at Tina, who stood in the doorway.

She smiled at me. "You can do this, Emmie. Just be honest and be yourself." She readied her bow and arrow.

I fingered my knife I had tucked in my pants at my back. I didn't want any weapons to show while I broadcasted over Kingsland, but I didn't want to be completely defenseless once security broke in. Stepping toward the computer, I hovered my finger over the enter key. I took a deep breath and, giving one last glance at Tina, I looked directly into the camera and pressed enter.

Each screen went to static for half a second and then my face filled every single one of them.

CHAPTER 14

I put on the most genuine smile I could muster. "Hello, Kingsland citizens. My name is Emmie Woodard and I am a resident of the city of New Haven."

I paused for a moment to take a deep breath. My voice bellowed from outside the president's home. I tried my best not to think about the fact that thousands of people were seeing my face and hearing my voice.

"I'm sure most of you are wondering who I am and why I'm here. Some of my fellow New Haven residents have joined me in coming here to rescue your city members who have been taken captive by your president. Your fellow residents who are hardworking people, trustful, honest, and kind. Members who have been faithful citizens their whole lives. People who have lived up to their potential and then beyond. Like all of you, they have only wanted the best for their families."

I twisted my ring on my finger, taking my time with each word that came out of my mouth. I didn't want to rush. "President Coleman has not been honest with all of you. He has deceived you and doesn't deserve your support. Your neighbors deserve your support. They have done nothing wrong, yet President Coleman has been holding them against their will. Instead of letting them leave, he has kept them under his control, even hurting and killing some who didn't agree with him."

Closing my eyes for a moment, I thought of Dante and his bruised and beaten body. "Dante Brown and his family left this city for a reason. Their lives were in danger. They only wanted to protect those around them and stand up for the greater good. I'm not sure what lies your president has told you about the Brown family, but I've had the privilege to get to know them this past year. They are decent people with amazing hearts. They have put their lives on the line to protect our citizens and to fight for their freedom."

The image of President Brown's death came into my mind. He was blown to pieces right before my eyes by a traitor, Steven, from my old city.

I shook the thought from my mind. "They are selfless, and they proved it yet again by coming here. They wanted to rescue those who'd been taken prisoner. They risked their lives in the hope of setting you free. They want everyone here to be happy. To be able to stand on your own two feet and make your own decisions without interference from the government.

"Obviously, we still need structure, and New Haven can offer that to you. We let our citizens choose their life choices. How many children they want. When and if they want to get married. What career they would like. Where they live and what they eat. But we also have laws that protect you and your property. We listen to our citizens and let them vote on leaders and laws."

The pounding on the front doors began. "I need your help. Dante, Vivica, and eight other New Haven citizens are being detained by President Coleman right now. We need to free them. We need to show your president that he can't do this to people. You need to stand up for what's right. Come out of your homes. Stand together, united as a city, and storm Headquarters. Take back what's yours. Take back your freedom."

Maya shouted orders from the hallway. Security must have been almost through the front door. I kept my voice calm as I continued. "In return, I offer you protection. New Haven is open to any Kingsland citizens that want to live there. You'll be able to have a say in your life. You'll be listened to and given opportunities to expand your knowledge."

"Fire!" Maya's command echoed in my ears. Security was in the home.

"I've heard some of your citizens are sick." I stared at the camera, trying to keep my eyes soft and inviting. "New Haven has a cure. Fight for us and you'll get that cure. Come together right now, outside, tell President Coleman you've had enough, and the cure will be put in your hands. You can save all your loved ones who are sick."

Commotion by the door tore my gaze from the camera. Joshua, Luke, Maya, and Tina were all at the doorway, firing off arrows. An arrow was lodged Joshua's arm, but he ignored it and kept firing.

I turned back to the camera. "I know I'm asking a lot. I

know you don't know me and I'm sure you're asking yourself why you should trust me. But you *can* trust me. Everything I'm telling you is the truth. I promise you. Fight with us. Save Kingsland from total demise and evil. Save everyone who is sick."

The door slammed shut. Joshua, Maya, Tina, and Luke all stood inside, holding the door closed. Joshua yanked the arrow out of his arm and tossed it on the ground.

Security banged on the door, pushing in with all their might. The door heaved in and out with each shove.

"Open the door!" The voice was muffled, but I could hear the security guard clear enough.

"Let us in and we won't harm you!" the guard shouted. I highly doubted that. We'd be lucky if they didn't kill us.

I looked desperately at the camera. "Please, come out of your homes. Save the Brown family and their legacy. I know they've worked hard for years to protect this city and only have your best interest at heart."

A rattling noise came from the ceiling. I looked up to see a vent cover being pulled away. Before I could react, a body jumped down into the room. The person stood up and approached me, a huge smile plastered onto their face.

He held up a document. "Look what I found." Bruce peered behind the paper, watching intently at my reaction.

I took the paper from his grip and glanced over it. For a moment, I'd forgotten that there was a camera on me. "What is this?"

Bruce flattened out his hair as he looked at the camera. He wiggled his eyebrows and winked.

I smacked him on the arm to catch his attention. "What is this, Bruce?"

"Read it." He smiled at the camera. "I'm Bruce. I'm a hero and a fighter. But I'm also an excellent hugger and listener."

The sound of wood splintering came from the door. They were almost in.

"Hurry up!" Luke shouted.

I read over the paper, not sure if what I was reading was correct. I went back over it again and again. I looked at Bruce. "Is this what I think it is?"

Bruce shrugged. "It depends on what you think it is. If you think it's a delicious lasagna recipe, you're sadly mistaken. But if you think it's a cure for the disease that has been taking over Kingsland, then you're right."

Shaking my head, I continued to read. "They have the cure?"

"Yes." Bruce flexed as he looked at the camera. "Apparently, President Coleman has had the cure for a while. He has a secret stash of papers in his office. It took me forever to find the safe it was in. He put it behind a picture. How lame is that?" He winked at the camera again and ran his fingers through his hair. "Then I had to find the key, which was in a secret compartment in his desk."

The door broke open and some security guards jumped onto Maya, Luke, Tina, and Joshua, taking away their weapons as they held them down. Bruce came and stood in front of me, putting himself between me and the guards.

I stared at the paper in disbelief. "If he's had the cure, why is he hiding it? It doesn't make sense. He could've cured all those residents of Kingsland." I put my hand on my head. "Why did he let them die?"

Bruce kicked at a security guard who tried to grab him. "You said yourself that President Coleman was a bad dude. Hi-yah!" He kicked the guard right in the face, breaking his nose. "This just proves it. He has the cure and has been hiding it in his office. From the looks of it, there were a lot of other things he was hiding."

He took his knife and thrust it at another guard. "What's even worse? He had the cure when Whitney was still alive. Instead of healing her, he ended her life. I mean, he didn't wait until she died on her own. He took it upon himself to decide it was time for her to go and had the doctor 'terminate the subject'." He kicked the guard and threw his arm around, slashing the guard's arm. Bruce turned at looked at me. "Those were the exact words he used. The guy is a total creep."

The guard seized Bruce and pinned him down on the ground. Bruce let out a yelp as the guard took away his weapons.

Zoe screamed out in the hall. She shoved her way into the room and jumped on a guard that was about to grab me. I was too preoccupied with the document in my hand and everything that Bruce had just told me.

"Leave them alone!" Zoe yelled. "They don't mean any harm! They're just trying to help!"

"Jordan, get Zoe under control!" A guard near the door had yelled that out to the man that Zoe was attacking.

Zoe kept hitting Jordan on the head over and over again. "Don't do this! My dad is the monster, not them!"

I looked up as Jordan twisted his body so he could get a good grip on Zoe. He took her firmly in his grasp and held her arms behind her back. She continued to squirm in his arms.

Another guard came at me. I turned the paper in my hand, so it faced the camera. "President Coleman has the cure. He's been hiding it from you. Come and get it."

I kept my gaze firmly on the camera, even as a guard threw me on the ground. I didn't fight back as he bound me up. I just stared at the camera hoping that was enough to fuel Kingsland citizens.

The guard picked me up off the ground, forcing me to walk on my own and out the door. My hands were bound tightly behind my back. They marched all of us outside and threw us in a van. Joshua was right next to me, pain filling his eyes. The broadhead was still lodged in his arm.

"How bad is the pain?" I asked him.

Sweat slid down Joshua's pale cheeks. "Nothing I can't handle."

We rode in silence the rest of the way. When we stopped and they opened the back door, Headquarters stood before us. The front doors were open, waiting for us to enter. The guard who pulled me out of the van was nowhere near gentle with me. He shoved me so hard, I fell, my face scraping against the pavement. The sting on my cheek made my eyes water as he picked me up and thrust me forward again. That time, I didn't fall.

Once inside Headquarters, we were forced down a bunch of halls until they finally started throwing us in a room. Before I got to the door, my guard pinned me up against the wall, putting his face just inches from mine.

His breath warmed my skin. "I hope you realize what a horrible mistake you've made. You just cost the lives of each one of your friends." He wrapped his large, callused hand around my throat, squeezing tight. "You will be last, of course, and I will make sure to take my precious time with you."

I struggled for air as he squeezed harder, his thumbnail digging into my skin.

He pressed his mouth against my ear. "You're awfully pretty, too. I'm sure the president will let me have some alone time with you before the torture begins." His slid his mouth along my cheek until his lips were at mine. Closing my eyes, I tucked my lips in as he talked. "I'm going to take you apart, limb by limb. I promise you will feel every ounce of pain." I breathed furiously through my nose as he continued to choke me. He put his lips back at my ear. "No one can save you now."

The guard pulled away and let go of my throat. Holding the knife he'd taken from me, he twirled it in his hand as he glared at me. Pressing the tip of the knife against my cheek, he slid it down, my skin slicing open underneath it. He pulled it away when he got to my chin. I tried to keep calm as he stared at me, his eyes full of hatred and lust.

The other guards were watching us. Everyone else had been thrown into the room already, which I was grateful for. I wouldn't want any of them to see what this guard was doing to me. He put one hand on my throat, more to hold me back than to choke me. With his other hand, he drove the knife through my stomach.

"Just to give you a taste of what's coming your way," the

guard said as he held the knife inside of me. I choked on my sobs as he pushed it in deeper. I didn't want to scream out in pain. I couldn't.

He finally yanked the knife back out and threw me into the room. I hit the ground hard, pain erupting in my arm as well as my wound. I closed my eyes and focused on each breath as the door slammed shut and the lock clicked into place.

CHAPTER 15
Janice

On a cold winter night nineteen years ago, I reached over and shook Philip awake. My water had broken, soaking my pants. Philip called the infirmary to let them know I was in labor. While we waited for them to arrive, he got dressed and went to wake Derek.

As soon as they knocked on the door, Philip picked me up and carried me outside. He pushed past the ambulance driver who had knocked and rushed me to the back of the van. Derek ran as fast as his little legs would let him. An infirmary worker picked Derek up and placed him in the back of the van with us.

The whole ride to the infirmary, I tried to focus on my breathing just like I did when I had Derek. But as I watched Philip coaching me the same way he did with our son, my heart broke. He knew it wasn't his child inside me. Our physical relationship ended shortly after I had Derek and started my job as Whit's assistant. But Philip treated the birth the same way he had with Derek's. He showered me with such love and devotion, making sure I had everything I needed.

Even after I had Emmie, he treated her like his own. He loved her unconditionally and was the father she needed. I loved Whit, but he didn't have the same compassion that Philip had. Philip adored Emmie and looked after and protected her. I wasn't surprised to learn that he had dropped everything and left with Emmie on her foolish mission.

I went back and forth on how I felt about Emmie leaving. I was still convinced it was a childish thing to do, but I admired her determination and her drive. She had an independent nature which helped as much as it did hurt her.

Emmie was different from the start. She watched Derek like a hawk and wanted to do everything he did. She crawled by five months, walked by ten months, and at seventeen months, she decided she was done with diapers. I caught her one day throwing all her diapers away. When I asked her what she was doing she responded, "No diaper. Toilet." She never once had an accident.

By the time Emmie was two, she had made it very apparent that she did not like Whit. I wasn't sure how their relationship would turn out, but it did not go the way I had hoped. Whit did come by to see me in the infirmary after I had her. He was mostly concerned about my health, though. He never once offered to hold her. He barely looked at her. I told myself it was because it was too painful for him, but in all honesty, he wasn't interested.

Every time Philip and the kids came by Whit's home to

see me, Emmie would give Whit a death glare. She would throw things at his head and stick her tongue out at him. At the age of five, she learned to just ignore him as he did her. They rarely acknowledged each other when they were in the same room.

It started to change when she turned fourteen. Whit took a sudden interest in her and asked me about her constantly. I thought maybe he finally wanted to be a part of his daughter's life, but he still never actually talked to her. He would just ask me or Derek questions about her. They eventually started having short conversations when they were out in public and people were watching. But they were doing all they could to be civil to each other. It wasn't until I heard about the prophecy that I realized that was the only reason why he was interested in her.

Over time, I realized that I had started treating Emmie exactly how Whit did. His feelings for her rubbed off onto me. I was cold and heartless to my own daughter. By the time I had figured it out, it was too late to undo the damage. There were so many times where I wanted to go back and fix everything. I desperately wanted the chance to have the relationship with her I should have had in the beginning.

A big part of me knew it was too late, but I still had this little ounce of me that hoped Emmie would let me back into her life. I couldn't repair all the damage, but maybe we could start over. We needed a fresh start, just like the city did. With Emmie and me working together, we could make history. The possibilities were endless.

Jen's mission had to be successful so we could put an end

to Austin's reign and start a new era.

A loud knock at the door took me from my thoughts. I sat up tall in my chair. "Come in."

Tami came in, throwing the door open and slamming it closed. She walked up to my desk and stood before me. I motioned for her to sit down, but she kept standing.

"What do you need, Tami?" I asked.

Folding her arms, she rested her weight on her hip. "I thought you should know that Austin just sent Amber, Dean, and a few others on a trip."

"Do you know where they're going?" I clasped my hands in front of me on the desk and kept my posture straight. She liked to stand to be taller than me, but I could keep myself refined.

"We're not entirely sure, but they are headed in the direction of New Haven," Tami said.

My eyebrows rose. "New Haven? Why would he be sending a small group there?"

Tami shook her head. "I don't know. There's no logic behind it."

"No, there isn't." I sat back in my chair, moving my clasped hands to my lap. "If he wanted to send a spy, he wouldn't send Dean or Amber. He must have a bigger purpose."

"But not that big of a purpose, because there are only five of them total," Tami said. "They took a jeep."

"When did they leave?" I asked.

Tami let out a frustrated sigh and shifted her weight to her other hip. "A little less than an hour ago."

I looked at her, startled. "What took you so long to tell me?"

"I was trying to put together a group to follow them," Tami said. "And then I got hungry."

Standing, I placed my fists on the table and leaned toward her. "Your appetite can wait. You're supposed to come to me right away with things like this."

Tami rolled her eyes. When my face didn't soften, she took a couple of steps back. "I didn't think it was that big of a deal."

"We came to an agreement," I said, keeping my gaze firmly on her. "We said we'd be open with each other and would work together to get even with Austin. But I think you keep forgetting that in the end, I'm the one in charge here."

"You can't tell me what to do." She came back to her original spot right behind the table. "I have no reason to take orders from the whore who ruined my family."

I slammed my fist on the table. "I don't care about your feelings about my private life! This was a business arrangement and nothing else. We put aside our personal feelings and work for the common good, which was to get our city back in order."

She leaned in so her face was inches from mine. "I don't care. You're lucky I even came and told you."

"Tami, I know you hate me, and I understand why you do." I took a few breaths to calm myself. "But we need to work together if we want to make this work."

"Maybe I don't want to make it work."

I leaned back. "Fine. You and your mother are welcome

to leave. I'm sure Austin would love to have you back." Straightening my shirt out, I sat down in my chair. "You can leave my office now."

She stood there, her breaths coming out in exaggerated huffs. I ignored her and went over some papers that were in front of me.

After a moment she flopped down in the chair on the other side of my desk. "I'm sorry I took so long to tell you. Next time, I'll be sure to tell you right away." Her tone was that of a child who'd just been scolded, reluctant to make an apology.

"Good." I took a sip of water from my cup at my desk.

"We sent a few men after them," she said as she crossed her legs. I could feel her gaze on me. "They were able to catch up and have been tailing them ever since."

I took another drink, still looking at my papers. "I'm assuming they're keeping their distance so they won't be spotted."

Tami sneered. "Of course. I'm not stupid."

I looked up at her then. "I know you're not. That's why you're still here and why I've wanted your help." I sighed. "Tami, I don't know what to say to you about my life choices. I know they weren't conventional. But what happened is over and done with. We can't go back to the past. I have said this countless times, and I will keep on saying it as long as I have to. We need to put aside our hatred for one another if we want this to work. Once we have the city back where it needs to be, we can go our separate ways and never speak to each other again."

"I look forward to that day."

"Trust me, so do I. Has Jen been notified?"

Her face twisted and I couldn't read her expression. "Yes, I had someone tell her. She'll be on the lookout."

"Any news on her end that I should know about?" I already knew what was going on with Jen since I gave her a personal communication device, but Tami didn't know that. I had to see if Tami was going to be honest with me.

"Nope," she said, shaking her head. "She's there, but Emmie hasn't come back yet."

"Have they been nice to her?"

She nodded. "They were reluctant at first, but Derek was willing to give her a chance until Emmie could actually talk with her."

"That's understandable." I shuffled my papers around and grabbed a pen from my drawer. "That will be all for now." I glanced at Tami. "Keep me informed, please."

Tami stood, giving me a little bow. "Of course." Her smile told me she was lying.

I kept my sigh internal. I would never be able to fully trust her or her mom. They would never be completely open and honest with me.

Tami left the room without another word.

Letting my posture slip, I put the pen down and ran my fingers through my hair. Life was difficult when you had no one you could fully trust. I used to think I could trust Whit, but as more was revealed about him after his death, I started to see that I couldn't fully trust him. I had thought he'd told me everything, but obviously, he hadn't.

My closest allies were my two worst enemies. I had just sent a possible spy, Jen, to seek my daughter's help. My daughter who didn't trust me. Everyone around her, including Philip and our son Derek, didn't trust me either, which meant I couldn't trust them.

The weight of the fact I had no one in my life I could trust came crashing down on me. And my list kept piling up. I had a horrible sinking feeling in my stomach, which was something I hadn't felt in years. Before Emmie had left and Whit was murdered, my life had been so perfect. I had absolutely nothing to worry about. Whit spoiled me and made sure I had whatever I wanted. He made me feel safe and comfortable.

All of that was gone in the blink of an eye. If Austin thought he was going to get away with it, he was horribly mistaken. I would not rest until I got even. I didn't want Austin taken out of his position; I wanted his life taken from him. He didn't deserve to live while so many lives had been altered because of his careless decisions.

I hoped my daughter would come to her senses and work with me. With her help, we could end the war. My life would never be completely whole again, but it would be a good start. I didn't like the fact that I had to depend on so many people, including ones who hated me, but I had no other option.

CHAPTER 16
Emmie

The cold, hard floor of the holding room pressed against my back. Shivering, I placed my hand over my wound, trying to apply as much pressure as I could.

"Emmie." Urgency filled Eric's voice. He came up next to me and tried to lift my hands so he could see.

"No." My voice was shaky and quiet. "It needs pressure."

"What did they do to you?" Dante asked, coming to the other side of me.

Eric wiped away the blood on my cheek from the long gash. I couldn't help but smile. He furrowed his eyebrows. "What?"

"If it doesn't heal well, we'll have matching scars on our face," I said. He didn't smile in return. I guess it wasn't that funny.

"Are you ignoring my question on purpose?" Dante asked. There wasn't a smile on his face, either.

"Mmmmmmm!"

Eric looked behind him, so I followed his gaze. Dee was on the floor, feet and hands bound, tape over her mouth. Eric removed the tape as gently as he could, which wasn't easy since his hands were bound, too.

Once the tape was off, Dee scooted closer to me. "What happened?"

"That's the question of the day, isn't it?" Dante didn't hold back his sarcasm. Eric pressed his hands down on mine, putting more pressure on my wound.

I turned my gaze to the ceiling. "A guard got a little carried away, that's all." My voice came out weaker than I'd wanted. I didn't need everyone worrying about me. There were more important things to think about. Like keeping all of us alive. I looked around for my brother. "Where's Joshua?"

"I'm here." His voice came from behind my head. I tried to crane my neck to see him, but I couldn't.

"How's your arm?" I asked him.

Eric and Dante both grunted and I chose to ignore them. We didn't need to talk about my wound.

"It'll be better once I get this stupid broadhead out," Tina said.

Joshua moaned. "Gentle, please."

"I'm trying to be," Tina said. "But gentle isn't working and you need this out."

"Let me try to help," Luke said.

I couldn't see what they were doing, but I could hear the groans and swearing coming from Joshua.

"Back to Emmie," Dee said. "You're bleeding pretty badly

and you're as pale as a ghost."

I tried to smile. "I'm fine."

"You've been stabbed," Eric said, his voice tight. "That doesn't qualify as fine."

"Hey, a little love and support here," I said. "You don't need to be so angry."

"We're not angry at you," Eric said. "Just at the situation."

I rolled my eyes. I said that to him all the time.

Dante moved his face so it was in my vision since I was still looking straight up. "Why did they stab you?"

I shrugged and then moaned at the movement. "Just trying to prove a point, I guess." I wasn't about to tell them what the guard had told me. What they didn't know wouldn't hurt them.

"This has gotten way out of hand," Gideon said. His head came into my view and then left. After a few seconds, it came back. He paced behind me. Besides Dee, everyone else only had their hands bound.

"What do we do now?" Hiro asked. I stopped trying to place where the voices were coming from. It took too much energy.

"If we don't get out of here soon, we're dead," Terrance said. "I'm sure they're getting everything ready for our executions."

"I don't like the sound of that," Bruce said. "There has to be a way to get out of here."

"How?" Will asked. "If there was a way out, don't you think we would have taken it already?"

"Everything's changed," Maya said. "There's a lot more

chaos out there right now."

"Ahhhh!" Joshua's scream pierced the room.

"It's out," Tina said. "You're going to live, Joshua."

"For now," Luke put in.

"Thanks for the optimism," Dee said.

"You're welcome," Luke said. "Sometimes being realistic is better than optimistic."

"No," Gideon said, putting the conversation back on track. "Maya's right about everything changing. With everything in pandemonium, it's the perfect chance to attempt an escape."

"It's the *only* time to attempt an escape," Terrance said. "And we have to take it."

"What are you thinking, Terrance?" Hiro asked.

"Now that we have everyone back together, I'm willing to make a break for it," Terrance said.

"I agree," Gideon said.

My breathing was ragged, but I forced out the words. "Okay, I'm just hearing voices …"

"Crazy …" Bruce whispered.

I ignored him. "But I don't think I've heard Vivica, Santiago, or Rachel's voices. Are they in here?"

"We're here," Santiago said.

"They're having a lovefest." Thunder Thighs grunted. "And it's grossing me out."

I smiled. "Good. Glad we're all here." My teeth clenched together from the pain.

"So, what's the plan?" Maya asked.

"The guards should be coming for us soon," Dante said.

"Once they come in, we need to attack and make a run for it."

"Emmie and Joshua will need help," Will said.

"I'll carry Emmie," Eric said.

I could see Dante's face in my vision, and he had opened his mouth to say something, but Eric had talked first. Dante snapped his mouth shut. His face had a mixture of sadness and anger.

"Tina and I can help Joshua," Luke said.

"How are we going to fight with bound hands?" Vivica asked. Apparently, their lovefest had finally ended. Or it was taking a slight pause.

"Ow!" I tried to turn on my side, but it hurt too much. I sucked in my breath from the pain.

"Easy there," Eric said. This time his voice was gentle.

"Sorry," I said. "I just remembered I took a knife from the guard while he was stabbing me. He had someone else's knife in his pocket, so while he was distracted, I pulled it out and slipped it in my pocket."

Eric went to reach for my pocket, but Dante stopped him. "Keep your hands on her wound. I'll get the knife." I watched the two of them, trying to read the look that passed between them. I had never seen it before. Or had just never noticed. I shook my head. The loss of blood played with my mind.

Dante reached into my pocket and retrieved out the knife. He motioned for Eric to lift his hands just a little so he could cut the cords. Once they were off, Eric took off his jacket and then his shirt, and then put his jacket back on. He gently moved my hands so he could get the shirt directly onto my wound and then replaced my hands and kept his hands on mine. He gave me a soft smile which I returned.

Dante had given the knife to Gideon so he could cut Dante's cords. Gideon continued to go around the room and cut everyone loose.

Shouting and loud thuds came from the hall. Whatever was happening was a distraction we could use to our advantage. Unless it was Kingsland security rallying together outside the room.

"Do you think you could sit up?" Eric asked me.

"Only if you held me," I said.

He let go of my hands and pulled me up until I sat in his lap. Wrapping his arms around my waist, he put his hands back over my wound. The room spun, so I closed my eyes.

"I love you," Eric whispered in my ear.

I moved my head, so it rested against his cheek. "I love you."

Clearing his throat, Dante stood and folded his arms. "If they've been watching, they will know we aren't tied up anymore and have a weapon."

"Then we better hope that whatever's happening out there is not good for Kingsland," Terrance said. He came and stood by Dante. "Once they open that door, we need to be ready."

Gideon still held the knife in his hand. "I think we should only use this as a last resort."

"I agree," Hiro said.

"No way," Santiago said. He stood next to Vivica, holding her hand. "They haven't been nice to us. We shouldn't hold anything back. We need to storm out of here, grabbing any weapons we can and use them on the guards." He eyed me sitting in Eric's lap. "Look at what they did to Emmie."

"He's right," Eric said.

Maya shook her head. "We don't need to make this worse. Piling up the body count isn't going to do anything."

"We should still be taking weapons from them." Luke stood tall, his arms folded, and his feet squared with his shoulders. "They'll be using them on us. We need to be able to defend ourselves."

"I don't like the idea of all these weapons." Dee's eyes held a terror I hadn't seen in a while.

"You were the one begging us to let you come." Tina quirked an eyebrow at Dee.

"I know." Dee bit her lip. "But seeing them actually used and the results …"

Thunder Thighs grunted from the corner of the room. "You're all a bunch of sissies. Why are we even waiting for them? Let's break down the door and get out of here. I'll be taking as many weapons as I see and anyone who gets in my way will be on the other side of that weapon with no hesitation on my part."

"Some of us actually value our lives," Bruce said, moving his hands dramatically.

"Enough." Dante's voice commanded the room. "We're wasting time. Everyone, get up and get ready to storm out of here. Once we're on the other side of that door, our only goal is to get out of here alive. If that means killing a few guards on the way out, so be it. That's why we came here in the first place. We're at war. If you don't like it, too bad. Next time we'll leave you home." He glanced at Dee when he said that.

Will put his arms around Dee and held her close, giving Dante a nasty look.

Everyone was on the verge of a breakdown. The unity we usually had was slipping away. We needed to regroup.

I turned my face toward Eric. "Help me up. Dante's right. We need to leave."

Eric kept a firm grip on me as he stood, doing it effortlessly. He placed one arm around my back and then scooped up my legs. I rested my head against his shoulder as he held me in his arms. It killed me not being able to stand on my own two feet and help fight our way out, but I also enjoyed being in the comfort of Eric's arms.

Joshua had his arms around Tina's and Luke's shoulders as they held him up. Dante and Gideon came and stood in front of Eric and me right as Maya and Santiago went behind us. I knew they were creating a barrier so no Kingsland guards could get to us. Terrance and Thunder Thighs went to the door, bracing themselves for when the door opened. Everyone else piled around us.

"Terrance," Gideon said.

When Terrance turned around, Gideon tossed him the knife, the hilt landing perfectly in Terrance's hand.

We only waited for a few minutes before the door to the room opened and Brandon walked in.

CHAPTER 17

Terrance punched Brandon in the face as hard as he could, knocking him unconscious. As soon as Brandon's body hit the floor, Thunder Thighs pulled his bow and arrows off him and slung the quiver around her back. Two more guards rushed in, but Terrance and Thunder Thighs easily knocked them down and they fell on top of Brandon. Dante and Gideon snatched up their bow and quivers.

We all piled out of the room, stepping out into a chaotic hall. More guards tried to seize some of our group, but we easily overpowered them and within minutes, everyone in our group besides me had a quiver around their back and a bow in their hand. We were even able to get a few of our knives back. Santiago and Maya had helped put the quiver around Eric's back so he could continue to hold me.

The halls were filled with security guards trying to hold off angry Kingsland citizens. They were all shouting and demanding to see President Coleman, wanting an explanation for my broadcast.

Terrance, Thunder Thighs, Dante, and Gideon pushed forward through the crowd, forcing their way toward the exit. Eric was right behind them and I could feel him being pushed forward by Maya, Santiago, and everyone else behind us.

"There she is!" A Kingsland citizen shouted out. The room went silent as everyone turned and looked at me.

"What happened to her?" Another member demanded. She looked at me with surprised eyes. Most of the citizens were looking at me that way. It was probably a mix of the fact that I was indeed an actual person, but also that I was injured.

"One of your guards stabbed her," Santiago said, anger lacing his voice.

Terrance and Thunder Thighs kept trying to push forward, but we had nowhere to go. The hall was squished with people. Some of the members gasped when they finally saw Dante and the condition he was in.

An elderly man pushed his way toward me. His cold hand landed on my cheek. I turned my head so I could look at him. His kind eyes reminded me of my father's. "Is it true?" His voice was soft yet pleading. "Do you have the cure?"

I closed my eyes and nodded. "Yes, we do." When I opened my eyes, tears were falling down his cheeks.

"My granddaughter," he said, his voice shaking. "She has the disease. Can you heal her?"

"It depends on how far into the disease she is," Maya said from behind me. Her voice was just as soft as the man's. "But we have the formula. If your doctors got to work right away on making it …"

"He has the formula!" A man shouted out from the

crowd. "President Coleman already has it! We want it!" Everyone shouted out in agreement. The sound hurt my ears. I leaned my head back into Eric and groaned.

"Just hold on," Eric said.

"Eric." My jaw clattered. "I'm so cold." Heat had left my body. The pain in my stomach throbbed.

"Stay strong, Emmie." Eric's voice was soft in my ear. "Stay strong for me."

"She's dying," the elderly man said. "We need to take her to a doctor."

"Is there one nearby?" Eric asked.

A female in the crowd raised her hand. "I'm a doctor. Bring her to me."

The crowd opened and the elderly man helped steer Eric toward her. My whole body shook. I was freezing cold yet sweat dripped down my forehead onto my cheeks. "Eric."

There were still guards trying to press through and get the crowd out of the hall, but no one would budge. When the guards wouldn't stop, the crowd turned on them and a fight broke out. Dante, Santiago, Maya, and Gideon stayed close around me so no one could hit us.

The lady who raised her hand came up to me and took my hands off my wound. She gently pulled the shirt away and examined the cut. Her black hair was pulled back in small braids all the way around her head. I couldn't tell for sure since I was being held up, but she seemed to be very short.

She looked at Eric. "It's bad. She's already lost so much blood. This needs to be treated right away or she'll die."

"Then do whatever needs to be done to save her," Eric said.

The lady nodded and then looked at me. "I'm Janette. Let's get you out of here. My house isn't far." She glanced at Eric. "Follow me."

Even though there was still fighting, the residents made sure to make room for all of us to get through. They lined up on both sides, keeping the guards away. If I wasn't so weak, I would've have smiled and thanked them all. Luckily Dee was with us, and I could hear her saying thank you to every person we passed.

Once outside of Headquarters, Janette broke out in a jog. I was surprised how easy it was for Eric to keep up with her. He didn't seem to be straining at holding me for so long. It was colder outside, so I curled into Eric, trying to soak in his heat. He kissed me on my head as he continued to run through the streets.

A large crowd had gathered outside. They were shouting and demanding answers. From what I could see, there seemed to be thousands of residents surrounding Headquarters. I smiled to myself, happy to see they had come through.

A few minutes later, Janette opened the door to her house, and we followed her in. She pointed to an old brown couch near the brick fireplace. "Lay her down there. I'm going to get my supplies."

Eric laid me down as gently as he could. The other fourteen New Haven residents with us piled into the small living area. Dee kneeled next to me. Tina and Luke set Joshua down in a chair. I tried to open my mouth to say he needed to be treated too, but no words came out.

"Don't try to talk," Eric said as he brushed a few loose

hairs out of my face. "I'll make sure she tends to Joshua after you're all fixed."

Janette came back in the room and forced Eric and Dee away from my side. "I need room to work." She looked at Eric. "Help me take off her jacket and shirt."

As they removed my shirt, a few coughs sounded in the room. When I tilted my head, I noticed all the guys in the room had turned around, giving me some privacy. I smiled for a moment and then flushed when I realized that Eric had still seen me. It was the first time he'd ever seen me with my shirt off. But when I saw the concern in his eyes as he stared at my cut, I immediately felt better.

A stinging sensation at my cut caused me to yell out in pain. Janette had started to clean my wound. "Sorry," she said. "This is going to hurt for a while." I bit back my screams as she examined the cut. "It doesn't look like any organs have been pierced. You were lucky. I'll just need to stitch up the cut." She looked at me and then Eric. "I never got your names."

"Oh, sorry," Eric said. "I'm Eric and this is Emmie."

"Nice to meet you," Janette said with a smile. She nodded to some towels on the wood coffee table next to the couch. "Why don't you go clean your hands in the bathroom, Eric, and then you can bring back some dampened towels for me and Emmie's hands? The bathroom is the first door on the left down the hall."

"Of course." Eric kissed me on the forehead and left the room.

Janette eyed my blood-covered ring. "Is that your husband?"

"Fiancé." I barely managed the word out. The pain was too much for me. I sucked in my breath and closed my eyes.

"You two make a cute couple." She didn't wait for a response before she continued. "My husband's the same as Eric. He's very protective and sweet with me. I kept thinking it would change as the years went by, but it hasn't. He still looks at me the same way he did when we were dating." I could hear the smile in her voice. I wanted to ask how long they'd been married, but I was too weak. Janette looked young to me, but I couldn't be for certain.

Luckily my mind reader was in the room with me. "How long have you been married?" Dee asked. That was a benefit to having a best friend like her. We'd known each other so long, we could read each other like an open book.

"Twenty-three years," Janette said. I let out another scream at a sharp pinch to my skin. "I'm doing the stitches now."

I still had my eyes closed, so I couldn't see what was happening.

Someone grabbed my hand and started cleaning it. I could tell they were Eric's hands, so I just lay there and let them both do their work. After Eric was done with that hand, he switched to the other.

"Do you have any kids?" Tina asked.

"Two," Janette said. "Jason is thirteen and Elizabeth is seventeen." She gave a small laugh. "Jason goes pale at the sight of blood, so it's a good thing he's in bed right now."

Eric finished with my hand and came up next to me, stroking my hair. Reaching for my hand, he took it in his, his warm lips kissing my skin, and then he held it up against his cheek. Having him right next to me helped me relax.

"Mom?" A girl's voice came somewhere to the right of me. She sounded sleepy. "What's going on?"

"Just helping some friends," Janette said. "Elizabeth, would you please find an old shirt you don't use anymore? Emmie here could use a new one."

"Of course," Elizabeth said. Her footsteps faded down the hall.

A small knock on the door made Janette's hands freeze. I opened my eyes to her staring at Eric, her eyes wide.

"I'll get it," Dante said. The front door squeaked open just a bit. "Oh, am I glad to see you." The door opened further and then shut. From the sounds of clapping on backs, I figured Dante was hugging whoever was at the door.

"Everyone, this is Marcus," Dante said. Sighing in relief, I closed my eyes. They were becoming too heavy to keep open.

I heard someone approach the side of the couch. "Here's a shirt," Elizabeth said. "Can I get you anything else?"

I couldn't force my eyes open. Dante and Marcus talked softly in the background, but I couldn't make out any words.

"Do you have a blanket we could drape over Emmie?" Eric kept his voice low, but I could hear the tightness in it. Something was bothering him, but I didn't know what. All the guys had turned their heads.

"Yes, there's one right here," Elizabeth said.

A few seconds later, a soft blanket covered my chest.

"Thank you," Eric said. He took a towel with his free hand and wiped the sweat from my forehead. I held on tightly to his other hand.

"Well," Dante said, "nice work, Emmie. Your broadcast worked." His voice was surprisingly close. I forced my eyes open and saw him standing right next to me. His eyes flickered between the blanket on me and Eric who kneeled beside me.

"Most of the city members turned on President Coleman," Marcus said.

I looked over at him. He was tall and strongly built like Dante, but he had a bald head. His brown eyes were tired. Just looking at them made me close my eyes again. I had kept mine open too long.

"There's still a lot of fighting going on outside," Dante said. "But at least there are now more people in our favor than in President Coleman's."

"We still haven't gotten our hands on him, though," Marcus said. "We need to come up with a plan."

"Once Emmie and Joshua are stitched up, we're leaving." Eric sounded upset.

"You're leaving?" Marcus asked. "Dante, I thought you were staying."

"We are." Dante's voice was rigid. "Emmie and Joshua can rest here a while, right Janette?"

"Of course," Janette said. "They'll both need rest." I heard a clip from her scissors. "Emmie, you're all stitched up now. Just take it easy for a few weeks. That was a nasty cut. It'll be sore for a long time, so no heavy lifting and no breaking into any other cities." There was a smile in her voice. Her weight left the couch and her footsteps headed toward where Joshua sat.

Eric's hand tensed around mine as weight settled on the couch again. Prying my eyes open, I saw Dante sitting near my feet. He smiled at me. "How are you feeling?"

I tried to open my mouth, but Eric spoke. "Let her rest. You two can talk later." He stroked my hand with his thumb. "And we're leaving. I'm taking her out to the jeep and driving her home so Samantha can tend to her. You can stay here if you want."

"There's still stuff to do," Dante said. He glared at Eric. "We came here to do a mission."

"I know," Eric said. "Which we accomplished. Marcus and his supporters are free to come out now. President Coleman's men are outnumbered. They can take it from here. They don't need an injured Emmie and Joshua to help out."

"But we could use you," Dante said. My eyes kept opening and closing. "And Emmie needs rest. Look at her; she can barely keep her eyes open. We shouldn't move her yet. You'll just make it worse by taking her in a vehicle on a bumpy road."

"We can take her home," Will said. He had his arm around Dee's waist. "You don't need us. Eric can stay and we'll go."

"I'm not leaving Emmie," Eric said.

"Dante's right," Elizabeth said. She was over near her mom, helping her with Joshua. He clenched his jaw in pain as Janette stitched up the opening in his arm from the arrow. "You shouldn't move her yet. You could break open the wound."

"I'll drive carefully," Eric said. I could tell in his voice that he knew they were right, but he wouldn't admit it in front of Dante.

"She's staying here tonight," Janette said, the tone in her voice closing the matter. "So is Joshua. They've both lost a lot of blood and just need to rest for now. We'll talk about it again in the morning."

Everyone was quiet as Janette finished up with Joshua. Once she was done, she sent Elizabeth back to bed and picked up all her supplies. "I hope you don't mind sleeping on the floor, Joshua."

"I don't mind." He looked over at me with a weak smile.

Janette left the room for a minute and then came back, bending down next to me. Eric scooted over to give her room but kept a hold on my hand. She cleaned off my cheek and then applied some glue to it. "This will hold it closed. It's too shallow to need stitches. It'll heal just fine."

"Thank you, Janette," Eric said, sincerity in his voice. "For all of your help. I can't tell you how much we appreciate it."

Smiling at him, she patted his shoulder. "I'm glad I could help out. Of course, I now expect an invitation to your wedding."

Eric laughed. "I'll give you front row seats. You saved her life."

"She still has a lot of recovery," Janette said. "You need to keep a close eye on her wound and clean it daily. The last thing we want is an infection or for it to break back open."

"I'll take good care of her," Eric said.

"I know you will." Janette squeezed my arm. "Sleep, Emmie." I tried to nod, but my head wouldn't move. I forced out a sound that I hoped sounded like I was saying I would. She stood and looked at Dante. "As for all of you, out. Emmie doesn't need the stress. The only people allowed in my home tonight are Emmie, Joshua, and Eric." She looked around the room. "I'm not trying to be rude, but they need rest, especially Emmie. She's recovering from a serious injury."

"Fine," Dante said as he stood. "We need to go help out at Headquarters anyway." He looked at Eric. "Are you coming with us?"

"No," Eric said.

Dante swore under his breath and then stormed out of the house. Everyone said goodbye to us and then left. Will and Dee were the last ones to say goodbye. As they were walking to the door, Janette stopped them.

"You're both welcome here, too." Janette looked at Dee. "I can tell you don't want to go back out there and I won't force you to. I just wanted Dante out of here. He seemed a little too worked up."

"Thank you," Will said.

Dee looked at me. "Is that okay?"

I got out a very quiet, "Yes."

Dee turned to Eric and he nodded. "You two are always welcomed around Emmie."

"I'll let Maya know," Will said. He went outside.

Joshua went over to the fireplace. There was a nice fire going, heating the small room. He lay down in front of it. "Goodnight everyone. Thanks, Janette. Love you, Emmie."

Before anyone could respond, he was breathing deeply, already asleep. Janette left the room and came back with some blankets. She handed a few to Dee and then draped one over Joshua. She smiled at me and Eric. "Goodnight. Sleep well."

"We will," Eric said. "Thanks again."

The door opened and Will came back inside. Taking off his shoes, he lay down next to Dee, who had already lay down on the floor. He covered them with some blankets and then threw Eric an extra one.

Eric stroked my hair. "I'm going to sit you up a little so we can put a shirt on you. I'll be as gentle as I can." I tried to help him as much as I could, but I was way too weak. Once the shirt was on, Eric moved as to lie down on the floor.

"No," I said.

Scooting me over on the couch, he lay down next to me. He put the blanket over us and wrapped his arms around me.

"I love you," he whispered into my ear. He gave me a soft kiss on the cheek and then I closed my eyes, snuggling into his chest. It wasn't long until I was asleep.

CHAPTER 18

When I woke in the morning, Eric was already awake. He held me close, his arms wrapped tightly around me. I looked up at him and smiled. "Good morning."

He kissed me on the nose. "Good morning. How did you sleep?"

"Surprisingly well," I said. "I love Janette's home. There's something so comfy and inviting about it."

They had one-story log homes in Kingsland just like we did in New Haven. Pictures of Janette's family hung on the wall near the brick fireplace.

"It reminds me of our home," Joshua said. With Eric's help, I slowly sat up. Joshua was in the chair he'd been in the night before. He had a blanket wrapped around him and a mug was in his hand. He smiled at me. "How are you feeling?"

"Terrible," I said. My stomach was incredibly sore and so was my cheek. Eric pulled me close to him and wrapped his arm around me.

Dee and Will came to sit on the couch next to us, both

holding mugs in their hands like Joshua. Dee patted my leg as she sat down. "I was beginning to think you'd never wake up."

"What time is it?" I asked. My muscles screamed at me to stretch, but I figured that wouldn't be good for my stitches.

"A little after eleven," Janette said, walking into the room. She handed Eric and me some mugs of hot chocolate. I breathed it in before I took a sip.

"That late? I really slept in," I said.

"You needed it." Janette lifted my shirt so she could see the stitches. "Everything looks good. We'll clean it up before you leave."

The front door opened, and a boy walked in. He looked a couple of years younger than Elizabeth, so I figured it was Janette's son. He had the same eyes as his mom and sister.

He froze in place when he saw me. "You're that girl everyone's talking about. We're all trying to figure out if you're brave or crazy. I was betting on crazy."

"Jason!" Janette shook her head at her son. "Manners."

"Sorry," Jason mumbled. He went into the kitchen, grabbed a couple of chairs and then came back into the living room, setting the chairs down next to his mom.

"Emmie, this is my son Jason," Janette said. She swatted him on the back of the head when he sat down.

With his eyebrows furrowed, Jason rubbed his head. "I said I was sorry." He looked at me. "There's a whole bunch of rumors going around about you. One is that you're dead, but by the looks of it, that one's not true."

"It sure feels like it," I said.

There was a small knock at the door, so Jason jumped up

to get it. When he opened it, Dante, Maya, Santiago, Terrance, and Marcus all walked in. Jason shut the door behind him and went to sit back down in the chair next to his mom, but she stopped him.

"Always offer a lady your seat," Janette said to Jason. She smiled at Maya. "You may sit here."

Before Maya sat down, she put her hand on Jason's arm and thanked him. He flushed and smiled shyly at her.

"What's the latest news?" Joshua asked.

Dante looked at me, but I couldn't read his expression. I was usually able to read him so well, but I'd been off the past few days. He cleared his throat and then looked over at Joshua. "We attempted to capture President Coleman last night, but he got away."

"So did Brandon and some of the other guards," Terrance said.

"Where did they go?" Will asked.

Santiago shrugged. "All we know is that they left Kingsland."

"You don't think they know where New Haven is, do you?" I asked. I would hate for them to show up when none of us were there to protect them.

Marcus shook his head. "I highly doubt that. I'm sure they're just hiding out in the woods somewhere."

"What's the plan now?" Dee asked.

There was another knock at the door. As Jason went to go get it, Janette laughed. "My house is really popular."

When Jason opened the door, Zoe came rushing in. She ran over to me and took my hand in hers, almost knocking over my cup of hot chocolate. "Are you okay?"

I forced a smile as I set my cup on the coffee table in front of me. "I'm fine."

Will stood and Dee scooted over on the couch so Zoe could sit next to me. She kept my hand in hers. "I heard you got stabbed and I freaked out. I wanted to come see you last night, but there was so much going on in my house and at Headquarters that I couldn't sneak away." She looked over at Dante and then back at me. "Then this morning they wanted me to let you rest."

I squeezed her hand. "Janette got me all stitched up. I'm going to be okay."

"As long as she rests," Janette said. "I cannot stress that enough."

"To answer Dee's question," Dante said, "Marcus is going to run Kingsland for now. He'll work closely with us and New Haven. But we still need to find President Coleman."

Zoe flinched at the mention of her dad. I rubbed her arm, hoping to give her at least some comfort.

"There are some out there searching for him right now," Marcus said. "And I'll keep people out there around the clock until we find him."

"We're headed back to New Haven," Santiago said. "As soon as Emmie's ready."

"Speaking of New Haven," Eric said. "Has anyone contacted them?"

Maya pulled a communicator out of her pocket. "We barely got our hands on these. I haven't turned mine on yet. It's been so crazy." She tossed it to me. "That one's yours."

Eric caught it and turned it on. The second he did, Derek's voice filled the room. "Hello? Anyone there? This is Captain Awesome speaking."

I took the communicator from Eric and held it to my mouth. "Hello, Captain Awesome." Zoe looked at me with raised eyebrows, so I tried to clarify. "He's my brother and he's crazy."

Joshua held up his good arm. "Other side of her family. I do not share any blood with the guy."

"Where have you been?" Derek asked. "You've had all of us worried."

"Things got complicated," I said. "But everyone's alive."

"What about President Coleman?" Derek asked. "And Marcus?"

"President Coleman and some of his security escaped the city," I said. "But Marcus is here with us and he has a lot more supporters than he started with."

"Thanks to Emmie," Eric said.

"Well, you'll have to tell us all about it when you get back," Derek said. "Which needs to be soon." His voice suddenly sounded urgent.

"What's wrong, Derek?" I asked.

"Are there a lot of people listening?" Derek asked.

"No," I said.

"Liar," Derek said.

I sighed. "Okay, so there are a few people in the room."

"How many is a few?" Derek asked.

"Fourteen," Zoe said.

"Who's that?" Derek asked. "I don't recognize the voice."

"Her name is Zoe," I said. "She's President Coleman's daughter."

Derek gasped. "Friend or foe?"

"Friend," I said. "She helped us out last night. Now just tell me what's wrong."

"Not with that many people in the room," Derek said. "How do I know I can trust all of them?"

"You can," Dante said, his voice loud to carry across the room. "Just tell us, Derek."

"Are you positive?" Derek asked.

"Yes," Dante, Eric, Santiago, Maya, and I all said at the same time. Jason laughed.

"I didn't recognize that laugh," Derek said, sounding alarmed. "Who's that?"

I fought the urge to swear. "Derek, tell me now!"

The communicator went dead for a minute. We all waited eagerly. Finally, Derek's voice came through. "President Mendes said I could tell you. First, someone showed up in New Haven yesterday."

"Who?" I asked.

"She said you know her," Derek said. "Her name is Jen."

Dee and I exchanged a glance. "As in my dorm leader, Jen?"

We had some run-ins with Jen during Recruitment. She broke up a few of my fights.

"Yes," Derek said.

"What's she doing in New Haven?" I asked.

Derek was silent again. He sighed before he answered. "She said Mom sent her."

The communicator dropped from my hand. I stared at it in my lap as if my mom might jump out of it. I hadn't thought about her in a long while.

"Emmie?" Derek said. "Are you still there?"

Slowly picking up the communicator, I cleared my throat. "Yes, I'm here. Why did Mom send her?"

"Are you sitting down?" Derek asked. "In fact, is everyone sitting down? And also, can you *really* trust everyone in the room?"

Janette stood. "Jason, let's give them some privacy." When they were out of the room, Dante and Santiago sat down in the chairs they had been using. Terrance leaned against the wall.

Giving my hand a quick squeeze, Zoe stood. "I'll be outside." She looked at Dante as she passed him and then stepped outside. Marcus followed her out, closing the door behind them.

"Derek, there's just New Haven residents left in the room," I said. "Please tell us what's going on."

"It's big news," Derek said. "I'm not even sure where to begin."

"Start with why Jen's there," I said.

"She didn't tell me much," Derek said. "Just that Mom sent her. She won't tell me why, though. She'll only talk to you. She did tell me …" He let out a long sigh. "Emmie, River Springs is split."

"What do you mean split?" Eric asked.

"It's divided in two," Derek said. "Mom is controlling one side with Amy and Tami Randall."

Joshua looked at me with startled eyes when he heard his mom and sister's name.

"And President Randall?" I asked. "Where is he?"

Derek cleared his throat. "Is Joshua in the room?"

"Yes," Joshua said. "I'm here."

Derek swore. "I was hoping you wouldn't be. Listen, I don't know how to say this, so I'm just going to say it. Joshua, Emmie, your dad … well, he's dead."

Joshua and I sat there staring at each other. I wasn't sure how to react. Joshua finally stood and went to stand next to the fireplace.

"How?" I had to force the question out. "When?"

"Last year," Derek said. "Not long after the battle with Juniper ended." He paused. "As for the how, this is where you *really* need to be sitting down."

I looked over at Joshua. "Joshua, do you want to sit back down?" He shook his head and stared at the fire.

"Tell us, Derek." I didn't realize my hand was shaking until Eric put his hand over it.

"He was killed," Derek said. "Shot in his office."

"Someone assassinated him?" Eric asked.

"Yes," Derek said. Joshua leaned his hand up against the mantle over the fire. "And that person is now leading the other side of River Springs. This is why they haven't come to attack New Haven."

"They know where we are?" Dante asked, his voice loud so Derek could hear it.

"Yes," Derek said. "They've known for a while. But with the split in the city, they haven't been able to go through with their plans."

"Who is it?" I asked.

"Is it someone we know?" Eric asked. Rubbing my arm, he pulled me closer to him.

"Uh, this is the major part I didn't want to tell you," Derek said. "Well, one of the major parts. But, um, the person who killed President Randall and who wants to destroy New Haven … well …"

"Just spit it out!" Santiago yelled.

"It's Austin," Derek said.

My heart stopped for a few beats. The communicator would have slipped through my hands if Eric hadn't been helping me hold it. The room spun. Putting my hand on my forehead, I leaned into Eric.

My voice was quiet. "That's not possible. He's dead."

"That's what we thought," Derek said. "But he faked his death. He made Luke think he'd been killed. He'd been working against us the whole time. Him and Amber."

Bile rose in my throat and I had to force it back down. "He's been working with Amber? How is this possible?"

"I don't know, Em," Derek said. "I really don't know. But it's the truth."

"It's what Jen told you," Eric said. "How do you know we can trust her?"

"I did the lie detector test on her," Derek said. "And she passed. It's all the truth. Austin killed President Randall and he and Amber have now taken over half of the city. Mom rallied a lot of the residents and they came to her side of the city. They've been at war this past year."

"No," I said. "It can't be true. Austin isn't capable of this." I looked at Joshua. He still stared at the fire. I turned to Eric. "Help me up."

"Emmie, just stay seated for now," Eric said.

I shook my head. "Please, Eric." He sighed and helped me to my feet. I walked over to Joshua, putting my hand on his uninjured arm. "Joshua, look at me."

He stared at the fire, his face completely blank. I shook him, but he wouldn't budge. "Joshua, tell me it's not the truth. Tell me you didn't know. Tell me something." When Joshua didn't move, I shook him again. "Joshua, please, talk to me." I gripped his arm as hard as I could. "Tell me!"

With tears forming in his eyes, he finally turned to me. "I … I …" He looked at everyone in the room and then turned back to me. "I didn't know he killed Dad, I swear."

Releasing my grip, I dropped my arm. "You knew he was alive? You knew Austin was alive and didn't say anything?"

Joshua's voice was barely audible. "He told me not to."

I stepped away from him. "I trusted you, Joshua. You betrayed me! You betrayed New Haven!"

"No!" Joshua pleaded. "No! I didn't know he wanted to harm New Haven." He came up to me and put his hands on my arms. "You have to believe me, Emmie. I didn't know Austin was bad. I thought he was going to help us."

"How would that help us?" I asked. "How would me thinking he's dead benefit me in any way?"

"I don't know." Tears fell down his cheeks and onto the floor. "I trusted him as much as you did. He made me swear that I wouldn't say anything. He's looked after me my whole life. I felt like I owed it to him." Choking on his sobs, he pulled his arms away from me. "It was only last month that I started to catch on that something was off with him. But by then I was too far into it. I wanted to tell you, but I didn't know how."

I slapped him on the cheek as hard as I could, ignoring the pain from the movement. "You walk into my room and tell me!"

With startled eyes, he placed his hand on his cheek. "I couldn't. After everything you've done for me …" He looked me in the eyes. "Emmie, I didn't want to lose you. I didn't want you to think I was a traitor. You coming into my life has been the best thing that has ever happened to me. I finally felt like I had family and I was accepted."

"What have you told him?" Eric asked. I looked over at him and his face was red, his hands balled into fists. If I wasn't standing between the two of them, Eric would have hit Joshua.

Joshua ran his fingers through his hair. "I don't know. We talk about basic stuff. I trusted him. I never thought anything I said would hurt New Haven, I swear."

"You said something changed over the last month," Dante said.

He, Maya, and Santiago had come up next to us.

"Yes," Joshua said. "He's seemed angrier. He's been asking more questions about our military and how we run things. He tried to make it sound like he wanted to know so he could make the same choices at Infinity Corp."

"And you told him?" Santiago asked.

Joshua shook his head. "No. I did at the beginning, but I quickly caught on to his behavior change. Austin gets horrible anger spells. He can lash out at any moment. I thought he'd gotten it under control. I haven't seen him angry in years. I learned growing up that you shouldn't tell Austin anything important when he's angry. When I wouldn't tell him anything, he started to get mad. He went off on a tirade. So, I made up some stuff."

"You swear you didn't tell him anything that could hurt New Haven?" Dante asked.

"I swear I didn't," Joshua said. "At least, not that I'm aware of. This last month I've been very careful and conscientious of everything I say. But before that, I can't be certain. But I don't remember talking about anything important like this. It was more talking about how our families were doing and the weather." He looked at me. "Emmie, I'm sorry. I've been trying to figure out how to tell you, but I just didn't know how."

"You're still communicating with him?" Maya asked.

Joshua nodded. "Yes. But I kept my communicator back at home. I don't have it with me now."

"Did you tell him we were coming here?" Eric asked.

"No," Joshua said. "I never mentioned it. We only talk once a week, so I figured it was safe to leave for a few days without him noticing."

"We might be able to use this to our advantage," Maya said. We all turned to her. "If Austin's still talking with Joshua, and he thinks that Joshua's on his side, then we can use it against him at some point."

"Are you on his side?" Dante asked Joshua.

"No!" Joshua said. "I believe in New Haven. I believe in

everyone here. I would never betray New Haven on purpose." He looked at me. "I'm not like our father and I'm not like Austin. I promise."

I just stared at him. I had no idea what to believe anymore. I had trusted Austin with all my heart, and it turned out I shouldn't have. How could I be certain I could trust Joshua? What if he was working with Austin?

"Emmie, please say you believe me," Joshua said. Fresh tears were falling down his face. "Please, Emmie. I can't lose you. I love you, and I would never, ever betray you. You have to believe me."

I looked away from him. I didn't have an answer for him. Taking hold of Eric's arm, I walked back to the couch and sat down.

"Emmie?" Derek's voice came through the communicator.

I picked it up. "Yes."

"There's one more thing," Derek said. "And it's bad."

A small laugh escaped my mouth. "How could it be worse than Austin still being alive, Whit being killed by Austin, the city split in two, and our mom leading the other side?"

"Amber and Dean Johnson also showed up," Derek said. "They came with a couple of other people and broke into our house in the middle of the night."

My whole body cringed at the sound of Amber's name. "What? Why?"

"They wanted you," Derek said. "They came on Austin's orders to kidnap you."

I looked at Joshua who was staring at me with pleading

eyes. So at least he was telling the truth that he didn't tell Austin we were going to Kingsland. Pulling my eyes away from Joshua, my gaze settled on the floor. "So, do you have them in your custody?"

"No," Derek said, choked up. "They got away. But they were angry that you weren't there, so they took someone else instead."

"Who did they take?" I asked.

I closed my eyes and covered them with my hand. From the sound of Derek's voice, it was someone dear to him and us.

Derek sniffed like he was crying. It took him a while to get the words out, but he finally did. "Emmie, they took Rosie."

CHAPTER 19
Austin

The vase shattered into hundreds of pieces as it smashed against the wall. Amber had run out screaming after I had pushed everything off my table and thrown my chair at the window. But it still wasn't enough. Rage still boiled inside.

How could Emmie have been gone when they went there? Joshua never told me they were leaving. I couldn't go off the assumption that he'd forgotten. He wouldn't forget something big like going to invade Kingsland. Somehow, they'd turned him. Or they'd caught onto him. I hadn't heard from him in almost a week. Maybe they found his communication device and took it away.

How was it possible that I had no one I could trust? Everything was slipping farther and farther away from me.

Someone pounded on the door and then came barging in. Dean slammed the door behind him. "What's wrong with you? You have my daughter scared out of her wits!"

"I don't care!" I yelled. "You blew the mission!"

"It's not our fault Emmie wasn't there," Dean said. "It was your intel. You should've known she wouldn't be there."

I went to him, putting my finger in his face. "You brought back a child with you!"

"I didn't want to waste a trip." Dean paused for a moment. "I figured they'd be willing to negotiate with us if we had someone they cared about."

"How do you know they care about this little girl?" I asked. "Who is she?"

Dean shook his head. "I'm not sure. She won't speak to us. We don't even know her name."

I shoved him in the chest and walked away. "You idiot. We can't get information from a child. If you really wanted to take someone, you should have taken an adult. A weak one who would break easily. Derek would have worked. But not a child. You should know better!"

Dean stared at the ground, shifting uncomfortably. That was when it hit me. I laughed as I leaned against my desk. "It was Amber who took her, wasn't it? You're just covering for the stupid move your daughter made."

"Leave her out of this." The veins on his head popped out.

"Oh, she's already too far into this," I said. "And now she's made the worst mistake."

"That's not true," Dean said. "I'm sure they wouldn't want something happening to a child. They'll come for her."

"You better hope they do," I said. "I'm holding you personally responsible for this. If it doesn't work in our favor, you're a dead man, you understand?"

Dean took me by my collar. "Do not threaten me. I could kill you right here and now with my bare hands."

"But you won't." I kept my gaze on him firm and steady. I would never let him see fear in my eyes. "Now put me down." Dean hesitated, but he finally did. I smoothed out my shirt and straightened my tie. "Where did you put the girl?"

"She's in a holding cell under Headquarters," Dean said.

"Bring her to me," I said. "I want to talk to her."

Dean shook his head. "You need to go to her. We can't give her an opportunity to escape."

"She's only around ten years old! How could she possibly escape?"

"She's feisty." Dean folded his arms. "She put up quite a fight when we first took her. She tried to escape multiple times. She even jumped out of the moving jeep. She's lucky she's still alive."

"Was she injured from the jump?"

"Broken arm," Dean said. "We already had a nurse attend to her. She'll be fine."

Standing up, I went to him. "You'll bring her to me now."

"Fine." He stormed out of the room, slamming the door on the way out.

I yelled out as I slammed my fist against the window. A few cracks ran through it from where I had thrown my chair. They spider-webbed out even more from my punch. I looked over at my ruined chair and sighed. I needed to calm down if I intended to question the little girl. She wouldn't trust me if I was rude or showed I was mad. I needed to get on her good side.

Five minutes later the door opened, and Dean walked in. He held the little girl in his arms, her hands and feet bound. I was about to ask why, but she squirmed in Dean's arms and screamed at him to put her down. I smiled on the inside. I liked her already.

"Dean, be a good man and set this poor girl down," I said, using the nicest voice I could. It was one my father used to use, and it worked like a charm.

Dean clenched his jaw, probably to stop himself from lashing out at me.

"You heard the man!" the little girl yelled out. "Put me down!"

Dean sat her in the unbroken chair on the other side of my desk. She kicked him in the shin and then tried to bite him. I couldn't help but laugh.

I slapped Dean on the shoulder. "Thank you, Dean. That will be all." I smiled at him until he finally grunted and left the room. Taking a knife from my pocket, I freed her hands and feet.

She rubbed the wrist on her good arm and then pulled her arm in a sling close to her. She looked up at me, swinging her legs back and forth. "Thank you."

"You're welcome." I leaned against my desk next to her chair. She was a beautiful young girl with long brown hair. Her large brown eyes were warm and inviting. She was still in her pajamas from the night before. There were some scrapes on her cheeks and legs, probably from jumping out of the jeep.

Crossing her legs, she clasped her good hand underneath her sling. She sat up tall and looked me right in the eye. "Now, would you please tell me why I was taken here and have been so rudely treated? I have done nothing wrong."

I folded my arms and gave her a warm smile, making sure it reached my eyes. "I really am sorry about all of this. I did not give them permission to take you or to bring you back here."

"Why did you send them in the first place?" she asked. I opened my mouth, but she cut me off. "And don't try telling me that you didn't send them, because I know you did, Austin."

Her comment surprised me. I raised my eyebrows. "How old are you?"

"How old are you?" she asked, raising her eyebrows in return.

I laughed. "Yes, I know a young lady would never reveal her age. Well, I sent them to talk to Emmie, if you must know."

She furrowed her eyebrows. "In the middle of the night?"

"I'll admit the timing was off," I said. She was quite difficult to work with. I wasn't sure how I would be able to get information from her. She was smart.

"You could've used a communication device," she said. "You didn't need to send people."

I sighed. "It was a sticky situation."

She stuck her head up in the air. "Oh, you mean a sticky situation where you made our city believe you were dead, when in fact you were actually alive? Yes, I could see how that would be sticky."

Oh, she was good. I really liked her. "What's your name?"

She sat back in her chair, getting as comfortable as possible. "Now, why would I want to tell you my name?"

"You know mine," I said. "It only seems fair."

That caused her to laugh. "Fair?" She snorted. "Please. You lied to us, kidnapped me, and now you want to bring up the word fair? Boys."

"Emmie has been a family friend for years." I tried to think of a way to work it in my favor, but she was too quick. "I felt I owed it to her to talk in person."

The little girl stood, walking over to look at the pictures on the wall. "Only you didn't go yourself."

"I had to stay here and lead my city. A leader can't just leave at any moment. I wanted them to bring her back to me."

Fury flashed in her eyes. "So, you wanted to kidnap her, not me?"

Anger crossed my face just briefly, but I reined it in. "That's not true."

She went to the picture of my father and studied it for a minute. Then she turned back to me and put her good hand on her hip. "You wanted to kidnap Emmie, it's so obvious. Otherwise, you would have contacted her yourself and asked her to come on her own terms. Not send her most hated enemy and her stupid, bald father to take her in the middle of the night." She tsked at me. "Your father would be so disappointed in you, Austin."

"He would not!" I swore to myself for snapping at her. Closing my eyes, I took a few breaths.

"I'm not sure what you want with me, but you won't get it. I'm not telling you anything. You're a liar and a bully. I don't like men like you. Do what you want with me, but my lips are sealed." She kept her hand on her hip, tapping her foot on the floor.

I took the deepest breath I could before I spoke, trying to keep my voice calm and even. "I don't want to hurt you. I just need to talk with Emmie."

"Then take your communication device and talk to her, dummy."

"She still has the one I gave her?" I asked, surprised. I thought she would have gotten rid of it since so much time had passed.

"I'm sure she does. Try it." She went back and sat in the chair. "I'm starving. I need some food, please." Crossing her legs, she looked up at me expectantly.

The smile came back to my face. She was quite charming, even though she loathed me. I adjusted my tie. "I'll see that some food is brought to you."

"Good." She pointed to her pajamas. "And since you claim you don't want to hurt me and didn't want me brought here in the first place, I would like a change of clothes and a change of rooms. That concrete room in the basement isn't going to work. I'd like something nicer and with a bed."

"As you wish."

Before I could speak into my communication device to give orders, the girl spoke. "Oh, and I don't want to see that evil brat Amber ever again. Keep her away from me. She's mean." She sniffed. "Also, keep her father away from me. He's like a meaner, uglier version of Mack. He kind of scares me."

I laughed. "I'll keep them away. I can't stand them either."

She eyed me for a moment. "Do you mean that? Or are you lying to me again?"

"Oh, trust me. I'm not lying. I can't stand either of them."

"Well, at least you don't have horrible judgment in people then. Just horrible judgment in choices." She turned to the picture of my father. "It's not too late, you know."

"What do you mean?"

She looked back at me. "To fix what you've done wrong. My father used to tell me that no matter what mistakes I made in life, it was never too late to fix them. I would always be given a second chance."

Staring at the floor, I rubbed my eyes. I'd had the hardest time sleeping. "I think I've already blown my second chance."

"Then there's always the third and fourth chance." She stood and touched me on the arm, startling me. "There are as many chances as you need. Just fix it. Make your dad proud. You owe it to him and Emmie. And to me. I'm still mad, you know. I don't like my sleep interrupted, and Amber and Dean are two of the noisiest people in the world. Next time if you want a mission to succeed, send someone who knows what they're doing. I'd still be at home if they hadn't woken me and piqued my curiosity." She tapped her lips. "Is that the right word? Piqued? I never know if I'm using that word right. I'm still getting used to it. Limited vocabulary sucks sometimes."

I couldn't help but laugh. "Yes, that's right. I really wish you'd tell me your name. I'm rather fond of you."

She sat back down. "Well, you'll just have to earn it." She patted her stomach. "Food?"

"Yes," I said. "Food."

She may have not revealed anything about New Haven, but she did reveal one thing. She was far too valuable for anyone to just let her go. They would be coming for her.

CHAPTER 20
Emmie

I dropped the communication device. It bounced off my lap and fell to the floor. It rolled a few times until it was underneath the table. I watched it tumble, trying to hold back the sobs.

Santiago dove for the communicator. He scrambled around under the table until he finally got a firm hold on it and then pulled it up to his mouth. "Derek, please tell me there's some mistake."

Derek's cry was painful to hear. "I'm so sorry, Santiago. When I ran out of my room to see what was going on, I saw Amber and Dean trashing the place. Dean came to me and threw me up against the wall, demanding to know where Emmie was. I wouldn't tell him. He hit me a few times and then dropped me."

It took Derek a while to speak again, he was crying so hard. "Rosie must have heard the commotion because the next thing I knew, she was in the front room. Amber picked her up and carried her out. I ran after them, but Dean stopped me. I fought so hard, but Dean's too strong. He finally had to shoot me just so he could leave."

I jumped, screaming out from the sudden movement, but still went to Santiago and grabbed the communicator. "He shot you? Are you okay?"

"I'm alive," Derek said. "Besides, that doesn't matter. They have Rosie. They got away with her. I couldn't stop them!"

Santiago took the communication device from my hands. "You can't blame yourself, Derek. You couldn't have stopped them without a weapon." Tears formed in Santiago's eyes and shoved the communicator into my chest. He sat down on one of the chairs, putting his head down as he cried. He'd lost his father and brother just the year before and now his little sister had been kidnapped. I couldn't imagine what he was feeling.

Eric steered me back toward the couch and sat me down. He took the communicator from me. "Derek, did they take anything else or leave some type of message?"

"No," Derek said. I barely heard his voice, it was so quiet. "I think taking Rosie was a rash decision on Amber's part. I don't think it was planned. They wanted Emmie."

"Then we need to trade," I said. "Me for Rosie."

"No," Eric said. "We're not doing that."

Tears fell down my cheeks. "We have to, Eric. She's only ten!"

"Eric's right," Dante said. "We need to come up with a plan. They'd never allow a simple trade like that."

"We don't know that," I said. "They might."

"It doesn't matter," Santiago said through his tears. He looked up at me. "We're not trading. We'll come up with a rescue mission. We'll save my sister, but we're not giving you to them."

"But …" I started.

Maya stepped in front of me. "This isn't open for debate, Emmie. We'll get Rosie back without giving you up. We can do it."

"How?" I asked. "We can't just walk in there and take her."

"Emmie," Derek said. "You need to come home. Come talk to Jen."

"We're leaving," Dante said. He pulled the communicator from Eric. "We'll see you in a few hours, Derek."

"Drive safe," Derek said.

Dante shoved the communicator in his pocket and looked at Eric. "Help her up. I'll tell the others we're leaving." He left without another word.

Maya, Santiago, and Terrance followed him out. Janette came out a moment later and saw Eric helping me up. "Are you leaving?" she asked.

"Yes," I said. "Something has come up. We need to get back to New Haven."

"Is everything okay?" Janette asked.

I looked at her, ignoring the question. "Thank you for all of your help. You saved my life and you offered complete strangers your home. We'll forever be in your debt."

Janette smiled and took my hands in hers. "I'm glad I

could help. If you ever come back to Kingsland, know that my door's always open to you and your friends." She lifted the bottom of my shirt and examined the wound. "This looks a little irritated. Have you been gentle with it?"

"Do you really want to hear the truth?" I asked.

Janette shook her head. "Probably not. Please be careful, Emmie. This is a serious wound. You're not healed yet. Your life's still at stake so take extra caution." She went over to Joshua who still stood near the fireplace. She looked at his arm, avoiding eye contact with him. From the way he stared at me, she could probably tell something was wrong. "This looks fine. But still, take it easy."

"Thank you," Eric said. He had his arm around my waist, holding me close. "For everything."

"Thank your daughter for her shirt," I said.

"I will," Janette said. "Safe travels. And please keep in touch. I would like to know how you and Joshua heal." She winked at me and Eric. "Plus, I still need that wedding invitation."

"Of course." I gave her a gentle hug and then had Eric help me outside. I heard Joshua follow us out, but I didn't look back at him.

The whole ride to New Haven, my head wouldn't stop spinning. I leaned into Eric, trying to stay as comfortable as I could in the back of a jeep on bumpy roads. Gideon drove as well as he could in the circumstances. Dante's and Santiago's jeeps went on ahead so they could get back to New Haven quickly. Maya kept pace with us just in case anything happened.

From my seat, I could see Joshua clearly. He had his eyes

closed most of the trip and tears fell down his cheeks now and then. I thought he had told me everything that went on in his life. I was convinced we had an honest and open relationship. I couldn't believe he would keep the fact that Austin was still alive to himself.

When Joshua had first come to New Haven, we had made a promise to not hide anything. We wanted to have a functioning family relationship. We both had that lacking in our lives growing up, so it was very important to both of us to be truthful. I wasn't stupid; I knew family members lied to each other all the time. But I thought Joshua and I had something different. I thought I could depend on him and trust him with my life. I desperately wanted to believe that he only had good intentions, but my trust in him had been fractured.

Joshua turned around and looked at me, his eyes full of remorse and regret. "*I'm so sorry*," he mouthed.

"*I know*," I mouthed.

A hint of a smile flashed across his face and then he turned around, facing forward.

Eric leaned in close to my ear. "How are you feeling?"

Being in the back of the jeep was noisy, but we still didn't want to be overheard by Gideon or Joshua. I put my mouth close to his ear. "I hurt. Both my wound and my heart."

"Samantha will be able to get you some pain medication," Eric said. "As for your heart, Emmie, I have no idea what to say. I'm not sure if we should believe Joshua or not."

"I know." I started to cry, more from the pain in my heart than anything else. "I can't believe Austin betrayed us like that. After everything we've been through. I trusted him, Eric, and

I trusted Joshua. If my faith in Austin turned out to be based on lies, how can I believe Joshua?"

Eric sighed into my ear. "I don't know, Em. It's confusing to me. You trusted Joshua a lot faster than anyone else did. But you've always been good at reading people."

"Not with Austin. I hadn't the slightest inkling toward his betrayal."

"No one did." He squeezed me. "With Joshua, it took me a while, but I thought I'd really come to know him. He's seemed so sincere, more so than Austin. I've always liked Austin, but I've never actually gotten to know him like I have Joshua. I studied Joshua closely for months and months. I was convinced he was good."

"We're going to have to keep a close eye on him," I said. "I don't want to, but it's necessary."

"I agree."

We hit a bump in the road, causing pain to ripple through my stomach. I clutched onto Eric's arm and let out a small scream.

Gideon glanced at the rear-view mirror. "Sorry, Emmie. That came out of nowhere."

Joshua had turned around and leaned toward us. He put his hand on my knee. "Em, are you okay?" The concern in his eyes was genuine. Or at least it seemed that way. When Eric eyed Joshua's hand on me, Joshua pulled it away, his face apologetic.

I smiled slightly. "It's okay. I'm fine. Just be more cautious."

"I will," Gideon said.

Joshua studied my face for a moment and then slowly turned back around. He kept his eyes focused on the road, looking out for anything that would cause the jeep to shake, pointing them out to Gideon when he thought it was necessary.

Closing my eyes, I pressed my lips against Eric's ear. "I can only see two options here."

"Which are?" Eric asked.

"Joshua really is a good guy but made a horrible mistake and a bad judgment call." I took a deep breath. "Or he's completely manipulated all of us and he's eviler and more calculating than his father."

Eric pulled me close and put my head against his chest. He kissed the top of my head. "Then we better hope it's the first option."

CHAPTER 21

When we pulled into New Haven, Samantha ran out of the entrance and came to my side. "Oh, Emmie, I heard what happened. I'm so sorry. I'll look you over when we get inside." She felt my forehead. "You have a slight fever. I'll give you some medication for that and the pain. But it'll make you drowsy."

"I can't afford drowsy right now," I said. "We have a situation on our hands."

Samantha furrowed her eyebrows. "We'll have a bigger situation if you don't take it easy."

"Can we start with a small dose and work our way up?"

"Sure, but I'm still in charge of it. If I say we're increasing the dose, then we are. Understood?"

I nodded. "Fine."

Once inside, they got me to a room and situated into a bed. Dee helped me change into the infirmary clothes and redid my braid.

She smiled when she was finished. "I was thinking of

adding some curl to your hair for the wedding and maybe a few small braids on the side. Then we can pull it back, but not too tight so some curls can hang loose."

"That sounds nice, Dee," I said.

Samantha came in and hooked an IV up to my arm. "I'll get these started and then you can work. But don't push it, Emmie. And only a few people in here at a time. The lady sure did a good job on the stitches, though. You're lucky she was there and willing to help."

"Her name's Janette." I tugged on one of Dee's curls. "You'll have to add her and her family to the wedding list."

"This is going to be the biggest wedding, ever." Dee clasped her hands together. "I'm excited and nervous at the same time. So much pressure for a wedding planner. Everyone wants to come! There will be thousands of people there."

My jaw dropped. "Thousands? Maybe we should consider just doing family and really, really close friends."

Dee let out a laugh. "Then I'll let you be the one to tell people they can't come. You're legendary here. You must have known that one of the revolutionaries getting married is a big deal. Everyone respects you."

"I still didn't think they would all want to come to my wedding." I glanced down at my ring, twisting it a few times. A sharp pain gripped my heart when I thought about my dad.

"What's wrong?" Dee took my hand in hers.

"I wish my dad was here." A few tears fell from my eyes, landing on my shirt.

A small knock sounded at the door. Eric and his dad, Alexander, peered in.

"May we come in?" Alexander asked.

"Of course," I said, quickly wiping my tears away.

Samantha held up three fingers. "Only three others in here at a time, Emmie. No more than that. I'll be back to check on you in a while."

When she left the room, Eric sat next to me on the bed. "Has anything kicked in yet?"

"No," I said. "Still feel all of the pain."

"I'll leave you guys alone." Dee kissed me on the cheek and left the room.

Alexander sat in a chair next to the bed. "I'm glad to see you're safe, Emmie." Sadness tugged at his eyes. "You kids have seen way too much for one life. Luckily, you're both strong individuals. I don't think I could've handled all you have had to deal with when I was your age."

"Times change, Dad," Eric said.

"I know," he said. "But every parent hopes their children will have a safe and easy upbringing." He sighed. "That was the whole point behind Infinity Corp, but it didn't turn out as it should have."

I intertwined my fingers with Eric's. "I can't say I'm happy with all I've had to go through, but I can tell you it has made me a stronger person. Each trial has certainly taught me a lot about life and myself."

I thought of my dad again. "I think everyone has to go through trials so they can truly appreciate what they have and understand the beauty behind it. It wasn't until I got here that I looked at my dad in a different light and started to appreciate everything he did for me."

Eric's mouth turned up into a smile. "It also made you get along with Derek."

"True." I smiled, a small laugh escaping my mouth. "I'm still not sure if that's a good thing or not."

"It's good," Alexander said. "Family's important. Even if it's not the traditional family or if it's a family you create, it's nice having that support."

I thought about Derek and Joshua, and my fellow revolutionaries, plus Dee and Tina. I had created my own family. I would trust any of them with my life.

Even Joshua.

"What are you thinking about?" Eric asked, stroking my hand with his thumb.

"Family." I looked over at Alexander. "I have a question for you."

Alexander smiled. "Ask away."

"I've been thinking about the wedding." I glanced over at Eric and then back at his dad. "Alexander, I was wondering if you would be willing to walk me down the aisle."

Alexander was quiet for a minute. I couldn't quite read his facial expression. With tears in his eyes, he cleared his throat. "I'd be honored, Emmie. Thank you for asking." His lips twitched into a frown. "I'm just sorry it couldn't be your own father."

"Me, too," I said. Eric squeezed my hand and gave me a soft smile. "But, Alexander, I consider you a father, too. You have been there for me this past year."

"Well, I already look at you as a daughter." He took hold of my other hand. "I know I'll never replace your real father, but I'll always be here for you, Emmie. No matter what."

I smiled at him. "That means a lot to me."

Tina popped her head into the room, her wet hair hanging down around her shoulder. "Sorry to interrupt, but Jen would like to talk with Emmie."

Jen walked into the room without waiting for an invitation. She looked exactly like I remembered her—petite with sharp features—only her face held some fading bruises and a couple cuts.

She wore a serious expression, without any hint of excitement at seeing me. "Hello, Emmie."

"Hi, Jen," I said.

Alexander stood and hugged me. "Rest, my dear Emmie."

When he went to leave the room, Jen didn't move out of the way, so he had to scoot around her, frowning the whole time.

Tina was still standing behind Jen, so she rolled her eyes at me.

"Why are you here?" Eric asked.

Jen looked at him sharply. "I'm only talking to Emmie. No one else."

Eric went to Jen, looking down at her. "I'm not leaving her alone with you."

Jen pursed her lips together. She finally sighed. "Fine. Tina can stay here with us."

"And me?" Dee asked, walking into the room. Her eyes were red from crying.

"Were you listening at the door?" I asked her. Whenever I talked about my dad, she always teared up.

She bit her bottom lip. "Sorry. I couldn't help it." She flashed a smile. "But, yay for Alexander walking you down the aisle!"

Jen turned around and looked at Dee, her sigh that followed completely audible for all to hear. "You've got to be kidding me. I know what happens when the three of you girls get together."

Tina pushed past Jen and sat on the bed next to me. She smelled like fresh soap and I suddenly wanted a shower. "Yeah, we beat the crap out of anyone that pisses us off. Don't do that and you'll be fine. But if you won't have Eric in the room, you get me and Dee. Your choice."

Jen mulled it over. "Fine. Tina and Dee." Sitting down in the chair Alexander had vacated, she waved her hand at Eric. "You may leave now."

Eric kissed me on the lips. "I'll be right outside if you need me. Love you."

"Love you, too," I said.

He shot Jen a spiteful look and then left the room.

"He's a charmer," Jen said after he walked out.

I laughed. "I could say the same thing about you." I adjusted the pillow behind me and then rested my head against it.

Jen sat back in her chair, clasping her hands together. "I swear every time I see you, Emmie, you're fresh out of a fight."

"I seem to attract trouble." Finally feeling the medication kicking in, I crossed my fingers Samantha didn't give me too much. I needed to stay coherent during the conversation. "So, what brings you to New Haven?"

"Derek gave me a nice tour." Jen eyed one of Vivica's paintings on the wall. A small smile formed on her tight mouth. "I have to say, this place isn't that bad. I'd take it over our city right about now."

Dee sat down, crossing her legs. "I heard it's bad over there. Is that true?"

Jen sighed. "Austin's gone completely crazy and, Emmie, your mom." She sighed again. "I have no idea what to think about your mom."

"You and me both." I hadn't talked to my mom in over a year, but she'd always been a difficult person to figure out.

Tina leaned forward, looking at Jen. "So why are you here?"

"Emmie's mom sent me," Jen said. "But before I talk, I want some answers."

"About what?" I asked.

Jen looked at me. "About why you're here. What started all of this?"

"It's a long story." And a hard one to explain to people.

"I have time," Jen said, shrugging.

Dee scoffed. "Well, we don't. We have a crisis on our hands right now. So, spill it!"

Jen looked down at her lap. "I heard about that." Rubbing her eyes, she sat forward. "This is all so crazy. I never thought life would end up this way. We were supposed to have an easy, structured life. Then Emmie goes all crazy and flees the city, taking people with her. Then Austin snaps. President Randall is dead. The city is split. What's going on?"

I sat up a little more and looked over at Jen. "Condensed

version? President Randall wasn't a good man. He killed and tortured to get what he wanted."

"How do you know that?" Jen asked. "Most of our city is in the dark. No one knows the truth."

"Well, we do," I said. "It's why we left. I saw President Randall and Dean Johnson kill Vice President Oliver."

"Dee and I were there, too," Tina said, running her fingers through her wet hair.

Dee started to cry. "It was awful. I still have nightmares."

I wanted to take her hand, but she was too far away. Tina sat between us.

"You saw it happen?" Jen shook her head, a look of disgust on her face. "Why did he do it?"

"He was a tyrant, that's why." I closed my eyes for a moment and pushed the image of Vice President Oliver's death out of my head. "President Randall wanted me dead, so we tried to escape, but got caught. After Vice President Oliver died, we were able to escape with the help of Mack and some others from River Springs."

"What else did President Randall do that was so bad?" Jen asked.

I thought back to why Luke came to New Haven. "President Randall took Eric hostage. They beat him pretty bad."

Jen looked over at me. "Is that what the scar on his face is from?"

I nodded. "President Randall tried to get Luke to beat information out of Eric, but Luke wouldn't do it. President Randall had just killed Luke's father right in front of him."

"Well, technically, Dean shot him," Tina said. "President Randall never did the dirty work himself. He made others do it."

"Luke took Eric and got Austin to help him leave the city." I ran my hand down my braid, twisting the end in my fingers. "We thought Austin had been killed during the escape, but apparently, he faked his death."

"I can confirm that he's still alive," Jen said. "He's turned his territory into a prison. There are guards everywhere, making sure no one breaks a rule. And your mom's territory is full of people who are scared and don't know what to do. Everyone's scared. I haven't slept well in a year."

Letting go of my braid, I reached for my butterfly pendant, twirling it in my hand. "That's why we created New Haven. We wanted people to have a safe place to live but aren't under strict commands. Does that answer your question?"

Jen slowly nodded. "I think it does." She sat back in her chair. "Emmie, your mom sent me to get your help."

My eyebrows shot up. "My mom wants my help?"

"Yes," Jen said. "As I've said, Austin's out of control. The man has a split personality disorder or something. He keeps talking nice to everyone, saying he wants our input and wants to make the city a wonderful place to live in. But then he keeps a tight security detail around the River and Ocean Precincts. People have been shot in their own homes for breaking a rule. Anyone who tries to flee to your mom's territory is either shot by Austin's men or by your mom's henchmen because she thinks they're a spy. I'm lucky to be alive."

"What do you mean?" Dee asked.

"Austin sent me over to Janice's territory to be a spy," Jen said. "I only agreed so I could get out of his territory. Stupid Tami Randall tied me up and then beat me before she took me to Janice. Luckily, Janice hates Tami and Amy as much as I do, so she cut my bonds. She sent me here to get you and bring you back to River Springs."

"My mom wants me to go back there?" I asked.

Jen nodded. "With your help, she thinks they can take back over Austin's precincts and get things back to how they were."

I shook my head. "I don't want things back to how they were."

"Emmie, what's your problem?" Jen glared at me. "River Springs was fine before. Our lives were safe. Things were easy. We all got along."

"No, we didn't." I rubbed my forehead. "Jen, you broke up our fights. Not everyone in the city got along with each other. There was too much tension. And what about our happiness?"

Jen shrugged. "What about it?"

I thought about my mom and my dad. "My parents were forced to marry each other and then when it didn't work out, they couldn't divorce. They were stuck in an unhappy marriage and had to pretend everything was fine. I understand having order and structure. But let people choose who they want to marry, what they want to do for a living, and where they want to live."

Jen shifted uncomfortably in her seat. I was about to ask her what was wrong, but she cut me off. "Listen, this whole thing is incredibly confusing to me. I'm still trying to wrap my head around it all." She took a communication device from her pocket and set it on my bed, right next to my hand. "You can contact your mom through that. She just wants to talk."

Jen stood and started to walk out of the room, but I stopped her when she got to the doorway. "Jen, who's side are you on?"

She looked over her shoulder at me. "No ones."

CHAPTER 22

The communication device sat there, next to my hand, willing me to hold it. I stared at it for a few minutes, not sure I wanted to talk to the person on the other end. It had been too long since I'd last heard her voice.

"Do you want us to leave you alone?" Dee asked.

I looked up at Tina and Dee, both staring at me, their faces sympathetic. Clearing my throat, I nodded. "Yes. I think this is a conversation I need to do on my own."

Tina stood. "I understand." She gently hugged me and then left the room.

Dee's hug wasn't as gentle. When she pulled away, she ran her fingers over my braid and pulled it forward, so it rested against my collar bone. "I'll be outside. Good luck."

"Thanks." I nodded at the door. "Will you shut the door on your way out?"

Dee left without another word, closing the door behind her.

I ran my finger along the edge of the communication

device, debating whether I should pick it up. The device itself was one I'd never seen before. Most of ours were black rectangles in various sizes, with different knobs and buttons for changing channels, volume control, and powering it on. The one near my hand was small, silver, and more of an oval, with only two buttons: one to turn it on and off, and one you held down when talking.

Closing my eyes, I rested my head against my pillow and took a few deep breaths. I hoped to calm my racing heart, but it didn't work.

I had mixed feelings about my mom. She hadn't had a big role in my life growing up. She just seemed to be there, in the background, coming and going as she pleased. One day she'd be talking to me like everything was normal, acting as a real mother would. The next day, she would be closed off, avoiding me like an earthquake that destroyed the earth.

My dad told me over and over again how much my mother loved me and wished she didn't have to work so much. But I'd never heard the words come from her mouth. I desperately wanted to believe my father, but I had no reason why I should.

The fact that she had cheated on my dad with the man I loathed most in the world didn't sit well with me. Plus, the fact that I was that man's daughter left me feeling sick to my stomach. I wasn't sure if I could ever forgive her.

But then again, if it weren't for the affair, I wouldn't have been born. I wouldn't have my amazing friends. I wouldn't have Eric.

Taking a few more breaths, I picked up the

communication device and turned it on. I held it up to my lips, pressed down on the talk button, and forced myself to speak. "Hello?"

The minutes following that one word were tortuous. I twisted my ring around and around on my finger, anxiously waiting to hear a response. By the time it came, my throat was completely dry.

"Emmie?" My mom's voice echoed throughout the room.

"Yes, it's me." My voice came out quieter and higher pitched than I had wanted.

The seconds ticked by, each one a tiny tear to my heart. Her voice was soft. "It's good to hear your voice."

"What do you want?" The question escaped my mouth without any thought. I hadn't meant to sound so snappy and rude. But I couldn't take it back.

"Can we catch up first?" my mom asked. "It's been so long since I've last talked to you. How are you doing?"

That question was too complex to answer. So, I settled with the traditional answer. "I'm fine."

"What about your brother? And your father?"

My sarcastic instinct was to reply, "*Which one*?" But seeing as my relationship with one brother was rocky at the moment and both of my fathers were dead, I reeled myself in. "Derek is doing fine."

When I didn't continue, my mother spoke. "And your father?"

She apparently hadn't heard about his death. It wasn't something I wanted to talk about. "What do you want, Mom?"

Her sigh was loud and sounded remarkably like my own.

"How much has Jen told you?"

"That River Springs is split, Whit is dead, Austin is a traitor, and you want my help."

"Need, Emmie," my mom corrected. "I *need* your help."

Unfortunately for my mom, she had caught me at a very ornery time in my life. I was too emotional. "Why should I help you? Seriously, Mom, I'd like one good reason why I should even be speaking to you right now."

"Because I'm your mother!" she snapped.

I laughed. "Funny, because you've never acted like it."

My mom swore, something I'd never heard her do. "Can we put aside our personal feelings for a moment? We have a crisis going on over here in River Springs and I need your help. I need New Haven's help."

"Why should New Haven even think about helping River Springs? That city screwed me over."

"You screwed yourself over, Emmie. You didn't need any help with that. You're stubborn and selfish."

"Where do you think I got that from?"

Maybe it hadn't been a good idea to send my friends out of the room. I was fuming and couldn't compose myself. They would have been able to calm me down.

"You sound just like your father when you're upset." My mom inhaled sharply after she spoke. She probably hadn't meant to say out loud.

It was a statement I couldn't avoid, though. "Which one, Mom? The one who raised me or the one you'd been sleeping with for all those years?"

"I'm sorry, Emmie, okay? I'm so sorry." She choked up.

I closed my eyes and thought of the man I'd considered my father my whole life. The man I loved as a father, even though genetically, he wasn't. He wouldn't want me acting like this. He'd raised me better. I still wanted answers, but I tried to keep my voice as calm as I could. "For what, Mom? I want to hear why you're sorry."

"Does it make a difference?"

I furrowed my eyebrows. "Of course, it does. Sorry is just a word. How do I know if you even mean it?"

"I mean it." She started to cry. "I'm sorry I wasn't involved in your life growing up. I'm sorry I never told you the truth about Whit. I'm sorry for never holding you when you were hurt or listening to you when you needed to talk." She gasped for air. The sound surprised me and made tears form in my own eyes. "I'm sorry for not loving you like a mother should love her child. I was depressed and I took it out on you and Derek. And your father. Philip."

Reaching over for a tissue, I wiped the tears away. "Why were you depressed?"

"I hated my life, Emmie. I hated who I had become. I didn't mean for everything to happen like it did. When I first met Philip, I was instantly drawn to his sweet and loving nature. I wasn't attracted to him, but I felt that over time I could come to love him as he did me. I believed in the city, so I married him and started a life with him."

She paused and took a few breaths to slow her tears. "But then I got my job working with Whit. The attraction was instantaneous. I had just found out that I was pregnant with Derek, so nothing physically happened between Whit and me.

We just flirted a lot and I worked long hours just so I could be around him. It was after Derek was born that we started sleeping together. Emmie, I was so young at the time. I didn't realize the effect our relationship would have on everyone. Especially Philip. I never wanted to hurt him. It wasn't until after you were born that I realized the full impact it had on him."

"But you still didn't end your relationship with Whit." I wiped my nose, threw the tissue away, and grabbed another one. "You kept it going all those years and left Dad, me, and Derek all alone."

Her voice was quiet. "I know. But Philip and I couldn't get divorced and I was in love with Whit."

I shook my head in disbelief. "You really loved Whit?"

"Yes, Emmie." Her voice was firm. "I loved him with all my heart."

"But he's evil. He tried to kill me. He killed Vice President Oliver."

"I can't say I agree with all of his actions, because I don't. But when he was with me, he was different. He treated me well and loved me unconditionally. He was sweet and generous. He made me feel special."

"Did you know? That he wanted me killed?"

"No, sweetie, I didn't." Her voice was sincere. "I never would have allowed him to do that. I may have been a horrible mother, but I do love you, Emmie. I know that may be hard to believe, but you must trust me when I say that I love you. I'll never be able to make up for everything I've done or the hurt I've caused you, your brother, and your father."

I wasn't sure whether to believe her. She had spent so many years around Whit. She could have learned to be deceptive like him. "That still doesn't explain why you shut me out."

"I don't have a good, solid reason. What I wanted more than anything was to be able to have a life with you and Whit. I pictured us having this perfect, happy family. The three of us living together was something I knew I could never have. Seeing you reminded me of him and how I'd never have that happy life I wanted." She let out a small laugh. "And you hated him so much. Watching my little girl loathe the man that was actually her father was too much for me. I thought I could handle it better if I stayed away. I felt it was the only way to get through my life without feeling the pain every single day."

"What about Derek?" He and I never had a good relationship growing up, but now it was different. We still joked around and teased each other, but now it was done out of love, not hate. The fact that my mom didn't include him in her perfect, happy life broke my heart. Despite his quirkiness, he was an amazing guy and brother. He had looked after and protected me, something my own mother couldn't do. "Why isn't he in your vision of your perfect life?" My tone came out defensive.

My mom sounded shocked. "You hate your brother."

"No, I don't. I love him. He has been there for me when you haven't. He's taken care of me this past year when all of my other family was gone."

"I don't understand," she said. "What about your father?"

I wasn't sure how to tell her, so I just spit it out, the words coming out fast and mumbled. “He’s dead.”

“Not Whit,” she said. “Philip. The man who raised you.”

“He’s dead.” I didn’t like having to repeat myself. The words tasted horrible on my tongue and I worried they'd never wash away.

“What? When? How?” She sounded shocked and saddened, which was more than I could have asked for. I wasn’t sure how’d she react.

“Last year,” I said. “We had a battle with another city. Dad was killed during the fight.”

“Oh, Emmie.” Her tears came back. I could hear her sniffles through the communicator. “I’m so sorry. I didn’t know.”

I fought back my own tears. “It was hard at first. But Derek, Joshua, Dee, and Eric helped me through it. Along with some new friends of mine.”

“I’m glad to hear you had such a big support system.” She cleared her throat. “How is everything with Joshua? Are you two getting along?”

That was another conversation I didn’t want to have right now.

It had been going well, but now I wasn’t sure. But I didn’t want anything to leak to Austin, so I lied. “It’s great. He, Derek, and I live together, and we all get along perfectly. Of course, it was awkward for everyone at first, but we adjusted and over time we bonded.”

“Derek and Joshua are friends?” I could hear the smile in her voice. “That’s surprising but good. That makes me happy to know that you have two brothers who are there for you.

And Eric. I'm assuming the two of you are still together?"

I twisted my ring on my finger. "Yes. We're engaged."

"Congratulations." Her smile sounded even bigger. "That's wonderful. You love him, right?"

I smiled. "Yes. More than anything in the world. He's amazing."

"Oh, good. I wouldn't wish upon you what I had to go through. I'm glad you got to choose the man you love."

"Me, too." Since I had finally calmed, I figured I should find out what my mom wanted. "Why did you send Jen here?"

"I was hoping for your help. Austin has split the city in two and innocent people have been killed. They're still being killed. He has taken complete domination of his territory. He hurts and kills those who step out of line. It needs to end. We can't keep living like this. Families have been ruined and shattered because of him."

I wanted to reply that Whit had done the same, but I didn't want to break out in another argument. "What do you need from us?"

"Support. With the combination of my territory and New Haven, we can take back over River Springs. We can restore it and put it back together."

"I don't want River Springs how it was before. I left because I didn't agree with the way it was run and my thoughts haven't changed."

"Emmie, it was fine before you left."

I sighed. "No, mom, it wasn't. I know you loved Whit, but he hurt and killed innocent people, too. There were too many rules and too many restrictions."

My mom's sigh matched mine. "People need rules and restrictions to keep them from getting out of line."

"That's not entirely true. New Haven has proved that to me. Our people are happy. Yes, we have laws they have to live by, but they get a say in those laws. They get to choose their career and their family. We work together to make our community safe and comfortable. I've never been so happy in my life. I love it here and the people. I have met so many wonderful people from different cities and different cultures. My mind has been expanded and my heart has opened."

"What would it take to get you here?"

I wasn't sure if she would like my answer, but I didn't care. It was the only way she'd get me to step foot in River Springs again. "I want a promise that things won't go back to the way they were. I want a promise that my fellow revolutionaries and I will be able to run Infinity Corp and River Springs."

"No." Her voice was sharp. "I can't hand over the city to you and some other children I haven't met."

"We aren't children anymore. We've seen more in the past year than you've seen in your whole life. We're smart and capable of running a city. We've proved that with New Haven."

"You have a president and vice president. They're adults and running your city."

"First, we are adults. We're nineteen. Second, we put them in charge of taking care of the day to day events for now, but we chose to have them. We've been hands-on the whole time. We've overseen protecting our citizens and fighting for their freedom and so far, we've won. And we'll continue to win. No matter what you say to me, we will win in the end, I can promise you that. So, if you want our help, you will hand over the leadership of your part of the city to us."

She swore again. "You know I can't do that!"

"You can!" I yelled. "The man you loved predicted this would happen, and look, Mom, it's coming true. We're here to make this world a better place. We're going to fix it, whether you like it or not. It's either now or later. So, you can hand it over and work with us to do what's right, or we'll take it from you. You know the second way would cause more bloodshed than there needs to be. We want to fix Infinity Corp as much as you do, but not Whit's way. We're doing it our way."

"Emmie!"

"This isn't open for debate. It's your choice, Mom. Give us full access to your side of the city and we'll end Austin's reign of power. We'll make River Springs a safe place to live. We'll give everyone the right to choose their happy ending, just like you wanted all along. You have twenty-four hours to think it over. Make the right choice, Mom. If you love me like you say you do, prove it. I'll talk to you tomorrow."

Turning off the communication device, I slammed it down on the bed.

CHAPTER 23
Janice

"Emmie!" I waited for her voice to come back through, but it didn't. I slammed the communication device down on my desk, letting out a frustrated groan in the process. Placing the palms of my hands on the desk, I lowered my head and took long, even breaths to control my temper.

I wasn't expecting my daughter to demand control of the city. There was no way I could just hand it over to her. It would be a sign of weakness and defeat.

Sitting down in my chair, I let out an exasperated sigh. I needed her help. We couldn't beat Austin without New Haven. But Emmie was so young. She may have considered nineteen to be old enough, but I didn't. And I'd never met her 'fellow revolutionaries.' I knew nothing about them or their way of living. How could I trust complete strangers? Especially when they were only nineteen themselves.

Whit would never have received help from anyone. He would have figured it out on his own. Sitting back in my chair, I rubbed my temples. As much as it pained me to admit it, not all of Whit's choices were right.

My Grandma Mae had always told me to never be afraid to ask for help. I was stubborn as a child and wanted to do everything on my own. Of course, I'd end up failing or messing up some of the time. I sighed. Most of the time.

She told me that was why we had families, friends, and neighbors. They were there when we couldn't do things ourselves. She also told me not to let my pride get in the way of doing what was right.

Was putting Emmie in charge the right thing to do, though? Her intentions were good, yes, but that didn't mean they would be right or work out for the best. The structure we used to have was necessary at the time. The rules needed to be enforced. They needed drastic measures to fix the world. But maybe over time, the rules needed to be altered to support the change in society.

I picked up the communication device and stared at it. My thumb ran along the button that would connect me to my daughter. My baby girl who wasn't a baby anymore. She was strong, focused, and had the drive to get her far in life. She was just like me and her biological father. She had a good mix of the two of us. Both Whit and I had wonderful qualities, but we also had our fair share of faults. I think our Emmie took only the wonderful qualities and left the faults behind.

I was about to press down on the button when someone knocked on the door. I put the communication device in the front drawer of my desk. "Come in."

Amy and Tami walked through the door, along with Nick and Sean. They were the two men who I'd appointed to lead our security detail. They were both tall and strong and had no problems being forceful when needed. I made them dress in nice suits. They probably weren't the most efficient for their job, but I liked the way it looked. Suits reminded me of Whit.

I had recently found out that Nick and his wife had taken Eric into their home after his father had disappeared.

"What brings you all here?" I asked.

Amy was about to speak, but Nick came up to me and cut her off. He and Sean hated Amy and Tami as I did.

Nick stood before me, his shoulders square. "We spotted some people walking into Austin's side of the city."

My eyebrows shot up. "How many?"

Sean shook his head as he came to stand next to Nick. "We didn't get a full count. Twenty to thirty, by the looks of it."

"Do you know who they were?" I asked.

"No," Nick said. "We've never seen them before. I don't think they're from our city."

Was Austin working with New Haven? I didn't think that could be possible. "Are you sure they aren't from River Springs?"

Sean nodded. "They were dark-skinned, had a different kind of weaponry and their clothing was nothing like what Infinity Corp issues."

Tami hurried to my desk and folded her arms. She didn't like how the two guys always acted like her and her mother weren't in the room. "Maybe they've come to destroy Austin and then we won't have to worry about it."

"Not possible." Nick kept his gaze on me, not giving any indication that Tami was the one who'd spoken. "They just walked in. The guards were expecting them. Austin has some allies from another city. Important ones, too."

I furrowed my eyebrows together. "How do you know they're important?"

"You could tell by the way they carried themselves," Nick said. "And there were a few who seemed to be guarding one man in particular. It was obvious by his stature that he was the leader."

That probably meant they weren't from New Haven. I knew they had a woman president, and the vice president was originally from River Springs. Plus, Emmie and her revolutionaries were young. I looked between Nick and Sean. "But twenty to thirty people doesn't add that much to their numbers."

"There could be more on their way," Sean said. "Maybe that was just the beginning."

I didn't like the thought of another city joining up with Austin. If it wasn't New Haven, that only left Kingsland. I'd heard Juniper had been destroyed and Scorpion had joined forces with New Haven.

"I need some fresh air." After I locked my drawer, I stood and went around the table, tucking my key into my skirt pocket. "Nick and Sean, I'd like you to join me." I snagged my coat hanging behind the door and pulled it on.

"What about us?" Amy asked.

"You're not needed." I left the room without looking back.

I moved down the hall, passing the security detail that guarded my door. Once I was to the stairwell at the end of the hall, I started down the stairs, hoping that Nick and Sean followed me like I had ordered. From the distinctive footsteps right behind me, it was them and only them.

When I got to the first floor, I pushed open the door leading outside, stepping out into the cold. I zipped up my coat and headed down the street. It was mostly deserted, just a few security guards scattered about.

Even with everything that had happened, I had made sure we kept our precincts clean. The streets were perfectly cleared of debris and all the lines had been freshly painted. The trees stood bare from winter, but the branches were neatly trimmed.

There was a sharp, bitter-cold breeze in the air. The sky was perfectly blue with some scattered white clouds, making the cold bearable. I walked for about a mile in perfect silence. I never looked back, but I could hear two sets of footsteps behind me.

When we arrived at the lake, I stepped onto the pebbled shore and stopped near the water's edge. Heels and pebbles didn't mix well. The two men stepped up on either side of me, Nick on my left, Sean on my right.

I could see my breath as I spoke. "I need your advice."

"What's on your mind, Janice?" Nick asked.

"It's been too quiet in Austin's territory," I said. "I know he likes to take time to plan his attacks perfectly, but it's been a year. Now with people from another city showing up, that means he's probably spent this past year gaining allies."

"I was thinking that same thing," Sean said.

I rubbed my arms for warmth. "I'm pretty sure those were Kingsland residents who showed up. They have a big city. If they've teamed up with Austin, we're in trouble."

Sean took off his jacket and placed it around my shoulders. I put my arms in the sleeves, thankful for the added warmth. I smiled at him before I turned my attention back to the crystallized lake before me.

Out of the corner of my eye, I noticed Nick look at Sean's jacket around me. He cleared his throat. "What have you heard from Jen? Has she talked with Emmie?"

Nick and Sean were the only ones I had told about my plans to have Jen talk Emmie into joining us. They were the only people I could trust.

I put my hands in the pockets of Sean's jacket, wishing I had remembered to grab my gloves on the way out. "I had just finished talking with Emmie before you walked into my office."

"What did she say?" Sean asked. "Did she agree?"

"That's why I need your advice." I kicked a little at the pebbles on the ground. I had thought I'd decided what to do but realized I couldn't make this decision on my own. My choice would end up affecting thousands of people. "She agreed, but only on one term."

Nick sighed. "Why don't I like the sound of that?"

"She wants total control of our territory," I said.

Both Sean and Nick swore at the same time.

Sean spoke up first. "No. No way."

"We can't hand over complete control," Nick said. "That would be reckless."

"Not to mention we've worked so hard to get this far," Sean said.

"And she's young," Nick put in.

"And so is everyone else with her." Sean had scooted so our arms were touching.

Taking my hand out of my pocket, I rubbed my forehead. "I've had those same thoughts. But we need help. We can't do this on our own and it looks like Austin has partnered with Kingsland, so that only leaves New Haven."

"Can we trust New Haven?" Nick asked.

"We have to." I lowered my hand to my side, brushing it against Sean's hand. He tried to take hold of my hand, but I put it in my pocket before he could.

"I don't like the thought of leaving the lives of our citizens in their hands," Nick said.

Sean took a step away from me. "Can we make it look like we're giving them control, but still keep the power ourselves?"

"I've thought of that, but I don't know how that would be possible." I scooted a little closer to Sean. "I don't like the thought of putting our citizen's lives in their hands, either, but New Haven has been in a battle before. The odds were stacked against them, they were extremely outnumbered, yet they won."

"They did, but another city showed up to help them," Nick said.

"All the more reason to trust them," I said. "They took the help of another city and they ended up winning. From what

I've heard, Scorpion handed over leadership to New Haven and both areas have been getting along nicely. The people are happy and safe."

Sean scooted closer to me, so our arms were touching again. "I don't know if I agree with the way they run their city."

I thought about Emmie and everything she had said to me. "I didn't think I agreed, either, but the more I think about it, the more I'm open to the change. They still have laws. They still govern their people, but they aren't as strict. Maybe letting our citizens have some say in their lives isn't a bad thing. You've met our residents. They're smart, capable people. I think they can handle New Haven's way of life."

I wasn't looking at Nick, but I could hear the smile in his voice. "It sounds like you've already made up your mind."

"I want to do what's best for our residents," I said. "I want to keep them alive. I think the only way to do that right now is to work with New Haven."

"Can we set some terms?" Sean asked.

"Like what?" asked Nick.

"We hand over control to them and let them plan the strategy," Sean said. "But only if they let the three of us work with them and get a say in what they do."

Nick sighed. "I'm not entirely happy with this, but I think you're right, Janice. It's the only way to save River Springs."

I turned to Sean. "I like your terms. I'll contact Emmie and let them know."

"I really hope this works," Sean said.

"Me too." I looked over at Nick. "On a side note, I have some good news from Emmie."

Nick turned toward me. "What is it?"

"Eric and Emmie are engaged." I wasn't sure what his reaction would be. Eric had only lived with Nick, his wife, and his daughter for a little over two years. But Nick thought highly of him and came to love him as a son.

Nick smiled, the sincerity showing in his eyes. "That's wonderful. Carla and Courtney will be so happy to hear that."

Sean stepped forward and reached his hand out to Nick. "Congratulations."

Nick shook his hand. "Thank you."

"Maybe this will be a good thing, teaming up with New Haven," I said. "That way, you can see them get married."

A few tears escaped Nick's eyes. "I'd like that. The girls would like that."

Sean was still standing in front of me. He looked down into my eyes. "You can be there, too."

I wiped away a few of my own tears. "If she'll let me. She's pretty pissed at me and for good reasons, too."

Sean put his hand on my arm. "Give her some time. She'll come around."

"Janice," Nick said. "Would you mind if I took leave for a half-hour so I can run home and tell the girls in person?"

"Of course." I reached over and hugged. "I don't know much about Eric, but from what I've heard from you, it sounds like my Emmie made a good choice."

"She did," Nick said, squeezing me. He pulled back. "He's an amazing young man. Just like his father, Alexander. I've had nothing but respect for their family. I'll be back soon."

He turned and left me and Sean alone. I looked up at him

and he was staring at me so intensely. I could tell he wanted to hug or kiss me. I wasn't sure which one.

Two years ago, Sean had lost his wife to the same disease I had lost my mom to. From what Nick had told me, it sounded like the same disease Eric's mom died from as well. I heard some New Haven residents had caught it and it was spreading like a wildfire in Kingsland.

Sean finally pried his eyes away from mine and stood next to me again. I debated for a moment, but I took hold of his hand, intertwining our fingers. We had grown close over the past year, leaning on each other for support. I was trying to get over Whit and he was trying to get over his wife. We had both been so deeply in love with our companions.

When the city first split after Whit's death, I had a hard time sleeping. I would find myself going on walks at night. Sean would do the same thing. We crossed paths a lot and started talking. Soon, we were taking our walks together. Whenever I was having a rough day, I would find myself seeking him out. He was so kind and listened to every word that came out of my mouth. He understood me. He made me feel safe and comfortable.

We hadn't done anything more than hold hands a few times and hugged now and then. Some nights we would sit down on a bench near the lake and I'd end up crying. He would just hold me in his arms until I stopped.

I could tell he wanted more and deep inside I wanted more, too. I just wasn't sure I was ready.

CHAPTER 24
Emmie

I was so deep in thought, I hadn't heard Eric come into the room. He was suddenly sitting in the chair next to me, holding my hand.

"Emmie? Are you okay?" Eric asked.

The metallic taste of blood filled my mouth. I had been so upset with my mom that I had bit down on my lip so hard, it had split open.

Panic sat in Eric's eyes.

I gently placed my hand on his cheek. "I'm so glad to see you."

Taking hand from his cheek, he kissed my palm. "What's going on? What did Jen say to you?" I instinctively looked down at the communicator. Eric followed my eyes. "Who did you talk to?"

"My mom." I forced the words out. Taking the device, I shoved it in my pocket. Eric sat down on the bed next to me, pulling me into his arms. I sighed into his chest. "I didn't know how hard it would be to talk to her."

He kissed the top of my head. "What did you talk about?"

"Everything." Fresh tears fell from my eyes and onto Eric's shirt. He rubbed my back as I spoke. "She apologized for not being there for me. She admitted she loved Whit and had wanted to be with him, not my dad. She wanted the three of us to live together; me, Whit and her, like one happy family."

"What about Derek?" Eric asked.

"That's what I asked." I sniffed and wiped away a few tears. "She never actually answered that question, so I don't know." The next words came out in a whisper. "She told me she loved me."

"Do you think she meant it?"

"I think so. It sounded sincere enough. But she wants something from me, so I don't know. Hanging around Whit all those years had to have taught her a thing or two about manipulating people."

"What does she want from you?"

I pulled back and looked up at him, our faces close together. "She wants New Haven to help her defeat Austin."

Surprise flashed on his face. "What did you say?"

"That we would under one condition."

His eyebrows rose. "What's the condition?"

"That she hands full control of her part of the city over to us."

Eric smiled and kissed my forehead. "Smart thinking, Em. What did she say to that?"

I started to laugh. "Oh, she wasn't happy. She didn't want

to do it. I told her she had twenty-four hours to make up her mind if she wanted our help."

"Well, you need to rest during those twenty-four hours." He stroked my cheek with his hand. "I need you fully recovered before the wedding."

I ran my fingers through his hair. "I will be, don't worry." He pulled me close and kissed me on the lips. He held me softly as we kissed, careful of my injury.

Two minutes later the door opened, and a bunch of people poured into my room. I pulled back from Eric and saw Dante, Santiago, Maya, Will, Dee, Tina, Luke, Jen, Derek, and Joshua.

"I thought I said no hanky panky?" Derek folded his arms and glared at us. Dante did the same, but I ignored them both.

"Please, everyone," I said, "just come on into my room." I tried to pull all the way back from Eric so I could sit up, but he held onto me. He and Dante were staring at each other. I tucked the information into the back of my mind, determined to talk to them alone when I had the time.

Dee stepped in front of everyone. "I'm sorry; I tried to keep all of them out. I told them you needed rest."

"She does," Eric said.

"Then why are you in here?" Dante asked Eric.

Eric opened his mouth, but I cut him off. "Enough," I said. "Why are you here?"

"Who is that question for?" Derek asked.

I grunted. "All of you. I'll start with you, Derek."

Derek smiled and stepped forward, a slight limp in his walk. He was wearing his, *I can't adult today*, shirt. "Thank you for asking me first, since I know I'm the most important person here. I just wanted to see how you were doing."

"I'm tired, my side hurts, I'm a little frustrated with certain people at the moment, I'm a little hungry now that I'm thinking about it, and I feel claustrophobic with so many people in here and all of them staring at me." I faked a smile. "Thanks for asking."

Derek clapped his hands together. "Good. Glad to hear it."

"Why are you limping?" I asked him.

"A big, bald man shot me in the leg," Derek said, waving his hand like it was no big deal.

"Oh!" I looked down at his leg, even though I obviously wouldn't see anything since he was wearing pants. "I forgot. Are you doing okay?"

He raised his eyebrows. "You forgot that I'd been shot? Thanks a lot, Emmie. And yes, I'm doing quite well, thank you. Naomi has taken good care of me. She actually remembers critical things that happen to me."

"I'm sorry," I said. "So much has happened in the past couple of days. But I'm glad you're well and that you have Naomi."

"Me, too. I'll leave you now. Goodbye, sweet sister of mine." Since I was still in Eric's arms, Derek raised his hand up for me to high-five. After I slapped his hand, he left the room.

I pointed at Tina and Luke. "You two?"

Tina looked at me apologetically. "We just wanted to see how you were doing. I also wanted to see how the conversation went."

"What conversation?" Santiago asked.

"She talked with her mom," Jen said.

"What?" Dante asked. "When?"

"Just a little bit ago." I glanced at Dee and Tina. "Do you mind if I talk to you two later about it?" I motioned to Luke and Will. "I'm sure Tina and Dee will relay everything I say to you."

Tina smiled. "That's true."

Luke shrugged. "Sounds good to me."

Taking Tina by the hand, they left the room. Dee and Will both smiled at me and then followed them out.

I looked at Jen. "I'm sure you already talked to my mom."

She nodded. "Yes. She hadn't made up her mind yet, though, when we spoke a few minutes ago. I'll keep you updated." She forced a smile and left the room.

That just left my fellow revolutionaries and Joshua all staring at me. Joshua shifted uncomfortably where he stood. He cleared his throat and looked at me. "We can talk later."

He was about to walk out of the room, but Dante put his hand on his arm. "Stay for a minute."

Joshua looked at me and then back at Dante. "I don't think I need to be here right now."

Slamming the door shut, Dante folded his arms. "You need to explain yourself."

"He already has, Dante," I said.

Joshua looked surprised that I had defended him. I still hadn't decided how I felt about the whole situation, but I was in a foul mood and Dante was starting to piss me off.

"He betrayed us!" Dante yelled.

Joshua's face was red. "I didn't! I never meant to cause harm to any of you or New Haven, I promise!" He turned to me. "Emmie, I swear on my life that I didn't mean for any of this to happen. I didn't know Austin was bad. I trusted him just like you did. I haven't told him anything that would hurt us."

Dante shoved Joshua hard in the chest. "You could be lying."

Joshua shoved him back. "I'm not lying! Do the lie detector test on me if you don't believe me."

Taking Joshua by the shirt, Dante threw him up against the wall. "How do we know you haven't been trained to make lies look like truths! Your father was President Randall! He was a monster!"

"Dante!" I tried to stand, but Eric stopped me. He stood up himself, went over to Dante, and pulled him off Joshua.

Joshua straightened out his shirt, his chest heaving in and out from anger. "I'm not like my father! I was never trained to deceive! I would never, ever hurt Emmie. She's my only family! I love her!"

Dante pushed Eric away and went at Joshua again. He took a swing, but Joshua ducked out of the way. Santiago stepped between Dante and Joshua, holding his hand up to stop Dante from coming forward again.

Taking Dante by the arms, Eric pulled him away. Dante turned to Eric, pulled his arm back, and punched him in the face.

"Dante!" I screamed. I got out of the bed way to fast, falling onto my knees. Eric, Dante, and Joshua all rushed to my side. There were way too many hands grabbing at me, trying to help me.

"Stop!" The sudden outburst from Maya froze everyone in their tracks. "Stop it right now. You're acting like a bunch of little boys."

Santiago pulled Dante away from me. "Let's go outside, Dante."

Dante shrugged him off. "No. I'm not leaving."

"Yes, you are," Maya said, stepping up to him. She slapped him hard across the face. "I don't know what's gotten into you, but you need to go sort it out." Dante opened his mouth to say something, so Maya slapped him again. "Out. Now."

Santiago took Dante by the arm and yanked him out of the room.

Maya looked down at Eric and Joshua, who were both still down on the floor with me. "Both of you out, too."

"What?" Eric clenched his hands into fists. "Why should I leave? I've done nothing wrong."

Maya bent down and helped me onto my feet and back onto the bed. "You've upset Emmie."

Tears fell down my cheeks. I shook from the pain of my injury, but also my emotions. Everything that had just happened completely confused me.

"You've done enough for now," Maya said to Eric and Joshua. "Emmie needs to rest. In case you've forgotten, she got stabbed yesterday and almost had her life taken away. It's getting late. She should have been asleep hours ago."

Joshua swallowed. "I'm truly sorry, Emmie. I cannot apologize enough, and I know I'll never be able to make it up to you, but I want you to know that I support you. Not Austin. I didn't know he had turned." He came up to me, even though Maya glared at him. He took my hand. "I love you. You've been the best sister and friend a guy could ask for. I hope one day you'll be able to believe and forgive me." He squeezed my hand and left the room.

Maya looked at Eric. "You have one minute and then you aren't allowed back in here until tomorrow. Tell everyone else that applies to them, too. I'll be standing guard outside her room tonight, so don't even think about trying to sneak back in here." She went to the door and turned her back to give us some privacy.

Eric stared at her with wide eyes and then finally came to my side. He took my hand in his. "I'm sorry, Emmie. I didn't mean to upset you." He wiped a few tears from my eyes.

"You didn't," I said. "It was Dante and Joshua. I'm so confused about Joshua right now. And I have no idea what's going on with Dante."

Sighing, Eric sat down in the chair. "I do. It's obvious. But first, let me say that I know everything with Joshua is confusing. I didn't know what to think at first, but I think he's telling the truth, Emmie. I believe we can trust him."

"That's what my gut is telling me." My laugh was strained. "But I trusted my gut with Austin and look how that turned out."

"But you never had a chance to talk with Austin in person. It's a lot easier to lie to someone over a communication device. There's a chance we could have caught on if we saw his face when he talked."

I nodded. "That's true. I do love Joshua. I've come to accept him as a brother, and I don't want to lose him."

"You won't." Eric glanced over his shoulder at Maya, but she was still giving us time. "Emmie, as for Dante …"

"He's been so ornery lately," I said. "But mostly with you, it seems. Did you do something to make him mad?"

Eric let out a laugh. "Yes. I loved you, proposed to you, and made you unavailable."

I shook my head. "I don't understand."

"He loves you, Emmie."

"I know. All of us revolutionaries have come to love each other. We're a family."

He held up a finger. "Let me rephrase that. He's *in love* with you."

"No." It wasn't possible, right? We were just friends. "He doesn't love me like that. He loves Whitney."

"Oh, I don't doubt he loves Whitney. But he has come to love you more than just as a friend. I don't think he meant for it to happen, but it did. He's confused."

"How long have you known?"

He shrugged. "It's progressed over the last few months. I think he tried to deny it for a while, but finally realized it himself not too long ago."

"That's just crazy. I can't believe it."

"Believe it." Maya turned around. "Sorry to interrupt, but it's true. Santiago and I noticed it, too."

"Does everyone know?" I asked.

Maya stole a glance at Eric and then shifted her gaze back to me. "I'm sure some have noticed. But don't worry about it,

Emmie. He'll get over it. Just give him time and some space."

"I should talk to him," I said.

Eric shook his head. "I don't think that's a good idea right now. Maya's right. Give him some space to sort it out."

I stared at my lap. "I don't want to lose him as a friend."

Eric took my chin and lifted my face to his. "You won't. He loves you enough to want to keep your friendship."

"Did it hurt?" I ran my hand over his cheek where Dante had hit him. There was a big red mark that was sure to become a bruise.

"Nothing I can't handle." Eric leaned in and kissed me. "You're worth it. I'd fight to the death for you."

I gasped. "Don't say that!"

He smiled at me. "It's just a saying, Emmie. Dante and I aren't going to duel it out. No one would let that happen. You saw how quickly Santiago and Maya broke this up."

I rested my forehead against his. "You know I love you more than anything in this world, right?"

"I know." His voice was a whisper. "And I love you even more than that." He kissed me again, holding his lips softly against mine. He finally pulled away and stood when Maya cleared her throat. "I love you. Sleep well and I'll see you in the morning."

"Okay," I said. "I love you."

When he left, Maya came over to me. "Sorry, but you need some privacy and there was too much bad energy in here."

"I'm glad you did it. I'm tired and just want to sleep."

"Then I'll leave you alone." Maya twisted the charm bracelets on her wrist. "I'll be right outside, so holler if you need anything."

She left me alone in the room, with just my thoughts and my mom's communication device burning a hole in my pocket. Reaching my hand into my pocket, I turned it back on just in case she tried to contact me.

Twenty minutes later, my mind still hadn't shut itself down. I closed my eyes and sighed, wanting more than anything to just sleep.

A voice came out from the communication device, so I pulled it out of my pocket.

"Emmie?" It was my mom.

I pulled it up to my lips and pressed the button. "Yes?"

"I'll agree to your terms, but under one condition."

"Name it."

"I want to be involved in the process, along with my two top security guys. We get to have a say in all the planning and will be there for every meeting and decision made. We have thousands of our people to think about and we can't just hand over everything to you not knowing if their needs are being met."

The thought of working with my mom made my stomach uneasy. I didn't know if I would be able to handle it, but I didn't have a choice. We needed to get in there so we could end Austin for good. I also shouldn't have made any arrangements without talking to my fellow revolutionaries, but I was too tired and seeing Dante right now probably wasn't a good idea.

So, I made the choice on my own. "Deal."

CHAPTER 25

Not long after I finished talking with my mom, I drifted off into the land of sleep. I would have enjoyed the rest if it hadn't been for all the dreams. Most of them I forgot right after I woke, but there were a few that stuck with me.

There was one where my mom, Whit, and I were living together. We had a beautiful, spacious home, with a white picket fence and porch that wrapped around the house. Cherry trees surrounded our home for miles, filling the air with their scent. We sat out on the porch, laughing and talking while the sun set. Whit kept throwing a ball out into the orchard and our golden retriever would run after it and bring it back to him. We acted like a real family without a care in the world.

I woke from that dream screaming.

In another dream, Eric and Dante had their chance to duel it out. Our friends circled them and cheered them on as they battled with swords. Everyone placed bets on who would win, like it was a game. In the end, Dante ended up driving his sword through Eric's stomach. I ran to him, falling on the ground, and taking him into my arms. My tears fell onto his face as I watched him die.

I woke from that dream with real tears streaming down my cheeks and yelling out Eric's name.

Then there was one where I was in an open field of blue flowers, just like the ones that bloomed in New Haven. Picking one up in my hand, I twirled it around with my fingers. Someone tapped my shoulder and turned around to see my father. I threw my arms around his neck and hugged him tight as he spun me around. When he set me down, Vice President Oliver was behind him. I ran to him and hugged him tight. As soon as I released myself from him, two big arms pulled me into a hug. I didn't have to see the face to know it was Mack. When he pulled back, he gave me a broad smile, one he hardly used when he was alive.

More people started to surround me. President Brown, Vice President Mendes, Javier, Eric's cousin Richie, and my Great Grandma Mae. Steven stood far off, watching us hug and reunite. He looked worn and tired. A hand touched my arm and I turned to see a woman I'd never met before, but I instantly knew that it was Eric's mom. She held me close, running her hand over my hair. She smelled like warmth and lilacs. I didn't want to let go.

That dream scared me the most. I woke up shivering, despite the sweat that ran down my face. They were all people that were dead, and I was there with them. They had been waiting for me and were excited at my arrival. I didn't know what the dream meant, but I could only speculate the obvious; I would be joining them soon.

It took me an hour to fall back asleep after that dream. Relief flooded my body when I looked at the clock and saw it was seven in the morning. I couldn't force anymore sleep.

Instead, I just lay there and stared at the painting on the wall that Vivica had painted. It was my favorite painting of hers. It was a field of wildflowers with butterflies scattered about. I played with my butterfly pendant as I soaked in the painting.

There was a small knock on the door, followed by the door opening and Maya peeking her head in. "You awake?"

I turned to her and smiled. "Yes."

"You up for a visitor?" Her hair seemed to be spikier than usual.

"Yes, that would be nice right about now."

A part of me hoped it was Rosie, just so I could see her smiling face and abundance of joy. Thinking of her reminded me she was gone, taken by Amber. The thought of how they treated Eric last year before entered my mind, making me sick to my stomach. I hoped they were humane enough to not treat a little girl the same way.

Maya stepped back and Dee entered the room. She sat down in the chair and took my hand. "I'm glad you're awake. I couldn't sleep anymore, and I wanted to see you, but didn't want to wake you."

Turning onto my side, I sighed. I didn't feel like sitting up just yet. "I had a horrible night, Dee. My dreams sucked. Some were more like nightmares."

"I'm sorry." She rubbed my hand. "I used to have bad dreams when I was sick last year."

"Do you still have them?" I didn't want these dreams to last.

Dee shook her head. "No, thank goodness. I think it might have been all the drugs in my system."

"I hope it's just that." I thought of my dream with Eric and Dante. "Have you seen Eric or Dante this morning?"

"Nope. Besides Maya, most of the city is still sleeping. Lazy people." She smiled and patted my hand. "As for your pain, how are you feeling this morning?"

"My side is still tender, but I'm much better." I touched my butterfly pendant. "There wasn't a fight last night after I went to sleep, was there?"

She scratched her head in confusion. "Not that I'm aware of. Were you expecting some sort of rumble?"

Letting go of my pendant, I covered my face with my hands. "Eric told me that Dante was in love with me."

"Wait a minute." Dee took my hands off my face. "You're just figuring that out? I've known for months. Tina's known for months. Everyone and their grandma have known for months."

"You've never mentioned anything to me," I said, my shoulders slumping.

She sat back in her chair and laughed. "I figured if you wanted to talk about it, you would. Besides, how do you fit that into a casual conversation? 'I'm really looking forward to the spring so I can start holding classes outside, and by the way, how awkward is it that Dante's in love with you?'"

I threw my hands back over my face and groaned. "This can't be happening. I don't need added drama right now."

"I know. But seriously, how awkward is it that Dante's in love with you?"

Removing my hands from my face, I took my pillow and threw it at her. "I should smack you, you know."

Dee hugged my pillow and rested her chin on it. "You wouldn't hurt little ol' me." She sighed and tilted her head. "Oh, what a horrible life you have, Emmie. All these men, swooning over you, willing to die for you. It must be dreadful to be so beautiful."

"Give me back my pillow." I glared at her and until she gave in and handed it back. I set it back on the bed, giving it a little fluff in the process. Resting my head back down on it, I looked at her. "You know, it wasn't awkward before because I obviously didn't pick up on it. But now it will be. How can I look at him now?" I gave her a half-smile. "And you're even more beautiful than I am. So are Tina and Vivica. All three of you have men swooning for you."

She took my hand. "I just wish my swooning man would propose already. I'm dying over here! It's agonizing. Does he realize what he's putting me through? We've been exclusively dating for a year now. He's told me he loves me. He talks about our future all the time. I know mini Will's and Dee's are in that said future of his."

My smile grew. "Dee, Will is one of the shiest guys we know. Give him a break. He's probably just building up the courage."

"Could you maybe say something to him?" She looked at me eagerly, squeezing my hand. "Like, he'd better propose soon, or I'll beat the crap out of him? Oh, and it better be romantic like Eric's proposal."

"I have no idea how Will could top what Eric did." I twisted my ring, my smile somehow getting even bigger. "It was downright amazing."

She sighed. "I know. He's ruined everything for all the other guys out there in the world."

I was about to say something when my mom's voice came out of the communication device. I took it out of my pocket. "Hey, Mom." Somehow, I was finding it a little bit easier to talk to her each time we talked.

"Hi Emmie," she said. "I wasn't sure if you'd be up this early, but I thought I'd try."

"I couldn't sleep." I finally forced myself to sit up in my bed. Dee moved my pillow up against the wall so I could lean my back on it. I smiled and mouthed, "Thank you."

"Me either," my mom said. "It's hard to sleep when you're under stress."

Lifting the bottom of my shirt, I checked the bandage covering my wound. "Or after you've been stabbed. I don't recommend doing that. It's not as glamorous as it sounds."

My mom's gasp surprised me. I'd forgotten I hadn't told her about that. Whoops. Her voice came out high and shrill. "When did you get stabbed? Who did it?"

I looked over at Dee, but she just shrugged. How much could I tell my mom? I wasn't even sure if I fully trusted her yet. "Um, it happened just the other day at Kingsland."

"Are you alright?" She sounded concerned and panicked.

"I should live. I just need to take it easy. I lost a lot of blood."

"Oh, Emmie," she said. "I wish I could be there with you right now. But, hey, you'll be leaving to come here soon, right? We're set up in the medical trade school building, so we'll have everything you'll need."

Dee looked at me, shocked. "You're going back to River Springs?"

"Is that Dee?" my mom asked.

"Yes," Dee said. "Hi, Mrs. Woodard." She flinched after she said the name.

"Please call me Janice." My mom sounded amused.

"Sorry about that," Dee said. "I wasn't sure what to call you. That came out faster than I'd wanted it too."

I was surprised by Dee's candor, but my mom just laughed. Dee had always been an honest person.

I looked at Dee. "I haven't talked with anyone about it, but I agreed to go help my mom out in River Springs."

"You mentioned Kingsland," my mom said. "Why were you there?"

"Uh …" I bit my lip, trying to decide what to tell her. "They needed some help, too."

"Did they send some people over to River Springs why you were there?" my mom asked.

I thought about President Coleman, Brandon, and all the others who escaped. "No, but some people ran away while we were there."

"Anyone of importance?" my mom asked.

"Their president," Dee said.

"That makes sense now," my mom said. "There were about twenty to thirty people who snuck into Austin's territory the other day. My security said one looked like someone important. They could tell by the way he was guarded."

"That's probably President Coleman." I shook my head. "But why did he go there?"

"I'm thinking he and Austin have formed an alliance." My mom swore, making Dee smile. "This can't be good. How big is Kingsland?"

"Pretty big," I said. "But they're split right now. More than half support New Haven."

My mom let out a little sigh of relief. "That's good. The more people on our side, the better. Em, I think you need to get here as soon as you can. They may be already planning something."

"Let me talk with my people here and get back to you. I haven't even told them what I've agreed to."

"What did you agree to?" Dante's sudden voice at the door startled me. By the way Dee jumped out of her chair, she was surprised, too.

"Uh, Mom, I'll get back to you." I put the communication device down next to me.

"Okay, talk to you soon," my mom said.

Dante cautiously approached the bed. "What did you agree to?"

I looked past him at the door, hoping to see Maya, but she was nowhere to be seen. Dee started to get up, but I yanked her back into her seat. I gave her a look that hopefully said, 'Please don't leave me here alone with Dante because I think it'll be too awkward and it's too early in the morning to deal with it.' Or something along those lines.

"Dee, could you leave us alone for a minute?" Dante asked.

"Uh …" Dee's gaze darted back and forth between me and Dante. She was probably deciding which look outweighed the other. Mine was a desperate, pleading one, and Dante's was one of, *get out of here now and I won't hurt you.*

Dante's eyes softened. "Please?"

She started to give in. I held onto her arm tightly. "She doesn't need to leave. Whatever you have to say to me you can say in front of her."

Dante looked at me, his eyes now pained. "I'm not sure about that."

Dee turned to me, mouthed, "*I'm sorry,*" and left me alone in the room with Dante.

I played with my butterfly pendant, twisting it so hard that I worried it might snap off.

He stood there for a minute, shifting back and forth on his heels, staring at me. I had the answer to Dee's question; I'd never felt so awkward in my life.

In one swift movement, he was sitting in the chair, holding my hand, leaning in close, and tears falling down his cheeks. "Em, I …"

"What's going on in here?" Eric stood at the door, a look of fury on his face.

Dante immediately stood, took a few wide strides away from me, turned his back to Eric and wiped his eyes and cheeks. He sniffled a few times, bouncing up and down just like he did before a boxing match.

I sighed in relief and reached my hand out for Eric. He

came to my side, taking a seat in the chair and grabbing my hand.

He brushed my cheek. "Are you okay?"

Slowly shaking my head, I opened my mouth to speak, but Maya and Santiago entered the room. Santiago looked back and forth between me and Dante. He cracked his knuckles. "Is everything good in here? It's never too early for a smackdown."

Eric glared at Dante, who still had his back to us.

I squeezed Eric's hand. "We're fine. I was just about to ask Eric to help me get up."

"No, Emmie," Eric said. "You need to stay in bed and rest."

"Well, I have to use the restroom at some point," I said with my eyebrows raised. "I'm not going to wear diapers."

Santiago laughed. "You sure? Because that would be awesome. Little Emmie in diapers."

I rolled my eyes at him but still smiled. The tension in the room needed a break. Eric helped me to my feet. I was perfectly fine standing on my own, but I leaned into him anyway. He put his arms around me, gently hugging me.

Clearing my throat, I threw the words out of my mouth so fast I could barely understand myself. "But then I need to go back to my place so I can pack because we're leaving today for River Springs. Okay? Great. Let's go."

Dante turned around and faced me. "What? Why are we going to River Springs?"

Sighing, I let go of Eric and plopped myself down on the bed. I grimaced at the pain from moving too fast. "My mom needs our help to take over Austin's part of the city."

"And you said yes without talking to us?" Dante asked.

"I was tired and all of you had already left when I talked to her," I said. "Besides, I only said I'd do it if she handed over her part of the city to New Haven. She agreed to the terms as long as she and her two closest security guys could be part of the planning."

Smiling, Santiago let out a whistle. "Wait, we have control of half of River Springs now? Sweet." He raised his hand for me to high five, which I happily did.

"Are you sure you should go, Emmie?" Maya asked. "I don't know if that would be good for your injury."

I shrugged. "It's probably not the best idea, but they're set up in the medical building, so there will be supplies. I don't have to go outside; I could just be behind the scenes making the plans." I looked at Dante, who was visibly upset. "My mom said President Coleman showed up. He and about twenty to thirty others went into Austin's territory."

Dante's face switched to confusion. "They're working with Austin? That can't be good."

"No, it can't," I said, shaking my head. "This is why we need to go help them. We can't let Austin get entire control of the city. We have to stop it before that happens."

Eric sat down next to me and took my hand. "You promise you'll stay inside? No top-secret Emmie missions?"

I scrunched my face together. I didn't like the thought of being stuck indoors and not being able to help. But I also didn't like the thought of dying. At the moment, the latter won. "Yes, I'll stay inside. No awesome missions."

Eric turned my chin toward his. "Promise?"

I stared into his blue eyes and I could tell how much he truly cared about me. It would be so much easier if he wasn't so hot. "Promise."

Santiago clapped his hands and rubbed them together. "I'll let my mom know. Let's go pack."

CHAPTER 26

Two hours later, we were sitting in the conference room. The four revolutionaries sat on one side, Terrance, Gideon, Hiro, Tina, and Vivica sat on the other, while President Mendes and Vice President Jennings sat on the ends.

Everyone agreed to let Eric sit in on the meeting. He didn't want to leave my side and I needed him to help me around. Normally I would have just had Dante do it, but things were different. He sat on the other end of the table, avoiding eye contact with me or Eric.

"So, Emmie," President Mendes said, "what exactly did you promise your mom we'll do?" She was sitting on the opposite end next to Dante.

I held on tightly to Eric's hand as I spoke. "Basically, I agreed to send our military to River Springs to help my mom's side fight Austin's. She's handing over control to us, but she and her two security guys will be working with us."

"So, it's not complete control," Terrance said. "It's just combining our two sides."

"Does it make a difference?" Tina asked. "There will be ten of us and only three of them making the decisions. We'll outvote them every time."

"If we all agree," Vivica said. "Some of us may side with them."

Maya sighed. "This isn't about sides. We need to focus on the big picture, which is stopping Austin and making sure New Haven is safe. He's the one that wants to destroy us, not Emmie's mom."

"She's right," Santiago said. "I think we should go and help them out. Let's put an end to our war with River Springs once and for all."

Gideon sat forward in his chair and looked at me. "When does she need us there?"

"As soon as possible," I said. His face turned somber after the words left my mouth. His wife had given birth to their first child only three days before. He already had to go on one mission and now I was making him go on another. "She's already sent some buses to come get us."

Dante swore and slammed his fist down on the table. "They're already coming to get us? You can't just make decisions without us, Emelia!"

I turned to him, my jaw dropped. Dante had always sided with me in the past because we'd always seen eye to eye. His words stung. I had to blink back my tears. "Dante, it's my mom. She made the decision on her own without asking. That's how she is."

He finally turned at looked at me. "And you want to team up with this woman? If she's going to make her own decisions, then what's the point of going there? She won't hand over control. She's using you and you're too blind to notice."

"Stop talking," Eric said. He had his hand that wasn't holding mine curled tightly into a fist. His knuckles had turned white.

Dante stood, the motion sliding his chair far back. "Don't tell me what to do."

Maya grabbed my other hand, a mix of comfort and protection.

Santiago stood, went to get Dante's chair, and shoved it under his legs so they buckled, and he was forced to sit back down. He clamped his hand onto Dante's shoulder. "Easy, man. Just chill."

Vivica glared at her brother. After a few deep breaths, she turned and looked at me. "I talked with Marcus before this meeting since someone put his ornery pants on this morning. He's willing to help us out. He'll send some of his men to help your mom's territory in River Springs if we want."

"That's good," Terrance said. "We can use all the help we can get."

"With Kingsland, plus half of River Springs, and New Haven, we'll outnumber them," Maya said.

"Then this shouldn't take too long," Vice President Jennings said.

President Mendes nodded in agreement. "In the end, it's the revolutionaries' decision, but you have my support. Take whatever and whomever you need. We'll be fine here until you get back." Her watery eyes looked at Santiago. "Bring my baby home to me." The thought of Rosie made me realize how necessary the trip was. Even if it wasn't to help my mom, we had a rescue mission we needed to carry out.

The president and vice president both left, leaving only military personnel in the room. Terrance nodded at me. "You have our support, too. Just say the word and we'll get going."

I looked down the table at Maya, Santiago, and Dante. Maya and Santiago were both smiling and nodding in agreement. Dante stared straight ahead, still fuming.

I looked over at Terrance. "We're going. The buses should be here in a few hours. Round up all the New Haven warriors, weapons, ammo, and any other supplies you think we'll need. I want everyone and everything outside and ready to go when the buses arrive."

"Would you like us to use our buses, too?" Hiro asked.

"Yes," I said. "There are a lot of us and a lot of supplies we need. The more we can get there at one time, the fewer number of trips we'll have to take."

"We'll get on it," Tina said as she stood. She left the room with Vivica, Terrance, Gideon, and Hiro.

When they were all out of the room, Santiago turned to Eric. "Can you leave us four alone for a few minutes?"

Eric shook his head. "I'm not leaving Emmie."

"It won't be long." Santiago stood and came over to me and Eric. He kept his voice low, running his finger over the cross tattoo behind his ear. "Listen, Eric, I'm on your side. But right now, the tension between the four of us isn't working out. We need to fix it before it gets worse."

I squeezed Eric's hand. "He's right. We can't function like this. The only way we're going to win the war is if the four revolutionaries chosen to do it are getting along and working as one."

Eric glanced at Dante and sighed. "Fine." He placed his hand on my shoulder. "I'll be right outside." He kissed me on the lips and left the room.

Standing, Dante moved toward the door. "There's nothing to talk about."

Santiago put his hand out and stopped him. "You're not leaving until we work this out, Dante. I've had enough."

"So have I," Maya said.

"You can't make me stay here." Dante pushed Santiago, but Santiago easily took control of him and forced him back in his seat.

"Enough!" Santiago yelled. "What's wrong with you, man?"

"It's none of your business!" Dante yelled out.

Maya went to Dante. "It is our business. You keep forgetting that we're all in this together. If you have a problem with Emmie, you have a problem with all of us."

Dante stood to leave again, but Maya took him by the shirt and threw him up against the wall, surprising all of us. She was much tinier than him, but she was strong. "Whatever's pissing you off, you need to let it go, Dante. We're about to go to war with River Springs. If you keep acting like this, you're going to get one or more of us killed. We need your head in the game."

Dante stared at the ceiling, clearly trying to fight back tears. He slammed his fists against the wall behind him. "I need five minutes with Em."

"No," Santiago said. "We're not leaving her alone with

you. You're way too out of control right now."

Dante looked at Santiago. "I'm not going to hurt her, if that's what you're thinking."

"Why should we believe that?" Maya asked. "Look at you! You're a mess and not in your right mind."

Tears fell down Dante's cheeks. "I would never, ever hurt Em. Ever."

"Leave us." I was still sitting in my chair. Both Santiago and Maya looked at me nervously.

"Eric won't allow it," Santiago said. "He'll be in here the second we step out."

"If Maya can stop Dante," I said, "then the two of you can stop Eric. Five minutes."

Santiago let a small smile form on his mouth. "Five minutes." He took Maya by the arm and they left the room.

Dante stayed standing against the wall, the tears still falling. He turned his gaze to the ground.

Putting my hand on the table, I used it to help me up. I walked over to Dante, taking his hand in mine. "Dante, what's going on?"

He wouldn't look up at me. He rubbed his eyes with his free hand. "I'm sorry, Em. I don't know what's come over me. I'm just so confused right now."

"About what?" I had a feeling of where it was going to lead, and it made my stomach queasy. But we needed to air everything out if we intended to still work together.

Dante's eyes finally found mine. "Us."

I swallowed and licked my lips. My mouth felt dry. "What about us?"

"Em." He looked up at the ceiling. "I think I'm in love with you."

I wanted to drop his hand and leave the room. I never thought I'd have this conversation with him. Our friendship had always seemed so stable and sure. I forced myself to stay where I was. "You think?"

He cracked a smile and looked down at me. "Yes, I think. It's so confusing. I can't explain everything I'm feeling. It wasn't until a couple of months ago that the feelings started."

"What kind of feelings?" I asked.

"Different kinds." He sniffed and wiped some tears from his eyes. "I started to get nervous when I was around you. At least I think it was nervousness. My stomach felt unsettled. I get jealous when I see you with Eric."

He let go of my hand, walked over to the table, and rested the palms of his hands against it. "Every time you get sad, or you're having a rough day, you always go to him. I understand why. He's your boyfriend. Fiancé now. But I wanted to be the one you came to. I wanted to be the one who held you and made you feel better." He turned his head to look at me. "Remember that one day a month or so ago when we were out target-shooting and you hit the bull's-eye five times in a row?"

I nodded as the blood rushed to my face. I'd never done it before. I was so excited after it had happened that I ran over to Eric and threw my body on his, wrapping my legs around his waist. Then I kissed him, even though a lot of people were watching. My happiness had gotten away from me. I didn't mind little kisses in public, but I normally left that kind of kissing to when we were alone.

"As I watched the two of you kiss, it all of the sudden hit me that I wanted to be the one you were kissing. I wanted to be Eric at that moment."

My voice was a whisper. "But Whitney."

Dante stood up straight. "Yes, I love Whitney. She'll always have a piece of my heart. But people change. Times change."

"I don't know what to say, Dante." I twisted the ring that Eric had given me only days before. "I'm in love with Eric. I want to marry him. I do love you, Dante, just not like that."

He nodded slowly. "I know, Em. I know you love him and would never leave him. I'm not asking you to do that." He approached me cautiously and took my hand. "This is something I need to work out on my own. Like I said, I'm confused right now. I shouldn't have let my emotions run away from me like that. I'm so sorry. Will you forgive me?"

"Of course, Dante." I smiled at him. "I'll always forgive you, no matter what you do or say. You're one of my best friends and you always will be." I thought of Zoe and how she was in love with him. "You'll find someone else, I know it. You're such a great guy."

"Just not great enough for you." His face was sad again.

"Dante …"

"Sorry. I shouldn't have said that." He pulled me into a hug. "I love you enough that I want to see you happy and I know that Eric's the right guy for you. He treats you well and loves you unconditionally. I couldn't have lost you to a better guy." He let out a small laugh. "Now, if it had been Santiago, then I would have fought for you."

A smile formed on my lips. "I would have asked you to fight for me if it had been Santiago."

"Good to know." He pulled back and looked down at me, brushing some stray hairs out of my face. "Please don't punch me, but there's something I need to do."

I almost opened my mouth to say something, but his lips were on mine in a matter of seconds. I tried to push him away, but he held on tightly. I finally just gave in and let him kiss me, thinking of anything else I could, like butterflies and chocolate and anything that would take me to my happy place. Like Eric. He was my happy place.

Dante pulled back, kept his eyes closed and scrunched his face together, ready for my punch.

I surprised both of us by laughing instead. "I'll let it go this one time since you're obviously having a bad day. But if you ever try that again, I will hurt you."

He stood there, staring at me, his face even more confused than when we had started our conversation.

"What?"

He scratched the back of his head. "I guess I was just expecting more."

My jaw dropped slightly. "Are you saying I'm a bad kisser?"

He put his hand over his mouth and laughed. "Not bad. I just didn't feel the chemistry. It was nothing like when I kissed Whitney."

"Normally, I would be totally offended by that statement," I said, folding my arms. "But since it just means you aren't in love with me like you thought, then you're off the hook."

His laugh started quietly and then got louder as the seconds ticked by. He sat down in a chair, holding his stomach as he laughed.

I glared at him as he laughed and waited for him to stop, but he didn't. He sat there, laughing, fresh tears forming in his eyes, but from happiness instead of sadness.

"Is it really that funny, Dante?"

He snorted, making himself laugh even harder. "Yes!" He wiped some tears away. "What was I thinking?" He looked up at me and snorted again. "I'm worse than Santiago." He took a few breaths, but it didn't stop the laughing. "Which is quite embarrassing."

He stood and took me into his arms, spinning me around a few times. When I yelled out in pain, he immediately put me down and his laughter finally stopped. "Oh! I'm so sorry, Em. I completely forgot you're hurt. Are you okay?"

Eric stormed into the room, pausing when he saw my lips pursed together from the pain, and Dante standing next to me with his hands on my arms, some tears from the laughter still resting on his cheeks.

Dante dropped his hands and looked at Eric. "I owe you an apology." He turned to me. "I owe both of you an apology."

Santiago came into the room, followed by Maya. Santiago folded his arms. "You owe us an apology, too. And a thank you, because it was quite hard to hold Eric back that whole time. The guy's freaking strong."

"What was all that laughter about?" Maya asked. Her gaze went back and forth between Dante and me, trying to read our faces.

I sat down and put my hand on my wound. The pain medication had worn off.

"I just realized what a fool I've been," Dante said.

Santiago laughed. "Hey, we could have told you that a long time ago."

"I'm sorry," Dante said. "I shouldn't have acted as I did. But Em and I talked it out and we're good. Everything will go back to normal. I promise." He held out his hand to Eric. "You're a good man and I'm happy Em has you."

Eric stole a glance at me, his face thoroughly confused.

I smiled at him. "Take it. Everything's fine."

He grabbed Dante's hand, shaking it firmly.

Santiago whistled. "Can I tell you how happy I am now that that's finally over? Now, let's get to work. We have a lot to do before we leave." He slapped Dante on the shoulder and then left the room. Maya and Dante followed him out.

Eric sat down next to me and started to say something, but I threw my arms around his neck and kissed him fiercely, until I was sure Dante's kiss was completely off my lips. Then I kissed him a little bit longer because I enjoyed doing it so much.

When we finally left the conference room, we'd only gone a couple of steps before Samantha called out my name. I turned around and saw her running toward me. "Marie wants to see you for a minute." She came to a stop and eyed my stomach. "How are you feeling?"

"In pain," I said. "I think the medication wore off."

Samantha nodded. "I'm sure it has. I'll give you some more right before we leave."

My eyebrows rose. "We?"

"Of course." She smiled at me. "You shouldn't be going at all, but I know there's no point in arguing with you, so I need to go to keep an eye on you. My father would turn over in his grave if I let something happen to you."

I thought about Austin. There was no way Vice President Oliver would have been happy with his son's choices. I hadn't talked with Samantha about it yet, but news spread fast around New Haven. "Are you sure you want to go?"

A frown formed on her lips. She had the same look of disappointment in her eyes that her father used to get when I did something wrong. "I'm going for you, Emmie, only as your nurse. You will be my only worry and the only thing on my mind when we're there."

"But your brother …" Eric started.

Samantha held up her hand to silence him. "I don't want to talk about him. He has crushed my heart and our mom's. I trust all of you to deal with it properly; I just don't want to be involved in the process. He's still my brother, after all." She looked me in the eyes. "And no matter how foolish our brothers can be, it's almost impossible to stop loving them."

I nodded. I felt the same way about Joshua. "So, Marie wants to see me?"

"Yes," she said. "She's still in her room. Follow me."

When we got to her room, Samantha left us. Eric stayed outside to give us some privacy. I walked into Marie's room and saw her sitting in the chair next to her bed, holding little Mack in her arms.

Marie recently got a haircut, her short brown hair in an A-line.

She smiled when she saw me. "I'm glad to see you're alive." She held out Mack. "Want to hold him?"

"Yes." I took the other chair in the room and slid it next to hers. Taking Mack into my arms, I sat down and leaned back in the chair. He slept peacefully, all snuggled in a blanket. I kissed him on the forehead, the smell of lavender soap filling my nose. "I swear that is one of the greatest scents in the world. Nothing tops that of a freshly washed baby."

Marie smiled. "I know." She touched my arm. "I can't get mad at you right now since you're holding my son." I looked at her in confusion as her face tightened. "In fact, that's why I handed him to you."

"I don't understand," I said, shaking my head. "I brought back Gideon alive and unharmed."

"Yes, you did. Which I thank you for. But that didn't mean that you had to get yourself hurt instead."

I furrowed my eyebrows. "It's not like I asked that guard to stab me. He just did."

Marie's angry look fell off her face. "I know, Emmie. I just wish it hadn't happened. But I'm glad you're alive."

Gideon and Eric both walked into the room. Gideon kissed Mack on the forehead and then kissed Marie on the lips. He sat down on the bed, motioning for Eric to sit next to him.

Marie took Gideon's hand and glanced between me and Eric. "Now that we're all here, Gideon and I have something to ask the two of you."

"What is it?" I asked.

Gideon looked at Marie. "Do you want to be the one to ask, or do you want me to do it?"

"I want to, of course." Marie laughed for a second and then pulled herself together. "Eric, Emmie, well, Gideon and I were wondering … no, we were hoping that the two of you would agree to be Mack's godparents."

My heart swelled. Even though no one had godparents in our old city, I had learned about them from my father.

"Of course, we'll give you time to think it over," Gideon said. "No rush. But we just wanted to throw the idea out there."

Eric and I looked at each other, both of us smiling big. We didn't need time to think about it.

"Yes!" We both shouted it out at the same time.

Gideon laughed. "Good!"

Marie leaned over and looked at her son lying in my arms. "Gideon and I love the two of you dearly and we want you to be involved in Mack's life."

Some tears formed in my eyes. "Thank you so much. We love you, too."

Eric kneeled next to me and Mack, kissing him on the cheek. "And we love this guy even more."

We all sat there in silence, watching Mack sleep, completely unaware of the troubles going on in the world. It was a few minutes of peace that all of us needed.

CHAPTER 27
Austin

Sighing, I rubbed my temples. "This isn't good."

We were sitting in a conference room in Headquarters. Since my office was in disarray, I had our security bring President Coleman, Brandon, and a couple of their guys there instead.

President Coleman sat opposite me at the end of the table. He was sitting up straight, doing his best to make himself seem more important than me. I may have been taller than him, but he was stronger. His hands were clasped together, resting on the table. "No, I'm afraid it's not. They've taken control of my city and I want it back."

"If you think I can help you," I said, sitting back in my chair, "then you're sadly mistaken. In case you haven't noticed, we have our own problem here."

"Then hurry and fix it," Brandon said. He was sitting next

to President Coleman with his arms folded to make his arms look huge, which they were. "Take back your city and then help us."

I adjusted my tie. "It's not as simple as you think. They have about the same amount of people I have. They have the means and the willpower to fight back. I can't just waltz in there and seize control."

"Brandon told me you have a spy in there right now," President Coleman said. "What have you heard from them?"

"She's already gained the trust of Janice," I said. "She's on a mission right now, but I haven't heard from her for two days."

"What's the mission?" Brandon asked.

I tried to keep my cool and hoped my face didn't give away my disappointment. "I'm not sure, but she said it could change the entire outcome of this war."

President Coleman scoffed. "What's the point of a spy if they don't give you valuable information? How do we know if this change will benefit us or them?"

I put my hands under the table so they couldn't see me ball them into fists. My rage was harder to control with each passing day. "Janice thinks it will benefit her, of course, but we have the advantage of knowing ahead of time what their plan is."

"That's if your spy tells you the plan." Brandon shook his head. "Do you know if you can trust this spy?"

"We can." Dean stood near the door. I'd forgotten he was there until he spoke. Apparently, he wasn't the sitting type. "President Randall has used her as a spy before to get information about Emmie. She never let him down."

Brandon looked at Dean but pointed at me. "She was a spy for President Randall, not him. There's a difference."

I needed to change the subject before I exploded. "President, how did they get control of your city? What happened?"

President Coleman shifted uncomfortably in his seat, straightening out his suit coat in the process. "Emmie did a broadcast to our entire city. She told them New Haven had a cure for the disease that's spreading around Kingsland. She bribed them."

"She told them if they rallied against us, she would give them the cure," Brandon said. I could tell it was hard for him to talk about it since he'd lost his sister to the disease.

"Do they really have a cure?" I asked.

"I believe so," President Coleman said. Something passed between him and Brandon that I couldn't pinpoint. Brandon seemed upset with him.

I shook my head in disbelief. I knew they had been trying, but to have the cure was amazing. "Impressive."

"So, Austin," President Coleman said, "how do you plan on winning back control of the other half of your city?"

My mouth turned up into a smile. "Well, simple, really. We need to eliminate the revolutionaries since they are the ones pulling the strings."

Dean didn't hold back his laughter. "I still don't think you can do that."

"I agree with Dean," President Coleman said. "How could you possibly kill the four of them before they kill you?"

I ignored Dean, even though I could feel him staring at me. "We have something of theirs that they will want back."

"What do you have?" Brandon asked.

"A girl," I said.

"A girl?" President Coleman furrowed his eyebrows. "How could a girl be leverage for you?"

Crossing my feet at my ankles, I clasped my hands together. "We took her from New Haven. I know Emmie well enough to know she'll come and get her."

"What does this girl mean to Emmie?" Brandon asked.

"Emmie would sacrifice her life for anyone in New Haven," I said.

President Coleman raised his eyebrows. "Is she really that reckless?"

I nodded. "And then some. She'll come for the girl herself. The revolutionaries will come to try to stop her. I'm sure they're already on their way. Once they get here, we'll set up a meeting so we can try to come to an agreement." I smiled. "Although, we won't because we'll assassinate them before we do. With the revolutionaries gone, New Haven will crumble. We'll be able to seize control."

"That's a mighty big assumption," President Coleman said. "But it's worth a shot. We don't mind helping out."

Brandon sat forward and looked at me. "But I get Dante."

"As long as I get Emmie," I said, "I don't care who kills the rest."

The door opened and Amber stormed in. "*I* want Emmie. *I* want to be the one who kills her."

I stood, letting my anger slip away from me. "Were you

listening at the door?"

Amber shrugged. "Of course. You wouldn't let me in, so I had to take matters in my own hands."

"It's my fault." The young girl walked in, her face completely shameless. "It's a habit of mine. She caught me listening, but when she realized how fun it was, she stayed." She had changed out of her pajamas and into a green dress.

President Coleman looked at the girl and then at me. "Is this the young lady you took from New Haven?"

"Yes." The girl held her broken arm close to her chest. She pointed at Amber with her good hand. "This brat kidnapped me in the middle of the night." She pointed at Dean. "And that oaf let her."

Brandon laughed. "I like her." He stared at her for a moment, tapping his fingers on the table as he did. "You remind me of someone. What's your name?"

She strolled over to an empty seat and sat down. "That's none of your business."

Amber stormed over to me, her hands clenched into fists. "I want to kill Emmie."

I sighed. "Can't you just kill Eric? Won't that be enough?"

"I don't care about Eric." She stomped her foot on the ground. "You promised me Emmie and I want her."

"And who is this delightful young lady?" President Coleman asked, eyeing Amber with obvious disdain.

"She's the oaf's daughter," the girl said. "They're equally annoying." She turned to me. "Speaking of which, you promised to keep them away from me."

"You what?" Amber eyes went wild.

I put my hand on her arm, but she shook it off.

President Coleman glanced at me like I was a child. "Quite the show you're running here, Austin. It seems some of your subordinates need to learn a thing or two about respect."

He was right. I didn't like how Amber and her dad were embarrassing me.

I looked at President Coleman. "If you'd excuse me for a moment." Taking Amber by her arm, I dragged her out of the room. As soon as we were out, I threw her away from me, causing her to fall to the ground. "How dare you talk to me like that in front of President Coleman!"

She scrambled to her feet, brushing off her clothes. "I can talk to you however I want! You forget we're together, Austin."

"Oh, trust me. I could never forget that. You remind me every single day!"

She came up to me so our bodies were touching, her lip turning down into a pout. "What are you trying to say? You don't want to be with me?"

No, I didn't. But I couldn't afford to piss her off. It would just piss off her dad and then he'd run over to help Amy, which would help Janice.

Sighing, I leaned down, putting my hand on the back of her head. "I'm sorry. This is too much stress for me right now. There's so much riding on this war." I ran my finger down her cheek. "And I want to impress President Coleman. We need him to help us out."

She reached her arms up, putting them around my neck. "It's okay. I understand. Just take it easy on me."

I suddenly realized that handing Emmie over to her

wouldn't be a bad idea. Emmie was stronger and smarter. She could kill Amber so I wouldn't have to.

I gently kissed her lips. "You can have Emmie. But let's keep it between us for now."

She smiled at me. "Thanks, and I will." She put her lips back on mine and I let her kiss me until she was finished.

"Hey, babe, I'm kind of hungry." I stroked her cheek. "Do you mind getting me some food? Maybe a sandwich?"

"Of course." She kissed me again. "I'll be back soon."

I watched as she skipped down the hallway. Taking a deep breath, I walked back into the room. Dean glared at me, but I ignored him. "Sorry about that. I think we're all just a little tired."

President Coleman nodded. "That's understandable." He looked at the girl with what he must have thought was a friendly smile, but it was forced. "So, young lady, are you really not going to let us know who you are?"

She yawned, more for show than anything. Her eyes said she wasn't tired. "Of course not. I'm not stupid. I'm the smartest kid my age."

"And how old would that be?" Brandon asked.

I almost told him that it wasn't worth his energy to question her seeing as she would never answer him, but I loved hearing her talk.

"Again," she said, "that's none of your business." She eyed President Coleman. "You were the president of Kingsland?"

President Coleman smiled. "You used the past tense like I'm no longer the president."

She nodded. "Yes, because you aren't. Otherwise, you wouldn't be sitting in that chair. It seems all of you boys have yourself in quite the predicament."

Brandon leaned forward in his seat. She was sitting across the table from him. He tapped his fingers on the table again. "You have any brilliant ideas to get us out of it?"

She raised her eyebrows and laughed. "Yes. Surrender."

"Surrender?" I couldn't believe she'd suggest that. "Why would we do such a thing?"

She looked over at me. "Because, *Austin*, you're going to lose. It's pretty obvious you're outnumbered and outwitted, so you might as well save everyone the time and energy and just surrender."

"You're quite sure of yourself for a nine-year-old," President Coleman said.

"Nice try, *ex*-president," she said, with great emphasis. "I'm not going to let you know how old I am. And, of course, I'm sure of myself. I'm right."

"You're not nine?" Brandon asked.

She rolled her eyes. "I never said that."

"So you are." President Coleman leaned toward her to get a better look at her face.

She leaned toward him, rolling her eyes dramatically. "I never said that, either. Man, you really know how to waste time, don't you?"

"She's right." Everyone turned toward me, including the girl. "We're wasting time. We need to attack the rebels."

"Others from our city should already be on their way," Brandon said. "When they get here, you'll have more people.

They're bringing weapons, too."

The girl laughed. "Yes, let's kill everyone because that will solve everything."

"We need them to surrender," I said. "It won't take long. They don't want to see innocent lives lost."

She raised her eyebrows, tilting her head to the side. "But you do?"

I stood and casually walked over to her. "Of course not. But I need to do what's necessary for the good of my people."

She stood, putting her good hand on her hip. "Then surrender. That's what will help your people. Not having a war is a great way to protect them."

"What should we do instead?" President Coleman asked.

She turned around so she faced him. "Talk it out. Like adults. Sit down with Janice and work out a way to make the leaders and the residents happy. It can't be that difficult. I do it all the time with the kids in my class. If a bunch of …" She stopped herself when she saw President Coleman looking at her expectantly. "… children of various ages can work out a problem by talking it out, then certainly adults can."

Putting my hand on her shoulder, I turned her back toward me. I bent down so I was at eye level with her. "That's what makes children so naïve. Sometimes you can't talk things out, so you need to take action."

"Well, if the world wasn't filled with a bunch of nincompoops like you, then maybe we could talk it out." She sat back down. "I'm starving."

Brandon smiled. "Me, too."

She looked up at me. "It looks like your guests need some

food. Start with that and then you can move on to destroying your part of the city because you can't be rational." She turned to Brandon and pointed to a leather bracelet he had on. "Did you make that?"

He nodded as he took it off. He slid it across the table to her. "Yes, I did. My sister had a matching one."

She picked it up and put it on her wrist, twirling it around. "Did she lose it?"

"No." His voice was quiet. "She died."

She stopped twirling the bracelet and looked up at him. "I've lost a couple of family members, too. It sucks, doesn't it?"

Brandon's mouth turned up into a small smile. "Yes, it does. I miss her every day."

"Well, at least heaven has another angel up there." Taking off the bracelet, she handed it back to Brandon. "You did a good job on this. I bet your sister loved hers."

"She did." He wiped a few tears from his eyes.

I cleared my throat. "I'll get some food sent up and then we can strategize. Every second that passes is valuable."

We needed to attack Janice's rebels and the sooner we did, the better.

CHAPTER 28
Emmie

We arrived at the outskirts of River Springs later that evening. A sense of dread washed over me as we got closer. I wasn't sure how I felt about seeing my mom. Our relationship growing up had been so strained but talking with her seemed like the start of a bridge for the gap between us. I didn't want to get my hopes up in case she let me down again. But the thought of getting my mom back warmed my heart.

I was sitting next to Eric at the front of the bus. I held his hand in mine, our fingers intertwined. Samantha sat across from us so she could keep checking on me every so often. It felt like every ten minutes, but it probably wasn't that much.

Gideon drove our bus since he knew how to operate the thing. They weren't as simple to drive as one would think. He pulled to a stop on the edge of the Lake Precinct. A guard opened the gate and let us in.

As we drove through town, my grip on Eric's hand

tightened. It felt like ages ago when we had been living River Springs, our lives completely free of any problems. Or so it had seemed.

When we pulled up in front of the medical trade school building, my mom was standing outside with two men. Her fifties-style red dress made me realize how much I enjoyed the shirts and pants we wore in New Haven. Although, she did look beautiful in it. At the sight of her, my heart fluttered. I didn't realize I had been holding my breath until Eric nudged me.

"You see that guy to the right of your mom?" he asked.

I stared out the window and noticed a tall, broad man in his late forties. His brown hair was perfectly combed, and he stood straight with his hands clasped together. His suit and tie were sharp on him. He had a kind face, even when he wasn't smiling.

"Yes."

"That's Nick." Eric couldn't hold back his smile. "He took me in after everything that happened with my dad."

"Oh." I turned to Eric, but he was looking out the window at Nick. He rarely talked about his other family, but when he did, it was always positive things. They had loved and cared for him like he was their own son.

Eric waved at Nick who returned the wave with a smile. When the door to the bus opened, Eric helped me stand and walk down the steps.

As soon as my feet hit the ground, my mom was right in front of me. We both stared at each other, uncertain of what to do. There were so many barriers between us that had multiplied as the years went on. Somehow, in just a matter of seconds, those barriers crumbled to the ground.

She took me into her arms, squeezing me so tight it hurt my wound, but I didn't care. We stood there hugging, both crying, relieved to be with each other again. All those years of resentment vanished; they didn't seem to matter anymore. I felt like her little girl again.

Mom pulled back and put her hands on my cheeks. "Oh, my Emmie. I'm so glad to have you here."

"I'm actually glad to be here." I couldn't help but smile.

She laughed a little and then turned to Eric. "I know we haven't been properly introduced, but would a hug be out of order?"

He smiled and took her into his arms. "Of course not. We'll be family soon, after all."

When he pulled back, Mom looked over at me. "Quite the catch you have. Nick here has had nothing but great things to say about Eric and his family."

Nick stepped forward and held out his hand to me. "I'm Nick. It's so nice to finally meet you, Emmie."

I ignored his hand and threw my arms around him. He was the man who had taken care of my Eric when his family had been taken away from him. If it weren't for Nick, I think Eric would have gone off the deep end. "It's nice to meet you, too."

He held me for a moment and then released me. Within seconds, he and Eric were embracing. As they were hugging, another man came forward. He was tall and strong like Nick, but his face wore a sadness that pulled at the heartstrings. He had thick, light brown hair that had a natural rumple to it. He pulled it off well.

"Oh, Emmie," Mom said. "This is Sean. Sean, this is my daughter Emmie."

He held out his hand and I shook it. "It's nice to meet you, Sean."

He smiled at me, but it didn't touch his eyes. "It's nice to meet you, too. Your mom talks about you all the time."

My eyes widened. "Good things, I hope."

He smiled again, only that time it did touch his eyes. "Yes, of course. She's so excited to have you here."

Someone cleared their throat at the steps of the bus. I turned around and saw Derek standing there, looking hopefully at our mother. We hadn't planned on him coming, but he insisted that we needed a technical guru who knew the ins and outs of River Springs. I knew he secretly wanted to see our mom as well, but he'd never admit it.

Mom threw her hands over her mouth and laughed. "Have you gotten taller?" She walked up to him, putting her hands on his arms. "And stronger? My goodness, look at you!"

Derek beamed and jumped off the bus. Mom pulled him into a hug and started crying again. He looked at me as they hugged, his eyes excited.

Naomi came down the steps and stopped beside Derek. When she found out he was coming, she insisted on going as well.

Derek pulled back and pointed at Naomi. "Mom, this is my girlfriend, Naomi." His eyes were still lit up. It was the same giddy look he used to get when we were kids and we would sneak candy from Vice President Oliver's office.

Mom's eyebrows shot up. "How on earth did you get a gorgeous girl like this?"

Naomi blushed as Derek shook his head. "I have no idea. I keep thinking it's a dream, but she keeps showing up every day, still looking happy to see me."

"I'm always happy to see you," Naomi said, giving him a shove. She held out her hand to Mom. "It's lovely to meet you."

Mom shook her hand. "And you as well." She looked over at Eric who was standing with his arm around me. "I must insist you both call me Janice. It's easier that way."

"Yes, it is!" Dee squeezed through Derek and Naomi and smiled at Mom. "Hello, Janice." She looked at me. "I'm sensing everything's okay now between you two so I'm good to hug her?"

I laughed. "Yes, Dee, hug away."

She squealed and threw her arms around Mom. After that, the introductions seemed to go on for hours. When I finally felt sure we'd introduced my mom, Nick, and Sean to all the right people, we went inside the building.

Mom led us to her office on the third floor. Nick and Sean went to get more chairs to accommodate everyone. Samantha had me sit in a chair near Mom's desk. She lifted the bottom of my shirt and peeled back a bandage covering my wound. The skin surrounding the cut was irritated.

"Is it supposed to be red and puffy like that?" Mom kneeled beside Samantha so she could get a good look herself.

Samantha gave her a small smile. "It's just from the

bandage rubbing up against her skin during the trip." Her eyes found their way to Gideon.

Gideon held up his hands. "I can't control the road conditions. They haven't been kept up in years."

"It's okay, Gideon," I said. "I'm fine. Oh!" A cold liquid touched my skin making me bite down on my tongue.

"Sorry." Samantha looked at me sheepishly. "I probably should've warned you about that. Just cleaning it up."

Nick and Sean came back into the room with folding chairs. Eric and Dante helped set them around the room, forming a circle in the middle. I only counted eight chairs, but there were a lot more people than that in the room.

Mom must have seen my expression. She put her hand on my knee. "I would like to have a private meeting. Just your leaders and ours."

Dante nodded at me, so I nodded at Mom. "Sure."

Samantha put the bandage back over my stitches and then handed me some pills for the pain. "I'll need to check on it in an hour." She looked over at Mom. "I hope that won't be a problem."

"Not at all," Mom said. "Just knock at the door and we'll let you in." She handed me a bottle of water so I could take my pills.

After I swallowed them, I stood and walked over to Dante, Maya, and Santiago.

I glanced at everyone else in the room. "If you don't mind, the four of us, plus my mom, Sean, and Nick are going to have a meeting."

"And us." The voice at the door caught my attention. My

eyes widened when I saw it was Amy Randall. Her daughter, Tami, stood next to her. They both wore fifties style dresses, but neither looked as good in them as Mom. Tami's wasn't flattering at all. She looked sloppy.

Joshua stood in the corner near Dee and Will. He tensed when he saw his mom and sister come in. He gave me a panicked look, which I returned. There were so many ways it could go and there was a good chance it wouldn't go well.

Mom put on a smile, but I knew that smile too well. It was the one she always forced when she was extremely upset. "That won't be necessary."

Amy stepped forward. "Yes, it will. Remember our agreement, *Janice*." So much hatred lingered on that last word that I flinched.

For some reason, I had an overwhelming need to defend my mother. "Surely we don't need both of you. Just one should suffice." Tami opened her mouth to speak, but I stepped forward, my voice cutting her off. "We have four from our city. We only need four from yours for this meeting. Three seats are already taken, so only one of you may come. That's our agreement."

Nick and Sean shared a smile. Nick covered his mouth and forced out a fake cough to cover up his laughter. Apparently, they hated the Randall's as much as everyone else in the room did.

Tami glared at me, her face turning red. "How dare you speak to me like that. You have no …"

Amy held up her hand to silence her daughter. When Tami stopped, she put down her hand. "I'll stay. Tami can take the others on a tour of our two precincts."

"That sounds like an excellent idea," Gideon said. He looked expectantly at Tami. "If you'd lead the way, please."

Tami's jaw hung open. She snapped it shut after a few awkward seconds. "Sure. If everyone would follow me, I'd be happy to give you a tour."

Luke stood closest to the door. He shoved Tina out of the room like he couldn't get them out fast enough. Gideon, Will, Dee, and the others followed them. Joshua stood in the corner, frozen in place. Eric went up to him and said something so quiet that no one else could hear.

Tami had gone out of the room but came back in when she realized Eric still hadn't come out. She glanced over at him and for the first time noticed her brother. "You!" She stormed over to him, but Eric stepped between them. She shoved him in the chest. "Get out of my way!"

"No." Eric kept his feet planted where they were. "We aren't going on the tour, so you may leave now and escort everyone else."

"You can't stay in here if I can't!" Tami had her hands on her hip. She had her hair pulled back, but some had escaped, making it look like a mess.

Eric's voice was firm. "I didn't say we were staying in this room. I said we weren't going on the tour. Now leave."

She tried to get past him, but he just held out his arm to stop her. Her strength didn't even compare to his. He hardly moved as she pushed him.

Rolling his eyes, he looked over at me. "This is going to get old fast."

"Enough, Tami." Until then, Amy had been quiet. She just stared at Joshua, her face unreadable.

Tami glanced over Eric's arm at Joshua. "This isn't over. We'll talk later." She stormed out of the room without looking back.

Eric looked at Nick. "Are Carla and Courtney at home?"

"They should be," Nick said, glancing at his watch.

"Good," Eric said. "I think Joshua and I will walk over there so we can catch up." He looked at me. "I have my communicator if you need us."

"Sounds good," I said. "Have fun."

Eric kept in front of Joshua as they walked out, putting a barrier between him and Amy. Once they were out of the room, Nick closed the door and we all sat down, eager to get started.

CHAPTER 29

Sitting in a circle took some getting used to. Usually, there was a desk in front of me where I could hide my bouncing leg or twirling thumbs. I felt fully exposed.

Mom sat on my left. Dante was on my right, followed by Maya, Santiago, Amy, Nick, and Sean. Mom turned to Sean and asked him to get waters for everyone. We waited in silence until he came back and handed them out. I still had the one Mom had given me for the pills, so I declined.

As he sat down, Sean scooted his chair closer to Mom. I looked at them, trying to see if I could get any insight on their relationship but I came up with nothing. Maybe he just didn't like sitting so close to Nick.

"First and foremost," Mom said as she crossed her legs, "I want to thank New Haven for coming to our aide."

Dante glanced sideways at me. "We didn't have much of a choice."

With her eyebrows raised, Mom looked at me. "Did you force everyone to come?"

I shrugged. "No, I just said we were coming, so we came."

"We don't have time for chit chat." Amy's tone was cold, reminding me of her husband Whit. Mom must have noticed my shiver because she stood, went to her desk, and opened a drawer. She pulled out a blanket and brought it over to me, wrapping it around my shoulders.

Santiago rubbed his hands together. "Let's get down to business, then. What do you need us to do?"

"I'm hoping to do this without bloodshed, but I doubt that's possible," Mom said.

"Austin will fight until the end," Nick said. "He won't surrender."

I put my hand over my mouth and sighed. I still couldn't believe Austin was capable of this. His father would never have done something so drastic. "Is he really that bad?"

Sean nodded, his face grave. "Unfortunately, yes."

"He sounds just like Whit." I tugged on the blanket, pulling it tighter around me. Dante scooted his chair closer and put his arm around me. I snuggled into him, grateful for the added warmth and grateful things were back to normal between us.

As I adjusted myself, I noticed an awkward pause hanging in the air. I looked over to see Amy and Mom both staring at me, their faces a mix of shock and anger. At first, I thought it was because Dante was holding me, but then it hit me.

"Oh." I sighed. "Let's just get this out in the open so we can work together. I hate Whit, so I call him Whit. I know my mom loved him, I know Amy had her own weird relationship with him, but I can't stand the man. He's a coward, a traitor, and plain pathetic. He stopped at nothing to get what he wanted. Amy and my mom hate each other. I don't like Amy. I love my mom. I have no idea how Amy feels about me, but judging by the look on her face, she doesn't like me either. Am I correct?"

Amy gawked at me but nodded. Mom shook her head and surprisingly a laugh escaped her mouth. She patted my knee. "I think that sums it up. Anyone else want to add to that?"

There were some shaking of heads and murmured nos. Smiling, Nick winked at me.

Mom kept her hand on my knee as she talked. "Now that the air is cleared, we need a game plan. I have a feeling Austin's going to strike soon."

"Emmie said President Coleman showed up," Dante said, looking at Mom.

Mom nodded. "Yes, just the other day."

"He's ruthless," Dante said. "Not as bad as President Randall, but close. He and Austin working together won't be good for anyone. Whatever you're thinking Austin might do, multiply that by at least two."

"I was afraid of that," Sean said.

"What's your weapon supply like over here?" Santiago asked.

Nick leaned forward and rested his arms on his knees. "We have guns and plenty of ammo. I was able to get my hands on a few grenades, but not much."

"We brought guns," Maya said, fingering the sword pendant on her charm bracelet. "In addition to swords and bows and arrows."

Sean raised his eyebrows. "Different weaponry?"

Maya nodded. "Yes. We used swords in my old city."

"And we used bows and arrows in mine." Dante pulled out our smaller version of the sword. He had it in a scabbard at his side. "We made these beauties, too. Much easier than hauling a regular sword around, but more powerful than a knife."

"Do you mind if I look at that?" Nick asked.

"Sure." Dante released his grip on me and reached his sword out for Nick to take.

Nick looked it over, examining the blade and the hilt. "These are nice."

Sean let out a forced laugh. "Yes, but I sure hope we don't have to get close enough to use them."

"I have a feeling we will," I said. Nick handed the sword back to Dante.

"Me, too." Mom removed her hand from my knee. "I think we'll need to set up our military along the edge that touches Austin's territory."

"Do we wait for them to come to us?" Sean asked. "Or do we go to them?"

"We need to go to them," Santiago said. "We don't have time to waste and the sooner we attack, the better."

Maya nodded. "It would be nice if we could throw them off guard."

I looked at Mom. "Do you think they know we're here?"

"Yes." She glanced at Sean and then Nick. "We have scouts watching their area, so we have to assume they have some watching ours."

"They could already be getting ready," Dante commented.

"We need to drive forward until we can get to Austin and President Coleman," Maya said. "Once they're dead, it will be easier to gain control of the rest of the city."

"What about numbers?" Nick asked.

Dante scratched his chin. "If we can get more buses back here with the New Haven warriors, plus the military personnel Marcus is sending from Kingsland, I think we might outnumber them."

"That's good," Mom said. "We need any advantage we can get."

I looked over at Santiago. "Don't forget we have a side mission."

His face fell. "Yes, we do. And that one we can't fail."

"What are you talking about?" Mom asked.

I turned to her. "They kidnapped Santiago's ten-year-old sister Rosie."

Mom gasped, her face genuinely surprised and concerned. "What? We had no idea. When did that happen?"

"When we were invading Kingsland." Maya eyed the sewing machine pendant on her bracelet. She'd been teaching Rosie how to sew.

"They went to New Haven to kidnap Emmie," Dante said.

Santiago sighed. "But when they realized Emmie wasn't there, they took Rosie."

Mom shot Amy an accusatory look. "You never said anything about them bringing back a little girl with them."

Amy's face twisted, anger lined on every inch. "Our scouts

didn't see a little girl with them."

Standing up abruptly, Mom approached Amy. "How could you not notice a girl with them?"

Amy was quick to her feet, standing inches away from Mom, her fist balled like she was ready to throw a punch. Sean forced himself between the two of them, pushing them away from each other.

He looked at Mom. "We don't have time for this right now. We need to focus on the rescue of Rosie and the upcoming battle."

I did my best to hold back my tears as I looked back and forth between Mom and Amy, my thoughts on an entirely different matter. "The things Whit did to Eric last year and how he killed Vice President Oliver …" I choked on a sob. "They wouldn't do that to a little girl, would they?"

Mom turned to me, her face softening instantly. She knelt in front of me, putting her hand on my knee. "Honey, I'm positive Austin would never do that to a girl. He may be an arrogant, prideful man, but he's not capable of anything that evil."

"Whit was not evil!" Amy yelled out. "He didn't even do those things. He's never killed anyone or hurt anyone!"

I turned to her, my tears now falling. My jaw clenched tight as I spoke. "How dare you defend him. He was evil. Just because he didn't pull the trigger or throw the punches himself, he gave the orders. He watched it happen. I watched him give the order to kill Vice President Oliver! I had to watch him die."

"Emmie …" Mom started.

"No!" I screamed. "I'm not going to sit here and listen to

anyone defend that animal. I don't care how much you loved him." I looked at her. "Do you know what it felt like to see Eric in the condition he was brought back in? He was bruised, broken, and still has scars from the torture he received. It took months for him to recover." I gasped for air. Dante put his arm around me and held me tight. "If Luke hadn't gotten there when he did, Eric would be dead."

"You don't know that." Mom's voice was quiet.

"He couldn't have survived much longer," Dante said. "We all saw him. He's lucky to be alive."

Maya reached over and handed me some tissues. I wiped away some tears and then looked back at Mom. "Do you know what he did to Luke's father?"

Mom slowly shook her head as she sat down in her seat. "I heard he died, but I'm not sure how." It looked like she was telling the truth. It made me wonder how many things Whit did over the years that she had no idea about.

"He told Dean Johnson to kill him," I said.

"No." Amy's voice was barely audible, but I heard it. She was back in her seat, her leg bouncing up and down. I remembered then that she and Dean had been sleeping together. How much had she known about Whit and Dean and the things they were capable of?

"Luke saw it happen," I said. "Whit ordered Dean to kill Carl right in front of his own son. That's why Luke left. That's why Eric's alive." I paused at the realization. "The only good thing that came from Carl's death was that it saved Eric's life."

Nick stood and ran his fingers through his hair. He walked away from the group, sniffling as he rubbed his eyes. All of us watched him, not knowing what to do. There was no one in the room close enough to Nick to be able to console him.

Mom cleared her throat. "Enough talk about Whit. It's obvious he did some horrendous things, but we need everyone focused on the task at hand. We need to stop Austin before he does something crazy. We need to stop him before more lives are ruined and more families are shattered."

"She's right," Sean said. He stood up and walked over to Nick, putting his hand on his shoulder. "Let's start getting all the supplies ready to go and prep our military."

"Emmie," Mom said, "you're staying inside, right?" She glanced at my stomach. "I don't think it's a good idea for you to fight."

"She's staying inside," Dante said. "She already agreed to it. We can have her running communication, sending messages between people and looking over maps for us."

"Speaking of maps." Mom stood and went to her desk. She pulled out a bunch of papers from the top drawer and sat them on the desk. "Emmie, come over here for a minute so we can look over these."

Dante helped me up and together we walked over to Mom. Soon everyone else joined us at the desk.

Mom pointed to the medical trade school building on the map. "This is where we are right now. Austin will most likely be in Headquarters calling the shots."

"Is there any other way of getting there besides taking the streets?" Santiago asked.

Sean shook his head. "Nope. I'm afraid that's the only way."

"We'll be so exposed," Amy said.

"There's no other option," Nick said. He gave me a sympathetic look and half-smile. His eyes were a little red, but he'd stopped crying.

"Then we'll just have to go as fast as we can," Dante said.

Maya looked at Mom. "What about the residents you don't want fighting? Where should we move them?"

"Good question." Mom traced her finger along the map until she stopped at the foot of the mountain in the Mountain Precinct. "Here. It's the farthest away from Austin. There's a trade school building where we can send everyone to."

Mom looked at Nick. "As soon as we leave this room, start the evacuation. We can use New Haven's buses to transport people there."

"We can have Samantha set up downstairs for the injured," Maya said.

"Should they be so close to the edge of the split?" Amy asked.

Maya ran her hand over her spiked hair. "No, but we need to get them checked out as quickly as possible."

I looked at Maya. "Maybe we can have Samantha check them over. Anyone with minor injuries can be treated right away and then sent back out to fight or sent to the building near the mountain with the others."

Dante nodded. "And people with serious injuries she can do her best to slow the problem and then transport them where they can continue to be worked on there."

"Derek and Naomi." I looked over the map. "Where should they set up their technical equipment?"

"Let's move them farther away from here, but not too far," Mom said.

"We can set them up at my house," Nick said. "It's a few blocks from here." He looked at me. "Emmie, you can stay with them there."

"Is everyone okay with these plans?" Santiago asked. Everyone nodded. "Okay, let's head out." We started to move, but he stopped us again. "Oh, prayer. Revolutionaries, let's move it in." He looked at Mom, Nick, Sean, and Amy. "You're welcome to join us if you'd like."

The four of us put our arms around each other. I glanced over at Mom. She had a confused look on her face but came over and put her arm around my waist. Soon Nick and Sean joined us, but Amy stayed back.

Santiago cleared his throat. "Lord, give us the strength to carry out our mission. Help us to keep our eyes clear and focused, our hearts full and open, so we can win this battle for New Haven, River Springs, and Kingsland. Amen."

"Amen," Dante, Maya, and I said at the same time.

Mom, Nick, and Sean threw in a rushed, "Amen," after they heard us say it. Since religion wasn't practiced in River Springs, it was all new to them.

As everyone started to leave, Nick came up to me and put his hand on my shoulder. "Is it true? Did President Randall really do all those things to Eric?"

I nodded. "Yes. It was bad, Nick, really bad. I could barely recognize him."

He blinked back some tears. "That scar on his cheek, is that from Whit?"

"Yes," I said.

"I can't believe it," Nick said. "And he had Vice President Oliver killed right in front of you?"

I nodded again. "I wasn't the only one in the room that had to watch."

He looked down at me. "Did Eric witness it?"

"Yes." I wiped away some tears. "Alexander had to see, too. Plus, some of my friends."

"Emmie …" Whatever he was about to say was cut off by the floor moving under my feet. A loud explosion came from behind us, debris flying everywhere, shaking the entire building. Heat consumed me as I flew back, my head colliding with a chair before I hit the ground.

CHAPTER 30

Someone said my name, but my ears were ringing from the blast, so I didn't know who it was or where it came from. From the burn on my stomach, my stitches had been torn.

Dust clouded the air, making it hard to see in front of me. I crawled toward where I thought the door was. Two hands pulled me up so I was on my feet. Wobbling around and coughing, I looked at where the outer wall should have been, only to see a large hole.

"Rocket." Someone to the right of me said the word, but I didn't know who. I was too busy staring at the debris.

Waving my hand in front of my face to clear the air around me, I tried to take a couple of steps toward the opening to see more but someone held me back. I looked down at the hands holding me and immediately recognized them. Dante was trying to take me out of the room, away from danger.

Giving in, I let him pull me away. Before we stepped completely out of the room, I noticed a body lying on the floor near the hole. My whole body stiffened as I stared at the lifeless form on the ground.

"Dante, look." My mouth felt dry. The heat from the blast crawled down my throat.

"Emmie, we need to leave." His raspy voice echoed through my ears. My gaze settled on his pleading eyes, but I just blinked at him.

I opened my mouth and tried to speak, but my throat felt like it was on fire. I licked my lips and swallowed. "Body."

He looked confused, but when he glanced back in the room, he saw what I was referring to. He let go of me and rushed back in. I stood there and waited for him.

When he came back out, he took hold of my arm and led me down the hall. Maya and Santiago were ahead of us, holding onto Sean. His left leg was covered in dust, blood, and the shredded material of his pants.

Another rocket hit the building, sending me and Dante into the wall. My body started to fall again, but Dante held me up. We continued forward as the building shook and tried to stop our progress. When we finally arrived at the stairs, relief flooded my body. Mom and Nick were both waiting for us to join them.

I looked up at Dante. "Amy?"

He nodded but didn't say anything. Without a word, Mom came to my side and she and Dante helped me down the stairs. Nick stayed right behind us the whole time. Before we started down the last flight of stairs, Samantha came running up, stopping when she saw us. Her eyes darted around frantically until they settled on me. A sense of calm washed over her but instantly vanished when she looked at my shirt. Glancing down, I noticed my shirt was soaked with blood.

"Keep moving," Dante said. "We need to get out of this building before it collapses."

Samantha nodded numbly and went back down the stairs and out the front door. Once outside, chaos consumed us. Residents were coming out of the buildings and homes, looking wild-eyed toward Austin's part of the city. Children were screaming and crying, while parents were demanding to know what was going on.

They rushed toward Mom, bombarding her with questions. She tried to yell over them, but no one would quiet down enough to listen.

Following the resident's gazes, I saw the reason for their concern. Smoke rose from the medical trade school building from the rockets that hit it. Troops from Austin's territory were headed toward us, their guns ready, some already firing.

"Listen up!" Dante yelled out, but it was useless. There was too much panic in the air.

Nick, Mom, Santiago, and Maya tried to push the residents back, away from the oncoming enemy.

Out of the corner of my eye, I saw someone running toward us. When I turned my head, Derek was just a few feet away. He stopped next to us and handed Dante a megaphone. "Use this."

Dante held it to his mouth. "Listen up!" He waited patiently until everyone quieted down. "Children on the buses, now. We'll escort you out of harm's way. Anyone willing to fight, follow them." He pointed to where Nick, Mom,

Santiago, and Maya were standing. "They'll get you weapons." He lowered the megaphone and handed it back to Derek. "Emmie needs help."

"I'm here," Samantha said. "We need to get her away from here."

Dante looked at me. "Do you know where Nick's family lives?"

I shook my head. "Maybe Nick can just tell us …"

"Emmie!" Eric's voice rang out. I searched through the crowd until I saw him. He and Joshua came up to us moments later.

"Eric," Dante said. "Can you show Emmie, Samantha, and Derek the way to Nick's house?"

Eric nodded. "Yes. Follow me." He took my hand and pulled me into his arms. His hand touched my shirt and he pulled it back quickly, noticing the wetness. "What happened?"

"My stitches tore open."

"You need to hurry!" Dante yelled. Shots rang out through the streets. The New Haven warriors that had arrived were already returning fire on Austin's troops.

Sweeping me up into his arms, Eric broke out into a jog. Samantha and Derek kept pace with us as we weaved through the streets. Naomi met us while we were running. Eric stopped in front of a door that looked exactly like mine growing up. All the houses were identical.

Samantha pounded on the door and a minute later, a woman in her late forties opened the door. She was tall and slender and had her brown hair pulled back into a ponytail. Her facial features were sharp and pointy but somehow suited her perfectly. When she saw Eric, she opened the door all the way and motioned for us to come in.

"What's going on out there?" she asked.

"Austin's forces have started their attack on us," Eric responded. "We need a place to set up our technical equipment and also to get Emmie some medical help."

She pointed to the kitchen. "You can set up everything in there."

"Thanks, Carla," Eric said.

Derek and Naomi immediately started setting their stuff up on the kitchen table. Carla pulled out a chair and Eric sat me down on it.

As Samantha started fixing me, I looked over at Carla. "Thank you for letting us invade your home."

"Of course," Carla said. She smiled softly at me. "This wasn't how I hoped we'd meet."

Eric ran his fingers through his hair. "Sorry, my manners got away from me. Carla, this is my fiancée Emmie. Emmie, this is my second mom Carla."

She took my right hand in both of hers, glancing at my ring. "It's beautiful." She turned to Eric. "Just like she is."

"I know." Eric smiled. "She's gorgeous."

Even with everything that was going on and the pain in my side, I blushed. "You're being too nice."

"It's the truth." A teenage girl stepped into the kitchen. She looked around fifteen and was practically identical to her mom. When she smiled at me, though, I immediately saw her father.

"Emmie, this is Courtney." Eric put his arm around her

shoulder. "My overly-nice little sister."

My side stung from Samantha's disinfectant she used, but I still managed a smile. "Hi, Courtney." I looked over at Carla. "It's so nice to finally meet both of you. Eric talks so highly of your family."

Eric knelt in front of me, taking my hand. "I'm sorry to cut this short, but I need to leave."

"I know," I said, squeezing his hand. "Go kick some butt so we can go home."

He leaned in and gently kissed me on the lips. "I love you."

I put my hand on his cheek and stroked it. "I love you."

Giving Carla and Courtney a hug, Eric left us to join the others. Derek and Naomi were still busy setting up their equipment. I had purposely avoided watching what Samantha was doing to me. I didn't want to know the damage.

Samantha stood and looked over at Carla. "Are you two going to stay here?"

"Yes. I would like to help out as much as I can."

"Good." Samantha talked as she piled her supplies back into her bag. "Keep an eye on Emmie. I need to go find and treat others who are wounded, but Emmie needs to lie down and she needs to stay put." She slung her bag over her shoulder. "She's not the greatest at following orders, so you might have to be forceful."

I gave her a fake pout. "I'm not that bad, am I?"

"Yes." Derek and Naomi had said it at the same time, making Courtney laugh.

"We'll take good care of her," Carla said, smiling. "Don't worry."

Samantha put her hand on my shoulder. "I'm serious, Emmie. It ripped open pretty bad. I had to redo the stitches. Take it easy. I'm sure everyone here in the room will agree when I say we want a wedding to attend soon." She squeezed my shoulder and left the home.

Courtney's eyes lit up. "Can we come to your wedding?"

"Courtney!" Carla tsked. "Don't be so rude."

Looking down at the floor, Courtney frowned. "Sorry."

She was standing near enough to me, so I reached out and took Courtney's hand. "Of course, you can come." I glanced over at Naomi who was busily working. "I haven't had much time to plan the wedding since we've been busy and, well, Eric only officially proposed a few days ago. But I've been reading some old traditions they used to have for weddings."

River Springs only offered a simple wedding. It was the bride, the groom, and their immediate families. You sat in a room, the president said a few words, declared you married, stamped the certificate to make it official, and that was it.

Courtney's eyes lit back up and she sat down in a chair next to me, still holding onto my hand. "What did you find?"

Talking about my wedding during an attack seemed incredibly silly, but it distracted me, which was what I needed. "I've found out a lot. They used to have extravagant weddings before the separation of the cities. All your friends and family would come to see you get married. People got married in churches, at the beach, in backyards. You could get married anywhere you wanted. Decorations were set up and after the ceremony, everyone would get together to eat and dance."

"That sounds amazing!" Courtney said. Carla had taken a

seat on the other side of me.

"Where are you thinking about getting married?" Naomi asked. She was looking at her computer screen, but still listening to the conversation.

"At the park near the school in New Haven." I looked at Courtney. "It's a beautiful area right up against the mountain. During the spring and summer, the grass is green, and these small, blue flowers line the area."

"How romantic." Courtney sighed making all of us laugh a little.

"Eric and I will be up front while our friends and family sit on chairs and watch the ceremony. We're not sure yet who's going to marry us." I adjusted myself on the chair, so I was more comfortable. "They have what they call groomsmen and bridesmaids. The bridesmaids all wear matching dresses and stand near the bride, all of them holding flowers. The groomsmen stand near the groom and have matching suits."

"What, no flowers for the guys?" Derek asked with a smirk.

I rolled my eyes at him. "Actually, they pin little flowers to their suit right near the heart." I looked back at Courtney. "Anyway, I was hoping that you and Naomi will agree to be my bridesmaids."

Courtney put her hand over her mouth and gasped. I glanced over at Naomi, who had stopped working and just stared at me.

"Are you serious?" Courtney asked.

I smiled at her. "Of course. Eric considers you his sister, which means you'll be my sister, too." I looked at Naomi. "And

I consider you a sister already."

Naomi shuffled some papers around in front of her. She wasn't one for showing emotion, but I could see her holding back the tears.

She finally gave up and came to me, putting her arms around my neck. "Thank you. I consider you a sister, too."

Derek froze where he was and watched us hug. When Naomi pulled back, he looked back and forth between us. "So, if you two consider yourselves sisters, does that mean …" He gulped. "I mean, Naomi, you and I …" The color drained from his face. "Are we getting married or something?" When Naomi widened her eyes at him, he cleared his throat. "I mean, I want to one day. And, well, I love you and all …"

Naomi's jaw dropped. "Did you just say you love me?"

"Wait." I looked over at Derek. "You've never told Naomi that you love her?"

He shook his head. "I've wanted to for so long, I just didn't know how."

My eyebrows rose. "And this was your ideal setting to tell her?"

"No!" The color rushed back to his cheeks. Naomi went and sat back down in her chair, staring at her computer. Fear and panic swept over Derek's face. He looked over at me and mouthed, "*Help me.*"

I motioned for him to take her hand. It took him a while to understand, but he finally reached out and took it. Naomi still stared at the screen.

Carla cleared her throat. "Courtney, why don't you and I help Emmie to the family room so she can lie down on the couch?"

I didn't want to leave, but I let them take me away. Luckily, I could still see them from the couch. Carla started to say something, but I shushed her. Courtney sat down on the floor near me and we both stared into the kitchen. I had to strain my ears, but I could hear the words.

"I didn't mean for it to come out like that," Derek said. He put his hand on Naomi's chin and turned her face toward him. "Naomi, you're the best thing that's ever happened to me. Beautiful girls like you aren't supposed to like guys like me." He wiped some sweat from his brow. "Naomi, I love you. Very much so. I want to marry you. I really do. I think our kids would be so cool." He closed his eyes and I could tell he was cursing himself for that last sentence.

Carla let out a laugh, making Courtney and I turn toward her. She just shrugged as she whispered, "Sorry, but this is some good stuff."

We turned back to Derek and Naomi.

"Marry me, Naomi," Derek said. "I promise I'll take care of you and do my best to make you happy."

Throwing her arms around his neck, she kissed him on the lips. Courtney covered her eyes, but I noticed she moved a couple of fingers so she could peer through.

After a minute, I couldn't take it anymore. "Is that a yes?"

Naomi pulled back and laughed. "Yes! It's a definite yes."

Derek threw his arms into the air. "Captain Awesome has done it once again."

I sighed and lay my head down on the arm of the couch. "And there went the whole moment."

Carla went and got me a pillow as Derek and Naomi went

back to work.

A few minutes later, someone knocked on the door. When Carla opened it, Joshua burst into the home. Carla just gaped at him, not knowing what to do.

He was walking toward the kitchen, so I called out to him. "Joshua."

He stopped and spun around, surprise in his eyes. He shook his head back and forth, making his blond hair bounce around. Muttering under his breath, he came and sat down on the floor next to Courtney. He looked upset, so I reached out for his hand, but he swatted my hand away. "They kicked me out."

"What?" I asked.

"Dante and them." Sighing, he ran his fingers through his hair and then took my hand. "They made me leave. Said they couldn't trust me."

I gently squeezed his hand. "Can you blame them?"

Joshua twisted his mouth as he thought. Closing his eyes, he leaned his forehead on our clasped hands. "No. But it still sucks."

"I know, but I could use the company right now." I shook our hands a little. "You forgot your manners, Joshua."

He snapped his head up. "What?"

Courtney snickered and Joshua turned to her, looking at her like he had just noticed her for the first time. He blushed deeply. "Oh, sorry. Uh, I'm Joshua, Emmie's brother."

"Other side of the family," Derek yelled out from the kitchen.

Joshua turned to look at Carla who was sitting on a chair

next to the couch. "Sorry for barging into your home like that."

Carla shrugged. "Don't worry about it. I understand. That's my daughter Courtney. She wasn't here when you and Eric came by earlier."

"Nice to meet you," Joshua said to Courtney. He cleared his throat. "And thanks again for letting me invade your home."

"I'm glad you're here," I said. "We're talking about my wedding. You all need to keep me entertained so I don't go crazy from being cooped up."

Courtney instantly filled the void, going on and on about my wedding. Gunshots and shouting sounded in the distance, but I tried to drown it out by talking more and more. After an hour, my eyes drooped.

I was almost asleep when Derek shouted out my name. "Emmie!"

Moaning, I pried opened my eyes. "What, Derek?"

He came over and handed me a communication device. "It's Austin. He wants to talk to you."

CHAPTER 31
Austin

My attack had surprised them. Dean had reported seeing buses pulling into Janice's territory. My plan to get New Haven here had worked. Planning the attack started immediately; we couldn't waste a single minute of our time.

Once our troops were in position, we fired the rocket launchers at the medical trade school building. Our source had told us that was where Emmie, Janice, and the stupid revolutionaries were having a meeting. I had hoped to kill them all at once, but somehow, they all escaped without any serious injuries.

I had to bring them to me, or at least bring Emmie to me. She was the one I wanted. One of our tech guys was easily able to contact Derek, who happened to be in the same room as Emmie. Everything was finally coming together.

"Hello?" Her voice came through the communication

device. A mixture of weariness and orneriness weaved through her tone.

"Emmie. How nice to hear your voice again." It wasn't, really, but my goal for the moment was politeness. Although, I wasn't sure how long it would last. My patience was wearing thin.

Emmie snorted. "I would say the same thing, but it couldn't be farther from the truth."

"Ouch," I said with a small click of my tongue. "I've missed you, too."

"Austin." She paused before she continued. "Why?"

I thought she would expand upon the question, but she didn't. Shifting myself in my new chair I retrieved from the conference room, I looked out onto the city from my office window. The cracks from my earlier outburst distracted from the otherwise marvelous view. "We don't have time for that right now. There's a battle going on out there, Emmie. Innocent people are dying."

"Then call off your troops." Her voice was flat and slightly irritated.

I held back a smile. "I will once we talk."

"We're talking right now," Emmie said.

"In person." I loosened the tie around my neck.

A few seconds went by. Then a few more. "I can't leave. You'll have to come to me."

"Not possible."

"Then we can't talk in person." Her tone made it sound like she was closing the conversation.

Only I wasn't done talking. "We have something that

belongs to you, Emmie. I know you want her back. Let's trade. You come to me and I'll let her go."

"How can I trust that you'll let her go?"

"You're just going to have to trust me."

Emmie laughed. "Yeah, I made the mistake of doing that before and look how that turned out."

I stood and went to the window. Smoke rose high in the air from where we had hit the medical building. "Emmie, do you know how this all started in the first place?"

"What do you mean?" She sounded intrigued.

"An arrogant teenage girl rebelled against her city. She fled, taking her loved ones with her. She got my dad killed in the process."

Emmie swore, surprising me. "Whit killed your father, Austin, not me."

"But it was your choice that led to the unfortunate event." A small knock at my door made me turn around.

The girl peeked her head into my office. "Can I come in?"

I almost said no, but I figured she might come in handy in my conversation with Emmie. "Sure. Close the door behind you." She came to my desk and sat down in my chair. She held her broken arm close to her as she stared at the window, wide-eyed.

"This isn't worth arguing about, Austin," Emmie said. The girl startled at the sound of Emmie's voice. From the look on her face, she cared deeply about Emmie. Perfect.

"No, it's not." I tore my gaze away from the girl and glanced outside. "Emmie, you started this whether you'll admit it or not. Lives have been forever changed. Some have been taken. I want to end this. We *need* to end this. But you need to come to me. You started it, now you need to finish it."

"I told you I can't come."

I held the communication device out to the girl. "Talk to Emmie."

The girl hesitated but finally took it from my hand. "Hi, Emmie. It's me. Don't say my name. I haven't told these stupid people what it is."

"Are you okay?" Emmie sounded worried. She cared deeply about the girl, too.

"Other than a broken arm and being around the rudest, creepiest people ever, I'm fine." The girl crossed her legs. "How are you?"

There was a smile in Emmie's voice when she responded. "Other than a stab wound and being stuck indoors while everyone else is kicking butt, I'm fine."

"Good," the girl said. "Emmie, don't listen to Austin. He's an idiot, a liar, not that cute, arrogant, stupid …"

I yanked the device away from her. "Emmie, if you want to see this *darling* girl again, come to Headquarters. You have thirty minutes. Otherwise, the next time you'll see her, she'll be dead." Turning off the device, I thrust it into my pants pocket. I shook my head at the girl. "That was foolish of you. You might have just gotten yourself killed."

The girl raised her eyebrows. "You'd kill a little girl? Are you really that evil?"

"I'm not evil."

"Uh, yes you are. You just threatened to kill a young lady. That's pretty evil. You might be worse than President Randall."

I slammed my hand down on the table, making her jump out of her seat. "I'm not like him!" My breathing was fast and ragged. I had to calm myself down; I was losing control.

The girl slowly backed away from me, fear in her eyes. "Well, you definitely have a bad temper, mister."

Before I could respond, the door opened, and Amber came in. For once, I was relieved to see her. "Hey, Amber."

"Hey, babe." Amber rubbed my shoulders. "Are you doing okay?"

"Stressed." I pulled her into my arms. "I'll be much better when this is all over."

Amber rubbed my back, trying to soothe me. "It's almost over. My father just reported that we're winning. Janice's side was completely blindsided by our attack. He said they're frantically trying to pull things together, but it's pure chaos."

"Good," I said with a sigh. I pulled back from Amber, placing my hands on her arms. "Emmie's coming to us. We need to get ready for her."

Amber's eyes lit up. "Finally! Is she bringing others with her?"

I shook my head. "No, she's not with the revolutionaries. She's injured so she's not fighting."

Amber stuck out her lip as the light left her eyes. "It won't be as fun if she's already injured."

"She's tough," I said, rubbing her arms. "You'll have plenty of time with her."

"I better." Amber jumped up and sat on my desk. "What's the plan?"

"When she gets here, we need to pull her into one of the

conference rooms so we can talk."

Amber swung her legs forward and backward as she sat. "Is anyone else going to be in there with us?"

"No," I said, shaking my head. "Just the three of us. We need to get as much information as we can out of her before we kill her, though."

"You're going to kill her?" The little girl's chin quivered. "Why?"

"Because she's a thorn in my side." I walked over to her. "She doesn't obey orders. She's reckless and selfish."

The girl shook her head. "No, she's not. Those are *your* characteristics."

"Well, you're wrong about me," I said. "Emmie's going to get what she deserves."

Amber hopped off the desk. "What if she doesn't come alone?"

"We'll have guards waiting to seize whoever comes through the doors. We'll see them coming." My tie still bothered me, so I took it off and set it down on my desk.

"What about me?" the girl asked. "You're letting me go, right?"

The side of my mouth curled up. "You said yourself that I'm a liar."

The girl backed toward the door, each step slow and deliberate. She held back tears. "What are you going to do with me?"

I shrugged as I walked, taking a step every time she did. "We'll use you to get information out of Emmie if necessary. Listen, I don't want to hurt you. You seem like a nice girl, but

I need to do what's best for my city."

"You wouldn't really kill me, right?" the girl asked.

I didn't have an answer to that question. I didn't relish the thought of killing children, but there were casualties of all ages in war. It was unfortunate but true.

I turned back to Amber. "Let's get downstairs and make sure everyone is in place. I want to be prepared for when she gets here. This is the final move, so we can't screw this up."

"We won't." Amber left the room, leaving me alone with the girl.

I bent down in front of the girl. "There's nothing to fear right now. Just be a good little girl and everything will be fine." I smiled. "Who knows? Maybe I'll be so happy when Emmie's dead that I'll let you go back to your family. Would you like that?'

The girl glared at me. "What I'd like is for you to NOT kill Emmie!"

"I'm sorry, sweetie, but that isn't a possibility." I reached out to touch her arm, but she yanked it away from me.

"Do not touch me and do not call me sweetie! You're a horrible person, Austin! Horrible, horrible, horrible!"

I clenched my teeth to hold in my screams. "One day, when you're older, you'll understand why I've done what I've done. It was all necessary for the good of mankind."

The girl stepped closer to me, the fear in her eyes completely gone. "You're wrong." She huffed. "You know what? Emmie's not going to die. You are. She's smarter, tougher, better looking, and all-around a better person."

Running my hand over my head, I smiled at her. "*Sweetie*,

being a good person won't help you win. Sometimes it can even be a weakness."

"*Sweetie*," the girl said, her voice filled with disdain, "haven't you read all the books? Good always triumphs over evil. Always. You're going to lose and trust me when I say I'll be doing a happy dance when you do!" She turned around and stormed out of the room.

It really would have been so much easier if the girl wasn't so likable. I followed her out and we made our way downstairs. Amber had already begun telling the guards to be on the lookout for Emmie. Once everyone was notified, Amber, the girl, and I stood there near the front door, anxiously waiting for Emmie's arrival.

It couldn't come soon enough.

CHAPTER 32
Emmie

"No." Derek came over to me and crouched down in front of me, making Joshua and Courtney scoot to the sides. "You're not going, Emmie, and that's final."

"Derek …" I started.

Derek turned to Joshua. "Back me up here."

"He's right," Joshua said. "We can't let you go. For multiple reasons. You're hurt, it's probably a trap, and Eric will kill us if we let you leave."

"That's if Dante doesn't kill us first," Derek said.

"Or Santiago," Joshua said.

"Or Maya," Naomi said from the kitchen.

Derek swept his hand out to emphasis his point. "The list could go on and on. Since I'm sure you don't want to be responsible for the death of your questionable half-brother, your awesome half-brother and his fiancée …" He snickered. "… and your soon to be sister and mother-in-law, you just can't go. It's a simple fact."

I sighed. "It's also a simple fact that if I don't go, this battle will continue. Hundreds, if not thousands, of lives will be lost." I looked up at the ceiling, blinking back my tears. "And Rosie. Derek, I couldn't live with myself if something happened to her."

"You don't really think Austin would do something to her?" Courtney asked. I turned to her. She was as pale as a ghost.

"I don't know," I said quietly. "But I can't take that risk." I took Derek's hand. "This is a chance to end this battle and I need to take it. It will get us on the inside."

Derek's hand shook in mine. "He'll kill you."

"Not if I kill him first," I said. "I have to take the chance."

"I'm going with you." Joshua stood.

"No," I said.

Joshua shook his head. "I don't care what you say, I'm going. I know this city inside and out. I can get you there by underground tunnels, so you don't have to go out in the open. They won't be checking the tunnels."

"How do you know that?" Derek asked.

"Not many people even know they exist." Joshua put his hands in his pockets. "When Austin and I were kids, we went exploring all over the city. We found secret passages and mapped them out. We used them so much, I have them all memorized. Besides, Austin doesn't know I'm with you."

Derek scratched his head as he looked at Joshua. "Did you hear the part where I said the 'questionable half-brother'? Yeah, I was referring to you, not me."

Joshua turned to him. "Come on, Derek. You've had a chance to get to know me this past year. I've been open and honest with you. You know that I love Emmie and would never hurt her. You have to believe me."

Derek stared at me, the wheels spinning in his head. He finally sighed. "I believe you, Joshua. I know you would never hurt Emmie. You love her almost as much as I do."

"Almost?" My eyebrows shot up. "You must love me an awful lot, Derek."

Derek rolled his eyes as he stood. "Whatever. You're taking a communication device with you so I can always keep track of you. Just make sure to leave it on so the tracking will work." He went back into the kitchen.

"Are we sure this is a good idea?" Carla asked. "I don't think we should let Emmie go."

"Especially with only Joshua," Courtney said. "You should take others with you." She blushed. "I could go with you."

"No," Carla and I said at the same time.

"It's too dangerous," I said.

Carla looked at me. "Which is exactly why we shouldn't let you go."

I held out my hand and Joshua took it, helping me up. "I have to go, Carla. My life isn't worth that much compared to everyone else here in the city."

"Try telling Eric and Dante that," Naomi said from the kitchen.

The corner of my mouth turned up. "That's why I'm glad they aren't here. They wouldn't think logically."

"Logically," Joshua said, "we need to leave. We're running out of time."

"Hold on just a minute." Courtney left the room and came back with some clothes. She held them out to me as she glanced at my blood-soaked shirt. "You'll probably want some new clothes. This way you won't stand out. They're clean and they're Infinity Corp approved. You'll blend in."

Joshua turned away so Carla and Courtney could help me change. It was nice to have clean clothes on again, but it was weird to be in a blouse and skirt. Courtney also brought me a blue coat, which I was grateful for seeing how cold it was outside.

I ran my fingers along the material, flashbacks to my childhood forming in my mind. I quickly shook them away. I needed to concentrate. "Thanks, Courtney." I hugged her and then her mother. "Thank you, Carla, for your hospitality. When this is all over, I'm looking forward to getting to know your family better."

"We are, too," Courtney said, still smiling.

"We need to go," Joshua said.

Derek came over to me and handed me a communication device. "Keep it on; keep it in your pocket." He hugged me tightly. "Please be safe, Emmie."

"I'll protect her," Joshua said.

"You better," Derek said, releasing me from the hug. "Or I'll kill you."

Joshua nodded. "Good to know." He took my hand and we left the safety and comfort of the home.

When we stepped outside, people were running around in

the streets. Gunshots echoed around us, along with screaming and shouting. For the most part, it seemed like they were finally getting things organized. Everyone looked like they had a sense of purpose and belonging.

Joshua held me close as we rushed down the street. I did my best to ignore the pain in my side and focused on each step and each breath.

As we got closer to the medical trade school building, Joshua slowed our pace until we came to a complete stop just a block away. We were up against another building, waiting for a clear path to the front door of the medical building.

"Why are we coming back here?" I asked, my voice shakier than I wanted it to be.

"We can get to an underground passage from there," Joshua said.

There were dozens of New Haven warriors lined up in the streets. They all seemed to be catching their breath and reloading their weapons. We were out of the line of sight of Austin's troops. People must have been coming here to regroup before they went back out to fight. So, our main worry right now was anyone we knew spotting us and trying to stop us from completing our mission.

I was so focused on the path to the door that I didn't hear the footsteps behind us until they were practically on top of us. The voices were what caught my full attention, though.

"Honestly, why can't you wrap your head around the functions of a gun?" It was Thunder Thighs.

"They're complicated!" Skinny shrieked.

Thunder Thighs grunted. "No, they're not. You fill the

magazine with bullets, you put it in here, point the gun at the enemy and pull the trigger."

"Not all of us are trained like you are, Rachel!" Skinny's voice was shrill and frustrated.

"You've been training as long as I have!" Thunder Thighs yelled.

I turned around, taking them all in. They were facing each other, probably only a couple feet apart, both with a gun in one hand and the other hand clenched tightly into a fist. Skinny's frizzy hair pointed out in all directions and her glasses lay skewed on her nose. Thunder Thighs had her hair pulled back into a ponytail so tight that she had to have had a headache. Their chests heaved in and out from their anger.

I turned back to Joshua. "Remember how Courtney said we needed more people with us?"

Joshua looked wide-eyed behind me at Skinny and Thunder Thighs. "No way, Emmie. You can't do that to me."

"We need help. They'll be a good distraction if you and I need to do something sneaky." I felt around my body and realized that I didn't have any weapons on me. "I need a gun or knife or something."

"Emmie?" Skinny said behind me.

I slowly turned around and smiled. "Hi, Angela." I glanced at Thunder Thighs. "Hi, Rachel."

Thunder Thighs let out an exasperated sigh. "You. Whenever I see you, trouble lurks around."

"Not always," I said. "Speaking of trouble, how would you two like to go on a mission with me and Joshua?"

Skinny shifted her focus to Joshua, trying to smooth out

her wild hair while she gawked at him. She was not the most subtle person. "What do you need us to do?"

"We're going to Headquarters to retrieve something of ours," I said.

"What is it?" Thunder Thighs asked.

I shook my head. "It's not important. But we're in a hurry and it would be nice to have some backup."

Thunder Thighs pointed her thumb at Skinny. "You sure you want her coming? She doesn't even know how to use a gun."

Skinny opened her mouth to protest, but I snatched her handgun away from her and she looked at me surprised. She held her jaw open as she watched me while I checked how many bullets were in it and then tucked the gun in the pocket of Courtney's coat. The outfit was not suitable for war.

I looked at Joshua. "We need two knives. One for me and one for Angela."

He glanced around until his eyes settled on two New Haven warriors walking by. "Hey, I need your knives."

One of them stopped walking. "Why?"

Joshua held out his hand. "I just do. Hand them over."

They both looked at me, waiting for my approval. When I nodded, they pulled them out and handed them to Joshua.

"Thank you," Joshua said. "And please don't tell anyone about this." He handed a knife to me and Skinny. "We need to go." He glanced up and down the street and when he was satisfied, he nodded for us to follow. We kept a close line and walked as quickly as we could to the front door to the medical building.

I kept the knife in my hand as we moved. A knife was a lot less noisy than a gun and we didn't want to risk being caught. But it also meant you had to be close to the source to use it, which I certainly didn't care for.

As soon as we opened the door to the medical building, smoke wafted out. The aftermath of the explosions lingered in the air. Joshua led us down the hall without any hesitation. Making a right at the end of the hall, he led us toward a hatch on the ground. He lifted it, revealing a staircase leading into darkness. I felt my pockets and cursed myself. I'd forgotten to take my supplies out of my pants when I switched to clothes. I always kept a small flashlight with me.

Joshua and Thunder Thighs pulled theirs out of their pockets, giving me at least some relief. Joshua went down first, followed by me, Skinny, and then Thunder Thighs at the rear.

We continued in silence in the underground tunnels. Now and then, we'd hear the fluttering of wings. Skinny shuddered behind me and I knew she was thinking of our challenge we went through during Recruitment. We were going down a pitch-black hallway at the time when we were suddenly attacked by a swarm of bats. It was a memory I'd been trying to forget ever since it happened, but I had a feeling I never would.

After fifteen minutes, Skinny's voice sliced through the air. "How much longer?"

"Not too far," Joshua said. His voice was calm and filled with confidence, which penetrated to me.

"It's freezing down here," Skinny said.

I'd been too busy concentrating on the sounds around me

that I hadn't even noticed the temperature. As soon as she mentioned it, I felt the cold all over me. My nose and fingers were starting to go numb.

I pulled Courtney's coat tighter around me. "Where will this take us?"

"East end of Headquarters," Joshua said. He had let go of my hand back on the streets and I missed the warmth and comfort it brought me. I wanted to reach out and take his hand, but he had his knife in one and the flashlight in the other.

"What are we going to do when we get inside?" I asked.

He was silent for at least thirty seconds. "I'm not sure yet."

Thunder Thighs huffed. "I'm sure glad you all know what you're doing." She let out a long grunt. "I better not die in there. Otherwise, I'm going to be pretty pissed off."

"You'll be dead, so who cares?" Skinny said.

I smiled to myself.

Three minutes of blissful silence lapsed until Joshua came to stop in front of a ladder. He shined his light up to reveal a hatch on the ceiling. "This is it." He went up the ladder first and slowly lifted the hatch so only his eyes could peer through. He waited twenty seconds before he pushed it opened all the way and called down to us. "Come on up. Be quiet."

I went up first, reaching my hand out to Joshua when I got to the top. When my feet hit the floor in Headquarters, I gripped my knife and pointed it in front of me. I really wanted my handgun, but that was back at Nick and Carla's house. I had the handgun from Skinny, but I knew my gun inside and out. It fit the curve of my hand perfectly. But I reminded myself that the knife would be quiet and best if we wanted our presence to remain silent.

After Skinny and Thunder Thighs were through the hatch, Joshua started forward down the empty hallway. He stopped at a T in the hall, turning his head around the corner. "Empty."

Once we rounded the corner, though, it wasn't empty. Dean Johnson walked straight toward us, stopping in the middle of the hall when he saw us.

"I was wondering where everyone was," Joshua said. He walked up to Dean and patted him on the shoulder. "Good to see you. Where's Austin?"

"He's waiting for Emmie at the entrance," Dean said, his eyes full of hatred as he stared at me.

Joshua shrugged. "Oh, we took a different way." Dean moved toward me, but Joshua held out his hand to stop him. "Nice try, Dean. She's my find, not yours. I get to take her to Austin." He ripped the knife from my hand and took the gun from my pocket.

His grip around my arm was tight as he dragged me down the hall. I stared at him, shocked.

When Joshua looked at me, no sorrow sat in his eyes. "Sorry, sis, but always remember one thing: You can never trust a Randall."

CHAPTER 33

Anger boiled over, searing every inch of me. Swinging my free arm around, I whacked Joshua in the face and twisted my body, freeing myself of his grip. I turned my body away, reached into my blouse, and flipped on the communicator I always kept in a secret pocket on the outside of my bra. I'd always hoped I wouldn't have to use it, but Joshua had brought up a great point. Although, it wasn't just Randalls I couldn't trust. It was everyone.

It took only seconds for Joshua and Dean to wrestle me back into their grip, keeping me from doing anything more.

When I'd turned around, Dean held onto Skinny and Thunder Thighs, his grip around their arms so tight I thought they might pop off. Fear sat in their eyes. It was the first time in my life I'd ever seen Thunder Thighs truly scared. I was sure the look on my face doubled theirs. There was still a chance that they could live. Austin and Amber wouldn't let me leave the building alive.

Joshua didn't hold back his smile when we rounded the

corner that led to the entrance of Headquarters. Austin and Amber were both waiting for us near the door.

Joshua released his grip on me when Austin came to him. They embraced in a brotherly hug, patting each other on the back and saying how good it was to see each other again. Amber yanked off my jacket and forced my hands behind me to cuff them. I was completely frozen in place as I watched Joshua and Austin. Two men I'd trusted with all my heart betraying me. Joshua's betrayal was much worse than Austin's. I'd given him two chances and he'd stabbed me in the back. I felt so foolish and naïve.

"How'd you get here?" Austin asked.

"Underground tunnels," Joshua said. "I had to make her trust me."

Austin laughed as he looked at me. "She's always been too trusting."

"She's an idiot," Amber said. "I think we've all known this for years."

"She's not an idiot." Those words coming from Thunder Thighs caught us all off guard. "She's smarter than the four of you morons combined. She's done more good for humankind in just the past year than any of you have done in your pathetic lifetimes."

Skinny nodded toward Thunder Thighs. "Yeah. What she said."

Amber stood close, keeping a firm grip on my arm. Her long fingernails dug into my skin and I had to do my best to keep my mouth closed.

Austin came in front of me, looking down at me with

piercing eyes. When I tore my gaze away from him, he took hold of my chin and pulled my head toward his, making me stand on my tiptoes. Amber helped to push me up.

"I've waited for this day a long time," Austin said. "We have some catching up to do."

I smirked. "Yes, we do. I want to hear all about how you became a lying, selfish, arrogant loser."

He squeezed my chin hard. "You need to be careful with your words, Emelia. You have four people surrounding you who want nothing more than to see you dead."

"And two that don't," I said. Not that it mattered. They were both being detained by Dean and I was pretty sure he'd taken their weapons.

"Three." When I heard Rosie's voice, I tried to turn my head so I could see her, but Austin's grasp on me made it impossible.

"You don't count," Austin said, not moving his eyes away from mine.

Rosie stomped her foot. "I do, too!"

Austin let me go and walked away from us. Amber pulled me along as we walked down a hall and into a holding room. Besides from one chair in the middle of the room, there was nothing else in it.

Amber threw me down in the chair and bound my feet to the front legs of the chair. Before she stepped away from me, she punched me in the jaw. Rosie went to her, pounding her fists on her back and screaming out that she was a brat. Amber responded by pushing Rosie down on the ground, not being the slightest bit gentle.

"Wow, Amber," I said. "Your dad must be proud to see his little girl picking on children." I smiled. "Although, she's closer to your height than anyone else in the room."

That at least made Rosie giggle. She sat next to Skinny and Thunder Thighs, who had been placed on the floor up against a wall. Rosie wasn't restrained, but the other two had their hands and feet bound. Dean stood next to them with his arms folded and his face free of any emotion. It was one of the first times I'd seen him without a smirk or a scowl.

Joshua tapped Austin on the arm. "I have to go see someone. I'll be right back."

"Who do you have to see?" Amber asked.

"A close friend of mine." Joshua winked at me. "You know her. Tiffy. One of the girls you and your friends tried to beat up last year."

I narrowed my eyes at him. "Yes, and if I remember correctly, we did beat them up. Tiffy got a tooth knocked out."

Joshua shrugged. "She got a replacement not long after. Anyway, I told her I'd contact her as soon as I got back."

"Can it wait?" Austin asked.

"Come on," Joshua said. "I've been gone for a year. I think I've waited long enough. I'll be back soon." He wiggled his eyebrows. "Just a brief visit to … catch up."

Austin smirked. "I understand. Ten minutes and then be back in here."

"Thanks." Joshua opened the door but looked back in before he left. "Have fun in here, kids."

When he slammed the door behind him, I tried not to think about how much he'd hurt me. I had more important things to focus on, like getting me, Rosie, Skinny, and Thunder Thighs out of there alive and fully intact.

Austin clasped his hands in front of him as he stood tall. "Now, Emmie, we can do this the easy way, or the hard way. I want to end the battle outside. I want my city back."

"I'm tied up to a chair, Austin," I said. "Not much I can do from here."

He bent down so his eyes were level with mine. "All you need to do is tell your side to surrender. Then this will be over."

"I highly doubt that," I said.

Austin nodded at Amber and she punched me in the face twice. The first landed on my left cheekbone, the other on my nose. I sat up straight, pretending like the blows had no effect, even though they were stinging like no other.

He held out a communication device, putting it right next to my lips. "Tell Derek to send out a message for your side to surrender."

"Never." I clenched my jaw, ready for the hits. They came, one to my left eye, one to the jaw, one to my nose. If my nose broke again, my fury would rain down on them.

"It's a simple sentence. Just say it." Austin pressed the button down.

"Derek?" I said. Surprise crossed over Austin's face, but he let it go just as quick.

"Emmie?" Derek's voice rang through. "What's going on? Are you okay?"

"Wonderful," I said. "I have a message for you."

"Uh, okay …" Derek said.

I stared at Austin as I spoke. "Kill every single person in

Austin's territory."

Four punches that time. One to the lip and one to the jaw from Amber. Dean's punches were the worst. Both in the stomach, both terribly close to my stitches. I struggled to breathe after his hits.

Austin looked at Amber. "What do you think, sweetie? Should we use tools on Emmie? Or do we hurt her friends?"

Amber jumped up and down, squealing. "Emmie!" She ran out of the room without another word. I had no idea how Austin could date a psychopath. But then again, maybe he was one, too.

"When she gets back," Austin said, "this is going to turn ugly. Call off your troops and you won't have to feel any more pain." He nodded at Rosie, who had started crying. "And she won't have to witness anything grotesque."

I turned to Rosie, my heart melting at her beautiful face. She wiped her tears away and sat up tall. "Don't do it, Emmie. You're tough. Don't call off the troops. They can't win."

Tears came to my eyes. She was ten. She shouldn't have to witness anything that horrible. She also shouldn't have been put in a position where she knew our sacrifices were worth the lives of all our family and friends.

"Listen to her," Thunder Thighs said. "They can do what they want with us. Don't surrender."

Skinny's whole body shook. I barely heard her words when they left her mouth. "Don't surrender."

Amber skipped back in with a bag. She set it on the floor next to me, pulling out pliers, files, a hammer, a screwdriver, and knives of different sizes.

She smiled at Austin. "What can I start with?"

Austin took a step back. "Your choice, darling."

Amber clapped her hands and then eyed all her choices. Her hand floated over them, moving back and forth until it hovered over the screwdriver. She picked it up and ran her finger along it. "I've always wondered what I could do with this."

Amber stood, hatred and giddiness flashing across her face. I closed my eyes and hoped the girls sitting along the wall did the same. Pain erupted in my right leg. My eyes ripped open as I screamed out. Blood oozed out where the screwdriver was lodged in my leg. She twisted it back and forth a few times and then pulled it out.

Austin put the communication device back in front of my face. "Surrender." Again, he pressed the button.

My chest heaved in and out as tears flowed down my cheeks. I could taste the salt from them on my lips. "Screw you." The corner of my mouth turned up at the pun.

I tried to hold back the scream when she drove the screwdriver into my left leg, but there was no way to keep it in. My mouth opened to tell them it was useless, but Dean's two punches to my face stopped me. Blood dripped down my nose and I knew it was broken again. I would make him regret it.

"Surrender!" Austin's scream echoed in the room.

"No!" I wanted to yell louder than I did, but it came out hoarse.

Amber had the hammer in her hand, and she went to strike, but Austin pushed her out of the way. He went at me, looking like every single ounce of aggression that he'd held inside his whole life was now pouring out onto me. His punches came so fast, I could barely keep track of where they landed. Left eye, cheek, eye, jaw, nose, jaw, cheek, eye. They kept coming. When he stopped, I was surprised I was still conscious.

Rosie's sobs filled the room, tearing at my heart. I glanced at her and was at least glad to see that she had covered her eyes. Skinny had moved her body up next to her and Rosie leaned into her. Both Thunder Thighs and Skinny had their eyes closed. I hoped it was just my screams that made her cry and not because she'd witnessed anything.

Austin stood in front of me, his fists clenched as blood covered his knuckles. It was probably a mixture of his blood and mine. His eyes were that of a mad man's. He had snapped. Turning his head toward the ceiling, he screamed at the top of his lungs, an animalistic rage I'd never seen before.

Amber tried to console him, but he pushed her away. Dean finally dragged him out of the room and Amber followed, taking all the tools with her. The door locked, sealing us in.

Only two things went through my head after they left. First, I was now terrified of Austin and what he was capable of. Second, his breakdown had bought me more minutes of my life.

"Are you okay, Emmie?" Skinny spoke in a whisper, a quiver in her voice.

Blood filled my mouth. One of my teeth on top had been knocked loose. Wiggling it with my tongue, I spat the blood out on the floor. I swallowed, gagging on some blood. I spat again, but that time it dribbled down my chin. "I'm fine."

"You don't look fine," Thunder Thighs said.

"Then close your eyes." Right after I said that, I leaned to the right and threw up. The smell alone made more bile come up my throat, but I swallowed it.

"I hate that smell," Thunder Thighs said.

"Do you know someone who actually likes it?" I asked.

Thunder Thighs grunted. "No."

"Well, I'm sorry." I wasn't really, but it felt like it needed to be said. The vomit on the floor wasn't the only reason I'd said it. "Hopefully this will be over soon, and we can all go home."

"We aren't going home," Rosie said. Her cries had calmed enough that she could speak.

I kept my face turned away from her so she wouldn't have to see me. "Don't think like that. We need to stay positive."

"How can we stay positive?" Skinny's shrill voice made me miss her whisper. "We're going to die in here! Tortured to death!"

Rosie's cries started again, making me swear. "Knock it off, Angela."

"How can I stay calm?" Skinny asked.

"You have to," I said. My chin fell against my chest and I left it there. I didn't have the energy to lift my head back up. Something on the floor caught my eye. "Rosie, sweetie, I need you to come here."

"I can't," she said. "I can't move."

"I know this is hard," I said, "but I need you to be strong for me. They left a scalpel on the floor. Can you come get it before they come back in here?"

Rosie didn't respond, but I heard tiny footsteps coming toward me. Her hand came into my view and she snatched it up and ran back behind me.

"Can you put it in my hands?" I asked.

Cold metal touched my skin. I gripped the scalpel the best I could, but I didn't have much strength left in me.

The door opened and Amber and Dean waltzed in. Their gaze went to my pile of vomit on the floor.

"Ewww! Seriously, so gross," Amber said.

"I'm sorry my bile isn't to your liking," I said. "I did it just for you."

Amber glared at me. "You know …"

Amber didn't have time to finish the thought. Loud popping sounds came from the hallway, followed by shouting. One voice I recognized immediately.

Dante.

CHAPTER 34

Dean shut the door and held his body against it. "Get the chair!"

Amber ran to me, pulled out a knife, and cut the ties holding my legs to the chair. She shoved my body off, and I fell to the floor. Amber placed the chair under the door handle. It wouldn't hold very long, so I didn't know why they tried.

That thought vanished from my mind when I saw Amber coming at me with a knife. They wanted to kill me before Dante could rescue me. Fighting through the stab wounds, I scrambled to get away from her, using my legs to push myself back.

When she was right in front of me, I threw my legs into her, my feet hitting her right in the groin. I wasn't aiming for that spot, but when my feet landed, I thought to myself, *How convenient.* The effect would have been better, though, if she were a he.

Amber stumbled backward before she started forward again. She lunged at me that time, her knife flying toward my face. I moved at the last second, barely avoiding the knife plunging into my eye. When the knife collided with the ground, she lost her grip, and it bounced away from her. She reached out for it, but I wrapped my legs around her waist and twisted her away.

Amber's fist barreled toward my face, but I maneuvered out of the way at the last second, making her punch the ground. I smiled inwardly when I remembered that same moment over a year ago when she punched the tile instead of my face. She yelped out in pain the same way she had back then, too, making my inward smile turn to the outside.

She tried to push my legs from around her waist, but I held on tight. She put her hands around my neck and squeezed. "Just die! Why won't you just die?"

"You'll never … kill me … Amber." I struggled for breath. Closing my eyes, I rammed my head into hers, knocking her away so her grip loosened. "I'm smarter." I twisted my waist and threw her body to the side, making her hands leave my neck. "And stronger."

I used the moment wriggle my arms along my legs until my bound hands were in front of me instead of behind. Amber flung herself at me. I threw up my arms and jammed the scalpel into her neck. Her eyes widened in shock as blood rushed out, pouring down on me.

Forcing myself to stay in place, I kept a hold on the scalpel, watching and waiting for Amber's life to fade. I hated killing. It wasn't something a sane person could get used to. But if I didn't kill Amber, she'd sure as hell kill me.

Amber finally fell to the ground, her body going limp. I

wanted to drop the scalpel, scamper away from the body, but Dean was still at the door, trying to hold off the others from getting in.

Rosie's round, tear-filled eyes stared at me. "Oh, Emmie."

"I'm okay, Rosie," I said. "I'm going to be fine. Dante's here. They can't hurt us anymore."

Rosie nodded, but her eyes told me she was still worried.

I searched Amber's pockets until I found the key to the handcuffs. Bending my wrist, I tried to get the key in, but I couldn't get the angle right. Rosie gently took the keys from my shaking hands.

Moments later, my hands were free. I threw my arms around Rosie's neck. "Thank you for being so strong."

"It's easy when I have someone like you to look up to. You're practically my hero." Rosie gasped. "Don't tell Santiago I said that."

I let out a small laugh. "I won't." I picked up Amber's knife and cut the ties off Thunder Thighs and Skinny.

"Thank you," I said to Thunder Thighs. She replied with a grunt.

Dean still held the door. I always knew he was strong, but that just proved it. I shuffled over to him, gritting my teeth through the unbearable pain, and tapped him on the shoulder. He glanced at me for a split second, but then fully snapped his head toward me when he realized it was me standing there. And I was holding a knife.

"Back away from the door," I said. When he didn't more, I pressed the tip of the knife into his side. "If you want to live, back away from the door." For a moment, I thought he wouldn't move. But then he looked at Amber lying on the floor.

He backed away from the door and it burst open, the chair sliding away. Dante rushed in, his eyes going wide when they landed on me.

Santiago pushed past him and ran at Rosie. Picking her up in his arms, he twirled her around. When he put her back down, he examined her body, his eyes going wide when he saw her broken arm.

"What happened?" Santiago asked her.

Rosie smiled. "I jumped out of the jeep when they kidnapped me."

Santiago shook his head but smiled. "That's my little sister." He hugged her. "I'm proud of you. You're stronger than I am."

Maya, Mom, and Sean stood behind Dante.

Mom pulled me into her arms. "What did they do to you?"

"Exactly what it looks like," I said. "How did you get in here?"

"We don't have time to talk," Dante said. "Austin's still somewhere in the building. We need to get to him before he does something crazy. I heard some of the guards saying he snapped."

The pain radiating from my face and stomach proved that fact. "He did." Mom still held onto me. "Mom, I'm okay."

She pulled back and looked down, her eyes stopping when she saw my bloody legs. "What happened?"

"A screwdriver," I said.

Mom, Dante, Maya, Sean, and Santiago all gasped at the same time.

"Who did that to you?" Dante asked. He pointed a gun at Dean who had dropped to the floor, screaming over his dead daughter.

My gaze traveled to Amber. Dante held out a gun to Thunder Thighs. It must have been Dean's because Dante was still holding his and I assumed he would have taken any weapons from Dean. Thunder Thighs took it and pointed it at Dean.

Dante paused near me and put his hand on my arm. "I'm glad you're alive."

"Me too." I put my arm around Mom's shoulder for some support. Maya came to my other side to help me out. Walking with a stab wound in each leg wasn't easy.

When we went out into the hall, there were a bunch of dead guards on the ground. Mom and Maya made sure to maneuver around them so I wouldn't trip on any. Thunder Thighs walked ahead of us, stepping on the bodies that were in her path. If I wasn't in so much pain, and it wasn't such an odd thing to do, I might have laughed.

Dante and Santiago stayed in front, checking the halls before we turned. Thunder Thighs still had her gun pointed at Dean, who walked next to her. Rosie and Skinny stayed right behind Dante and Santiago, scampering to keep up.

Sean kept at the rear of the pack, walking with a slight limp. Whatever injury he received during the explosion still bothered him. It made me wonder if it would be permanent.

The hallways were eerily silent, making my hair stand on end. Silence in Headquarters wasn't a good thing.

I turned to Mom. "Where is everybody?"

She shrugged. "We're not entirely sure. It wasn't too packed to begin with. We killed anyone we came across, but there was less than we thought there would be."

There were a couple of dead guards in each hallway we went down.

"They're probably out fighting," Maya said.

"That's if Austin didn't scare them all away with his madness," Sean said from behind us.

We stepped into an open area filled with desks. There were computers at each station and monitors lined the walls. It looked like the main security area. But there wasn't a single soul in the room.

"This is weird," Mom said.

"Why?" Dante asked.

"This place is usually buzzing," Mom said. "I've never seen it empty. Ever."

We glanced around at all the screens, but they were filled with static. Santiago, Sean, and Dante walked around all the stations, looking for anything that might tell us what had happened.

Mom and Maya helped me sit down in one of the chairs. Maya removed the bag she had slung around her back and pulled out some gauze and medical tape. Placing a piece of gauze over the wound on my right leg, she wound the tape around a few times to hold it in place. She repeated the process on my other leg.

"This isn't much," Maya said, "but it'll have to do for now. Samantha can fix you up when we get out of here."

A throat cleared to the left of me and I looked up to see

Austin. Joshua, President Coleman, and Brandon stood next to him, along with several other security guards, some from Kingsland. They circled the entire area.

None of us heard them coming.

CHAPTER 35

Austin smiled. "I'm glad to see we're all together now." He stepped toward me. Dante pointed an arrow at him, but then several guns trained on Dante. "What is that thing, Dante? Whatever it is, put it down."

"No," Dante said.

Santiago raised his shotgun, Maya lifted her sword, and Mom, Sean, and Thunder Thighs all pointed their guns at Austin. Rosie and Skinny squatted down next to me, out of the line of fire.

"Fine, we'll play it your way," Austin said. "But the minute any of you move to attack, you'll all be dead."

"That's a risk we're willing to take," Santiago said.

Austin waltzed over to me, not acknowledging all the weapons that moved with him. He lifted my chin to look at him. "Any last words, Emmie?"

"Last words before what?" I asked.

I had Amber's knife in my hand, hiding behind my back. I didn't want to use it, but I wouldn't hesitate if it came down to it. What I really wanted, though, was my handgun. Dante, Santiago, and Maya had all brought the weapons they were trained with from their home cities.

Austin tsked. "You keep saying I'm arrogant but look at you. You're full of yourself."

"Well, if these are my last words, I would rather you talk." I stared into his eyes, forcing myself to not look away. "Why? That's all I want to know. Why?"

Austin took a couple of steps back. "My whole life I was in the shadows. No one noticed me. People loved my dad, but they never looked at me like I was good enough to be his son. Do you know what that's like?" His mouth turned up a little, more of a smirk than a real smile. "I guess you would. You had a mother who didn't want you. And a father that wanted to kill you."

"That's not …" Mom started.

Austin held his hand up to silence her. "This isn't a time for arguing. I'm just stating simple facts." He bent down in front of me. "Emmie, you and I together, I think we could change the world. We understand each other. We're the same. Unwanted children with bright ambitions. We've been overlooked. Let's make a stand. Let's show them they were wrong."

His words confused me. He went from wanting to kill me to wanting to be my partner? His expression didn't give much away, so I couldn't figure it out.

"What are you talking about?" I asked. "You hate me."

"No, I don't." Austin gently rubbed my cheek. I flinched at his cold touch. What was wrong with him?

“How did you become so evil?” I asked, trying to ignore his hand on my face.

Austin’s twisted smile sent shivers through me. “Well, as my dad used to say, some people are just born that way.” His finger trailed down my face and neck. “No matter what you do or how hard you try to teach them to be good, the evil is just too strong.”

Removing his hand from me, he rubbed his forehead. “It consumed me. I tried to fight it. I tried to be good, but it ate away at me.” He looked at his hands and arms. “It crept around inside of me, moving around.” He pointed to his head. “It started here and then moved down. My dad tried to get me help, but nothing worked.” He examined his arm closely and then held it out to me. “Can you see it, Emmie? Can you see the evil? It’s right there, under the skin, calling my name.”

“Austin, are you okay?” I asked.

Austin tilted his head in confusion. “Why wouldn’t I be?” He leaned in like he wanted to kiss me, but I pulled back.

I glanced at Dante, who wore the same confused expression I did. As I looked around the room, everyone was wearing that expression. Except for Joshua. I couldn’t be certain, but it almost looked like he’d winked at me when my gaze went past him.

Austin lost his bearings for a second and almost fell over. He shook his head, trying to focus himself.

When he looked at me, he blinked rapidly. He leaned in and out, swaying as he did. “Emmie, you and I …” His words were slurred. “Me … you … conquer …” He stared at his hands. "The evil has taken over."

Out of the corner of my eye, I saw a flash of black soaring at me. I stood, dropping Amber's knife behind me, reached out my hand, caught my handgun, and pointed it at Austin. I didn't see who had thrown the gun.

The moment my gun landed in my hands, Santiago stepped forward, keeping his shotgun aimed at Austin. Maya came between me and Santiago, holding her sword, pointing it at Austin. Dante rushed between me and Santiago, his arrow cocked and ready to fire at Austin's heart.

Us four revolutionaries created a circle around Austin. A power surged within me, blocking out the pain from all my wounds. I embraced it, using the strength to finally end the war. The war that had done too much damage and ripped families apart.

The four of us stood tall and strong, united as one. There was no doubt, no fear to be seen.

I lifted my chin ever so slightly. "It's over, Austin. Tell your troops to back down."

"You're outnumbered!" Austin raged. Veins popped from his face and neck, his eyes holding a crazy fury I'd never seen before.

"So are you," I said, my voice even and calm. "You either surrender, or you'll be dead. Your choice."

Austin's chest heaved. Letting out a war cry, he lunged at me, his fingers like claws wanting to rip me apart. I didn't want to hurt Austin. He'd betrayed me, but he was still an Oliver. A family I held close to my heart.

I think the other revolutionaries could feel my hesitancy. They understood. But they weren't connected to the Oliver's like me.

Austin's eyes bulged. Right before he got to me, he fell to the floor, an arrow sticking out of his neck, a sword in his side, and a shotgun blast on his back.

The four of us swept around, backed into each other for a mere second, and then charged. A few of the Kingsland guards who had been standing with Austin and President Coleman, turned on them, apparently their alliance with us.

It ended as quickly as it started. The second the last Infinity Corp guard fell, Joshua lunged toward a table, pressed a button, and began to yell. "Stand down! This is Joshua Randall and I order all the Infinity Corp troops to stand down. Retreat to Headquarters."

"Do you think that will work?" Santiago asked him.

Joshua shrugged. "It's worth a try. They think I'm allied with Austin."

My eyes turned to Austin. "What happened to him there at the end? He was acting so odd." My legs buckled beneath me, so I reached out and grabbed a chair, rolled it toward me, and sat down.

"I drugged him." Joshua bent down in front of me, his eyes full of sorrow. "I'm so sorry, Emmie. I didn't know they'd torture you like this." He swore. "Although, I guess I should have. I always underestimated their evilness. Especially Amber." He looked at my legs. "What the hell did she do to you?"

"It doesn't matter." I stared at him, not sure what to think. "What happened? I thought you betrayed us. Again?"

"Why would you think that?" Dante asked. He glanced over at Brandon's body, regret and pain on his face. It made me wonder if Dante had been the one to kill him. Or if he was just sad to see someone he once considered a friend dead. Maybe both.

I looked at Dante. "What? He handed me over to Austin and Amber. He left me alone with them. He told me that he was working with Austin."

Dante scratched his head. "Okay, now I'm confused. He's the one who told us where you were."

"Well, we had already started in the tunnel," Maya said. "We heard your communicator and knew something was wrong. Someone told us they spotted the four of you go into the medical building, so we went to check it out and noticed the open hatch on the floor."

"Thank goodness Joshua contacted us." Santiago whistled. "Those tunnels were confusing as all get out. I don't think we would have found Headquarters in time if it wasn't for him."

I turned back to Joshua. "What are they talking about?"

Sighing, he sat down on the floor next to my chair. "I figured the only way we'd get out of here alive is if we had help. I figured Austin would want you dead and I didn't think the four of us could do it on our own. But I needed a way to be alone so I could contact Dante and the others. That meant letting Austin think I was still working with him." He eyed my face and then my legs. "If I'd known they'd do all this to you, though, I wouldn't have left. I figured I'd be back in enough time to stop them from going too far."

"I don't mean this in a bad way, Emmie," Dante said, "but I'm glad Joshua did what he did. If he hadn't of left, we would have never made it here in time. You, Rachel, Angela, and Rosie would all be dead."

"Then these injuries were worth it." I looked at Rosie. "I love that pretty face too much to ever part from it."

Rosie blushed. "Thanks, Emmie. Maybe one day I'll be as pretty as you."

I laughed as I touched my face. "Yes, I'm sure I'm gorgeous right now." I raised my eyebrows at Joshua. "So, you and Tiffy?"

"Oh, hell no," Joshua said, disgust on his face. "Never in a million years. I have better taste than that."

I let out a sigh of relief. "Thank goodness. I wouldn't want her as a sister-in-law."

Joshua took my hand. "We're okay, right? You're not mad at me?"

"I understand now that everything's been explained." I squeezed his hand. "Stop doing sketchy things and we won't have to question you."

He squeezed my hand back. "Deal."

"Can we go?" Thunder Thighs asked. "My arm hurts. I was shot." We all turned to her. She pressed a bloody hand against her left arm and grunted. "And. It. Hurts."

Joshua stood and helped me onto my feet. He put his arm around my waist to hold me steady. "Emmie needs to be looked at, too."

"Yeah, I've got two stab wounds, I'm pretty sure my nose is broken, and I'm going to need a new tooth."

Dante came to me. "Really?"

I opened my mouth, wiggling the tooth with my tongue. "See?"

"That's gross!" Rosie exclaimed. Then she smiled. "Do that again."

Maya cleared her throat. "We should contact Gideon and Terrance. We also need to contact Austin's head of security, if they're still alive. We need to end the battle out there. It's still going on."

Dante nodded. "True." He turned to Mom. "Would you know who to contact over here?"

"Yes," Mom said. "I'll get on it."

We waited until all the right people had been contacted before we did anything else. Most of the Infinity Corp guards had retreated at Joshua's broadcast.

When the battle had stopped, we announced that New Haven was in charge of Infinity Corp and River Springs and we'd keep the residents informed of any changes. We sent them back to their homes until we could come up with a plan.

Though the sky was perfectly blue and clear when we stepped outside of Headquarters, it was still chilly. I wished I still had Courtney's coat.

A bus pulled up and Samantha and Eric jumped out, running over to me.

By the look on Samantha's face, I thought she might slap me. "I specifically told you not to leave the house! Do you ever obey orders?"

"No." I patted her on the arm. "You should've picked up on that by now."

Eric stared at my face, practically frozen in horror. He finally pulled me into his arms. "How could they do that to you?"

"The same way they could do it to you," I said. His body shivered against mine and I knew it wasn't from the cold.

"There you are."

I pulled away from Eric and turned toward the source. Tami stood there, one hand clenched in a fist, the other behind her back.

Mom was standing right next to me. "Who are you talking to?"

"Both of you, actually," Tami said. "You and Emmie have ruined my life."

"That's not true." Joshua approached us.

"And you!" Tami yelled at Joshua. "You're a traitor! You're all traitors! Because of you, my father and my mother are dead!"

"Welcome to the club." Santiago leaned against the bus with his arms folded. "Almost everyone standing here has lost one or both of their parents. So, get over it."

Tami gaped at him. "How could you be so heartless?"

Santiago yawned, completely bored of the conversation. "I've met both of your parents. You're probably better off."

"What he's trying to say," Maya said, glaring at Santiago, "is that you're not alone. This war has been brutal to all of us. We've all lost people we love."

Tami groaned. "But you started it all! If the stupid revolutionaries hadn't gone off and …"

"Then we'd all be living in cities that controlled our every move," Dante said, cutting her off. "People would still be dying, Tami. Your dad killed many people before this whole thing started."

"That's not true," Tami said.

Joshua sighed. "You can live in denial all you want, but it's true."

Tami's focus landed on me. "What was the point of all of this? What did you want to get out it?"

I thought about it for a moment before I responded, but only one word came to my mind. "Freedom."

"Are you happy?" Tami asked. "With the results?"

"Yes," I said. "Obviously, there are things I wish didn't happen and lives that shouldn't have been lost, but that's the cost of freedom. It's the cost of war." I stood tall, keeping my chin up. "And I'd do it all over again in a heartbeat."

Tears fell down Tami's cheeks. "That's one thing you and I will never agree on." She wiped away some of her tears. "I hope you've enjoyed your life, Emmie, because now it's over."

Tami brought her hand out from behind her back and lifted a gun, pointed it straight at me, and pulled the trigger. I yelled out as my body crashed onto the ground. Gunshots rang out around me.

Mom was on top of me, her eyes full of worry. "Are you okay?"

I blinked a few times, trying to figure out what had happened. "I … I didn't get shot."

"No," Mom said.

She had jumped in front of me and pushed me to the ground. Blood fell onto my hand and at first, I thought it was from my previous wounds. Then I looked into Mom's eyes.

"You're hit," I said. She nodded slowly. I rolled her onto her stomach and saw her back. Blood seeped out from the bullet hole. "Help! Someone, help us!"

Eric bent down next to us, removed his jacket and placed it against her back. Samantha tried to push me out of the way, but I couldn't move.

I turned Mom's face toward me. "Mom, stay with me."

"Stop moving her so much," Samantha said, kneeling next to me. "We need to keep her still." They laid her flat on her stomach while Samantha checked her.

I bent down so I could see her face. "Mom, please stay with me."

"I love you … sweetie." Mom gasped for air.

I put my hands on her cheeks. "I love you, but you need to stay quiet." I rested my forehead against hers. "I can't lose you. I just got you back."

"I've … always loved … you … I always … will …"

"Mom!" My tears fell onto her face. "Don't leave me! Please, Mom!"

Her eyelids fluttered until they closed, and her body went limp.

"Mom!"

CHAPTER 36

The next few weeks passed in a blur. We disbanded Infinity Corp and put Nick in charge of River Springs until we could get everything sorted out. We gave him everything he needed and all the personnel he wanted so they could get the city repaired. People were sent back to work and the children back to school.

Marcus did the same for Kingsland. With New Haven and Scorpion included, we were in control of all the cities.

President Mendes and Vice President Jennings were released from their duties. Once everything was settled, we would vote on a Mayor for each city. For the time being, everyone reported to the revolutionaries.

"I say we add that boxing is a required sport in each city." Santiago leaned back in his chair and propped his legs onto the table in the conference room.

Maya rolled her eyes. "We're not adding that as a law." She was sitting in between me and Santiago. Dante was on the other side of me.

Santiago shook his head, making his shaggy hair flop around. "You're no fun sometimes."

"But we can have sports." I had my legs propped up on a box beneath the table. They were still healing from the stabbing. My side was finally starting to recover since I was able to rest for once. The swelling in my face had gone down and the scar from the cut to my face was almost invisible. I had taken the bandage off my nose yesterday. For being broken multiple times, it didn't look too bad.

"I agree," Dante said. "I've done a lot of research and I noticed they used to have a bunch of different sports back in the day."

Maya sat forward and rested her forearms on the table, her charm bracelets clinking against the wood. "We have so many laws we need to go over and you want to focus on sports."

Santiago shrugged. "So?"

"We've gone over most of the basics," I said. "No killing, no stealing, no breaking and entering, no vandalism."

"Add no arranged marriages." Dante folded his arms. "I'm not being told who I have to marry. Or even if I have to marry." He looked at me. "You know, you look pretty good with makeup on."

I shoved his arm. "Thanks."

It had been a long time since I'd worn makeup. With our limited supplies in New Haven, that wasn't a priority. But now that we had everything back in order, I had started using just a little to cover up my bruises and cuts. But Vivica had shown me how to make my green eyes pop so I'd been wearing it more.

Maya wrote things down as we talked. When she was done, she tapped her pen on the table. "I think people should live in whatever city they want. And if it doesn't work out, they can move to another one."

Santiago nodded. "I agree. And let people choose their careers."

"Speaking of careers," Dante said. "Should we start a bartering system or create currency?"

"I think we should." I crossed my ankles. "Let's start paying people for their work."

Santiago let out a whistle. "We're going to be here forever, man. We have to create rules and laws, even when we have freedom."

"People can't have complete freedom," Maya said. "Think of what the world would be like. With people like Amber out there, it would be a scary place."

Dante shivered. "No kidding."

Maya glanced around at all of us. "How would you feel about me scouting around and trying to find an area where we can build up a new city?"

"Do you think there are other places that are safe to live out there?" Santiago asked.

"There's only one way to find out," Maya said.

Dante shook his head. "I don't know. According to all our historical documents, most of the world was uninhabitable, which is why our cities were placed in such a limited area."

"Things change, though," I said. "Maybe some places that weren't safe before are safe now. So many years have passed."

"I'm willing to take the risk," Maya said.

"If you're willing to do it," Dante said, "then I say go for it."

Maya ran her hand over her spiky hair. "What about you three? Do you want to stay here?"

"I do." I didn't even hesitate. "New Haven is home to me now. I love it here."

"It's nice," Santiago said, "but I'd rather go back to Scorpion."

Dante nodded. "I want to go back to Kingsland. I love the area."

I didn't like the thought of being parted with all of them, but it had to happen someday.

Dante reached over and took my hand. "We'll still see each other. We're within driving distance."

"I know." I squeezed his hand. "I'll still miss you guys. You're my family."

Santiago smiled. "Yes, one crazy family, but I love every single one of you."

"We'll need to hold monthly meetings." Maya squeezed my other hand. "At least. Maybe every other week."

I raised my eyebrows, my eyes hopeful. "Every week?"

Dante laughed. "Every week works for me. Since New Haven is central to all of us, we'll hold them here. We can come here, have the meeting, and still be able to get home the same day."

A small knock sounded at the door.

"Come in," Dante said.

The door opened and Eric walked in. "Sorry to disrupt you, but I need to borrow Emmie for a few minutes."

Santiago stood and stretched out his body. "We need a break anyway."

"Good." Eric came to me and scooped me up, holding me in his arms.

"I can walk, you know," I said as I snuggled into him.

"Yes, but this is much nicer, don't you think?" Eric asked.

I smiled. "Yes. Maybe I'll have you carry me everywhere from now on."

Eric kissed my forehead. "Don't push it." He carried me out of Headquarters, heading toward the park near the school.

Dee and the children from her class were outside, sitting on some blankets that were scattered about. All the snow had melted, but the grass was still dead from winter. The sky was blue, with some white clouds forming random shapes. Dee was reading them a story as they all watched intently. Some were sitting crossed legged and some were lying on their stomachs, their chins rested on their hands.

Eric set me down and put his arm around my waist. When Dee was done with the story, she closed the book and looked over at the two of us with a big smile on her face. "I didn't know we were going to have visitors today."

I looked up at Eric. "She didn't know we were coming?"

Eric shook his head. "Dee, do you mind if we sit here for just a moment?"

"Sure." Confusion crossed Dee's face, but she gestured to the blanket she was sitting on. We sat beside her and watched the six and seven-year-old kids. They were all smiling at us and a few waved.

"What are you doing here?" Dee whispered in my ear.

"I have no idea," I whispered back.

One of the boys came to Dee and handed her a drawing. "I made this for you, Miss Jennings."

"Thank you, Doug," Dee said as she took it from his hand. The picture was of a boy sitting at a desk with a frown on his face. A lady knelt beside him, pointing at a paper on the desk and smiling.

Doug pointed at the boy. "That's me trying to figure out math." He pointed to the lady. "And that's you, staying after class to help me understand it." He blushed and ran back to his seat on the blanket.

A girl came up next, handing her another drawing. "I made this for you, Miss Jennings."

"Thank you, Alice," Dee said, taking it from her hand. The picture was of children and a lady outside on the grass. They were all standing in a circle, holding hands.

"That's all the students and you outside playing Ring Around the Rosie," Alice said. She smiled at me. "It's my favorite activity Miss Jennings plays with us." She went back to her seat as another kid walked over.

They kept coming up, handing her drawings of Dee with the kids, either helping them or playing a game with them. When the last kid sat down, Dee was holding back her tears.

She had handed me each drawing after she looked at them. Something on the back caught my eye, so I turned one of them over. The letter R was written on the back. I started turning them all over, noticing a letter on each paper. Placing them on the blanket, I spread them out so we could see each letter.

"Why are there letters on the back?" Dee asked the

students. They all just snickered.

"Maybe they spell something?" I suggested.

Dee and I sorted through them, trying to piece them together.

It didn't take long for me to figure it out. "Oh."

Dee glanced at me. "Do you know what it says?"

I nodded as I rearranged the letters until they formed a sentence. I watched Dee's face as she read it out loud.

"Will you marry me, Dee?" Her eyes went wide. "Oh!" She threw her hands over her mouth, but I could see her huge smile underneath.

Footsteps approached. Will bent down on one knee and took Dee's hand. His face was bright red as he adjusted his glasses. "Dee, this past year has been the best year of my life." He swallowed and licked his lips. "I, uh …" Reaching into his pocket, he pulled out a ring. Small diamonds circled all the way around the silver band. "I love you more than anything in this world and I want to spend the rest of my life with you. Dee Jennings, will you marry me?"

"Yes!" Dee threw her arms around his neck and he held her tight. All the students were smiling, and a few snickered. When she pulled back and kissed him on the lips, all the children giggled.

I turned to Eric. "You knew about this?"

Eric nodded, not holding back his smile. "Will came to me for some advice and together we worked this out with the students. I thought you'd want to be here to see it."

"Plus, I was so nervous," Will said. Dee had pulled back from him and was staring at the ring on her finger. "There was some comfort to having the two of you here."

Dee smiled. "Well, Emmie and I are practically attached at the hip, so you two boys better get used to being around each other all the time."

Eric laughed. "We already are. Luckily, we've had a year to adjust to this before either of us tied the knot."

I shoved him away from me playfully. "We're worth it."

"Yes, you are," Will said. He blushed, making Dee's smile get bigger.

"Miss Jennings?" Alice called out.

Dee looked over at her. "Yes?"

"Does this mean we have to start calling you Mrs. Sanders?" Alice asked.

Dee let out a laugh. "Not until we're married."

Eric and I left and went to my house. When we got there, I opened the door and stepped inside. "Anyone home?"

"In the kitchen!" Derek yelled out. "You're just in time for lunch."

We walked into the kitchen and I smiled when I saw everyone at the table. Derek, Naomi, and Joshua sat on one side of the table. Eric's dad, Alexander, sat at the head of the table, while Sean and Mom sat on the other side. I took a seat next to Mom and Eric sat down opposite his dad.

"I made potato soup." Mom smiled. "And it actually turned out okay."

"It's more than okay," Sean said. "It's delicious."

Mom set her left hand on his, the diamond from her wedding ring glinting in the light. They had decided to get married right after she got out of the infirmary. The shot she took to the back paralyzed her from the waist down. Sean still had a limp in his left leg from the explosion at the medical building. They had spent so much time bonding over the past year, and both needed help, so they thought who better to help them than each other. I loved the way Mom looked at him, so I was happy with it. Plus, I had grown to like Sean over the past few weeks. Even Derek and Joshua had taken to him.

I glanced around the table and smiled, happy at my newly formed, slightly dysfunctional family.

After lunch, Eric and I went for a walk. He helped me up the ladder to the alcove and we sat down on a rock, looking out over New Haven.

"I love it here." I leaned into Eric, who had his arm around me.

"Me, too," Eric said. "I never want to leave."

"Good, because you'll never get me to leave."

He laughed and kissed the top of my head. "You know, now with Derek and Naomi engaged, and Will and Dee engaged, we need to get married soon so they can focus on their weddings."

I smiled. "I think a spring wedding would be nice, so what? May?"

"March?" Eric asked.

I shook my head. "Too soon. Dee hasn't finished my dress yet."

"April then." He gave me a hopeful smile.

I thought about all the preparations and shook my head. "May."

Eric sighed. "Fine, May, but the beginning."

"Pick a day," I said, running my fingers through his hair.

"The second," Eric responded.

"Why the second?" I asked.

He smiled as he ran his finger down my cheek. "Because I knew you'd say the first was too soon." Before I could respond, he bent down and kissed me gently on the lips.

When he pulled away, I curled into his arms and looked out over the city. It had taken a while to get where we were. We'd lost so many good people along the way. I still thought of my dad, Vice President Oliver, and Mack every single day. They had shaped me into the woman I'd become.

Every bump in the road, every life lost, every injury I'd received, all of it had been worth it in the end. Our city was free. Our citizens were happy. Everywhere I went, I saw people smiling and heard laughter. That wasn't something I had noticed when I lived in River Springs. Thunder Thighs had smiled on multiple occasions, even if it was a little deformed.

Eric kissed me on my forehead. "I love you, Emmie Woodard."

I squeezed him tight. "I love you, Eric Greene."

We sat there for hours, talking about anything and everything we could think of, until the sunset. Then we sat there a little longer, watching the stars come out and light up the sky.

EPILOGUE

May 2

"Would you hold still?" Dee was trying to get my dress buttoned up in the back.

Standing, I stared in the mirror at Dee, who was behind me. "Sorry, my foot itched."

She rolled her eyes and shook her head, making her brown curls bounce. They seemed extra curly and extra perfect that day. "Too bad. This is more important than an itchy foot." She glanced at me through the mirror. "Emmie, this is my first wedding dress. I need to wow people. If I want to start a side business, I can't screw this up."

Tilting my head, I looked at my dress in the mirror. When I'd first seen it, I about had a heart attack. Dee thought it was because I loved it so much (which I did), but it was because there were no sleeves. My whole life I'd worn very modest clothing. Everyone in River Springs did. It was the style. So, wearing no sleeves almost felt scandalous. When I'd said that out loud, Vivica told me I needed to lighten up. Plus, she said I had nice shoulders. I thought it was a weird compliment, but I thanked her anyway.

Dee informed me that a heart attack was not necessary. She hadn't finished it. She added a lace covering over the entire dress that had sleeves that went down to my wrists.

The lace opened at the waist, however, exposing the white silk material underneath. She had used a light lilac and light green stitch to embroider vines with flowers on the bottom half of my dress. The silk material stopped just below my ankles, but the lace continued in the back to form a short train.

I let out a yawn as I watched her work. She tsked at me. "No yawning."

Rolling my eyes, I yawned again. "Dee, you woke me up at four this morning. Four!"

She stopped what she was doing and put her hand on her hip. "Listen, lady, we had a lot to do. Hair, makeup, getting this dress put on you perfectly, so don't mouth off. You look simply stunning, so you should be thanking me."

"You think I look stunning?"

Dee nodded. "Absolutely. Eric might be the one to fall over with a heart attack when he sees you." She went back to finishing off the pearl buttons in the back.

"She's right." Mom rolled herself into the room in her wheelchair. She stopped next to me and took my hand. "You're gorgeous."

"And downright sexy," Tina said.

She was sitting at one of the desks in Dee's classroom. We'd set it up for my dressing room since it was right next to the park where I was getting married. Maya, Naomi, Vivica, and Courtney were sitting near her. I'd asked the five of them to be my bridesmaids. Dee was my maid of honor.

Rosie skipped into the room, gasping when she saw me. "Emmie! You're beautiful! I love your hair." Her arm had finally healed, and the sling had been removed.

"Thanks," Dee and Tina said at the same time.

They'd both spent hours on my hair. They started by doing loose ringlets all around my head. Then they put some thin braids throughout and a thicker braid that ran along the top of my head. Once they were done, they pinned my hair up so it was above my neck, making sure some of the curls hung loose.

Rosie held out some small blue flowers that had bloomed around New Haven. "Can we put some of these in your hair?"

I smiled at her. "Of course."

"As soon as I'm done," Dee said.

I twisted my butterfly pendant. Vivica had done my makeup. I was worried since sometimes she could go overboard, but she ended up going simple, yet elegant. The light gray and purple eye shadow she'd used made my green eyes stand out. She used a light, shiny lip gloss that had the slightest bit of pink to it.

Dee finished and stood next to me, eyeing her work. She was smiling until she noticed me playing with my pendant. She creased her forehead in concern. "Emmie, don't take this the wrong way, but you aren't going to wear that, are you?"

My mouth fell open. I'd worn it every single day since Eric had given it to me. He had hand-carved the butterfly himself. Wrapping my hand around it, I pressed it against my chest.

Dee flushed. "I love it, you know that. It just doesn't go with the rest of your ensemble."

"Oh!" Mom said. "I completely forgot." She handed me a small box. "Eric wanted me to give this to you. He wanted to bring it in himself, but I told him that was out of the question. The groom can't see the bride before the wedding."

"Why not?" Rosie asked. She swished her dress back and forth where she stood. She was wearing a lavender dress that Dee had made her. It poofed out from the waist down, where the silk material hung to her knees. At least Dee had given her sleeves that weren't see-through.

Mom smiled at Rosie. "They say that it's bad luck."

"Well, open the box already," Tina said, walking up next to me.

I removed the lid and gasped. Inside was a necklace made of the same silver as my ring, the pendant a small butterfly with little purple gems on the wings. There was a set of purple diamond earrings, too. Santiago had pierced my ears last month, but I didn't have any earrings that seemed nice enough, so I wasn't wearing any.

"Wow," Tina said as she looked over my shoulder at the jewelry. "They're beautiful."

Removing the earrings, I handed Mom the box and put the earrings in. When I was done, I bent down next to Mom, which was surprisingly easy. I wasn't sure how Dee had done it, but my dress was effortless to maneuver around in, which I appreciated more than she probably knew.

I took off my wooden butterfly necklace and handed it to Tina. “Keep a close eye on this.”

Mom placed my new necklace around my neck and clasped it together. It went perfect with my dress.

“Seriously, Emmie,” Vivica said, “you’re going to turn heads today.” She looked at Dee. “You’re doing my dress when I get married.”

We all turned to her.

“Do you have news you need to share with us?” I asked.

Vivica shook her head as she laughed. “No. I said *when* I get married. I hope to one day, but not yet.”

Naomi smiled. “Well, I have a wedding coming up and you’re doing my dress, too.”

Dee beamed. “Clients already! This is awesome.”

Maya and Courtney stood by us, so we were all looking at my dress in the mirror.

Courtney smiled. “I think everyone will want Dee to do their dress when they see Emmie.” Her eyes locked with mine. “You do look stunning.”

“Can I come in?” I turned around and saw Marie standing at the door holding little Mack in her arms. He had just turned three months old and had started smiling. He had the cutest dimples on his chubby cheeks that amplified when he smiled.

“Of course,” I said.

Marie gasped when she finally saw me in my entirety. She whistled. “You look hot!”

That made me laugh. “Thanks.” I held out my arms. “Come here, Mack.” He leaned toward me, smiling big.

"No!" Dee's outburst surprised us all. "What if he spits up on your dress?"

"I fed him a while ago," Marie said. "And he's been burped. Nothing will happen."

Dee didn't look satisfied with that answer, but I didn't care. I took little Mack into my arms and hugged him. "You wouldn't spit up on me, would you Mack?" He tried to grab some of my loose curls, smiling the whole time. I pulled him close and kissed his cheeks repeatedly. His giggle filled the room, making everyone else laugh.

"Now I'll have to fix your lip gloss," Vivica said, rifling through her makeup bag.

I kissed him a few more times. "He's worth it." Sighing, I handed him back to Marie.

"Can we put the flowers in your hair now, Emmie?" Rosie asked.

"Sure." I sat down on a nearby chair while Rosie, Dee, and Tina placed them throughout my hair. Vivica took the opportunity to reapply my lip gloss.

Marie looked at all the bridesmaid dresses. "Dee, you did an amazing job with these dresses as well."

All of them wore a sleeveless lavender dress made of silk that hung just past the knees. She did a lace cover like she did for me, but the shade matched their dress. The lace opened at the waist off to the right, instead of the middle like mine did. Dee's dress was the same, except her lace cover was cream.

When they were done with the flowers, Dee placed my veil on my head. It was made of the same lace material that she used for my dress.

Bending down, Maya put my shoes on my feet. Vivica and Dee had tried to talk me into wearing high heels, but I refused. I didn't need to trip and fall at my wedding. Maya and Tina were my voice of reason and talked them into letting me wear white slip-ons. They were comfortable, which was exactly what I needed.

Dee helped me up and looked me over. "Dress. Check. Hair. Check. Makeup. Check. Jewelry. Check. Shoes. Check. Veil. Check." She looked at everyone. "Are we forgetting anything?"

"Your ring," Rosie said, holding out her hand.

"Oh, yes." I slipped it off and placed it in her hand. She took it over to a small pillow and used a ribbon to tie my ring and Eric's ring to the pillow.

Marie took the pillow and held it in front of Mack. "Are you sure he's not too young to be the ring bearer?" He reached out and squeezed the pillow, a big smile on his face.

Vivica laughed. "I heard that back in the day some people used dogs to be the ring bearer, so using a three-month-old can't be that weird."

"Besides," Dee said with a shrug, "you'll be holding him." She eyed my original ring made of twine that still sat on my ring finger.

"It's staying on, Dee," I said, twisting it around my finger.

She held up her hands. "I wasn't going to say anything."

"Knock, knock." Alexander stood in the doorway. "It's time, ladies."

Mom put her hand on my arm. "I'll see you out there." I bent down and kissed her on the cheek before she wheeled herself out of the room.

The groomsmen walked into the room. Santiago whistled when he saw us. "So, this is where all the hot ladies are hiding."

"No time for chit chat," Dee said. "We all need to line up."

Santiago saluted her. "Yes, ma'am." He ran over to me, giving me a quick hug and a kiss on the cheek. "You look amazing."

Dante came to me next, giving me a big hug. "I'm so happy for you, Emmie." He kissed my cheek. "Love you."

"Love you, too," I said.

"Coolest brother first," Derek said, pushing past Joshua and pulling me into a tight hug, making it very difficult to breathe. "Remember to name your first-born child after me. And any others you have. Love you, little sister from another mister." He hurried away before I could tell him no child of mine would ever be named after him.

Joshua rolled his eyes and then embraced me. "You look beautiful, Emmie." He pulled back. "Promise me you'll never name a kid after Derek."

I laughed. "I wasn't planning on it. I'd name a kid after you before I would him."

"I heard that," Derek yelled out.

"Seriously, people!" Dee yelled. "You love Emmie, she looks stunning, we all know this! Places!" She tossed each bridesmaid a bouquet and then practically hurled mine at me. I had to jump to catch it.

Will shrugged and gave me an apologetic smile as he linked his arm with Dee's. Rosie stood at the head of the line, holding a basket of the same blue flowers that were in my hair. Marie stood behind her, holding little Mack in her arms, who was now sucking on the pillow. As long as he didn't swallow the rings, I was fine with it.

Courtney and Joshua were behind Marie, followed by Derek and Naomi, Santiago and Vivica, Dante and Maya, Tina and Luke, with Dee and Will right in front of me. Luke turned around and gave me a thumbs-up, turning back around quickly when Dee glared at him.

Alexander pulled my veil over my face and linked my arm with his. He gently placed his other hand on my hand that rested on his arm. "You look exquisite, Emmie."

"Thank you …" I paused. "Do you mind if I call you Dad?"

His smile reached up to his eyes like Eric's always did. "I would be honored."

"Good." I kissed him on the cheek. "Thanks, Dad."

"Lip gloss, Emmie!" Vivica yelled out.

"If you were facing forward like you should've been you wouldn't have noticed!" Dee said.

I turned to Alexander. "This is going to be fun."

He winked at me. "Yes, yes it is."

We filed out of the room, one couple at a time, and walked toward the park. We had picked the perfect day. Winter had gone, but the summer heat hadn't arrived. Pink, puffy clouds were scattered throughout the sky. The sun was beginning to set, painting pink and orange hues above the mountains.

My friends and family filled the rows of white chairs that had been placed on the grass. I was able to talk Dee down to only a couple hundred people with an agreement to record the event for anyone who wanted to watch it later.

Rosie went down the aisle first, dropping the flowers on the ground as she did. Then Marie followed with Mack, who very easily charmed the crowd with his dimples and a small bowtie around his neck.

As Courtney and Joshua started walking, I looked out over the guests. Mom, Sean, Bruce, Gideon, and Terrance sat in the front on one side. On the other side were Nick and Carla. Next to them, as promised, was the nurse who saved my life, Janette, along with her family.

The row directly behind them remained empty. We reserved those seats in honor of my dad, Mack, Vice President Oliver, President Brown, and all those who had given the ultimate sacrifice for New Haven.

Among the crowd were Samantha Oliver and her mom, Dee's family, Carmen Mendes, Dr. Stacey, and Hiro. Marcus, Zoe, and Michael came down from Kingsland to be there.

Dante had been contacting Zoe quite often. He kept saying how young she was, but something was starting to develop.

Near the back, Thunder Thighs and Skinny sat next to each other and for the first time since I'd known them, they weren't fighting. They weren't talking, either, but I'd take that over fighting.

"You ready?" Alexander patted my hand.

I nodded. "More than ever."

The crowd stood as Alexander and I started down the aisle. There seemed to be some sort of archway in front, but my eyes were only on Eric.

His blond hair was freshly cut and perfectly styled. He wore a black suit with a white, button-down shirt and a solid lavender tie. Seeing him so polished took my breath away. He was utterly handsome.

Keeping my focus on his blue eyes, my smile broke records as I sauntered toward him. I probably would have sprinted, but luckily Alexander was there, helping me go at a reasonable pace.

As we got closer, Eric blinked back tears, which made my eyes water. Somehow, his smile was even bigger than mine.

When we got to the front, Alexander lifted my veil back and kissed me on my cheek. He put my hand in Eric's and went to sit down next to Nick.

Eric leaned in, gently kissing my cheek. "You look positively radiant."

Still holding hands, we turned to Archie who stood under the archway. I took a moment to look at the detail on the arch. It was made of oak, handcrafted by Archie. Even with one hand, his craftsmanship was remarkable. Vines that held the New Haven flower were sketched all along the arch, along with small butterflies.

Archie smiled at us before he began. "I'd like to welcome you all today to this blessed occasion of the union of Emelia Woodard and Eric Greene. I've had the privilege of getting to know Emmie and Eric over the past year and the one thing I've noticed more than anything is that their love and commitment to one another has never faltered and never wavered. They have stayed by each other through more than any of us wanted to see or should have to see in a lifetime.

"We all know how trying the quest to win New Haven was. So many things happened to Emmie and Eric that in hindsight had a good chance of ripping them away from each other. But the opposite happened. They grew more with each obstacle. Their devotion multiplied with each barrier that threatened to get in their way."

Eric reached out and wiped some tears from my eyes.

"Their bond is the perfect example of how a marriage should be," Archie said. "They stand by each other through thick and thin, support and fight for one another, and they never speak badly of the other. They talk out their problems." He smiled. "And they do it rationally. They take the time to understand each other. Their relationship is built on faith and trust. They're starting their marriage on a firm foundation that I have no doubt will remain intact."

Archie's voice trembled. He cleared his throat before he continued. "The same loyalty Emmie and Eric have shown to each other, they have shown to this city. New Haven wouldn't be where it is today if it weren't for them. They fought hard for our freedom, never backing down, even when their lives were in the balance. I think I can safely say on the behalf of New Haven that you will forever have a special place in our hearts."

A small cheer broke out among the crowd. It probably would have been louder if it weren't for Dee shushing the crowd. Eric and I smiled at each other.

"I believe the two of you have written your own vows," Archie said.

Eric nodded, smiling at me. "Ladies first."

I had no idea what I wanted to say. There weren't any words to describe my feelings toward Eric or how much he meant to me. So, I did exactly what I had done for my father and Mack at their funeral. I followed my heart.

"Eric, I don't think you know the impact you've had on my life. Before I met you, I wasn't sure what I wanted in life or who I even was. I lacked confidence in myself and my abilities. But you …" I squeezed his hands. "You've never doubted me. Ever. You've always believed in me. You've given me strength when I thought I'd lost hope. You've given me something to live for. You've stood by my side through everything, never losing faith in me. What Archie said about our foundation we've created, it's firm because of you, Eric. You're my rock, you always have been, and you always will."

I took one of my hands out from his and ran my fingers through his hair. "You've taken such good care of me and showed me love and constant devotion. But you've done it without treating me like I was weak or couldn't do things on my own. I appreciate that more than you'll ever know. I love you, Eric Greene, and I promise that love will never fade."

Eric took a few deep breaths as he blinked back some tears. Bouncing up and down a little on the balls of his feet, he intertwined our fingers. "Maybe I should've gone first." His mouth twisted and he gave me a mischievous smile like the one he gave me when I was standing in the Recruitment office the first day we met.

"Emmie, I've looked at you like you're strong because you are. That's what I love about you. You never back down to a challenge and I feel sorry for any person who tries to get in your way. I'll never lose faith or hope in you or us. Given everything we've been through, I'm positive we can now stare anything in the face and come out on top.

"Emmie, I'm the luckiest guy in the world to have a woman like you. You've made me want to be a better person and gave me a reason to live when I thought everything had been taken from me." He closed his eyes, probably thinking about his mother and father.

When he opened his eyes, a few tears fell down his cheeks. "I believed I had no reason to continue. No reason to live. I didn't care what happened to me, so I became reckless. That changed in an instant with one look at you. To see the love and commitment you showed to your friend and your Recruitment partner blew me away. Your loyalty is unbreakable. You stand up for what you believe in and for what's right."

His smile twisted again. "Not to mention you're downright sexy." When I rolled my eyes, he put his hand on the back of my neck and pulled our heads together until our foreheads were touching. "I love you, Emmie Woodard, and I would do anything or go anywhere for you. I will always be here for you, no matter where life takes us."

Eric kissed my forehead and intertwined our fingers again. Archie motioned for Marie and Mack to step forward. Still sucking on the pillow, Mack let go and blew spit bubbles at me when I untied Eric's ring. I kissed Mack's cheek, turning his spitting into laughter.

Eric's solid band was made as the same metal as mine. Engraved on the inside was our initials, plus a small butterfly.

He held out his hand and I slipped the ring onto his ring finger. "With this ring, I pledge my love and commitment to you, never yielding, never wavering, and never-ending."

When Eric took my ring from the pillow, Mack scowled at him. It quickly changed to laughter, though, when Eric blew a raspberry on his cheek. Mack took a fistful of Eric's hair and started spitting bubbles again. Marie had to finally pull little Mack's fist away from Eric's hair so we could continue. She gave me an apologetic look, her cheeks bright red, but both Eric and I were laughing.

After giving my ring made of twine a twist, Eric slid my real ring over it. "With this ring, I pledge my love and commitment to you, never yielding, never wavering, and never-ending."

"I now pronounce you husband and wife." Archie's smile was the biggest I'd ever seen it. Mine was even bigger. "You may kiss your bride."

Eric winked at me before he dipped me down and kissed me. I wound my fingers through his hair as we kissed, soaking in the warmth that spread through me.

Santiago whistled next to us, along with a few others in the crowd. When Eric finally pulled me back up, he winked at me again, making me smile.

Archie motioned to the two of us. "Ladies and gentlemen, I present to you, Mr. and Mrs. Greene!"

Eric took my hand and raised our arms in the air as everyone stood and cheered. We started to walk down the aisle, but Eric swept me off my feet and carried me down instead.

The rest of the evening was filled with dinner, laughter,

and lots and lots of dancing. They had strung up lights around the park like the ones Eric had used during his official proposal. Hanging from the strings of lights were paper butterflies that the children at the school had decorated. Overall, everything was simple, yet so perfect.

I was off to the side drinking some water when Derek approached, took my drink, sat it down, and pulled me out onto the dance floor. Right when we started dancing, he pulled out one of the paper butterflies from Eric's proposal.

He turned it over in his hands. "Did you ever look at my butterflies?"

"Sorry," I said with a shake of my head. "I never had the chance."

Taking my hand, he twirled me a few times. When I came to a stop, he held the butterfly in front of my face. On the back, in Derek's terrible handwriting, was a 3E. In the bottom corner was a CA.

I raised my eyebrows. "Okay. What does that mean?"

Derek pointed to the 3E. "Three E's. Emmie, Eric, Eternity." He then pointed to the CA. "Of course, I had to trademark my marvel so everyone would know it was done by Captain Awesome." When I didn't respond right away, he sighed. "Okay, it's cheesy. I wanted to add something to set mine apart."

I pulled him into a hug. "It's wonderful, Derek. Thank you."

"Oh." He cleared his throat. "You're welcome."

Someone tapped on Derek's shoulder, so he pulled away. Luke stood there with an awkward smile on his face. "Do you mind if I cut in?"

Derek shrugged. "Sure. I'm done with her." He high fived me. "Have a nice life, sis." He scanned the crowd until his eyes settled on Eric. "I need to have a talk with the groom anyway."

"About what?" I asked.

Derek adjusted his tie. "A little thing called the birds and the bees."

Before I could stop him, he was gone.

"Well, that's going to be awkward," Luke said, pulling me in to dance. He put one hand on my waist and took my other hand in his. "First of all, Emmie, let me say you look beautiful tonight."

"Thanks, Luke." Since my free hand was on his shoulder, I took a moment to fix his shirt collar. "You look quite dashing yourself."

He smiled, but it didn't reach his eyes. "Has Tina talked to you at all?"

"About what?" I asked. That was a pretty open-ended question.

"About us," Luke said. When I raised my eyebrows, he continued. "I mean, about me and Tina, not you and me."

I shook my head. "Not recently. Why? Is everything okay?"

He looked over my shoulder and when I turned around, I noticed Tina was behind us talking with Dee and Will. She waved at us when she saw us staring.

Luke shifted his gaze back to me. "Yes. Everything's fine. It's just." He sighed. "Everyone's getting engaged or in your case, married. I'm just not ready for that kind of commitment.

We're only nineteen—"

He would have kept on going if I hadn't stopped him. "Luke, it's fine. Tina hasn't mentioned anything about marriage. She's happy with the way your relationship is right now. Just because other people are getting engaged doesn't mean you have to. You need to do what's right for you and Tina. I know Eric and I are young, but we were ready. Don't ask Tina to marry you unless you know for certain that you want to be with her for the rest of your life."

Luke nodded, looking only slightly relieved. "I guess you're right."

"I'm always right," I said.

Luke finally relaxed and laughed. "True. Hey, have you ever told Eric about me and you? I mean, what happened during that challenge?"

I thought back to when Luke and I were trapped in that room, thinking we were about to die. We had shared a pretty intense kiss. "No. There never was a good time to tell him. This past year has been crazy. And now ..." I glanced over at Eric who was talking with my brother. Derek was using very animated hand gestures and Eric had a look on his face that was a mixture of being entertained, yet horrified. "Too much time has passed to bring it up now. I say we just take it with us to the grave."

Luke nodded. "I like that idea."

"Although," I said, "never tick Joshua off. He knows about it and could use it as a weapon against you."

"Good to know," Luke said. The song ended, so we pulled away, clapping softly toward the band.

A faster song began, so I went to walk to the side, but Eric was suddenly at my side, pulling me close. "Your brother is officially crazy. I'm signing your 'Derek is crazy' document myself and putting about a thousand stamps of approval on it." He spun me out and then pulled me back in, setting his hand on the small of my back and resting his cheek against mine as we danced.

"This is a fast song," I said.

"Um, hmm." Eric held me close, swaying back and forth slowly.

I pressed myself closer to him. "Do I want to know what he said to you?"

"No." Eric kissed my cheek. "But he did make me start thinking about tonight. I think I'm ready to leave." He turned his head and pressed his lips to mine.

Running my fingers through his hair, I stared up at him. "Where are we even going to go?" I shook my head, surprised I hadn't thought about it earlier. "If we go to my place, Derek and Joshua will be there. If we go to yours, Luke and your father will be there."

The corner of his mouth turned up into a smile, his eyes telling me that he was hiding something. "I've taken care of it. But first, we need to get you out of this dress."

"Wow. Can you at least wait until we're not out in public?"

He tsked. "My goodness, Emmie. That mind of yours is always in the gutter." I rolled my eyes as he laughed and guided me off the dance floor. He took me to Dee and Tina, who were talking with Luke and Will. "Dee, Tina, can you get her out of this dress." He eyed the buttons on the back of my dress. "It looks way too complicated for me and I don't want to ruin it."

"I don't want you to ruin it, either," Dee said, taking my hand. "Or then I'd have to kill you, which would create an awkward wedge between me and Emmie."

As Dee and Tina worked at getting my dress off me, I thought of something. "What am I supposed to put on once you get this off?" I rubbed my forehead. "I really didn't think ahead."

"That's why you have me, my dear Emmie," Dee said. I put my hand on Tina's shoulder as I stepped out of the dress. Dee opened a box sitting on one of the desks in the room. She pulled out a pale green dress and brought it over to me. "Arms up."

I threw my hands in the air and Dee pulled the dress over my head. It was made of a light cotton material that fell nicely against my curves. I was relieved to see sleeves and slightly dismayed to see it only came to my knees. I looked at my white legs. "Are you sure about this, Dee?"

Dee waved her hand. "You have nice gams. Get over it and flaunt those things."

"Gams?" Tina asked.

Dee grinned. "Legs. Gam is another word for leg."

"You sound like my Great Grandma Mae," I said, still eyeing my legs.

"She's right, though," Tina said. "You do have nice legs. You need to get over your insecurities."

Dee clapped her hands. "Speaking of insecurities." She looked around the room until her eyes settled on a bag in the corner. She went over, grabbed it, and brought it back over to me. "A little something to wear tonight. Let me know what Eric thinks."

Tina and I glanced in the bag and I gasped when I saw a very limited amount of silk material in there. "I'm supposed to wear this?"

Dee nodded. "Yep. It's called lingerie. Vivica was telling me about it."

"Oh," Tina said, her smile mischievous. "I'm positive Eric will like that."

I started laughing.

"What?" Dee asked with a frown on her face. "You don't like it?"

"It's not that," I said. "I was just imaging how bright red Will's face would be if he saw you in something like this."

"I know," Dee said. "He'd probably faint." She smiled. "I'm already working on mine."

I kicked off my wedding shoes, wiggling my toes around. "Much better. Now I'm ready to leave."

Eric was waiting at the door to the school when we came out. He eyed the bag I was holding. "What's in there?"

Dee slapped his arm. "Something you'll be thanking me for." She hugged me and kissed me on the cheek. "Have fun, kids. I don't want to see you for at least a week."

"I'm keeping her for three," Eric said, pulling me off the ground and holding me in his arms.

"See you in three weeks, then," Tina said. She smiled at us before she and Dee walked away.

I kissed Eric's cheek as he carried me to a jeep. "Shouldn't we say goodbye to everyone?"

Eric shook his head. "No way. The goodbyes would never end." He opened the door to the jeep and set me inside.

"Where are we going?"

"You'll have to wait and see." He ran over to the other side, hopped in, and started the jeep. We drove through town until we ended up near the cemetery. I stared at the sky as Eric drove up the mountainside. It was a beautiful night with stars painting the clear sky.

When the jeep came to a stop, I pried my eyes away from the stars and saw a log home sitting up against the mountain. It was two stories, with large windows on the front and sides of the home. In front, a bench hung from the covered porch that wrapped around the home. From my seat, I could see the cemetery clearly, along with a perfect view of New Haven.

Eric opened my door and pulled me into his arms. "Welcome home."

My eyes darted back and forth between him and the house. "Is that?"

He nodded, his perfect smile glowing in the moonlight. "Our home. It's a little secret project Archie, Dante, Santiago, Luke, and I have been working on."

I stared at the log home with my mouth slightly open. After a moment, I turned to Eric. "It's wonderful."

"I'm glad you like it. I'm going to put the arch used in the ceremony on the top of the steps, so we have to go under it every time we enter our home." He carried me to the front door and turned the knob, kicking the door open with his foot. "Welcome home, Mrs. Greene."

I kissed him gently on the lips. "Thank you, Mr. Greene."

He held me close as he carried me over the threshold and into our home.

The End of the New Haven Series

Other Books by Sara Jo Cluff

YA Dystopian:

NEW HAVEN SERIES:
RECRUITS
RECKONING
RISE

YA Contemporary:

Filler Friend

The Kiss List

Middle Grade:

THE IMMORTAL LIFE OF COTTON WYLEY

ACKNOWLEDGMENTS

A big thanks to everyone who loved and supported the New Haven series. It was by far my favorite books to write, probably because I wrote them for myself.

I went through a phase where I was mad at every series I read because they never ended the way *I* wanted. So, I decided to write a series myself. And, hey, it ended exactly how I wanted! I never thought anyone would read them. They were my preciouses. But you did read them, and you loved them. Thanks for all your support. Because of you, my beloved series is now in print.

Now I just need them as a Lego videogame, and my life will be complete.

Chad, you'll always be my favorite person ever. Your support means the world to me. You're the Eric to my Emmie, and I love you more than life itself. You always know exactly how to cheer me up on my bad days and handle my craziness so well. I'm excited for the many adventures we still have ahead of us. I'm lucky to share eternity with you.

Thanks, Mama, for being the biggest fan of this series. Your love for it is the greatest feeling ever and I knew I had to put in in print, even just for you. Well, and my own personal collection.

Princess Buttercup, thanks for being my writing companion and being there through the whole process—the first draft all the way to the final printing. Eight years in the making, but it was all worth it. I love you, kitty.

Always and forever, Dr Pepper. You fuel my writing, and I will forever be thankful. #PepperPack #Ambassador #DrPepperislife

www.ingramcontent.com/pod-product-compliance
Lightning Source LLC
Chambersburg PA
CBHW060552310726
48982CB00008B/1096/J

* 9 7 8 1 7 3 2 1 8 3 2 6 1 *